BY JESSICA CLUESS

THE KINGDOM ON FIRE SERIES

A Shadow Bright and Burning

A Poison Dark and Drowning

A
POISON
DARK
AND
DROWNING

KINGDOM ON FIRE BOOK TWO

JESSICA CLUESS

Random House 🏠 New York

Text copyright © 2017 by Jessica Cluess
Jacket photograph copyright © 2017 by Christine Blackburne/MergeLeft Reps

Visit us on the Web! randomhouseteens.com

Educators and librarians, for a variety of teaching tools, visit us at RHTeachersLibrarians.com

Library of Congress Cataloging in Publication Data
Names: Cluess, Jessica, author.
Title: A poison dark and drowning / Jessica Cluess.
Description: First edition. | New York : Random House, [2017] | Series: Kingdom on fire ; book 2 | Summary: Even though she is not the chosen one—the sorcerer destined to defeat all seven Ancient demons terrorizing humanity in Victorian England—Henrietta Howel battles alongside the sorcerers in the war against the demons, journeying to find mystical weapons, gather allies, and uncover secrets about herself and her enemies.
Identifiers: LCCN 2016043364 | ISBN 978-0-553-53594-5 (hardcover) | ISBN 978-0-553-53596-9 (ebook) | ISBN 978-1-5247-7099-0 (intl.)
Subjects: | CYAC: Magic—Fiction. | Demonology—Fiction. | Great Britain—History—Victoria, 1837–1901—Fiction. | Fantasy.
Classification: LCC PZ7.1.C596 Po 2017 | DDC [Fic]—dc23

Printed in the United States of America
10 9 8 7 6 5 4 3 2 1
First Edition

Random House Children's Books supports the First Amendment and celebrates the right to read.

To Mom, Dad, and Meredith,
FOR A LIFETIME OF MAGIC AND LOVE

A girl-child of sorcerer stock rises from the ashes of a life.
You shall glimpse her when Shadow burns
   in the Fog above a bright city.
You shall know her when Poison drowns
   beneath the dark Waters of the cliffs.
You shall obey her when Sorrow falls
   unto the fierce army of the Blooded Man.
She will burn in the heart of a black forest;
   her fire will light the path.
She is two, the girl and the woman,
   and one must destroy the other.
For only then may three become one,
   and triumph reign in England.

—Taken from the Speakers' Prophecy

A
POISON
DARK
AND
DROWNING

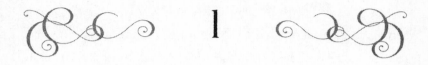

1

LONDON WAS WAITING, AND SO WAS I.

Tonight was an official gathering of Her Majesty's sorcerers—
my first since being commended to the royal Order—and as the
city's church bells tolled seven o'clock, my stomach fluttered
with nerves. We were a country still at war with monsters, but
at that moment attacking hellbeasts were the furthest thing
from my mind. The thought of going inside the palace made
me wildly uneasy.

From out Blackwood's carriage window, I watched the sorcerers as they rode up to Buckingham Palace on horseback or
floated out of the evening sky to alight upon the ground with
ease. They adjusted robes and ran hands through their hair as
they hurried inside, trying to look presentable. I stayed hidden
inside the carriage, my gloved hands folded tightly in my lap.

Two months before, when I'd arrived at the palace, it had
been blazing with lights, ready for a grand ball. Now it was
darker, more somber. It was a place of business. *My* business
now.

"Your first Order meeting," Blackwood said, sitting opposite me. "You must be excited, Howel."

"Excited or numb with terror?" That was a joke. Mostly. "What should I expect?" I still felt awkward in my black silk sorcerer's robe. It wasn't designed for a woman. I was the first female to be inducted into the royal Order by a monarch, at least in recent memory. And so I fidgeted, pulling at the collar.

"I've never been inside." He patted the handle of his stave. "Only commended sorcerers may enter. But I have heard," he said, attempting to sound all business and knowledge, "that it's quite impressive."

"Something that might impress the great Earl of Sorrow-Fell?" I said. Flicking my gloved fingers, I shot a few embers at him. The cool night air quickly swallowed my fire. Blackwood laughed, bolstering my courage. He wasn't much in the practice of laughter, though I liked to think he'd got more used to it after months of living with me.

"Do I have to worry about you bursting into flames every time you mock me?" he asked, wiping at his sleeve as the footman opened our carriage door. Blackwood stepped out and handed me down. I shivered. The evening was cool, a reminder that summer was nearly done.

"Don't be absurd. I mock you far too often to set fire to myself every single time." I took his arm, and we made our way to the palace's entrance. Around us, sorcerers were greeting each other. I searched for my friends, Dee or Wolff or Lambe, but saw none of them.

Blackwood cut through the crowd gracefully, men twice his age stepping aside for him and nodding. I'd never have imagined this was his first Order meeting. He moved about in his robe with ease, as if he'd been wearing it all his life. Perhaps he'd practiced? Or it could be that he was simply good at everything to do with being a sorcerer.

I was surprised how many of the sorcerers were young, my age or only a few years older. I knew I should have expected it—a group of tottering old men couldn't be expected to win a war—but seeing others plucking awkwardly at their robes, laughing too loudly and then ducking their heads in embarrassment, made me feel less alone. We entered the palace through a large, arched doorway and turned down a carpeted hall before making our way outside again, into the grand courtyard. In the center of the yard, a great black dome awaited us. We filed through the door, and I gasped as we entered a room of pure night.

I'd been inside obsidian rooms before, but this was an obsidian *cathedral*. The ceiling soared above us, fifty feet at least. No windows interrupted the smooth, dark expanse of stone on either side. The only source of natural light came from the large, round glass ceiling. It allowed the moon to cast a baleful eye upon the proceedings. Sconces lined the walls, the flickering fire lighting the way to our seats.

Whoever had designed this room had taken inspiration from the Senate of ancient Rome: tiered seating, much like an amphitheater, went up several floors in a semicircle. Most of the younger sorcerers clumped together in the back rows.

It felt rather like the day I'd first come to Master Agrippa's, only so much worse. At least when I'd first arrived in London, everyone had thought I was their great prophesied girl destined to bring about the end of the Ancients. Now as they turned to stare, we all knew that was not true. I had played a key part in destroying one of the seven monsters—Korozoth, the Shadow and Fog—but at the cost of shattering the protective ward around the city, leaving us all vulnerable to attack.

Yes. Feeling all the sorcerers' eyes upon me, it was *definitely* worse.

"Howel, ease up. I prefer to keep my arm." Blackwood's voice was tight with pain.

"Sorry." I relaxed my grip and began the calming exercises Agrippa had taught me months before. *Imagine a stream of cool water running down your hands.* The exercises kept me from going up in flames at bad moments.

The room was rather bare, all things considered. The only other things of note were a raised dais, upon which stood a backless obsidian seat—for the Imperator, I shouldn't wonder—and a large square pit with four compartments. One compartment held burning coals, one a pool of water, one rich earth, and one was empty save for a floating white feather that perpetually hovered inches from the ground. I'd read about this; it was an elemental square, like an altar in a church. Holy to sorcerers.

Everyone who entered walked up to the square, knelt, and touched their forehead to the edge. Was it wrong to find the whole thing a bit silly? We moved toward the square. Blackwood genuflected, and then I followed.

Kneeling before the elements, my body settled into profound stillness. I could feel the quiet whisper of the earth resonating through me, could sense the fire that pulsed below the surface of my skin. It was as if a cool, invisible hand had been laid on my shoulder, assuring me that I belonged. Gently, I touched my head to the obsidian. When I stood, I felt a bit dizzy and grabbed on to the edge. A sorcerer in his late twenties helped me to stand.

"It's a bit of a rush the first time you experience it. You'll find your feet," he said, not unkindly. I thanked him and then went to join Blackwood. He was seated in the second tier and looking about at the crowd expectantly.

"I don't think *everyone* will be here," he mused as I sat down. "But whoever's in London will come."

I might see some of the boys after all. It had been months since Lambe had been in town, and I'd barely spoken to Wolff since the commendation. God, I hoped they'd be here tonight. Them, or Dee . . . or Magnus.

Then again, perhaps I didn't need to see *everyone*.

"The Imperator should begin with formally inducting all the newly commended sorcerers," Blackwood said. "But he might not. I've read that Imperators past—Hollybrook, for example, who held the title from 1763 to 1801—sometimes required a small blood oath. Apparently it was a grisly mess." Blackwood's eyes seemed to glow as he looked at the Imperator's still-empty throne. "Don't be afraid to speak up if you wish. There's no formal structure for these sorts of things. Whitechurch is our leader, and he may ask for specific advice from the Masters, but everyone in the Order has a right to question or offer opinions."

"You know quite a bit about the Imperator's office," I said.

Blackwood looked a bit sheepish. "I confess it's a job that's always interested me. Though there's an unofficial rule that says Blackwoods can never be Imperators—we're too influential already."

"They'd be mad not to consider you," I said. Blackwood would be one of the best choices for a leadership role. Even though he'd only just turned seventeen, he had a cooler head than most men twice his age. He sat up even straighter, his green eyes brightening.

"Howel!" Dee bolted up the stairs toward Blackwood and me, as excited as an overgrown calf in clover. I didn't care. *Someone* from my old Incumbent house was here, besides Blackwood. Dee ducked into our row, jostling a pair of sorcerers, and sat on my skirt. It took a couple of tugs to get it out from under him.

"Dee! I didn't think you'd be back from Lincolnshire. Did you battle Zem?" I said, stifling a laugh while he tried to yank his robe into propriety. Dee's red hair was a brambled mess. He must have flown here.

"I didn't get up close, but the Great Serpent was at work burning down masses of fields. Suppose the Ancients want to destroy crops, what with the winter coming. I got to work in the rain unit, you know. Even managed some lightning." His round face flushed with pleasure. Well, he should have been proud. Summoning lightning was a bloody challenge.

"You must have won a great victory." I smiled at him.

"We put the fire out, at least. How is everyone at home?" he asked, painfully trying to sound casual.

He was clearly asking about Lilly, my maid. He'd liked her since we'd all lived in Agrippa's house together, though he'd never made his feelings known. Normally I'd have been worried about a young gentleman chasing a maid—those sorts of things didn't usually end well for the girl. But I knew Dee would sooner cut off his own hand than harm Lilly. And if he didn't, I'd do it for him.

"Everyone is very well. Everyone," I said with a wink. Dee blushed harder, if such a thing were even possible. His skin practically glowed.

"What was that about?" Blackwood whispered.

"I don't have to tell you *all* my secrets," I said primly, fluffing my skirt.

"Pity. I'd like to know them."

I couldn't tell if he was joking, and I studied him a moment. Blackwood's profile was strong and distinguished in a shaft of moonlight, and the look in his eyes utterly distant. No matter how much time I spent with him, he could be as inscrutable as the dark side of the moon.

"All rise," a sorcerer called at the door. Instantly, I was on my feet, alongside Blackwood and the rest of the room. We were silent as a black-robed man entered, walked up the steps of the dais, and seated himself upon his throne. Horace Whitechurch, Imperator of Her Majesty's Order.

When I'd first met him, I'd thought him the thinnest, most unassuming old man, with white hair and wet black eyes. Now I could feel how his strength radiated outward. In this room, coupled with the power of the elemental square, I imagined him as the beating heart of a great body, his life force nourishing each one of us in turn. This man *was* strength.

"Be seated," he said, and we all obeyed in a whisper of silk. "To business. I shall be brief." He paused, as if gathering his words. Then, "There has been an attack on the queen."

He said it so matter-of-factly. Sharp cries sounded throughout the room, echoing off the high walls. Blackwood, Dee, and I looked at each other with horror. Whitechurch cleared his throat, restoring silence.

"Her Majesty is well. She herself has not been assaulted, but a message was found in the queen's bedroom," Whitechurch continued. He took something from his robes and held it up for all of us to see. It looked an ordinary type of letter. "From R'hlem."

Holy hell. The Skinless Man, the most fearsome, the most intelligent, the most ruthless of the Seven Ancients, left a message *in the queen's bedroom*? This time, there was no outcry. The room, as one, held its breath.

Finally, one young man in front of us stood. "How can we be certain it's from him, sir?"

"The message was found," Whitechurch said, unfolding the paper, "pinned to the body of one of Her Majesty's footmen." My stomach tightened to think about it. "A shadow Familiar was found painting on the walls with the poor man's blood."

I unsheathed Porridge and held it in my lap. I swore that the stave warmed in my hand, as if giving me comfort.

A shadow Familiar, he'd said. Could it have been Gwen? I recalled her the night of our commendation, laughing wildly as she pulled Agrippa away into the air. My heart twisted. Even now, the thought of Agrippa hurt. He'd welcomed me into his home, trained me. He'd been the first to believe in me. True, he had also betrayed me, but that part didn't seem to matter any longer.

"What became of the Familiar?" someone else called out. Blackwood was right: Order meetings were quite informal.

"We burnt the thing. It did not return to its master." White-church turned his eyes down to the paper in his hand.

A cold sweat broke out along the back of my neck. It was as if I'd gone back to that night months before, when I'd come face to face with the Skinless Man. It had been an illusion, and a damned good one. The monster had caught me by the throat and nearly choked me to death. Thinking about that one burning yellow eye in the center of his forehead, the bloodied stretch of his muscles, the . . . I nearly vomited.

The worst part of all this was that if one of R'hlem's agents had gained access to the palace and the queen's bedroom, then we were not nearly as safe as we'd hoped. After the ward came down, we'd erected barriers all around the edges of the city, barriers patrolled day and night. But clearly it hadn't been enough.

At least the queen was unharmed. At least he hadn't succeeded in attacking her. Unless it was R'hlem's plan to instill fear in us.

I knew from experience that fear could lead people to do terrible things.

Whitechurch began reading, "'My dear Imperator, I pray you'll excuse the messy delivery of this salutation. One must always make an impression.'" Even though Whitechurch spoke those words, I could hear R'hlem's voice saying them, his tone deep and soft and sinister on the edges. "'It has been rather a dull summer, wouldn't you agree? I admit that my dear Korozoth's destruction was a bit of a puzzle to me. But if there is anything I enjoy in this life, it is a challenge.

"'I've decided to give you fair warning: I am preparing an onslaught to bring your Order to its knees. I will show you horror, my dear Imperator. I will give you the very taste of fear. And you know that I am a man of my word.'"

I scoffed at that; R'hlem was *hardly* a man.

Whitechurch continued, "'There is one measure that you may take to spare yourself, your queen, and your loyal sorcerers from this coming apocalypse. Give me what I ask, and I shall perhaps not crush you beneath my boot. Be assured that if you refuse me, nothing can prevent your destruction.'"

Without thinking, I rested my hand on top of Blackwood's. He slipped his fingers through mine for an instant.

Whitechurch glanced out at the room. " 'I asked my servant to leave behind my demand.' "

With that, Whitechurch spun his stave and swept up the water from the elemental pit into a ball. He flattened it out into a thin, shimmering square and touched his stave to it. The surface rippled, and an image appeared. Agrippa had shown us this once—a way of looking into other locations, like a scrying mirror.

Again, I wished Agrippa were here now.

The image settled upon the queen's room. I could see the foot of her canopied bed. A great splattering of blood covered the floor and sprayed up onto the pale walls, still fresh enough to be dripping. I imagined a shadowy demon slicing the poor footman's throat, the servant's life bleeding away. *Monster.*

Whitechurch expanded the image. Above the mess, the Familiar had used the gore to write a few crude words:

Give me Henrietta Howel

2

WHEN I WAS A VERY LITTLE GIRL, MY AUNT AGNES
took me to the seaside. I raced through the waves, my head
filled with the pounding surf. It was like that now as I looked on
the horrible words. Were people talking? Arguing? Shouting?
I'd no idea. All I heard was the pulse of blood in my ears.

Why? Why did he want me?

Several months ago, R'hlem had wished to take me for one
of his personal Familiars, to "train me for great power." But he
couldn't want that now, not when I'd destroyed Korozoth. His
intentions had to be grisly. Had to be punishment.

I found my feet. As I rose, the hubbub around me died.

"Did he say why?" My voice sounded surprisingly clear,
considering I was about to burst into flame. Sparks trailed from
my fingertips; embers glinted at the bottom of my sleeves. I
could feel Dee and Blackwood inch away.

The Imperator shook his head. "He did not."

"We won't do it!" Dee shouted, standing beside me. To my
shock, many sorcerers surged to their feet in agreement, ap-
plauding Dee.

"We don't negotiate with demons!" someone cried.

"Perhaps R'hlem knows," one lone voice called out. The cheering quieted as a sorcerer stood. He was a short young man with hooded blue eyes and an imperious sort of air.

"Wonderful, it's Valens," I muttered.

Of course it would be him. Valens was the captain of my squadron. All newly commended sorcerers were formed into squadrons to be overseen and trained for battle, unless they went to the navy or the Speakers' priory. Valens had never made any secret about disliking me. Not only was I a liar, a magician, and *not* the chosen one, but I'd been involved in Master Palehook's death. Though Valens had joined the Order in speaking out against the horrible things Palehook had done to keep our ward up—killing innocent people and draining their souls didn't sit well with sorcerers—he'd still been one of Palehook's old Incumbents. He probably felt a deep loyalty to his Master, the way I felt for Agrippa. While I could understand that, Valens thought the Imperator showed favoritism by not punishing me.

So he'd decided he'd punish me *for* the Imperator. Whenever we ran drills at the barracks yard, he searched for any flaw of mine. Was I even slightly out of step when forming a waterspout? Do it fifteen more times. He would force everyone to join in another set if I made even one mistake, which made me *very* unpopular.

It didn't surprise me at all that he was speaking out now.

Valens stared me down from across the room. "Perhaps he knows that Howel is not truly one of us."

"I was commended, the same as you," I said. Perhaps it wasn't ladylike, but I refused to let him run roughshod over me. "I can use a stave, just the same as you. And *unlike* you, I helped to destroy Korozoth."

"Yes, that again." Valens sighed. *That again,* like I'd insisted on showing everyone my embroidery for the eighth time. "We never fail to hear of that particular exploit. But it's been months since your commendation, Howel. What have you done since?"

I've stopped myself from blasting you in the face with a fireball.

"Everyone, be seated," Whitechurch boomed. I sat, and Blackwood nudged me with his elbow. To support or to chastise me, I couldn't tell. "It shocks me that *any* of our members would attempt to sow discord at a time like this." He stared at both Valens and me, respectively.

The two of us kept silent, though Valens threw angry glances at me across the room. Glances that I returned, happily. Bother being demure.

"Where were the queen's guards?" Blackwood asked, frowning. "Our soldiers know better than to leave a room unattended, and Mab's court was supposed to help guard Her Majesty's chambers."

Indeed. The dark Fae had agreed to send more arms and soldiers now that the ward had fallen. They'd also set up an enchanted ring around the city, adding to the sorcerers' barrier. The faerie knights and our own sorcerer elite *should* have been at the chamber door.

Whitechurch sighed. "There seems to have been an error

with the changing of the guard." If the naturally unorganized Fae were helping to run things, that didn't surprise me. "I wished to share this news before proceeding with the meeting. We must discuss strengthening the barriers. Now, our warders—"

It was my first meeting, and I should have been paying attention. I should have hung on the Imperator's every word, riveted. But all I could think of was R'hlem ordering his creature to write those words in some poor servant's blood. That person had died for a stupid message targeted at me. My temples throbbed; my fault. It had been my fault.

What would R'hlem do if he got me? Tear me apart piece by piece? That was one of the kinder things he could do.

When the meeting was over, I rose with Blackwood and Dee. We started to file down the steps, but Whitechurch called, "Howel. Blackwood. Meet me in my chambers." With that, he turned and walked through a small door directly behind his throne.

"Best of luck," Dee murmured. Gritting my teeth, I marched down the stairs, Blackwood behind me.

I'd expected the Imperator's rooms to look as grand and austere as the obsidian palace outside. I'd imagined a stone chamber with Grecian pillars and scowling busts of Homer. Instead, Whitechurch's private office was rather homey. The Turkish rug was worn and threadbare, with bright reds and yellows that had faded over time. Two green-striped and over-stuffed chairs slouched before the fire, their cushions frayed at the edges. A brown-spotted porcelain bulldog sat on a table, and Whitechurch absently touched its head as he took a seat.

"So," he said to me, as if starting a normal conversation. "How do you feel?"

I didn't expect the lord of all the magic in England to care about my feelings.

"Guilty." I cast my eyes to the carpet, noticing some crumbs sprinkled near the Imperator's chair. "I don't understand what he wants."

"You wounded R'hlem's pride as well as his army when you killed Korozoth," Whitechurch said. "He wants to punish you and hurt us."

"Should I go to him?" All I could picture was that poor servant, dead on the floor. "Perhaps he won't hurt me. Perhaps we could set up some sort of operation where I spy on him, or he . . ." My voice trailed away. My breath wasn't coming right; perhaps my corset was too tightly strung. I pressed my hands to my stomach, and when my hands trembled, I forced them to stop.

"Agrippa told me about this quality of yours," Whitechurch said. His gravelly voice gentled a bit. "You couldn't bear to feel useless, he said. I saw his pride even before you . . . mastered your abilities."

Whitechurch knew I'd lied to him about my magician birth. When the queen had first commended me, it was no secret that he disliked me. At first, he'd been cold whenever we met or spoke. But it had changed these past few weeks, as I kept pace with my squadron—despite Valens's best efforts—and patrolled the barrier with the others.

"I don't want anyone else to suffer on my behalf," I mumbled. I was *not* going to cry.

"Which is why you must not think of going to him." Whitechurch cracked his knuckles. "He believes you are our greatest asset. He probably wants to show the public that we are so weak we could not protect the person we've raised up as our salvation."

That was smart. As far as the people of England knew, the sorcerers *had* found their prophesied one. When we walked through the rubble-filled streets of the city or in the shanty-towns near the barrier, I could see how people's faces brightened when I passed. Sometimes little girls would run up with a gift of a flower or a bit of ribbon. While it made me happy to see *them* so happy, that nagging guilt would return at once. I was *not* their savior, but I pretended to be. And now that I had R'hlem's attention, I put every person around me in greater danger, danger that I couldn't bloody protect them from.

I had to shut my eyes tight and will myself back under control.

"What should we do?" Blackwood asked.

"We must keep our chosen one safe," Whitechurch said. There was no mockery in his voice. "Blackwood, as you are Howel's guardian, we should discuss."

I bristled at that. Blackwood was my age, and not that much more skilled at magic than I. But he had to assume "responsibility" for me, since I was an unmarried girl running around wild.

"Heavens, imagine what a lost lamb I would be without a strong young man guiding me," I muttered.

"I always pictured you as more of a kid goat," Blackwood said. "Always butting heads." Despite everything going on, I couldn't help but smile.

"Enough." Whitechurch picked up an amber glass of whiskey from beside his bulldog and sipped. "Besides Howel's security, fortifying our defenses is our first priority now that R'hlem has breached the barrier."

Defenses again. We'd come out from under a ward after more than a decade of hiding, and now Whitechurch wanted to go right back under it. Meanwhile, the war raged outside London. R'hlem savaged the land, and his army of Familiars grew. I thought of Brimthorn, my old school, lying open to attack. I imagined little bodies in simple gray dress laid out on the grass, unnaturally still while the school behind them burned.

No. I had to shake those images, or I wouldn't get anything done.

"We shouldn't talk about defense, sir," I said. "We can't afford to wait for R'hlem to make good on his promise to destroy us."

"What exactly are you proposing, Howel?" Whitechurch asked.

I hadn't even considered the words until they were flying

from my mouth. But as soon as I spoke them, I knew they were right.

"We must destroy R'hlem before he can come after us," I said.

The room was quiet. I slid into the chair opposite Whitechurch as neatly as I could. His white eyebrows had shot up into his hairline.

"Of course we should destroy R'hlem," Blackwood said slowly, as if tasting the words. "How else are we to win this war?"

"Forgive me. I meant that *I* should do it," I said. This time, both of them gaped as if I'd sprouted a second head. "There might be something, er, outside our sorcerer magic that could help." I folded my hands in my lap. When in doubt, appear very prim.

"What resources do *you* have?" Whitechurch asked. His expression went stony. "The magicians." He did not sound pleased.

"There could be books," I said, trying to speak lightly. "Books never hurt anyone."

"You are no longer a magician, Howel." That calmness was a sure sign danger lurked ahead. "You swore to it at Her Majesty's commendation."

I had to be careful now. "Her Majesty told me that I could use what I needed from my past in order to help." I watched how each word landed. Whitechurch didn't hurl me across the room, which I took as a good sign. "Magicians have a strange ability, don't they? Perhaps there is something in their teachings?" I kept saying *they* and *their*. Hopefully, distancing myself would keep Whitechurch on my side.

"We don't know much about R'hlem," Blackwood admitted, coming to stand behind my chair.

"You agree with Howel?" Whitechurch's disapproving gaze made me feel like we were children being scolded.

"We're running out of time," Blackwood said. "Howel has a point."

I didn't love the idea of having Blackwood as my guardian, but as my ally he was doing quite well.

"I know that you want to help," Whitechurch finally said to me. He was using that smooth tone of his again, which meant the answer was no. "But you must do your part and nothing more. Train with Valens, and fight when we need you."

"We should make certain Valens doesn't hand me over himself," I grumbled.

"He knows what he may do," Whitechurch said, standing. "And so do you, Howel."

I didn't argue. He was the Imperator, after all. I would train, and I would fight. But no one could stop what I read in my spare time. And if I happened to find something useful? Well, better to beg forgiveness than ask permission.

Making trouble was becoming a regular habit, it seemed.

AS A SERVANT TOOK MY GLOVES, I HAD TO MARVEL at how in charge I felt in Blackwood's house. At Agrippa's, I'd been his ward and Incumbent, and while he'd been a generous host, I'd always known who was master. But here, Blackwood and Eliza and I were given supreme authority.

Lady Blackwood, their mother, was a reclusive woman who lived upstairs in her suite of rooms; I'd never actually met her. The door to her chambers was permanently closed, the scent of camphor and dried rose petals faintly emanating from it when I walked past. Though I was technically here as her ward—it would have been unseemly otherwise—we lived as though she did not exist. If I wanted a fire lit in any particular room, I gave the order; no need to check with Blackwood. If I wanted to go out, I could. Blackwood mightn't approve, but I didn't need his permission. Freedom was as intoxicating as strong drink, and I sometimes felt that the Blackwood siblings and I were playing an elaborate game of house.

As soon as we entered, Blackwood went to go find his sister. I gave the footman my gloves, bonnet, and robe, and then a smile. He accepted the first three and bowed swiftly to the last before leaving. The house ran like clockwork, organized but impersonal.

"You'd a rather busy night, I take it." Rook stepped out of a shadowy doorway and into the light, his brilliant yellow hair glowing like the sun in the dark Blackwood house.

"Too busy, really." I sighed.

Rook came to me, his eyes shining with ease. I felt myself relax. Despite everything that had happened tonight, the moment I saw him I felt as though I'd truly come home. He was warmth to me, and safety.

He also had one hand behind his back, his mouth quirked in a smile. "What do you suppose I've got here?"

"Twenty gold doubloons? The elixir of life?" I sighed again. "Really, don't I have enough of those already?"

Rook tossed me a shiny red apple. Good lord, this might have been even *more* valuable. I marveled at the fruit's glossy shine. Apples were more precious than gold these days.

"Working in a stable will give you the most fantastic riches." Crossing his arms, he nodded. "Go on, then. Take a bite."

"No, not yet. I want to savor it a little." I brought it to my lips and inhaled, enjoying the heavenly scent. "Few things are sweeter than anticipation."

As soon as I'd said it, I felt my cheeks warm. These past months, since Rook had survived Korozoth's attack, I'd kept hoping we would . . . well, that we would become closer than before. I thought he wanted to—I knew *I* wanted to—but the moment hadn't arrived. At this point, I was afraid one or both of us had lost our nerve completely.

Rook closed the distance between us. My breath lodged in my throat.

"When we were little and got that bowl of pudding at Christmas, I'd gobble it down and you'd make every bite last." His smile was easy. "You don't change, Net—Henrietta."

I loved hearing him say my full and proper name. Rolling the apple between my palms, I murmured, "Maybe I'll share it with Lilly. I know she loves apples, too." Then I felt myself flush even more. But Rook only laughed.

"That's a good idea." He took one of my hands. "Are you worried about the Skinless Man?" He grew serious in an instant.

"How did you know?" I asked with a start.

"Lady Eliza had a letter from one of her friends. She told me what that monster did." His voice held a low current of anger. He sounded as if he might simply go out there and challenge R'hlem himself. I looked down at our joined hands. His sleeves were buttoned, hiding the circular scars that still dotted his left arm.

"Well, I've some work to do regarding our skinless friend."

"Then I'll let you work." He pressed his lips politely to my hand. God, I wanted him to be not *quite* so polite. "Eat your apple." With a wink, he vanished down the hall. My body screamed to follow him, while my brain reminded me that was a frightening, uncertain prospect, and I needed to start my work anyway.

Blast. To business, then.

I went up the stairs to my room and dragged Mickelmas's trunk out from under my bed. To the untrained eye, it looked like a perfectly serviceable wooden box with a rounded lid. A bit splintered and battered, perhaps, but good for storing linens. As with all things, though, appearances could be deceiving.

At my knock, the lid swung open and I took out the papers I had spent the past few months sorting. A thrill ran through my body whenever I handled Mickelmas's spells. The cracked scrolls and books bound in red and green leather, gold lettering still visible along their faded spines. There was a sense of home when I held them in my hands. It wasn't simply because I was born a magician; books offered a sense of safety for me. Taking my papers, I slid the trunk back under the bed and went downstairs. The chair by the library fire was comfortable, and I knew I'd be reading for a while.

As I headed along the halls, I wished the grand house weren't so silent, like a mausoleum. The Blackwoods' London manor had tiled floors, high vaulted ceilings, pillars of gold-veined green marble, and stained-glass windows with the distant remove of a church. This wasn't a place designed for cheer. Black velvet and green damask curtains muted whispers and shut out light. Portraits of starch-collared, disapproving ancestors from different eras of English history lined the walls. Every alcove displayed some chiseled bust or sorcerer relic. A stave that had belonged to Blackwood's father rested on display in a glass case by one of the windows. The ivy carvings upon its length were typical for Blackwood sorcerers.

And me, apparently. My stave bore a similar design.

Entering the library, I found Blackwood seated on the sofa and Eliza, standing before him, her white forehead creased.

"But why should you speak with Aubrey Foxglove?" She played with a bit of lace at her skirt, a nervous gesture. In her cream gown, with her pale skin, rosy lips, and jet-black hair styled in a pretty chignon, she looked like a modern Snow White.

"Don't fidget," Blackwood said, smiling as he took her hand. "His family seat is in Ireland. You'll be safe there." It sounded as if he'd rehearsed this speech. I coughed to make my presence known, and Eliza waved me into the room.

"George and I are only talking." Her tone sounded forcibly cheerful. I stood a bit awkwardly looking through my papers. Yes, very fascinating papers.

Eliza continued. "You can't be serious about Foxglove. He's ancient!"

"Forty-two," Blackwood said, "and in good health."

"You told me I'd have a say." Eliza's voice held a warning.

"You'll be sixteen in less than three weeks." Blackwood was pretending to be easy and careless about the whole thing, which was so painfully stilted that I winced. "It's tradition to announce your engagement at your debut ball."

God, yes. Eliza's ball was going to be massive. The war

might be raging outside, but the sorcerers must have their traditions, particularly the Blackwoods.

"I know that," Eliza said, her voice tightening. "That's not the problem. You *said* I could have a choice in the matter. My choice is: not Foxglove." Eliza sounded matter-of-fact. "You may come to me with any other suitors you'd like." Blackwood said nothing to that, which relaxed her further. "Now. May I still go to the assembly tomorrow? It's only at Cornelia Berry's house."

"I won't be able to take you, and you know the streets are dangerous." But he was weakening already. No matter how hard he tried to be stern, Blackwood always bent to his sister's will. At least, he bent a little bit. Eliza swept behind him and wrapped her arms around his neck.

"I've been inside for three days. I'm so *bored*, George. Please? Please." She pressed her cheek to his. Blackwood, already smiling, tapped her arm.

"Fine. I'll arrange an escort."

"I adore you." She kissed the top of his head. "I'm off upstairs. Good night." She came over to kiss my cheek. Blackwood stood and watched her leave the room.

"That's not the last we'll hear of Foxglove, is it?" I asked as I went to sit before the fire. Poor Eliza. All her privilege came at a price: doing whatever her father or, in this case, her brother told her to do. The thought of it made me ill.

"I don't want to worry her about it. Not yet." He sighed. I opened my papers to an interesting discussion of eighteenth-century magicians in pre-Revolutionary France. Blackwood took up one of the pages. He read it, then reread it, his face going blank. "These are from your magician's chest, aren't they?"

I cleared my throat. "They're interesting. You should read some."

"Whitechurch *told* you to stay away from these. Do you ever actually listen to your superiors?"

"Yes. When I think they're right."

He all but groaned. "Why can't you read novels instead?"

"I've categorized everything by date. Come see." Creating systems for things made me happy. When I was a little girl, I loved alphabetizing the Brimthorn library shelves. Sometimes, for a treat, I'd sort them by color. I'd tried to show Rook how fun it was, but he'd always fall to the floor and pretend to be dead.

Blackwood pinched the bridge of his nose. But then he sat on the sofa, his weight beside me a comfort.

"Do you think there'll be anything to help us?"

"Any detail about R'hlem, no matter how insignificant, could give me something." I turned a page. I would have dearly loved to stay on the Napoleonic Wars, but I needed to work fast.

"And what insignificant details are you looking for?"

"Any books I've read on the Ancients and their tactics came from sorcerer scholars. No one's investigated magician theories in all of this."

"Magicians don't much care about the war." Blackwood didn't say it dismissively. "The Order made sure of that."

Public use of magician craft had been banned in England for over a decade. Terrible things were done to those caught practicing. It was why I'd been so desperately afraid when Mickelmas revealed my magician heritage to me. "Then think. If I find something useful, it could change the Imperator's mind about magicians." I wasn't holding my breath on that, but why not hope?

The door opened, and one of the footmen carried in a tray laden with an exquisite china set. He placed it on a table before us and poured steaming chocolate into two delicate cups. The scent warmed me at once, and—yes!—he'd even included a plate of fresh gingerbread. My favorite. Blackwood handed me a cup, looking pleased with himself.

"How did you know I'd be reading in here?" I immediately snatched up some of the gingerbread.

"You always read in the evenings. I know you too well."

"Oh? I must be very dull."

Blackwood considered this a moment. "No. I believe I like anticipating you."

"Am I that easy to predict?" I blew on the chocolate and sipped.

"I like a good routine." He was reading another of the papers intently and placed his hand on the sofa, brushing the edge of my dress. I moved myself a bit farther down the couch. He meant nothing by it, of course, but one could become too comfortable.

"Do you want to help me?" I had a large pile of papers to

get through, after all. But Blackwood quickly put down what he was reading.

"I really shouldn't involve myself." He handed me the paper delicately, as though it would bite him. "But tell me if you find something." He knelt on the floor to pick up some scattered pages. He got caught up in one of them—they *were* interesting, after all—and sat there quite at ease and informal. When I'd first met him, the idea of Blackwood sitting on the floor would have been a ridiculous one. What a difference a few months made.

"If I find anything important, you'll be the first person I tell," I said.

"Good," he replied. He gazed back into the fire, a distant expression on his face.

"What is it?" I asked. He shook his head.

"It's nothing. Read as long as you'd like." He was on his feet with a speed and grace that bordered on feline, and was gone.

The only sound in the room was a log snapping in the hearth as an hour crept by. I ate the gingerbread, careful not to get crumbs everywhere, and read until my eyes were blurry.

For the next two days, that was my routine. Wake, train with Valens, patrol the barrier when it was my turn, and in the evening read in the library. I went painstakingly through every scrap of paper, but while they were fascinating, they were also fundamentally useless.

The magical trunk regurgitated the oddest bits and bobs. I found a tin soldier that turned into a living caterpillar when touched. There was a powder that made my skin itch and turn green, twenty empty snuffboxes, and a tiny hand mirror with what appeared to be a crystallized thumbprint in the center. When I touched the print, for two seconds I had the most intense flash of an image: a young girl, approximately my age, with dark skin and beautiful bright eyes. She smiled in a pink silk gown. The image vanished when I dropped the mirror in surprise.

Indeed, Mickelmas had millions of secrets.

Stories of famous and irascible magicians filled the pages of his books; histories of the great Washing Tub War of 1745, in which two magicians, Esther Holloway and Tobias Small, engaged in a duel to see who could scrub all the linen in London by magic alone. There were mentions of Ralph Strangewayes, the founder of English magicianship, and his wild abilities to summon beasts from the air and bring forth gold from the ground.

When it came to the Ancients' war, though, only the standard order of events could be found: Mickelmas and Willoughby (and Blackwood's father, Charles, but no books contained *that* piece of information) opened a tear in reality twelve years ago. R'hlem and his creatures came through that tear. Even after all this time, little was known of R'hlem himself. His powers included the ability to rip all the flesh from someone's bones with nary a thought, and he clearly had some other psychic abilities—I had met him on the magicians' astral plane, after all. But suppose he had *other* powers, ones he had not yet shown to us all? Our knowledge of him was so sketchy, even compared to how little we knew of the other Ancients.

On the third night of reading well past the time I should have been asleep, I was growing frustrated with myself. The fire was low, and my temples throbbed. I rubbed my eyes before standing to stretch, my corset pinching me in the ribs.

I should go up to Lilly soon and prepare for bed. It wouldn't do to keep her waiting too long.

But I couldn't help looking back at one of the pictures of R'hlem's victims. I'd stumbled upon a rather grisly description of *how* he liked to skin people. He started with the hands, ripping the flesh away while the poor bastard watched himself being flayed alive. I imagined myself screaming as he peeled me like an orange.

The door creaked open. My fingers burst into flame on instinct.

"Henrietta?" Rook came to me, cap in his hand. "I didn't mean to scare you."

Groaning, I put my fire out and flung my arms around him, my heart hammering. "I was just scaring myself. I'm very good at it," I muttered. Rook squeezed me back. For one sweet moment I didn't think about monsters. Rook released me, taking a polite step away.

Again, always the image of politeness. Sighing, I grabbed the book I'd been reading from off the floor.

"I was afraid I'd miss seeing you," he said, stepping toward me again. This was our dance now: he would move near, and then shy away like a colt. Frustration churned inside me.

Perhaps all he needed was a little encouragement? But I didn't even know how to begin. Flutter my eyelashes? Pretend to trip and get him to catch me? Somehow that didn't seem like, well, us.

"How was your day?" I asked, feeling stiff and awkward. "Were the horses happy to see you?" Lord, what kinds of stables were open this late at night?

"Very happy." He laughed, passing a hand through his golden hair. "They all insisted on an extra handful of oats."

"You spoil them." I drew a little closer, and he let me. Yes, that was much better.

"I'm happy to have the work." His mouth tightened. He hated living off Blackwood's charity. In the first days after he'd nearly died, he'd kept trying to get out of bed so he could march outside and begin looking for a job. "And you?" he asked, his expression softening.

"It's been the most beastly day," I murmured.

"Still reading, then." He took the book from me and flipped through the pages. "You think there's a way to stop the Skinless Man in here? Truly?"

"Do stay quiet about it," I said, blushing. "I don't want word spreading."

"No one will know." He caught my hand. There was a hard

light in his eyes that hadn't been there yesterday. "I *still* don't understand why R'hlem wants you."

Gently, I released myself and sat on the sofa. "It's a way to show the people the sorcerers can't even protect their great 'chosen one.'" My eyes rolled inadvertently whenever I said those stupid words. "Who knows? Perhaps he thinks I can do something for him."

"He'll never have you." Rook sat beside me, his cap bunched in his hands.

"Of course he won't. I'm notoriously difficult to catch," I said lightly. That made him smile.

"You recall when we were thirteen, and your powers had just shown themselves? The things we had to do to hide them from Colegrind?"

God, the days when I'd set fire to just about anything. "When I scorched his parlor drapes?"

Rook smiled. "When you set fire to the rhododendron in the garden." He looked rather proud. "I convinced Colegrind it was an exploding bird. 'An act of God,' he said."

I pictured the pompous expression on our old headmaster's face and burst into a giggling fit. Rook and I drew nearer. If I reached out my hand, I could touch him. Turning my head, I looked up into Rook's eyes.

His black eyes. The sight of them made me shudder. They had once been a pale blue, but the color had shifted. Part of his gift from Korozoth. Part of his transformation. Fenswick and

I had slowed it with our studies and potions, but we could contain it only so long.

Rook said, "I helped you then, and I can help you now. I could use my powers to protect you." His hand covered my own. My heart leaped as I watched the fire's glow play over his face, the strong line of his jaw.

I wanted to make some teasing comment, but the firelight began to die. Shadows slunk from the corner to play about our feet. Instantly, I pulled away from Rook, and the darkness vanished. He stood, cursing softly.

"We can't play with your powers until we know how they'll be received," I said. Though I knew how the sorcerers would receive them; we both did.

"Of course," he said, his tone distant.

"One day the war will be over. We'll be free." I got up and went beside him.

"One day," he echoed. He touched me, only a hand on my waist. "Henrietta," he whispered, sending a thrill down my back. And then, his black eyes searching mine, he leaned closer. Closer still.

He wasn't going to stop.

Trying not to tremble, I slid my hand up his shoulder, tilted my head back . . . until he twisted away with a thick and bloody cough. Heart sinking, I watched as the shadows slithered toward Rook's feet.

"Help," he whispered, turning back to me. His eyes had gone full black, shining and depthless.

4

"DRINK THIS DOWN," FENSWICK SAID, HANDING Rook a wooden cup filled with a steaming liquid. The hobgoblin doctor took up Rook's wrist and felt it, tapping his clawed finger to mark the pulse.

I'd brought Rook to the hobgoblin's apothecary, at the very top of the house. The room was under a sloped wooden eave, loops of garlic and bunches of dried flowers hanging from the rafters. A small stove squatted in the corner, unwashed copper pots strewn about it. Pewter bowls and wooden pestles, covered in pollen and rose paste, were littered across a long wooden table. The place was homey and comfortable, not at all where one would expect to find a rabbit-eared, bat-nosed little hobgoblin in fashionable trousers.

Rook rolled his sleeve down. His face still looked a bit green.

"Should I be worried? I've had more control," Rook said. I winced. Fenswick and I knew that gaining more control was a bad sign. Rook's body was accepting his abilities. He was changing.

When I'd helped him through the dark house below, his arm slung about my shoulder, I had prayed that no one would see as the shadows had flared and rustled. They'd caught at my skirt with inky hands as I'd helped Rook up one painful step after another. Every day they grew stronger.

"No need to worry right now," Fenswick lied smoothly. My stomach knotted. "Get some rest."

"I'm sorry," Rook said to me. "I hate that you had to see such things."

"I don't care." It was the truth; I didn't give a damn about his powers. I only cared about him. I wanted *my* Rook back. Gently, I put my hand on his cheek. His skin was hot to the touch. Rook squeezed my wrist, kissing my fingers quickly. My body thrilled for a brief instant, and then he stood.

"Good night, Doctor. Thank you," he said, and left. Fenswick approached me. He wanted to talk, and I guessed the subject.

Avoiding his gaze, I picked up one of the pestles for grinding herbs. It was still covered with yellow powder—he'd been mixing dandelion root. It was supposed to help suppress infection.

"I'm afraid he's getting worse," Fenswick said. Worse. As though this were some cold, or a chill that was mildly dangerous. *Worse* didn't seem the right word for a boy who had shadows at his beck and call. A faint buzzing started in my ears. I dropped the pestle, which hit the table with a hard thunk.

Rook was being swallowed by darkness, and I hadn't done a damned thing to help him.

"What about that mugwort extract? If it's purified and

honeyed, it's supposed to be very effective." I'd finally found that damned recipe after tearing through every one of the Blackwoods' botany books I could lay hands on, and even then it had been in Latin. I'd had to double-check my translation.

"We've gone through every tome on herbalism I know," Fenswick grumped. "We've even used forbidden practices from Faerie. Do you know how hard it was to get powdered bat eyeballs?"

"We're missing something." *I* was missing something, but if I only worked a little harder . . .

"He's coughing black blood." Fenswick pricked up his rabbit-like ears. "What further proof do you need?"

No. *No.* I put my face in my hands.

"We have to keep trying. Please." I remembered being out on the moor with Rook that day when everything changed. Maybe if we hadn't gone away from the school, if Gwen hadn't found us, if Agrippa hadn't saved us, if, if, if. Memories danced through my mind. The time we'd gone swimming in the miller's pond, daring each other to leap into the cold water first. The day I'd revealed my powers at our meeting place on the moor, and the wonder on his face as he regarded the patch of scorched earth in front of me. Screaming as I erupted into flame when the shadow Familiars tried to take him away. His battle with Korozoth to save me. The apple he'd given me only a few days before. The moment in Agrippa's kitchens when we'd nearly kissed—all those moments leading to nothing?

No. I wouldn't allow it. "Please," I said again, with more force.

"I doubt anything will change." Fenswick began to stack some pewter bowls.

"Then I think we should tell him what's happening." I'd had my fill of lying to those I cared about.

"Don't," Fenswick warned. "Such honesty could prove fatal. Fear and anger accelerate the poison."

I cast a weary glance over the apothecary. The same herbs and fungi, the same bowls and bandages as always. We'd tried new remedies nearly every night for months, and nothing had changed.

"Give him some peace," Fenswick said with a sigh. "He deserves that."

"All right," I muttered, rubbing my burning eyes. "Would you mind if I read in here for a while?" Fenswick's ears flapped in surprise. Shivering, I said, "I don't want to be alone."

"Fine," he said, gently.

I went downstairs, gathered my papers from the library, and then let Lilly help me prepare for bed. It would be cruel to keep her up much later than this. Afterward, I took my wrap, lifted Mickelmas's chest onto a cushion of air, and brought it upstairs to Fenswick's apothecary. I was going to go through the whole damned thing if I could. Anything to keep my thoughts preoccupied.

I read as the bells outside struck midnight. Tired, I cupped my chin in my hand and listened.

Bells were a necessary part of my life now. After the ward fell, the Order agreed that it needed a way to signal to every sorcerer in the city simultaneously. The result was a system of bells, which would ring in simple patterns to instruct and assemble us. Two long, solemn tolls, three quick, light ones, and one more loud peal? That would mean R'hlem was on the outskirts of town. We'd not heard that pattern yet, thank God.

Tonight, after the twelfth bell, I waited. And yes, four long, rolling chimes followed. A simple changing of the guard along the barriers. I'd have to take a shift tomorrow afternoon.

Fenswick cleaned his spoons and measuring cups and lined up glass vials of fungi and unsavory-looking animal parts. He took such joy in all his little oddities, but seeing a dish filled with cold jellied goose intestine did make me a tad ill.

"What exactly are you trying to find?" Fenswick asked an hour later as he poured me some hot black liquid that smelled like licorice. I took a sip, gagged, and swallowed the whole thing. It worked; the tiredness rushed out of my body. I felt as though I could climb several mountains in one go, and rummaged through the trunk again.

"A clue." Hissing, I sliced my finger on a paper, and a bead of blood welled on the tip. I laid my head on the table and forced myself not to start banging it.

"Why should your magical trunk help you there?" Fenswick took a thimble of that licorice stuff for himself. "Surely whatever you want won't simply spring to your fingertips."

His words struck me. *Whatever you want.* I grabbed my

packet and fished out the note Mickelmas had left me. His last communication, two months ago, read: *Never what you want, ever what you need, until we meet again.*

Perhaps it wasn't simply a note. Trust that old devil to slip a spell in where I least expected it. Blood welled on the tip of my finger again, and I remembered one of the old pamphlets I'd read from Zachariah Hatch, Queen Anne's favorite magician: *Blood oils the hinge of reality, swinging open the door between what is wished for and what is.*

I bled onto Mickelmas's note, then grabbed Porridge—it sat on the table beside me, as I never went anywhere without it—and laid the bloodstained note into the red velvet lining of the trunk. I shut the lid and started swirling Porridge in slow circles. This was a standard sorcerer move, one that I found helpful when trying a new spell. The more basic the stave movement, the greater clarity I had in working the magic.

I'd been practicing in secret over the past two months. Seeking out little spells from Mickelmas's trunk, I'd continued my unusual education in mixing sorcerer and magician magic. Words didn't work for me, unlike most magicians. Perhaps it had to do with my stave. But finding the proper movement and focusing my will tended to help.

Now, instinctively, I sent Porridge in a slow, gliding figure eight over the lid. This was a maneuver designed to bring something up out of the depths of the water. I focused on the Ancients. Images of hideous Molochoron, a great moldy lump of jelly; fierce On-Tez, with her black wings and sharp teeth;

Callax, with his great height and muscled arms; fire-breathing Zem; Nemneris, the giant glittering spider—visions of all the monsters coursed through my brain. Tingling began, starting in my elbows, shooting down to my hands. My blood and magic were responding.

How could I beat them?

My focus narrowed to R'hlem. I could feel it again, the slimy, bloody coldness of his hand on my throat. My feet slipping for purchase, and the way he squeezed and squeezed, choking the life out of me. The burning ugliness of his yellow eye, taking in my face as he strangled me.

A bloom of hatred warmed my blood. Embers sizzled against the lines of my hands. I imagined slamming a knife hilt-deep into his bloody chest.

How? *How?* Where do I start?

Porridge pulsed, and the lid swung open on its own. It had worked. With a cry of excitement, I looked inside to find a rolled-up canvas.

Not a book. Not a knife. If I was supposed to battle the forces of darkness with an oil painting of some lively spring countryside, I was going to hurt somebody.

"What are you?" I grumbled, unfurling the thing. "A portrait of dogs dressed in amusing outfits?"

"I love those," Fenswick said, brightening at once.

I looked down at the painting . . . and my body went numb. Hastily, I knocked some bowls out of the way and laid the canvas out on the table.

Dear God.

"What in the Undergrowth?" Fenswick murmured, twisting his head back and forth to get a better look.

"The Imperator needs to see this." My voice shook with excitement as I rolled the picture up and tucked it beneath my arm.

UNFORTUNATELY, WHITECHURCH WAS IN DEVON ON business, so I had to wait. Two days later, the Imperator sat in his chamber in the obsidian cathedral, the painting open on the table before him. His thin, veined hands traced the canvas. First, he flipped to the back, as I had, to make certain he'd read it right. *Portrait of Ralph Strangewayes, at his home in Cornwall. Taming the bird. 1526–1540 or thereabouts.*

He turned the painting over. It showed a bushy-bearded man, dressed in standard clothes of the Tudor era. He was a long-faced fellow with a gold-beaded cap and a doublet of forest green.

This was Ralph Strangewayes, the founder of magician craft in England.

Strangewayes stood in the foreground. Behind him, there was a small house, the magician's home. The house wasn't what had captured my attention, though.

It was On-Tez, the Vulture Lady. I knew the sight of her immediately: a large black vulture's body with the head of a sharp-toothed, hook-nosed old woman. She flew high in the air above Strangewayes. Her horrible sharp teeth were bared in a dreadful grimace, her black wings fully extended.

Strangewayes didn't appear discomfited by this at all. In fact, he was blithely holding a chain—a chain that stretched all the way up to connect to On-Tez's ankle.

Here was a painting of one of the Ancients three hundred years before the war began. And Ralph Strangewayes, father of all English magicianship, apparently had not only dealt with the Ancients but been able to control them. To keep them, like pets.

Taming the bird, indeed.

I waited for Whitechurch's response, trying not to bob up and down with excitement. After all, he could be angry with me for disobeying his orders. Well, they hadn't been orders exactly, had they? More like suggestions. That's what I'd told Blackwood on our way down here; he'd insisted on coming, in case he needed to speak up for me.

He waited by the doorway like a disapproving shadow.

"Where did you say you found this?" Whitechurch finally looked up at me.

"In my father's collection, sir." Blackwood lied easily. I hated that he had to do it, but mentioning Mickelmas's chest was impossible.

"Mmm." Whitechurch rolled up the painting. I held my breath. "Are you certain of the date?" he asked us quietly, looking from one to the other.

"I'm no expert, sir, but it looks real. I researched Ralph Strangewayes's Cornwall home," I said. No need to tell him my information came from one of Mickelmas's books, *The Ascent of Magic*. "It's in Tintagel."

"You want to go there." Whitechurch leaned back in his chair, absently stroking his chin.

"Yes," I said. He stayed silent. Oh dear. "Strangewayes must have been able to control these creatures, if this painting is anything to go by. If there's something we can learn . . ."

"You had better do it." Whitechurch nodded. "Blackwood, you are in charge of this particular assignment. Go with Howel."

I shut up at once, stunned. That had been far easier than I'd expected. Even though *I* was the one who'd found the blasted painting in the first place, I found I couldn't get too frustrated that Blackwood had been given the lead. At least we'd be doing this together.

"When should we leave, sir?" Blackwood said. He sounded rather dumbfounded. But if the Imperator assigned him something, he'd get it done.

"The *Queen Charlotte* is stationed in St. Katharine's Docks. She leaves to patrol Cornwall against the Spider today, I believe. I'll write to Caius and have him wait upon you."

Today. I wouldn't be able to say goodbye to Rook before I left—I'd missed him at breakfast. Fear of returning from a mission to find Rook gone reared its head. But if there were some key in Cornwall to end this madness, then it would be worth it.

"If you don't mind my saying, sir, I can't believe you're allowing this," I blurted out.

"I might not have, but for the letters I've received." He looked rather uncomfortable. "Word has spread amongst the queen's government. They are petitioning Her Majesty to give in to R'hlem's demands."

Parliament would hand me over on a silver platter if it could, no doubt. Bloody cowards. The government and the prime minister, Lord Melbourne, did not like me. They blamed me for opening their city to slaughter and the queen to danger. Once again, I imagined cool water running down my hands, calming myself.

Perhaps leaving London was a good idea.

"YOU SHOULD BE AT HOME," BLACKWOOD told Eliza, sounding exasperated as our carriage pulled up to the docks.

Eliza plumped the large emerald silk bow of her bonnet. In a forest-green velvet gown that highlighted her beautiful eyes, she'd dressed especially nicely to see us off.

"Honestly, George, you make me feel as though I shouldn't care about your going to war at all," she said.

"Eliza's right. You should be more charitable," I said.

Eliza beamed at me, and Blackwood grumbled as he got out of the carriage and handed us down. On the ground, I waited for the coachman to set my satchel on the dock, then hefted it onto my shoulder—despite Blackwood's trying to take it—and walked. It banged against my back with every step. I'd attempted to pack light, but I hadn't been sure what I'd need. The journey to Cornwall would take at least five days by boat if the weather stayed good. Even if we had extraordinary luck in finding Strangewayes's house, this whole expedition would last the better part of two weeks.

Two weeks away from Rook. My stomach lurched to think of it. I'd left a note for him before I'd gone, hastily scribbling it while Blackwood waited.

I have to attend to the Order's business. I'll be back as soon as I'm able.

I'd sat there a full two minutes, debating whether to write the word *love,* and how to write it. Blackwood had had to remind me that the tide waited for no one.

The cool breeze snatched at my skirts as I walked along. Ships were anchored and waiting in the water, their sails tied up. Men climbed up and down the rigging, while barrels and other cargo were loaded. Sailors swarmed the decks, their sleeves rolled to show sunburned arms decorated with tattoos of frolicking mermaids or rude parrots. One of them caught me looking and winked.

Was it my imagination, or was the dock moving beneath my feet? My stomach rippled. I'd never been sailing before. My father was supposed to have drowned at sea, after all, which hadn't made me especially keen on it. But then Mickelmas had denied that story, right before he'd vanished that terrible night in St. Paul's Cathedral, when the world fell down around our ears.

Bloody Mickelmas.

I'd tried writing letters to him, putting them in his chest and hoping that they'd reach him. I'd kept asking what on earth he'd meant about my father, but nothing ever came of it. I wasn't sure if he'd received the notes, or if he simply didn't care.

Speaking of the chest, I touched the strings of the reticule at my wrist. I'd brought a few magician spells. Not all of them, of course, but one never knew when they could come in handy.

"There," Blackwood said by my ear, pointing to a rather grand vessel. She was lacquered black and trimmed in gold along the sides, sporting enough masts to seem a veritable forest. *"Queen Charlotte."*

"We're looking for Captain Ambrose, yes?" I asked as we dodged around a pair of men wheeling a barrow. One of them looked after Eliza and muttered something I *hoped* I hadn't understood.

"Whitechurch said they'd have someone assigned to help us."

"To take us to the cliffs, or all the way to Strangewayes's house?" I asked as we arrived at the—what was it called? Gangplank? Really, my knowledge of all things nautical could fill a small thimble.

"All the way. He's supposed to be a great soldier."

"Bless my soul," a familiar voice cried.

Blackwood's head snapped up as Magnus sauntered down the walkway toward us. "Is this a reunion? We should have invited all of Master Agrippa's former Incumbents. Though I believe Dee vomits at sea."

Magnus stepped onto the dock, smiling easily. He hadn't changed a bit in the months since I'd seen him. His hair was still a shining mass of auburn curls, and his gray eyes still sparkled with irreverence. Yes, he'd the same square jaw, broad shoulders, and infuriatingly informal expression. My spirits plummeted. Blackwood looked as though he'd swallowed a raw turnip. Eliza was the only one who appeared delighted.

"*You're* here?" Blackwood sounded exasperated already.

"I *am*, Blacky, though I appreciate the philosophy of the question. After all, are we any of us here? Can existence be truly proven? You've given me much to think about." Magnus sketched me a short bow. "Howel. A pleasure."

"Yes," I said stiffly. Magnus wore a tightly fitted blue naval coat with tan breeches. Looking more closely, I noticed his hair sported streaks of gold. His tan face had reddened a bit at the tip of his nose and the sharp lines of his cheeks; his body had grown leaner. Perhaps he *had* changed in the months we'd been apart. The boy I'd known in Agrippa's house had experienced only the briefest moments of combat. He'd been far busier helping me train, showing me the city, and growing closer than I should have allowed. He'd kissed me one night, quickly reminding me that I could only ever be a toy for him—he was already engaged, after all.

True, Magnus had come to aid me in the final battle against

Korozoth, and I'd wanted us to start over as friends. But the last time I'd seen him, he'd held my hand and whispered that he couldn't let me go. I'd walked away and hadn't seen him since.

I'd been perfectly comfortable with that.

"Oh, Mr. Magnus," Eliza cooed, extending her hand. "I'd no idea you'd be here." The over-the-top way she said it indicated that she'd perhaps had an inkling. Her insistence on coming to see us off made a great deal more sense now. Blackwood's whole face seemed to contract as Magnus kissed Eliza's hand.

"My lady, you are more charming than ever. Is it possible you're still not sixteen?" He *tsked*. "Inconceivable."

Eliza giggled. "We're planning a splendid party for my birthday. I hope you'll be one of the guests?"

Blackwood and I exchanged a look. As if this expedition weren't stressful enough.

"How could I refuse such an invitation?" He all but winked at her. Right. He hadn't changed at all.

"Come along," Blackwood muttered, taking Eliza's arm and practically dragging her back to the coach.

"Goodbye, Eliza." I waved to her.

"Goodbye!" She smiled at me, and then, "Farewell!" she cried to Magnus. I wondered if she'd toss him her handkerchief as a keepsake. Magnus kept grinning roguishly. Bloody fool.

"Don't worry, Howel," he said, turning to me. "You get me all to yourself on the boat."

I wanted to strangle him.

"How is Miss Winslow?" I asked. At the mention of his fian-cée, Magnus's face fell, but only slightly.

"She's well. And Rook?" The humor vanished from his voice. He knew about Rook's "condition." Granted, he didn't know everything. Part of me wanted to tell him what was hap-pening, to tell *someone*.

But I only replied, "He's wonderful." He was going to be. I was going to make damned sure of it. I walked hastily up the plank, wobbling a little bit, and gripped the ship's railing. Corn-wall. We only had to sail to Cornwall. Less than three hundred miles; surely they would fly by. Magnus's hand brushed my back to steady me, and I practically jumped.

"What's the matter?" Magnus looked rather surprised. "I thought we were friends."

I can't let you go. His last words to me, and he wondered why I was nervous? Did I not understand men at all?

Blackwood stumbled up the walkway, cursing under his breath. Magnus couldn't resist. "You'll get your sea legs yet, Blacky."

"Tell me you're not taking us to Strangewayes's." Black-wood didn't bother to conceal his hostility. Unfortunately, that was the sort of thing Magnus relished.

"I would, but I hate to lie to you." Magnus clapped Black-wood on the shoulder. "Just think. We'll be as close as we ever were." Blackwood looked as though he might commit murder. Granted, that *was* as close as they'd ever been.

"Howel. Blackwood." A man dressed in the blue coat of a

naval officer approached us. His long brown hair was tied back from his face. The only thing that marked him as a sorcerer was the stave by his hip. "Captain Ambrose, of Her Majesty's navy. So. We're to sail to Cornwall on the Order's business? Then there's no time to lose."

5

THE SALT BREEZE CHILLED ME AS I CLUNG TO THE railing and stared into the waves lapping against the side of the ship. The world tilted with every lurch. Everything I'd read in stories suggested that sailing was supposed to be relaxing, filled with lemonade and laughing people in attractive outfits. Frankly, I thought I was going to vomit up everything I'd eaten this morning, and maybe everything I'd ever eaten after that.

Behind me, men climbed the ropes, adjusted the sails, and kept a lookout high above. There were seven sorcerers aboard, excluding Blackwood and myself. Several of them hovered near, what was it, the crow's nest? They watched the coastline and the open sea, in case Nemneris, the Water Spider, attacked.

"I don't care if there is a party of Ancients waiting for us when we land," Blackwood muttered as he came up next to me. "I will be so bloody happy to get off this ship." His handsome face was tinged as green as I felt.

"We're land creatures, I'd say. How is Magnus doing so well?" I sighed as, speak of the devil, Magnus clapped his hands and called attention to himself. We all watched as he flew up, up to the, ah, oh hell, some *other* mast and fixed a line of rope, then somersaulted back down to land on the deck. He accepted the men's cheers the way a cat laps up cream.

"Some people are good at everything," Blackwood said darkly. "At least this war is pleasant for one of us." He launched himself off across the deck to speak with Ambrose, who was arguing with the helmsman.

I looked back into the water, my spirits sinking. I felt rather useless here. While I knew that was to be expected, seeing as how I was not and never had been a sailor, it still made me feel ridiculous.

Of course, being aboard this ship wasn't the sole source of my unhappy thoughts. When I'd tried so desperately to be commended, I hadn't considered what it would mean for the country. Now that I had taken the place of their prophesied one, I had increased the danger and offered the men and women of England no real protection in return. Scanning the coastline, I thought of all the people to whom I'd given hope . . . and how cruelly those hopes would be dashed.

Enough. I'd come to Cornwall to find the answer to our problems; there was no going home without it. I took Porridge in hand and twirled a spell to distract myself from my thoughts.

The magic stretched over my skin, radiating out from the core of me to my arm all the way along my stave. With a few twists, the water crashing along the ship's side formed into white-capped dolphins. One of them gave a playful spin through the air before plunging back into the deep.

"Impressive," said Magnus, appearing beside me. He leaned against the railing, as casual as ever.

"Any sign of Nemneris?" Thoughts of the Water Spider shoved my nervousness around Magnus out of my mind. Mostly.

Magnus's cocky smile died.

"She doesn't usually come out this far from shore." He pointed toward the coast, a smudged line of green and gray in the distance. "That's where she sets her traps. She weaves an underwater web, you see, that snares unsuspecting ships. After that, all she has to do is smash the unfortunate vessel, and . . . eat her prizes." His hand went down to an item upon his belt, a carved wooden charm in the shape of a star. Perhaps it was a favor from Miss Winslow.

"Have you ever seen her up close before?" I asked.

"Not yet," he replied. "But she always leaves a few survivors. Maybe to let the tales circulate."

"Perhaps she'd let us draw straws," I said.

Magnus laughed, sounding as he had several months before, when we'd been real friends. Before the ward collapsed and the war came crashing down on us. Before that night in my room, when he'd whispered in my ear, held me against his body, pressed his lips to mine. Apparently some things were more easily forgotten than others.

Blushing, I looked about for my escape.

"Did I say something wrong?" Magnus asked.

"It's nothing."

"Howel." But that was as far as it went. Blackwood walked carefully over to us, still looking peaked and wretched.

"We're sailing closer to shore. Ambrose says we should move to the rowboat in ten minutes."

"You'll be on dry land again soon, Blacky. Here." Magnus picked up an empty bucket and shoved it into Blackwood's hands. "Just in case." Then he walked away, whistling.

"I don't know what we've done to deserve this," Blackwood growled.

Soon the three of us were aboard a rowboat being lowered into the sea. The wind had picked up, lashing the waves into white-capped frenzy. The sorcerers and sailors watched us from above as the boat met the water, jolting violently. I bit my lip as I caught the sides, steadying myself.

"We'll provide cover if something should happen," Ambrose called.

Marvelously reassuring. I sat at the front of the boat while Magnus and Blackwood took the rear. Magnus's jacket was off, his sleeves rolled to his elbows. Blackwood kept his coat on. He wouldn't even take off his hat.

Magnus skimmed his stave along the top of the water, and a single wave picked us up and carried us toward shore. The ship grew smaller in the distance. They'd patrol the coast, then come back to this spot in two days' time. We'd have to make it back for the rendezvous, no matter what. The last thing any of us wanted was to have to trek across the country to get back to London. The roads were extremely dangerous now, more so than ever before.

We rode swiftly to the shore, where Magnus and Blackwood leaped out and dragged the boat up the beach. The waves crashed around us, pearly foam breaking upon the dark sand. Ahead of us, the cliffs waited, shrouded in mist. Getting out of the boat, I studied the craggy rock formations. We'd arrived near a sea cave at low tide—Merlin's Cave, if I recalled correctly. Tintagel was heavy with Arthurian lore. I'd wanted to see this place ever since my aunt told me the stories when I was a little girl. This was supposedly the cave where Merlin had found Arthur as a baby. I peered inside. The place was covered in barnacles and algae, the scent of brine and salt so strong I nearly gagged. The toes of my boots grew damp at once, and the bottom of my skirt trailed in the water as I looked up to the top of the cliff.

"How do you suppose normal people go up and down these things?" Magnus mused as he struck his stave in several points around his feet. "Climb?"

"How very dull," I said with a smile. As one, we rose upon columns of air, and I had to force myself not to look down at the shore and the boat as they grew smaller and smaller. I kept my ankles straight, wobbling only a bit as we reached the top.

The area around us lay covered in dense fog. To the left, stone rubble dotted a grassy field. The outline of a large building was visible among the weed-choked wreckage.

"What's that?" Magnus followed my gaze.

"The ruins of Tintagel Castle," I said sadly. This was supposed to be where Arthur's home had once stood. To think Ralph Strangewayes had made his house in such a storied place. Magnus slid his pack from his shoulders and onto the ground, opening it and retrieving a map with a well-thumbed, weathered appearance.

"We're here," he said, pointing at the edge of the coastline. "Strangewayes's house is supposed to be five miles inland to the east." Not the worst walk ever, but we'd likely have to make camp; the sun was already heading toward the sea, and no one wanted to be stumbling around here in the dark. "You're certain the house is still there, Howel?"

"Mostly," I admitted. Whitechurch had drawn up a water glass to find the location and make sure *something* was there before Blackwood and I left. Thankfully, Strangewayes had been famous enough that his house used to be a popular tourist destination. As such, its location was listed upon maps. In the scrying glass, we'd found an area shrouded completely in mist, so thick it was difficult to see through. But there'd been the outline of a building, enough to send us out here.

We headed along the rocky path, the sea at our backs. As we made our way deeper into the countryside, the mist sat heavily on my clothes, chilling me. It felt as though the mist were *touching* us, as though it were sentient. As though it wanted to keep us.

"I'm just glad the Spider didn't turn up," Magnus muttered.

"She doesn't come up the cliffs, does she?" I asked.

"You never know." His expression hardened.

"Are you all right?"

"Do you always talk this much when you're on a quest, Howel?" I'd never heard him sound snappish before. He cleared his throat. "Forgive me. It's just—"

"Quiet." Blackwood stopped in his tracks and slowly took out his stave. On instinct, I grabbed Porridge from its sheath as well. "Do you hear that?" His green eyes narrowed as he surveyed the terrain.

"No," I said, then instantly shut up. The world about us seemed to be holding its breath. No birdsong, no breeze. Only dead silence.

I could feel it, the movement of something in the mist. Something incredibly wrong. Blackwood warded a blade on his stave; I saw the dim yellow outline of it.

"Get down!" he shouted as a Familiar with eight horrid legs and gnashing fangs attacked.

6

I EXPLODED IN BLUE FLAME, THROWING A FIREBALL at the monster. It dodged far too nimbly and sprang into the air with its legs splayed wide. Magnus and I rolled out of its way as it landed, jaws clicking.

This was one of Nemneris's lice. I'd seen them before, but only from the safety of a water glass in Agrippa's library. Their bloated abdomens and eight legs were spiderlike, while their pale, grotesque torsos, bald heads, and arms were almost human. This monster had gnashing pincers where a mouth should have been. A long, gooey stream of venom dripped from its fangs.

The louse screeched as it leaped for Blackwood. He weaved and slashed with his blade. A plume of black blood gushed from the creature's leg, and it retreated a few steps, clicking in pain.

Magnus slammed down his stave and sent a shock wave through the earth, throwing the beast off-balance while I fired again. This time my magic found its mark, and the Familiar shriveled as the flames consumed it, the eight legs curling into its body. There was a grotesque popping noise as its black eyes exploded, gushing viscous ooze. The acrid smell of its death burned my throat.

"Howel, look out!" Magnus barreled into me, shoving me roughly to the ground. Another louse leaped out of the mist, landing on top of Magnus. My movements were too slow, too sluggish.

"Hold on!" Blackwood shot warded force at the thing and got it in the chest. It tumbled off Magnus, who lurched to his feet, clutching a bleeding arm. But he was alive. Thank God.

I twirled a spell I'd designed before, a blend of my sorcerer and magician powers. The earth formed a great hand to drag the monster down, but the Familiar scrambled out of its grip too fast. Damn it all.

Magnus lifted his stave . . . and collapsed onto his back. His head lolled to the side, his body limp. The Familiar raced forward, pincers clicking with glee. I screamed, trying desperately to think of another spell.

Something sliced out of the fog, slamming directly into the Familiar's head. The louse jerked backward as black ichor sprayed over the ground. The beast twitched once and became still, its hideous face cleaved neatly in two by an ax. I hurried to Magnus and knelt by his side.

"Who's there?" Blackwood called, whirling around. A small boy, no older than twelve or thirteen, approached out of the mist. He was clad in worn trousers and a threadbare vest, a cap atop his head. The boy looked to Magnus, who was groaning in pain.

Magnus. His arm sported two swollen puncture wounds, hot and already throbbing with infection. The Familiar had poisoned him.

"No," I whispered, thinking fast. Were there healing spells or medicines I'd brought with me? What had I learned from Fenswick about slowing poison? There was no bloody time to lose.

"If we don't treat it, he'll die." The boy echoed my frantic thoughts. He yanked his ax out of the monster's skull. It came away with a wet sound, like pulling a knife from a pumpkin. "We'd best leave. They hunt in packs." The boy wiped the ax blade on the grass. "Follow me." He motioned to us to follow, and Blackwood and I each took one of Magnus's arms. We hoisted him to his feet and pulled him along between us.

The boy led us back to the ruins of the castle, dodging over the piles of rubble and moss-covered stones. Entering what had been the castle's outer wall, he uncovered a cellar door that led belowground. The boy pulled the door open with a loud creak and waved us ahead.

We were following an ax-wielding stranger underground, where the air smelled stale and damp, but all I cared about was Magnus's racing pulse as I helped lower him inside, my cheek pressed against his neck. Carefully, Blackwood and I laid him onto the muddy ground.

Lit candles had been wedged into the rocky walls. Once the boy closed the door, the only natural light came from a crack in the rock ceiling. Blackwood had to duck to avoid hitting his head as I knelt beside Magnus to watch the boy at work.

The boy stripped Magnus's coat off and ripped his shirt open, exposing his chest. I nearly turned away from the immodesty of it but checked myself. Magnus was dying, for God's sake. I remained focused on his face.

"Who are you? How do you know what to do?" Blackwood's voice echoed in the cavern.

The boy didn't answer. Instead, he took a knife and cut into the wounds on Magnus's arm. Clear liquid welled out of the bites. The boy took a deep breath, then sucked at the marks, spitting the poison onto the wall.

"Can you do that?" I asked, stricken with horror.

The boy pulled his cap off his head. Wild bright red curls tumbled down. With the addition of the hair, the boy's entire appearance changed. His lips seemed fuller, the tilt of his eyes more feminine. This was a young woman, not a little boy. She looked at me; there was a hard knowledge in her gaze. "Aye. If you'd like, pass me that bag." She nodded at a leather pouch by my side. "Then go above and keep watch. There's precious little else you can do."

The lilt of her voice sounded northern, Scottish perhaps. I passed her the bag while Magnus began to wail and claw at the air.

"No, get away. He might still be alive!" He spoke to invisible phantoms. Foam flecked the corners of his mouth. His whole body went rigid, and he began to seize violently.

"Magnus!" I tried to touch him, but the girl struck my hand.

"Go now!" she cried. Blackwood threw the door open, pulling me after him. I could only listen to Magnus's delirious screams and sobs.

Blackwood and I sat at the edge of the cavern, our staves in hand. My knees would not stop shaking, and I looked to the sky above. The light had purpled, and the sun had reached the lip of the horizon. My teeth began chattering, which had nothing to do with the night's oncoming chill.

"He'll be fine." Blackwood sat on the balls of his feet, ready to spring into action. "Magnus has far too much absurd luck for it all to run out now." But he sounded unsure. Blackwood stood and walked forward, cautiously checking the open area around us. I could feel it, though. The Familiars had moved on. The air didn't seem so very still and awful now.

Slowly, Magnus's screams began to die down. *Please, God. Let that be a good sign.*

"The Familiar should have bit me, not him." I rolled Porridge in my hands, tracing my fingers along the carved ivy leaves that decorated the stave's length. The faintest trace of blue light shimmered in one of the tendrils.

"Don't start thinking like that." Blackwood sat beside me again.

We listened to the roar of the waves far below us. I dug the toe of my boot into the soft earth, drawing arrows and circles. There was no hell quite like waiting.

"I know you wish we hadn't come here," I said at last, unable to bear the silence.

Blackwood shrugged, a strangely casual motion for him. "We weren't any use in London. We might find something here, at least."

My thoughts turned to what Whitechurch had said, about how I couldn't stand to feel useless. Blackwood definitely had a similar drive. What else would compel him to rise and train every morning in his obsidian room before the sky was light? I gazed at the carvings on my stave, and then looked at his. Identical in every way. "Sometimes I think we're quite the same."

"Yes." The faintest hint of a smile graced his lips. He took Porridge from me for one moment and traced his fingers along some of the carvings. The hair along my neck stood on end. It felt oddly intimate.

"All right. Come in," the girl called at last.

We crawled back inside to find Magnus lying with a jacket rolled up beneath his head as a makeshift pillow. His arm was bandaged, and he appeared to be resting. His chest, now covered, rose and fell evenly with his breathing. He smiled weakly when Blackwood and I entered.

"Strangest doctor I've ever seen," he murmured, eyeing the red-haired girl. She poured water over some crude-looking utensils to clean them and looked at Magnus pointedly. "And by far the most skilled," he added.

"Best not forget that." But she grinned, slipped her instruments into a satchel, and hoisted it over her shoulder. "Bit close in here. Need some air." Without another word, she swept past us and out the door.

"I'll thank her." Blackwood left. I'd the feeling he also wanted to get a better sense of our mysterious savior.

Even with the burning candles, it was growing horribly dim in the cavern. Night was coming on fast; the glimpse of sky in the crack above had darkened to a deep violet. I fashioned a flame into a burning orb and suspended it overhead.

"Howel?" Magnus murmured.

I forced him not to move. "You need rest."

"Then stay with me. Laugh at my jokes and tell me I'm wonderful." He winced with pain.

"I'm not sure how much help I'll be," I said, a rush of relief flooding me. It didn't sound as though he were at death's door.

"I need to tell you." Magnus swallowed, then continued, "I'm sorry about how I was on the ship."

I didn't know what to say. To busy myself, I took one of our waterskins and poured a cup.

"I only wanted things to be normal between us." He shifted, wincing, and this time I helped him slowly sit up. His body was warm against me. "The last time we saw each other, I . . . said things I shouldn't have. I miss you, Howel." He smiled wearily. "It's such hell not being able to joke with you." I'd missed joking with him, too. "Friends?" he asked.

I did not speak as I gave him the water and he drank. Finally, I said, "I want to be. But . . ." I bit my lip and forged ahead. "I want nothing more than friendship. Truly." I meant it: there was Rook, after all, and even without him any desire I'd felt for Magnus was still tainted by what had happened. He nodded solemnly.

"On my word, I'll never speak to you of anything more ever again. We'll have a real fresh start this time."

He was all openness and sincerity, and damn it, I'd missed that.

I sighed in relief. "Well, I suppose it would be wrong to say no to the person who shoved me out of harm's way."

His face lit up.

"Indeed. Rather heroic of me, wouldn't you say? And I've received such a flattering wound." He groaned as he moved his bandaged arm. "I appear to have got my shirt off at some point. That poor girl must have been on the verge of swooning."

Speaking of, Blackwood's and the girl's voices rose and fell above us. I made Magnus take another sip of water.

"Well, I shouldn't have been so cold to you at the dock. I was shocked to see you," I said quietly. "Then you were the same Magnus as before."

"The same," he repeated. His mouth lifted in a weak attempt at a smile. "I know you see me as the laughing fool." He winced. "I'm more than some fellow who flirts with every pretty girl, you know." I'd never seen him so serious.

Who knew what he'd seen in the two months since we parted?

"I know," I said. Magnus stretched out on the floor, gingerly putting a hand behind his head.

"Rocks make an excellent pillow," he said. I laughed harder than I meant to.

Blackwood stepped into the cavern and unceremoniously dropped a satchel beside Magnus.

"Supper," Blackwood said, giving what could charitably be called a scowl.

Magnus cracked open one eye and patted the earth beside us. "Come nurse me, Blacky. I require your healing touch."

Blackwood squared his jaw. Apparently he wasn't nearly as sentimental about Magnus's brush with death as I. "We can't light a fire, but there's some dried meat." He handed me a strip of it. "Everything all right?" He looked grim, as if something desperate and scandalous might have been going on. Honestly.

"I think I might get some air. You can play nursemaid," I said. With that, I went for the entrance while he crouched next to Magnus.

"Will you lovingly feed me from your own hand?" Magnus sighed. Blackwood muttered something as I crawled out of the cavern, barking a curse as my head struck the ceiling. My eyes watered from the pain as I made it outside, and I looked down in dismay. The front of my dress was filthy, and my hands were cracked with dried blood. I should have brought that water-skin with me. Dusting my skirt the best I could, I spied the trousered girl and walked over to her. She sat atop one of the stones, looking out at the horizon. The mist had burned almost completely away by now, and the brilliant orange and violet of the sunset was glorious. I paused, unsure what I could say to this girl. Thank you, obviously, but what else? She'd a look of intense concentration on her face.

"Come along." She gestured me over. I smoothed my skirt and sat down on a rock beside her, shuffling to get comfortable. She noticed, and grinned in amusement. "Best eat that." She nodded to the food in my hand. "Never know when you'll need your strength."

My stomach growled in agreement. I tore into the dried meat, wincing at the salty taste. A few days ago I'd been eating gingerbread in a parlor. My, how things change. I didn't want to become some pampered idiot, so I made an approving noise. "It's good," I said.

The girl laughed, picked up her ax, and started cleaning it with a cloth. She regarded her weapon with a loving expression. Her eyes were a soft brown—unusual color for such bright red hair. There was something in her gaze that felt familiar, though I couldn't place it.

"I'm Henrietta Howel," I said, pounding my chest to make the food go down. "We're—"

"Sorcerers. You've the magic sticks." She held up her ax and studied it. "Maria Templeton." She offered her hand to shake, and I took it. Her grip was firm, her skin rough.

"Miss Templeton," I said, which made her laugh heartily. She shook her head, sending her beautiful curls tumbling.

"Wouldn't feel right answering to that. Far too grand. Maria will do. Now then," she said, "the moody one said you're lookin' for a house."

"Yes." I didn't want to give too much of our plan away. "Something like that."

Maria snorted. "No one lives in these parts anymore. Come across a few villages, but they're empty. Homes for the dead."

I shuddered. "You don't travel with anyone?"

"What's the point? I'm more than enough." She blew a red curl from her eyes. "You sorcerers forget that magic can't solve everything." She patted the handle of her ax. "Good blade does wonders."

Here was a girl about my own age, living in the ruins of a castle, wearing trousers, killing monsters. I felt as though the ability to set oneself on fire paled in comparison.

"Thank you for helping us. Magnus would be dead without you; most likely all three of us would be."

Maria nodded. She gazed out at the sea again, the cool wind blowing her hair back. The ax that rested on her knee gleamed in the low light. She was handy with it, no question. The look in her eyes was confident and competent.

"Would you like to come with us?" I blurted out. Maria raised her eyebrows in surprise. "I only thought that we could help each other."

"You could use another blade, then?" she asked.

"Certainly. And a healer. If we happen upon an Ancient, you could use *us*. I don't think an ax would do so much in that situation."

Maria considered this. "You're on a quest, are you? The brooding lord in there doesn't seem like the type to camp for sport." She regarded me shrewdly. "What are you searching for?"

"Something magical," I said. That much was true. Maria grinned.

"Don't trust me yet. No, I don't blame you," she said, holding up a hand to stop my reply. "Shows you've some sense. All right." She stood, brushing off her trousers. "Sounds like a bargain." Her grin died as she winced and clutched at her stomach. Oh no.

"Are you well? Is it the poison?" I stood up quickly.

"I'll be fine." She stretched and looked up at the pale moon, which had just appeared in the sky. "We'll take turns keeping a lookout for Familiars." She hefted the ax over her shoulder. "I'll take first watch."

I AWOKE IN THE NIGHT TO the sound of someone muttering outside. Heart hammering, I bolted upright and looked around. Magnus and Blackwood were huddled on opposite sides of the cave, dead asleep. Even with his injury, Magnus had sprawled himself out, claiming space. Blackwood's arms were protectively tucked against his body. Unconscious, they still revealed themselves perfectly.

The voice outside continued to speak. Maria. From the sound of it, she was pacing away from the cave. Slowly getting to my feet, I crept to the door and opened it gently so as not to make noise.

The moonlight overhead was strong, casting the world

around us in harsh silvery light and beautifully outlining the ruins of the castle. The clouds had swept away, and the sky was a dense tapestry of stars. Shivering, I stopped in the doorway. Ahead, I caught a glimpse of Maria's white figure.

Her arms were over her head, and her mouth hung open as though she were silently screaming. Even from here, I could see how pale she looked. She brought her arms down to hug herself. Kneeling to the ground, she waved her hands over a flowering shrub next to the castle.

"Blessed be the earth beneath, mother of mercy, mother of life." She kissed the ground. Something in my blood responded to her call. Maria stretched back to the sky.

She was ill. She must have taken too much of the venom. I wanted to go to her, but something inside me whispered to stay out of sight and watch.

She put her hands to the shrub again and spoke. Some of her words were lost, but I heard, "May this sacrifice honor you and heal my wounds." She bowed her head again, placing her palms on the earth.

The shrub withered and died before my eyes, the leaves shriveling and turning brown and the small flowers rotting and falling to the earth. Maria arched her back, hair billowing in the wind. Her skin glowed alabaster beneath the moon. I could *feel* the poison burning out of her body. The power she had awoken in the ground still pulsed through me, as sure as my own heartbeat.

It was different from sorcerer magic, which I felt as a cool rain on my skin, or magician magic, which hummed in my blood and my brain. This was magic of the earth's foundation echoing in my bones. I crawled back inside, shut the door as quietly as possible, and lay down again. I couldn't stop the thought that was exploding through my mind. What I had seen . . . There was no denying it.

Maria was a witch.

7

AS WE TROMPED THROUGH THE MIST THE NEXT morning, I kept stealing glances at Maria. How ordinary she appeared in the daylight—that is, apart from her habit of wearing trousers and carrying weapons. Hard to believe that she'd stood beneath the moon mere hours before and healed herself through forbidden magic. Harder still to believe how calm, even cheerful, she was. While she looked about, on the alert for another Familiar attack, she hummed a carefree tune.

What if she knew that I knew? What would she say? I had never seen a witch before. When the war started, witches had been hunted down and burned in record numbers. Punishment for Mary Willoughby, the witch who'd helped open a gateway and let the Ancients through. I'd been too young to see the burnings, but living in Yorkshire had put me close to many of them. I could recall waking up to the morning air smelling *cooked*.

Maria would have been a small girl when it happened. Had she lost anyone? Friends? Family? The very thought made me sick.

We went up one hill and down another, and my boots sank

into the mud. I conjured a spell from the air to dry them, and the bottom of my skirt as well. While I tended to my clothes, Maria motioned to me with an air of bewilderment.

"Who goes into battle wearing ladies' things?" she said.

"There's nothing wrong with being a lady," I said, blushing. Granted, she had a point, but the Order would have had collective heart palpitations to see me dressed like a boy.

Or associating with a witch, but they didn't need to know everything.

"Why do *you* wear trousers?" Blackwood asked. Maria shrugged.

"Ever tried to climb a tree in a dress?" she asked.

"No." Blackwood rolled his eyes.

"Once." Magnus grinned. "It was for a wager. I won."

God, what an image. Maria laughed and slowed down to walk side by side with Magnus. They seemed to get along well, and not in the usual, flirtatious way Magnus got on with young ladies. As they walked, she showed him how to handle her ax. It didn't take long before he was throwing it in an expert arc through the air and straight into a tree, even with only one good arm. Blackwood trudged beside me, shifting his pack from one shoulder to the other.

"How can we be certain she's *not* a spy?" he murmured, continuing an argument we'd started that morning. When Maria had officially volunteered herself as our new companion, Magnus had been delighted and Blackwood withdrawn.

"We need to be cautious with whom we accept," he'd told her when she'd noticed his less than enthusiastic reaction.

"What was the better introduction? The saving your life bit," Maria said pointedly, "or the saving *his* life bit." She'd nodded at Magnus.

"My life. Without question." Magnus had shaken hands with her. "Welcome to the party."

Blackwood said nothing further, but now here we were, still softly arguing about it. He was the stubbornest young man alive.

"We could use a physician. Besides, would you have felt comfortable leaving a girl underground all alone?" I whispered, lifting my skirt and leaping over a muddy patch.

Blackwood made his mouth a thin line but finally shut up about it. We walked, on alert for more Familiars as we passed one abandoned village and then another. The sight of them made us all uneasy. There was no scorching, no destruction to signify why the people had all left. It was as if they'd simply got up and vanished.

At midday we stopped for a small rest, and to allow Blackwood to form a scrying glass. He summoned water from the muddy ground and projected Strangewayes's house's location. It took a couple of tries, but with the help of the map, we soon saw it: a veritable wall of mist around what looked to be a small house.

"It's close now," he said, letting the water rain back to the

ground. He pointed ahead. "That copse of trees looks familiar."
Indeed, we were on the border of an ancient-looking wood.

The second we entered the trees, the mist enveloped us,
so thick I started to cough. Magnus cursed, and I lit my hand
on fire to give us some light. It did little to help, only allowing
us enough visability to move a foot or two at a time. It felt as
though the mist were trying to drive us out.

Then we saw the house.

An old wooden fence gated a land grown wild with weeds.
The fence was splintered and sagging on its posts, the barn beyond it in a dilapidated state. The wood was swollen with water
and bleached from the sun. To the right, a moss-covered gray
stone cottage had sunk into the ground. In short, it looked like
any other abandoned farmstead to be found in Cornwall.

But the *magic*.

It simmered in the air, coating the inside of my throat like
honey. Blackwood closed his eyes tight. He felt it, too.

"There's glamour upon it." Putting out his hand, he touched
only mist and air. "The enchantment is powerful."

"Magician enchantment?" Magnus walked forward, leaping over the fence. He turned around, and then came back
wearing a puzzled expression. "It feels off, doesn't it? Not quite
human."

Agrippa had schooled me in only the most rudimentary
form of enchantments, but the boys had learned more. An enchantment went deeper than a mere illusion—it permeated the
reality of an area, soaking it in deception. If I went inside that

stone cottage right now, it would look like any other ordinary, abandoned house. Whatever Strangewayes was hiding would remain cloaked from the naked eye.

Enchantments, to put it mildly, were tricky.

"It might be Fae in nature." Blackwood sounded confused. "But they don't usually bother with areas this close to the sea."

Indeed, the Fae were a woodland folk. Great amounts of salt water repelled them.

"Cut the air," Magnus said, readying his stave. A simple warded blade could sever weaker enchantments.

I slashed Porridge twice but got nowhere. Blast and damn. Magnus followed with his own attempt, though he was a bit clumsy with his arm bandaged up. Blowing out my cheeks, I paced in front of the fence. Maria chuckled.

"Sorry. But you all look so cross." She shrugged her pack off and set it on the ground. Her little fingers played along the top of her ax; she seemed to rely upon it for support, the way I relied upon Porridge. "Have you no other powers to use?"

Have you? I wanted to ask. Who knew what talents witches had for breaking enchantments? Then again, perhaps they'd never had much experience with them. Magicians, after all, were the race known for dealing in these kinds of deceptions. Right now, Mickelmas would have likely been a great deal of help.

That gave me a thought. Grabbing my reticule, I rummaged through it for . . . Yes! I unfolded one of Mickelmas's trunk spells. Maria studied it, wearing a puzzled expression.

"It's magician work, isn't it?" Blackwood sounded dismayed.

Magnus only peered over my shoulder to read.

BRING TRUTH FROM A LIE

A blade, obviously

Thread, if you've got it (if you haven't, I don't know how to help you.

Are you not wearing clothes?)

Soak thread in blood—MUST BE MAGICIAN'S OWN BLOOD.

Cut straight through.

What is false becomes true; what is hidden may be revealed.

Pig Latin works especially well. Or ancient Sumerian.

Whichever comes more naturally.

I searched my sleeve for a stray thread, found one, and pulled. Cutting it with my teeth, I handed it over to Maria, who looked at the thread like it would bite her. Then, taking a deep breath to prepare, I lightly sliced my thumb with my blade. I'd been as delicate as possible, but the sting still made my eyes water. Blood welled up and ran down my hand. Maria gasped in shock as I took the thread, bloodied it, and handed it back once more. She looked at me as though I'd gone mad.

"Hold the thread out tight in front of me."

"Eh?" But she obeyed, furrowing her brow at handling the bloody thing.

My thumb throbbed, but I put it out of my mind. Closing my eyes, I thought, *What is false becomes true. What is false becomes true.* I pictured an invisible curtain lifting off the farmhouse, and my blood began to hum softly. Using Porridge, I sliced the thread and opened my eyes.

A slit rent the fog down the center, clean as if done by a blade. Buttery sunshine poured out of the wound in the air. Magnus cheered while a gaping Maria poked her hand through. Blackwood's eyes widened, but he made no sound.

"Sorcerers can't do . . . that," Maria breathed.

We took a moment for Maria to pour water on my cut and bandage it. Then, one by one, we stepped through the hole and into a strange, surreal wonderland.

The grass, which before had been weedy and sparse, now grew emerald, lush, and knee-high. Plants I could never hope to identify bloomed in abundance. One shrub displayed flowers with spiky petals of a grayish-bluish-purplish color; the sight of it lowered my spirits. Another hedge contained leaves that were a riotous shade of pink, flowering buds opening and closing as we passed. If you looked closely, you could catch tiny, jeweled eyes peering out at you from inside the depths of the flower. Extraordinary.

"Look at the house," Blackwood said, his voice soft with astonishment.

The squat, mossy cottage was gone. In its place stood an elegant house done in the Tudor style, with a gabled roof, leaded glass windows, and an arched entryway of brick. One side of the house was covered in a lush growth of ivy. Weather vanes decorated the roof, elaborate iron designs that took the shapes of giant whales and squids fighting, and a decapitated man juggling his own head. The house was so soaked in magic that it made one dizzy, the waves of power that radiated from the building an almost physical force.

I could *feel* it, the pressure on the inside of my skull, the sensation of something slithering over my skin. Raw magic. Not elemental, but from some other world.

Like the Ancients.

I led the way up the path. Entering was difficult; the door was a thick metal, strangely orange in color. It had been closed a long while, because it squealed when the boys tried forcing it. Eventually, it began to yield. Cautious, I watched for a sign of . . . anything.

"Together now," I said as Magnus readied himself. "We're not entirely sure what's in here."

"If we're lucky, it'll only be some sort of black mold," Maria said, balancing on the balls of her feet. She was as alert to danger as a cat.

"That's *luck*?" Magnus grunted, throwing open the door. A burst of sour air met us, as if the house had exhaled. Wincing, I waited. Nothing came screaming out to attack us, so we moved in, one after the other. I entered first, flinching when a cobweb brushed my face.

I stopped dead in the entryway, so Magnus accidentally bumped into me. We all grouped together, gazing about in wonderment.

The room was enormous, four stories high at least. The

house we'd glimpsed from the outside was not big enough to support this.

Magicians.

A collection of melted-down tallow candles waited on a table right by the door, jammed into iron candleholders shaped like fists. I lit them, and we each took one. The floorboards creaked loudly as the four of us walked through the stillness of the room. Long tables covered with strange-looking objects stretched out on every side. My eyes watered; the place did smell faintly of mold but also of something sickly sweet, like a burnt cake.

The room was filled with the most extraordinary creatures. Glass cases covered with a fine layer of dust crowded the walls and tables. Wiping the dirt from one bell jar, I discovered a tiny creature, suspended forever in silence. Its face resembled a very large dragonfly's, bulbous eyes gazing blindly at the world. One lone fang hung from its open mouth. Wings like a bat's had been posed to resemble flight. The beast could fit into the palm of my hand, though I wouldn't want to pick it up.

It looked like an Ancient, only writ small.

"Look at this bloody thing," Magnus whispered. Hanging on the wall above our heads was a great skull, the size of a large dog. Three curving tusks protruded from its mouth. This was not a monster anyone would care to anger. Blackwood whistled softly and pointed to the ceiling. A stuffed creature, ten feet long and serpentine, hung suspended there. Silver and blue scales decorated the length of the monster, which appeared to be an eel—only with some kind of feline face.

Jars of yellow liquid held pickled monstrosities, hearts, eyeballs, organs. Stuffed heads of horned and thorny and spined beasts were mounted on plaques. Here was a bowl of serpent scales; there, a tray bristling with clipped claws and talons.

So Ralph Strangewayes hadn't merely summoned Ancients; he had *hunted* them.

"Let's be smart about this." Blackwood passed his candle from one hand to the other, the flame thinning. "Record everything you see. Once we go over the room, we'll continue exploring the rest of the house."

Yes, the rest of the house. On the far wall, two closed wooden doors awaited us, each decorated with elaborate carvings. The one on the left showed unicorns and goat-hooved satyrs capering among flowers and trees in leafy countryside. Maria threw it open to reveal what appeared to be an everyday dining room, complete with slate stone floor, wooden table, carved chairs. Perfectly standard.

The door to the right, however, was more menacing, its carvings less wholesome. The trees were leafless and barren, great, pendulous clouds forming overhead. Sharp-horned devils danced around young, half-dressed women who screamed in fright.

Charming.

Maria went straight to the other door, yanked it open, and vanished down a pitch-black corridor. What the devil was she up to? The boys were too transfixed with the Ancients to pay any mind, but I moved after her.

"Maria, where are you going?" I called, though I parked myself at the threshold. The darkness beyond felt, well, rather *furry*. I shrank from the black as though it might touch me.

"There might be more of them," she yelled back. Her bobbing light vanished around a turn. "I want to see where this goes."

"Wait for us!" But she had gone ahead, ignoring me. I was about to chase her when Blackwood called my name.

"Come look at this." He sounded awestruck. Well, blast it all. Maria was an ax-wielding witch. If she needed help, I got the feeling she'd call.

Magnus and Blackwood stood before a painting of Ralph Strangewayes. He'd the same bushy beard he'd sported in the painting from Mickelmas's trunk, the same small, dark eyes, the same long face. Another creature had been painted beside him. This one was insect-like, just as the one under the glass case had been, only large enough to sit at Strangewayes's feet and come up to his waist. Dragonfly wings erupted out its back. The thing was a vibrant shade of blue.

"It looks like Holbein painted this," Blackwood said, finally finding his voice.

"King Henry the Eighth's court painter created *this*?" Magnus said in amazement. He started cutting the portrait out of its frame. The canvas curled as he took it.

"What are you doing?" Blackwood sounded horrified.

"Whitechurch may want to see." Magnus rolled the painting up and shoved it into his pack. He cocked an eyebrow. "I never knew you were such an art lover, Blacky."

"Don't argue," I said before they really started sniping at each other. "We should go after Maria. She—"

A scream shattered the quiet, echoing from the open doorway.

Without pausing to think, I raced across the room and into the corridor. My candle flame quickly went out. It was as if I'd entered some black, alien world. I set myself burning as I moved forward along the hallway. Twisting and turning, I searched for doorways, for windows, for anything. But there was nothing, no decoration or natural light. Sometimes it seemed the blackness gurgled. It was like traveling into some great loop of intestine, as if the house had digested me and was enjoying its meal.

Stop that. It was enough to make one's hair stand on end. Where the bloody hell was Maria?

Rounding a corner, I nearly stumbled over her. Maria was huddled against the wall with her hands over her ears, her face taut with fear and pain. Her candle had gone out—God, how long had she sat in the dark?

"You feel it, don't you?" she cried. Her knees tight against her chest, her brown eyes wide and fearful, she looked nothing like the warrior I'd first met on the cliff.

"Feel what?" Then my vision blurred. I nearly put a hand to the wall to steady myself, but as I was still on fire it didn't seem wise. Through my veil of flame, I looked where Maria pointed.

The hallway had come to a dead end, and there in the wall was a door.

On the outside, it appeared perfectly normal. But magic pulsed behind that door, calling to me. Even more so than the room of monstrosities I'd left behind, I knew it deep in my bones: *this* was what we had been meant to find.

Opening the door, I stepped inside before I could lose my nerve.

The room screamed with magic. Runes had been carved into the wooden floor, the walls, the ceiling. Circles, swirls, and lines of runes unfurled around me. My stomach soured. Though I couldn't read anything in this place, I knew, somehow, that it was obscene. That it was against reason.

Looking more closely, I saw that some of these runes had been scratched out and burned. I was afraid to think what this room was like before they were eliminated.

Words of jibberish had also been carved into these walls with a childish, uneven hand. Most of the words were not English, but two phrases were clear, yet frightening.

All hail the Kindly Emperor read one sentence. Then, beside it in screaming block letters, *WITNESS HIS SMILE.*

My brain throbbed in my skull, the pressure too intense. I clamped my hands over my ears, and that eased the pain somewhat. Apart from the swirls of runes and jagged writing, only two other things were in this room.

One was a cage, about as large as would hold a person. The bars were bent and mangled, rotted with rust. The door appeared to have been blasted open from the inside. My eyes tracked to the second thing: a body, stretched out on the floor.

At least, it *had* been a body. The remains were skeletal. The gaping skull's mouth grinned, teeth crooked and yellow. My eyes tracked over the clothing, now moldering and moth-eaten. The puffed sleeves and doublet looked familiar, like those in the painting Magnus had just stolen.

"Hello, Ralph Strangewayes," I whispered.

The body of the father of English magicianship lay at my feet, and I doubted his death had been natural. The shredded back of his doublet suggested something had ripped into him. Likely, whatever had been trapped in that cage. I placed a handkerchief to my mouth and continued looking about the room. The others had arrived but would not enter. Magnus stood in the doorway, his mouth hanging open. In the pulsating firelight, he looked wraithlike, his shadow warping over the floor. "Don't come in," I said, my voice throaty and hoarse.

"I won't," he said. "Howel, get out of there. It feels . . . evil."

I stopped burning, plunging the room into that thick darkness once more. It was broken only by Magnus's candle, which he'd somehow kept alive. Crossing to him, I took the candle and raised it over my head, examining the room more thoroughly.

There was *something* here; I could feel it. I spotted a dagger hanging off Strangewayes's belt. It was an odd-looking metal, tinted gold-orange, but not rusted in the least. As quickly as possible, I unhooked the belt from around the skeleton's middle. I'd never stolen from a dead man before, and I hoped never to repeat the process.

There. Surely that was what I came here to find, wasn't it? I wanted to get out of this room, but as I made to leave, something wedged in beside the cage caught my eye.

It was a book. Ordinary as anything, yes, but still a book. Unable to resist, I yanked it out and I hurried from the room, throwing the door shut behind me. The pounding in my head eased the minute I left that cursed place and handed Magnus his candle. Blackwood had helped Maria to her feet, though she still had her hands over her ears.

"What is this place?" he said.

"Strangewayes had something captive in there, and it took its revenge," I said, handing Blackwood the book. As one, we all hurried back the way we'd come, following the impossible turns of the hall. What if we became lost in here? What if we wandered forever, until we became of the dark, and the dark became us?

Where had that thought come from? We ran until light pierced the darkness ahead and we reemerged into the Ancients' showroom. Magnus kicked the door shut. Panting, I swore to myself never to go down there again. Cold sweat beaded on my forehead, and my hands were clammy. I had felt like a small child again, clutching the blankets and waiting for storied monsters to come for me out of the dark corners of the room.

Blackwood stepped away from us and turned the book's pages, his expression blank. Putting an arm through Maria's,

I walked her about the room. Color began to return to her cheeks.

This horrible place was a monument to Strangewayes's perversions, nothing more. What had we gained by coming here?

"My God," Blackwood murmured. He turned the book toward me. "Look."

Sketches of the monstrosities Strangewayes had left hanging in his display room graced the pages. But I saw what had caught Blackwood's eye: a bloblike form, bristling all over with dark hairs. It looked—no, it was *exactly* like Molochoron, the great jellylike Pale Destroyer. I snatched the book from his hand and read, my mouth falling open.

To drive away, employ cariz, the book said, the script somewhat legible. What "cariz" was, I'd no idea. There were arrows showing points of attack onto Molochoron's body, porous areas I had never noticed before.

Drive away. Flipping another page, I found an illustration of a chain, one that fitted itself rather nicely around the leg of some lizard-like creature.

Ralph Strangewayes had not only written a book about the Ancients; he had shown us how to defeat them.

8

"WHAT THE DEVIL DOES HE MEAN BY A CAR-whatsit?" Magnus looked over my shoulder and pointed at the page. My hands trembled as I leafed through the book. I had to be delicate; the paper felt fragile beneath my fingers.

"This, I believe." I showed Magnus and Blackwood, now standing about me. There was a sketch of a flutelike instrument with an oddly formed mouthpiece.

Blackwood took the book from me and flipped through it. "Does it say anything about R'hlem?" He searched the pages, but no. For some reason, the Skinless Man was the only one of our Seven Ancients who did not appear in Strangewayes's book. What did that mean?

"Look back at the weapons," I said, pointing to more sketches. One weapon resembled a wicked sort of scythe, with multiple metal teeth on the edge of the blade. It looked oddly familiar. "Wait a moment." I turned back to the walls.

Yes. When we'd first entered, I'd been too stunned to notice. But hanging all around us were the cruelest-looking weapons imaginable.

There was the scythe, hooked beside a glass case that

contained a horned skull. Curved swords, their blades fashioned like corkscrews, were also displayed on the walls. Daggers with three prongs sat upon a table. We discovered three of those "flutes," a hand-sized lantern that gave off a soft, eerily persistent glow, and a whistle carved from some kind of twisted bone on a velvet cushion under a glass case.

Magnus took one of the warped-looking swords off the wall. He tried swinging it, but the twisting shape of the blade, plus his injury, hampered his movement.

The blades were all formed from that same dusky orange-gold material, exactly like Strangewayes's dagger.

Blackwood had started collecting all the weapons he could lay his hands on, the scythe, the spears, the daggers. Maria picked up the lantern, though she didn't try opening it. I used Porridge to break the glass case and snatched up the whistle.

"We ought to leave." Maria frowned. "There's something *alive* about this house." She looked back at the door with the carved devils.

I walked back to the front door to peer out at the garden. The sunshine was still bright here, and the breeze crisp with salt from the ocean. Despite the wonders of this house, already I was desperate to leave. Maria was right. Something was off about this place.

"Henrietta," Maria called. "Come and look at this."

I joined her by an expanse of wall.

"What do you think these are?" She pointed.

Hundreds of names had been carved into the wall. Some

were etched in large, looping letters, some crammed close together. A familiar name caught my eye: *Darius LaGrande*. He'd been an eighteenth-century magician, a Frenchman who'd escaped the Revolution and come to England to research alchemy.

"These are all magicians," I said. Gingerly, I traced my fingertips along LaGrande's name.

"This house is a place of pilgrimage, then?" Maria asked.

"It looks like it. Perhaps this was a way of paying honor to the father of their craft." I looked over the names until another one caught my eye. Sparks shot off my hand involuntarily.

"Careful now!" Maria brushed at her trousers.

"Sorry," I murmured, knitting my fingers together. I drew closer to make absolutely certain I was right.

William Howel. The handwriting was even and neat, and carved for all the world to see. A flush of goose bumps spread over my body. My father had been here. Touching the letters, I imagined him standing in this very spot. I pictured him taking a knife and cutting his name into this wall. When had he come here?

"Howel? Turn around," Blackwood said. He sounded calm, but the stiffness of his voice couldn't be denied.

A shadowy figure waited in the open doorway. For one heart-stopping moment I was afraid it was a Familiar or, God forbid, R'hlem himself.

Then I noticed the leafy branches protruding from the thing's head. It was not terribly tall—only coming up to Blackwood's chest—but the fierce, glistening black eyes made me decide not to misjudge its strength. Its skin had a greenish tint, the same color as bog water. Tree bark was strapped in plates over its chest and legs like armor. The smell of damp earth and peat moss permeated the air, strong enough to make me gag. The creature raised its weapon, a sharpened stick, over its head.

Not any creature—a faerie. Clearly, this was from one of the lower orders of the dark court. The lowlier a faerie's blood, the less human it appeared.

"Cain's subjects. You trespass," it declared in a gurgling voice. *Cain?* Of course: the biblical figure who killed his brother, Abel. Faeries did not have a high opinion of man.

"Hail, fellow. Well met." Blackwood sketched a low bow, his body graceful as a dancer's. "Goodfellow, does your fair queen sit under the hill?"

"Hail, fellow. Well met." The faerie returned the bow, though its movements were stiff. Its joints creaked, like wood swollen with water. "My queen abides. You are trespassing on her land."

"Trespassing?" I couldn't stop myself. "This isn't Faerie."

"Howel." Blackwood's voice tightened with warning. The faerie grumbled. Brackish water dripped from it to pool on the floor.

"My queen takes lands given over to the forest. Lands given over to the rot," it said, its gurgling voice growing sharper. "Did you not notice the glamour upon the place? You must pay the penalty, Cain's subjects." The beetle-colored eyes glimmered. "Death."

Oh, damn everything.

"Goodfellow." Blackwood bowed deeply again. "I request a parley with Queen Mab."

"My queen dines under the hill tonight," the Goodfellow said. "Be careful, for her appetite is great." Blackwood breathed in sharply; I got the feeling that was not good. If only once, just once, we could meet some kind, cheerful creature that wanted to hug us.

"We request to see her at table," Blackwood replied.

"You will follow me," the Goodfellow said, and walked out the front door. Magnus, Maria, and I all exchanged looks, ranging from bewilderment to a sort of mute terror.

"Have we any choice in the matter?" Maria asked.

"Have you ever been hunted through Faerie woods by a baying pack of hounds and goblins?" Blackwood muttered. "The choice is parley or execution." Blackwood stepped over the house's threshold, his pack in one hand, several of the weapons tied to his back or around his waist. I checked my own collection—the bone whistle, Strangeways's dagger, the glowing lantern—and went after him. "Listen. This is important," Blackwood said when we were all outside. "If they offer you food or drink, say no. If they offer to dance, say no. If they offer *anything*, be polite when you refuse, but do not say thank you. They'll take that as a sign that you've accepted."

"I wish we'd run into the light court, not the dark," I murmured.

Blackwood walked beside me as the Goodfellow led us.

"Common misconception. People often think the light good and the dark evil. They are different, yes, but not entirely dissimilar. Mab is more chaotic than Titania, the light's queen. But Titania is colder. She does not even pretend to care for humans."

Truly, I learned something new and unsettling every day.

We followed the faerie as he disappeared behind a large willow tree on the edge of the property. What had Agrippa told me once? Entrances to Faerie existed on the edge of a shadow, or out the corner of one's eye.

"Watch your step," Blackwood whispered to me.

We brushed aside a curtain of leaves and stepped over the roots. My feet gave out from under me, and I fell into the earth.

GNARLED TIPS OF ROOTS DRIPPED ABOVE our heads, and the walls were rich, damp earth. My hands and knees were already soaked. Climbing to my feet, I could just make out the others as they oriented themselves in the near darkness. Magnus and Maria stayed behind Blackwood as he kept a hand to the earthen wall, steadying himself. The Goodfellow waited for us at the cavernous mouth of a large, uninviting tunnel.

"You will not stray from the path," the Goodfellow declared. Faintly luminescent toadstools lined either side of a narrow, twisting walkway. Blackwood motioned for me to come forward. Once we'd assembled as a group, he led the way for us. I was quite happy to let him.

The Goodfellow moved slowly, his legs too stiff to easily

bend at the knee. He guided us around twists and circles and bends, until I feared we'd lose our way. Hadn't I heard stories like this as a little girl? The faeries would lead children into a never-ending maze with the promise of silver buttons and sweets, releasing them after two hundred years had passed.

The Goodfellow finally brought us into a great domed enclosure. The high ceiling was festooned with winking faerie lights, adding dim illumination to the dining hall below. A ridiculously long table stretched from one end of the cavern to the other. The cloth covering the table was moldering, water-stained green silk. Delicacies had been piled all along the length of it. At first glance, the fare looked normal enough: there was roast pheasant, wild boar, and clusters of small cakes with glittering icing. When I looked again, I noticed that the food was distinctly more odd than I'd thought. The roast pheasant was in fact a large bat; the wild boar, some sort of lizard-y, piglike creature; and the clusters of pretty cakes were dotted with shining eyeballs, which glanced wildly about the room.

Blackwood's warning not to eat anything sounded extremely wise.

At least the guests were enjoying themselves. Raucous laughter filled the enormous space. The faeries were all splendidly and bizarrely dressed. The ladies' outfits were especially fragile concoctions. One gown appeared to be constructed from thousands of fluttering gray moth wings; another's consisted of mere whispers of smoke that glided over her pale skin. The gentlemen wore old-fashioned white wigs that gleamed with spiderwebs, and moth-eaten velvet suits of red and green. The music, piped from creatures that floated through the air, was off-key and out of time.

As we made our way across the room, Blackwood pressed me against him, one arm tightening around my waist. Unthinking, I nearly slapped him away.

"We must be partnered, or they'll try to make us sit," he whispered. Magnus took his lead and grabbed Maria. We followed the Goodfellow, but hands plucked at my elbow. Two women of ferocious, black-eyed beauty smiled benevolently at me.

"Join the feast," one of them cooed.

"Heavenly tarts," the other said, biting into one. A blood-red jelly oozed from the pastry. I prayed it *was* jelly.

"This was a mistake," Magnus said through his teeth, flinching as a woman with long, sharp talons pawed at him. The faeries' appearances slipped and shifted the longer I regarded them, as though their handsome human visages were masks in danger of dropping away. Perfect noses grew longer, pearly teeth sharpened. Eyes became red or molten gold.

The Goodfellow mercifully turned and shouted, "They are the queen's distinguished guests. Let them pass." The faeries pouted and returned to their plates. Heart pounding, I clung to Blackwood as we walked toward a throne positioned at the head of the table.

"Is that my little lordling?" a female voice trilled. "Come, Georgy. It's been absolute ages."

The throne was situated above the floor, accessible by six earthen steps. A woman sat with one leg slung over the chair's arm. Even slouching, she appeared regal. This had to be Mab. The queen was a small, exquisitely beautiful girl who looked no more than nineteen, with bare feet and white, cobwebby hair that floated aimlessly about her head. A diadem of pearl and moonstone sat daintily upon her brow, glowing even in the low light.

"Where is my lordling?" She giggled as Blackwood came to the foot of the steps and knelt. "Still as handsome as ever. Beauty doesn't last on you humans, but I think that makes it all the more precious." Mab sniffed. "We're having quite a party, my little mortals. Such delightful music." She picked at her teeth and took up one of the pale cakes on a plate by her side. "I like these," she said conversationally, spreading jam across one with a knife that appeared to be made out of bone. In fact, all the plates and utensils I'd seen had been fashioned from bone. "Though I do miss the old delicacies. You people used to leave me the heart of a Roman legionnaire cooked in brandy. So scrumptious and perfect for an autumn evening."

"My queen, we humbly request use of your roads to return to the mortals' realm. We did not mean to trespass upon your Cornwall lands," Blackwood said.

Mab sighed, got off her throne, and traipsed down toward us. She wore no corset that I could see, only a billowing white gown that appeared to be made from spider silk. One capped sleeve slipped from her pale shoulder, giving me a glimpse of far more of the queen than I wanted. Mab stalked over to Blackwood and waved her jam-smeared butter knife in his face.

"You know there has to be a toll, my pet. I can't have people running willy-nilly across my lands. What would happen then?" She narrowed her eyes and pouted. "I'd have to eat them all is what."

"If Your Majesty wishes, what might the toll be?" Maria asked. The girl had no bloody fear. Mab grinned at her.

"This one speaks to me. Perhaps she can be a pet." She reached for Maria, and I stepped in front of her. Mab scowled. "No. Not you. You're too tall to help pull my walnut carriage."

I hated faeries.

Taking a cue from Blackwood, I tried to be my most polite. "Majesty, I am Henrietta Howel, the burning rose of England, the sorcerers' prophesied one destined to bring about the Ancients' destruction." Faeries liked long, showy titles. I curtsied. "We are your allies in this war. Giving us safe passage through your lands would illustrate the nobility of your character . . . and fully highlight and complement your matchless beauty." Queen Mab beamed, blackberry jam smeared all over her teeth.

"I like this tall one," Mab said, poking me in the stomach.

"Your Majesty is perfection, as generous as you are beautiful," Blackwood said, his voice silk. He nodded at me. Apparently I'd done well.

Mab studied Maria again—I think she was serious about

taking the girl—but Maria patted her ax, and the queen turned away. Of course. Faeries detested iron.

"You aren't like that mean Imperator of yours, Georgy. That's why I like you. Did you know he came to see me last week and *demanded* I open my roads to his Order? 'Easier to get sorcerers about the country,' he said. 'Takes less time and costs fewer lives,' he said. Well." Her cobwebby hair rose in her passion. "I don't even let my *sister* use my roads, so why does he think he gets a right?"

"We are allies in this war, Majesty," Blackwood said smoothly.

"I've already given so many of my lovely subjects to the stupid war. Do you know that eighteen hundred goblins were slaughtered near Manchester, not two weeks before? And still the Imperator demands more." Her eyes glinted with tears, presumably for her fallen soldiers. It made me soften toward the queen.

"My apologies, Majesty, for any indelicacy." Blackwood sounded sincere, and Mab appeared mollified.

"That doesn't change things, though. There *has* to be a toll." She huffed, and considered. "Heartbreak. The pains of the heart are so delicious to me. That would be a token, yes, a very fair one." She began to sniff at us, one after the other. She paused before me. Oh damn. "Mmm, such complexity." Mab stood on tiptoe and brushed a hand through my hair; I kept still. "Women's hearts are more complex than men's, I find.

Less virile, less passionate, but so utterly complicated." She trailed a delicate pink tongue across her bottom lip. "How delicious."

I had to force myself not to push her off. My toes curled with the effort.

"What do you want from me, Majesty?" I would not be afraid.

"A piece of your heart," she cooed, patting my cheek with her small, dry hand. Her eyes glittered, animal and wild. "One of those moments that gives you a scrap of hope on a gray day."

My mind rebelled. What would she take? A stolen moment on the moors with Rook? An evening playing chess with Agrippa? *How* would she take it? Mab must have read the resistance in my eyes.

"You won't get out of here otherwise." Her voice was sweet to the point of insult.

"Perhaps I might—" Blackwood began, but Mab dismissed him with a wave.

"You've nothing to interest me, Georgy," the queen said flatly. "Your feelings are always so mundane." Blackwood tightened his jaw; suppressed anger danced in his eyes. We had to finish this.

"Fine," I said shortly. "Do what you must." I clasped my hands together so she wouldn't see them shaking. Mab put her fingers to my lips. I was preparing myself when Magnus strode forward.

"Majesty." He gave an elaborate bow, as deep as Blackwood's had been. In his naval coat and breeches, with his skin golden from the sun, Magnus looked like a small scrap of light in this underworld. "You say a young man's heart is more virile. Why not taste mine?"

"No, Magnus," I said quickly, but Mab's nostrils flared. She crept closer and nestled against him, twining her small hand through his wild auburn hair. The queen pressed her cheek to Magnus's chest.

"Such pain." Mab swooned and chattered her teeth. "How did I miss it?" She wrapped her arms around his neck, her feet dangling off the ground. Magnus grunted. "Oh, I have to taste this. Give me a memory," she whispered in his ear, her voice turning guttural. Magnus flinched.

"Please. Take one of mine," I said.

"No, no. I want this." Mab kissed Magnus's temple. "Such a beautiful face. One of the most beautiful I can recall. I would love to see you chained with all my other pets."

If she tried to put him in chains, I'd have *her* heart.

"I prefer other forms of diversion to chains, ma'am," he said. His reserve didn't falter.

Mab laughed, the tinkling sound of breaking glass. "Your pain is so exquisite, my little warrior." She passed a hand along his arm. "It's the taste of someone unused to defeat."

Magnus closed his eyes. "If you want something, Majesty, please take it," he said, his voice tight.

"Then give me a most cherished memory," she whispered in his ear.

Blackwood caught my eye. "Don't move," he breathed.

"Quickly, if you please," Magnus said. Mab touched his lips, pressed a hand over his heart, and pushed. Magnus grunted, pain etched on his face as she pressed deeper, harder. I winced as I listened to him cry out. I felt as helpless as if I were watching it through the bars of a cage.

Maria came up beside me, keeping close. "Poor fellow," she whispered, holding on to my arm. I could sense it: she was both comforting and controlling me, should I decide to act.

"There it is," Mab cooed, holding some strange *thing* in her hand. It pulsed with light. The sheen was soft and delicate, milk white and tinged with blue. Magnus grimaced, one hand on his chest. He watched with desperation as the queen handled whatever small piece of his soul she'd taken.

And then she ate it. Gobbled it down like a small piece of cake. Magnus buried his head in his hands.

"You bitch," I snarled, tears springing into my eyes. Maria dug her fingers into my arm. Mab smiled.

"I know," she said in a singsong way. Traipsing up the steps to her throne, she returned to lounging. "You may use my roads. Remember not to stray from the path," she called as we walked out, following her tree-barked knight.

I slipped beside Magnus. "Are you all right?" I asked. When I tried to hold his arm to steady him, he pulled away with a shake of his head.

"I hate this quest," he whispered.

"Thank you," I said.

"Indeed. You were . . . brave," Blackwood said as he came up behind us. He sounded unsteady, as if complimenting Magnus required physical effort. Maria said nothing but put a comforting hand on his shoulder.

What a wretch I was. I should have forced Mab to take something from me. As Magnus walked ahead, I felt ashamed.

The road twined ahead of us, growing rockier and more uneven. There was barely space for us to pass single file. As the path grew narrower, whispering voices on either side called out to us. Listening to them, I could feel my eyes growing heavier. My legs felt weak; I wanted to turn, to sit and rest—

"Keep moving." Maria grabbed me by my collar and steered me straight. "They've a way of tricking you." Once she'd put me right again, she clapped her hands over her ears.

I murmured my thanks, slapping my cheek to bring myself out of the daze, and covered my ears as well. The road inclined steeply up, up, and up. My temples ached, as if someone had looped a leather band around my head and was tightening it, degree by degree, until I was on the verge of going mad.

We emerged aboveground between one heartbeat and the next. One instant, there was only dark earth above us. The next, the sun was so brilliant that my eyes watered and stung. Shouts of surprise erupted as a great crowd of people materialized out of nowhere. Maria was standing next to me, looking at the cobblestones beneath our feet with an expression of wonder.

"By the Mother," Maria muttered. "Where are we?"

"In London," I said, my eyes adjusting enough that I could recognize the streets. We'd come out close to St. Paul's Cathedral, in the heart of traffic. A hansom cab came to a clattering halt mere feet from us, the horse rearing on his hind legs. A red-faced driver shouted obscenities at us, until he got a better look. Then he went pale.

"Sorcerers," he murmured.

Maria huddled closer to me, like an animal seeking shelter. Had she ever been in a city before?

We quickly made our way out of the street. Thanks to the Faerie roads, we'd returned to London in record time. Now I could feel how odd we must look, with scythes and flutes strapped to our backs, daggers and swords dangling from our belts, a bone whistle around my neck, and a glowing, slightly sinister lantern in my hand.

"What do we do now?" Magnus said. He smiled at the crowd.

"We send word to Whitechurch and the queen," Blackwood replied, adjusting the scythe across his back. The sharp teeth that hung from the edge of the blade were dangerously close to his head. Perhaps putting these weapons down would be a good idea. "First, we go home."

BACK IN BLACKWOOD'S FRONT HALL, WE SLOUGHED off packs and unbuckled weapons with sighs of gratitude. The footmen said nothing as they helped us, but I watched their expressions of shock as they managed the curling swords and daggers. I checked my pack; yes, Strangewayes's book was still in there.

The moment I'd removed the weapons, I scanned the hall, hoping for a glimpse of Rook. Unfortunately, there was none to be had.

"Is Rook here?" I asked the butler.

"I believe he's out, miss," the man replied, holding the lantern as far from his body as possible. Rook was at work, most likely. Damn.

Maria slipped quietly to the sidelines, watching all of this with wide, wary eyes. She shifted her weight from foot to foot.

"Make yourself at home," Blackwood told her, sounding distant as he walked away. I imagined he was already composing a letter to Whitechurch in his mind. *Dear Imperator, we found a museum of monsters and Strangewayes's skeleton. What would you like us to do with the weapons?*

Then again, perhaps he would take a subtler approach.

Maria went to Magnus. "I should see to your arm," she told him, but he shook his head.

"It doesn't hurt, and I need to be off to see my mother. She'll want to know I've returned." He nodded. "Send word when Whitechurch replies," he told me, and left. The front door closed, and the hall was quiet once more.

Now it was just Maria and I. In this grand room, among polished brass fixtures and rich velvet hangings, I supposed she felt out of place. Indeed, her next words were, "I should be on my way."

"Where will you go?" I tried not to sound too interested.

"Might head east, then north. Point is to keep moving." She shrugged.

"By yourself?" I crossed my fingers. "Isn't there anything that could persuade you to stay?"

"Your gracious, brooding Lordship might not approve." She blushed. "Besides, I don't feel comfortable. No disrespect intended." She glanced at the stately surroundings as though they would attack her, a look I understood all too well.

"I felt the same when I first came to London, you know. I used to teach at a charity school," I said.

"Oh? So you were not always a great lady?" She meant it sincerely. I shouldn't have laughed.

"I used to get ten lashings for imperfect penmanship. I'm far from a great lady."

"You were beaten?" Maria's face cleared in surprise. Now was the time to act.

"May I show you something?" I asked.

She followed me upstairs to the very top of the house, down the corridor toward Fenswick's apartments. I opened the apothecary door and led her inside. At the sight of the dried herbs and flowers, the pots and bowls and pestles, the copper spoons and pans, Maria's whole expression changed. She knelt on a bench and studied the mashed herbs that lay before her.

"Is this powdered primrose? I can tell by the scent." She gave a gleeful shriek. "Whoever's chopping this has a fine hand. Why should she be playing with stinging nettle, though?"

"Who said anything about a *she*?" Fenswick grumbled, entering with a loop of garlic cloves twined around his neck. He hopped on a bench and then pulled himself onto the table, slapping pollen from his trousers. "How on earth did you recognize the nettle?"

"Smell's too sharp to be anything else." Maria leaned her elbows on the table. Cradling her face in her hands, she beamed in delight. "You're a hobgoblin, are you not?"

"And you're a red-haired miscreant," Fenswick said, ears flattening on either side of his head. He thought Maria was poking fun.

"They say hobgoblins know the secrets of every plant under the sun and the moon. Marvelous healers."

That seemed to do the trick. Fenswick scuffed his shoes

with pride while Maria moved around the room, touching a curling loop of tendrils that sprouted from a hanging planter. "Most sorcerers don't have such apothecaries. Too much like—"

"Witchcraft?" I finished for her. Here it was. I felt the tingling of embers blooming in the lines of my palms, a warning to be careful. Maria went still, like an animal trying to decide whether to fight or to flee.

"Wouldn't know," she said cautiously.

Fenswick looked up from chopping the garlic. Maria's fingers trailed to the ax at her side.

I forged ahead quickly. "I need your help."

"Meaning what?" All the friendly light was gone from her brown eyes.

"Someone dear to me is sick." I moved before the door, in case she tried to bolt.

"Dying?" Maria's look softened by a degree.

"Worse," I whispered. Maria snorted at that.

"What's worse than dying?"

"Henrietta." Fenswick's voice had a note of warning, but for Rook, I could not stop.

"Transformation." Quickly, I told about my own path to London, my fire abilities, about being found and brought here. I told her about discovering my magician roots, the fear of being found out, my brief imprisonment and betrayal. And I told her about Rook, his shadow powers, and what Fenswick and I had done for him.

While I relayed the story, Maria sat down, and Fenswick

brewed lingonberry tea, bitter but refreshing. My cup cooled beside me while I talked. When I'd finished, Maria was silent for a while. "You're not their chosen one, then?" She sounded amazed. "And you think I can save your friend?"

"I saw you heal yourself of the Familiar's venom," I said.

She shuddered. "My . . . gifts . . . are natural. The Ancients' aren't."

God, I couldn't lose her. Thinking fast, I said, "Listen. The road outside is dangerous. It's a miracle you've stayed clear of the Ancients thus far." I stepped closer. "What happens if you meet one, use your power, and someone sees? Sorcerers are not the only ones against witchcraft." Indeed, after Mary Willoughby's treachery had been revealed, the common folk had rioted, particularly in the north. They had done things that, well, made the sorcerers' burnings look restrained.

Maria chewed on her bottom lip. I could see she was weighing what I said.

"No one will discover you here. If you help me, I'll give you anything you want in return."

Just then the door opened, and Rook rushed inside. He was breathing fast, as if he'd been running up the stairs. The color in his cheeks was bright. When he saw me, a wide smile stole over his face.

"You're back." His arms were around me in an instant, and he lifted my feet from the floor. I buried my face in his neck, breathing in the sunlight on his skin. His embrace lasted too brief a moment. "Thank God," he said, putting me down. Rook noticed Maria and quickly bowed. "Apologies. Didn't know a, er, lady was present," he said, scanning her trousers.

I saw her notice the few visible scars that peeked out of his sleeve at the wrist. Today, they were red and inflamed.

"Maria Templeton," she said curtly. "Beg your pardon." She made her way around Rook and out the door. Damn. I followed and closed the door behind us, ready to beg—

"I'll help him." She folded her arms tight across her chest.

"You will?" My voice rose in excitement, and she shushed me.

"There are things we might try, if the hobgoblin allows it."

"He will," I said quickly.

"One more thing. I'd like a cot up here. I wouldn't feel comfortable in one of your grand rooms downstairs."

"Of course." I'd give her half my own blood if it would make her stay. "Why did you change your mind?" Apart from my brilliant reasoning, obviously.

"You love him." She said it boldly, without question. My face flushed. "There are few who love the Unclean in this world. Makes me feel I can trust you." She extended her hand. "Congratulations. You've the services of a very skilled witch."

WHITECHURCH REPLIED TO BLACKWOOD WITHIN HOURS. The ink on the letter was spattered, the words smeared—evidently, he'd written it hastily and shoved it into a messenger's hand without bothering to blot it. Even though it was afternoon, bordering on evening, Her Majesty had invited us all to meet at Buckingham Palace immediately. Blackwood and I pulled up to the palace to find Magnus already there, pacing outside the entrance with his hat in his hand.

Fae warriors and a unit of sorcerers guarded Her Majesty's door. The faeries were of the same rank as the Goodfellow, moss and lichen covering their wooden faces, carrying wooden shields and clubs studded with wicked-looking thorns. They said nothing as we passed them by.

The queen's private sitting room had an ornately carved wooden ceiling and shuttered windows to keep out the now-waning afternoon light. Lamps had already been lit, and in the corner, beneath a painting of the old king, a bell-shaped brass cage sheltered a pair of singing yellow canaries.

The queen was seated on a velvet sofa; Whitechurch stood behind her. I couldn't find a clue to his mood in his blank expression. His eyes, however, regarded each of us keenly.

Blackwood, Magnus, and I stood side by side and waited on the queen's command.

"Show us," she said at last.

Together, we laid Strangewayes's weapons out on a long, polished table. Her Majesty got up and drew nearer, staring at the weapons in astonishment. The lantern especially interested her. She picked it up before putting it down again quickly, as though it would bite. Finally, I placed Strangewayes's book.

Now what would she do? What would she say? It was one thing to discover these oddities, and quite another to be allowed to use them. Anticipation welled up inside me.

Whitechurch frowned as he studied our strange wares, but

the queen looked excited. She touched a finger to one of the orange-gold daggers, her mouth forming a soft O of surprise. In a lavender gown, with her hair pulled back in a simple style, she looked less like a sovereign at the head of a terrible war and more like a young woman admiring a carnival trick.

"Tell us about these," Whitechurch said, sweeping his hand over the assorted objects. Magnus and Blackwood allowed me to answer for all of us. It was no secret that the queen seemed to favor me. I tried not to let that go to my head.

"This is Ralph Strangewayes, and his otherworldly assistant," I said, unrolling the painting delicately. The queen gasped at the sight of the monster. On the back, elegant handwriting declared this was Ralph ("R.S.") and his servant Azureus, the Latin for "blue." Aptly named, as the creature was the color of a high summer sky.

"And this book details the Ancients?" Queen Victoria flipped through the journal, using only the tip of her finger to turn the pages.

"How could Strangewayes have had such knowledge?" Whitechurch didn't sound pleased. Damn. He wouldn't love what I was about to suggest.

"I believe magician craft comes from the Ancients' world," I said. The queen dropped the bone whistle. "We know that Strangewayes was trying to give King Henry a son, and discovered a source of unnatural magic." I crossed my fingers. "He must have found a path into the Ancients' domain. These weapons are specifically designed for creatures not of this earth."

"What are you proposing?" Whitechurch asked, though I could tell he knew and did not like it.

"We must learn how to use these weapons," Blackwood said, though he did not sound enthused.

Already, Whitechurch was shaking his head. "This is how it begins," he warned. Her Majesty remained silent. "This is how magicians gain a foothold in our society."

Was that so terribly wrong? I had to bite my tongue.

"Sir, we've battled these creatures for over a decade," Blackwood continued. "What if these weapons *do* contain the key to R'hlem's destruction?"

Whitechurch frowned deeper than ever. Here it was, our potential salvation, and he didn't want it because magicians could not be trusted? I had to stifle the urge to start shouting.

"Howel," the queen said, her voice soft. "Do you know how to use these?"

"Not yet, Majesty," I replied. Please, let her see how important this was. Let her agree. "Your Majesty said that I was a sorcerer." I decided to blunder ahead; it was time to be bold. "I am. But I used sorcerer *and* magician magic the night we defeated Korozoth, and Your Majesty said that I must control both sides of my power."

"I believe I said control, not use." The queen wasn't smiling.

"This could be our best chance," I said. Standing before the queen, I recalled once more the servant dead at the foot of her bed. His blood had been used as a message to me; I had to answer it. I *had* to strike at R'hlem, chosen one or not.

Whitechurch's power stirred. I could feel it on my skin, and it made me light-headed. "This is not our way," he thundered.

"But it might be the best way," the queen said. That stopped the Imperator. "This is dangerous, Howel." For one moment, I held my breath. Finally, she sighed. "Who would assist you in this?"

Oh, thank God and Strangewayes and even bloody Mickelmas.

"I would, Your Majesty," Magnus said. "Captain Ambrose doesn't want me back on board until my arm is fully recovered. Allow me to be of service."

"And I, Majesty," Blackwood said, though he sounded far more reluctant.

"There might be others who would agree," I said. I'd write to the boys, Dee and Wolff and Lambe. There was a small, selfish part of me that wanted us all together again.

"Very well," the queen said. Whitechurch kept silent, though I could read his disapproving thoughts. "But these weapons must work. If they don't, you will put them aside." She closed the book's cover. "Or you will face dire consequences."

"Yes, Majesty," I breathed.

Once again, I was playing with fire.

10

THE NEXT DAY, BLACKWOOD AND I ARRIVED AT THE Camden Town barracks with the weaponry and the few scratchings of a plan. The barracks themselves were two stables remodeled into sleeping quarters, with a wide, oval-shaped training yard for practice. Apart from a select few—Blackwood and myself included, since I couldn't well sleep in bunks with men all about—this was where the younger, unmarried sorcerers lived, trained, and waited to be called for battle.

Men ran drills as we entered, lunging forward seven, eight, ten times on command. Squadron leaders blew whistles, sending their men into different formations: the diamond patterns best suited for weaving nets of flame, the circles that anchored sorcerers as they made the earth tremble and shake. I blushed watching; it was a humid day at the end of summer, and some of them had their coats off. Even after all the weeks of living in Agrippa's house, I'd not got used to men without proper dress. If Agrippa were here, he'd say . . .

He wasn't, though.

Agrippa betrayed you. Those were the words I repeated to myself whenever the pain of missing him grew too great. I had tried to hate him, but his betrayal had been partly my own fault: I had not trusted him, and that had made him not trust me.

And now I was stuck with an annoyed-looking Valens coming over to meet us.

"There you are." His mouth tightened at the sight of the magician weapons. "The others are already arrived." He led us around the buildings to a smaller, more secluded area. This yard was walled, the cobblestones small and unevenly laid.

I held a packet of papers in my hand, instruction sheets I'd spent the night working up. Reading through Strangewayes's book had proven slow going; the ink had become blurred in many places, and the language and spelling were antiquated. Still, I'd done my best. Strangewayes's "introduction" had been particularly interesting:

In approaching these beasts, one must remember: they are not cattle, nor deer, nor anything that can be cudgeled or cajoled into obedience. They are monsters from the depths of nightmares. No mercy must be shown them, no compassion, and no hesitation if death is the only option. Whip the creatures until the blood flows, beacon them into a stupor, pipe until they are at the brink of despairing madness, but do not stop. Do not yield. One cannot look into the Devil's eyes and expect to glimpse his soul.

Not the cheeriest language. The very back of the book wasn't uplifting either, for Strangewayes had written in it when he'd gone well past the brink of despairing madness himself. A thick black circle had been drawn over and over again, with such strength that the pen had broken through the paper in some places. *The stars are black,* he'd written above it, along with mentions of that Kindly Emperor, the maker and unmaker of worlds.

WITNESS HIS SMILE was scrawled over three pages. I'd decided to leave these sections out of our training.

Dee was seated on a bench against the wall, examining one of the daggers. Magnus stood in the center of the yard and kept trying to get his corkscrew sword to behave itself. Whenever he tried swinging it, it whined in the air like a sick dog.

"I believe I'm an expert," he called. He'd already taken his arm out of its sling. Now it was bandaged tightly, and he winced when he moved it. Hopefully, he'd let Maria take another look at it.

"Some things never change." Blackwood went to lay the scythe against the wall. He would not be in an approving mood for any of this. Still, he'd sat with me in the library, helping to make copies of the instructions. He'd seen the weapons loaded carefully this morning, checking each in turn. Duty. He'd told me once that was his lifeblood. His queen gave an order, and he would see it done.

"It's like a homecoming." Magnus put his sword down. "We should have got the other fellows involved. Maybe brought some cider as well." He stretched his arms above his head, giving his back a satisfying crack.

"There's no time for games," Blackwood said.

"My favorite part of all this has been spending so much quality time with you, Blacky." Evidently, a large part of these meetings would involve keeping them from killing each other.

I handed out the papers and set the copies down on the bench. One could never have too many copies. I'd enjoyed making them, really. It took me back to my teaching days at Brimthorn. While I didn't have many fond memories of the place, the excitement and relief I saw in the girls' eyes when I helped them understand a particular equation or conjugate a certain verb in French had made me happy.

"I've created a lesson." I beamed.

"Huzzah," Magnus said dully.

For a few moments, the boys were silent as they read. I could tell they were confused; I didn't blame them. There were some terms I simply didn't understand, and others I wasn't entirely sure I could read. Strangewayes had bizarre names for his weapons, and no system for matching weapons with titles. I was fairly certain the whip was a *cariz*, the daggers *martlets,* but couldn't be sure. I'd done my best, guessing and filling in the gaps as I went. For the most part, I thought I'd done a fine job.

For the most part. The point of today was to have a go at each weapon. Even with spotty knowledge, we'd get nowhere without practice.

"Let's see this demonstration," Valens said, picking a thread from his sleeve.

Hopefully, this would be enough for a start. Dee and Blackwood began sorting out the weapons.

"We've got two twisty swords," Magnus said, checking the paper for the name. "Er, *deckors*." And that was that. He put the sheet by the wayside and didn't consult it again. "Then there's the thing that looks like a scythe with teeth, a bone whistle, two normal-sized daggers, a tiny, tiny dagger." Magnus picked that one up, frowning at it. It was about as long as my palm, blade and hilt and all. "There're also the three flutes, a whip, and some kind of lantern." He picked up the last one, then put it down just as quickly. There was something about that particular object that both intrigued and repulsed people.

I looked back at my paper. "Strangewayes didn't write about how to use most of them, but he did say that the lantern was ideal for 'beaconing' a creature."

Magnus took the whip from Dee. When he cracked it, a flash of violet light exploded in our faces. My eyes stung for several seconds before I could see properly again. Blackwood held out one of the swords, his knees relaxed, his arms out straight. He tried swinging it, but the weapon twisted in his hands and fell to the ground, making that sick-dog noise when it struck. My eardrums rattled at the very sound. Valens's pen scratched as Dee picked up one of the flutes. It really was the oddest-looking contraption: slender, with finger holes along the length and a cruel-looking mouthpiece that resembled a large metal thorn.

"What's this do?" Dee asked. I looked at the sheet I'd prepared. Strangewayes had said very little in the way of how to use it, only that the right tune would drive a beast away.

"We need a melody." I frowned. "Give it a try."

Dee shrugged, put his lips to the thing after wiping it down with a cloth, and blew.

A moment later, when my ears had finally stopped ringing and my head felt as though it was no longer going to explode, I got up off the ground. The damned sunlight pierced my skull like a knife. Blackwood was on his knees, his hands gripping the back of his head. Poor Dee, tears in his eyes, kicked at the flute where it lay on the ground.

"You stupid bastard!" Dee yelled.

"Don't touch it! It could make the noise again," Magnus yelled, tackling him. The flute's "music" had sounded like the demonic screams of a million cats burning in a furnace, but worse.

Valens had dropped his notebook and was working his jaw, testing his hearing. There were angry shouts from around the other side of the barracks as bootless men in their shirtsleeves came rushing around the corner to gape at us. One fellow sported half a face of shaving cream.

"No more of the flute today," Valens ordered, his voice cracking.

Blackwood grabbed the moldering sheath that the flute had come in, and gingerly slid the instrument back inside.

"Does anyone want to try the daggers? I mean, *martlets*?"

I asked, determined to use the vocabulary. Weaving as though drunk, Magnus picked one up. I took another.

"Do you know how to handle it?" he asked.

"It can't be too different from a warded blade," I said, though not with much confidence. Strangewayes's book had detailed the two sides of the blade—*upperside* for a blunter edge, *downwind* for the bottom, extremely sharp edge—but hadn't gone to the trouble of explaining how best to use the damned thing. It had to be like any normal dagger, yes?

Probably not.

"Gently," Magnus said, reaching back. We parried, and the blades met.

When the edges touched, a violent, invisible force shoved me back onto the ground, my skirt and petticoats flying about in a damned unladylike fashion. Magnus kept his feet better than I did. Swearing, he helped me up.

"I don't want to use the scythe," Dee said, dropping the thing like it would bite him. I examined the little dagger; what the devil did one *do* with such an insignificant item? I turned my eyes to the lantern, still pulsing with light.

Given our luck so far, I decided I'd rather not play with it.

Sighing, I picked up the bone whistle. It was the only thing here, besides the lantern, not made of that strange orange-gold metal. Finger holes had been carved along the length of it, for playing tunes.

Oh God, rather like the flute. Making a face, I put it to my lips.

"Everyone prepare." Blackwood put his hands over his ears. Valens's pen stopped, and I blew.

Absolutely nothing happened. I tried again, once and twice. Nothing. Not a sound.

"Well. At least it's completely useless as opposed to hatefully murderous," Magnus grumbled.

"Off to a good start, then?" Dee asked hopefully.

Valens continued scribbling, wearing a satisfied smirk.

11

BY LATE AFTERNOON, WE'D EXHAUSTED THE WEAP-
onry. Dee did attempt the scythe, as he was the only one of
us big enough to properly wield it. He appeared to handle it
well. However, the scythe made a muffled, sobbing sound as
it slid through the air, rather like a crying child. The noise was
so miserable that I begged him to stop and Blackwood had to
leave the yard.

"That was . . . fascinating," Dee managed as the four of
us made our way out of the barracks. He sounded like he was
thanking me for a rainy garden party.

"It was dreadful," I said. No point trying to pretend, especially with how ill everyone was. My vision had blurred as we'd
progressed through the day, and now there was a persistent
ringing in my ears. I'd had to step behind the barracks at one
point, press my forehead against the wall, and wait to see if I
would vomit. Dee *had* thrown up, becoming sick inches from
Valens's shoes. Magnus's nose had begun gushing blood for no
reason. As for Blackwood, I'd never seen him more wild-haired
or wild-eyed.

Our bodies had to *adjust* to handling the weapons. We all sensed it, and it made me horribly uneasy.

"We need something to lift our spirits." Magnus clapped a hand on Dee's shoulder. "Come to my mother's for tea."

"Tea?" Dee sounded faint with longing. My stomach growled, rudely butting into the conversation. Still, stomachs had a way of talking good sense.

"Would it be wrong to turn up uninvited?" Blackwood sounded as though he was looking for an excuse not to go. But *tea*.

"Nonsense. *I* invited you." Magnus extended his hand to help me into the carriage. Perhaps I should have gone back home to continue reading up on the weapons. But my stomach growled again, winning the argument. And as Dee was practically drooling, it seemed impolite to say no.

As the carriage came to a halt outside the house, my stomach knotted up. Meeting new people always unnerved me.

"Are you *sure* your mother won't mind?" I asked for the tenth time as Magnus helped me out of the carriage, Dee and Blackwood following behind.

"There's nothing she loves more than company." He swung open a little iron gate and gestured us to follow him. Magnus's mother lived in a small redbrick house, on a quiet but pleasant street. A gravel path cut across a bright square of lawn to the entrance. When Magnus knocked, a maid opened the door. Her hair was streaked with gray, and she squinted at us over a pair of spectacles.

"Polly, my dear," Magnus crowed. "How are you?"

"Mister Julian! And guests! Come in, come in!" She waved us into the foyer, fluttering about so much that I feared she'd fall over. "I'll summon the mistress," she said, and hurried off up the stairs.

I smiled as I untied my bonnet. "She's very enthusiastic."

"Yes. Very," Blackwood murmured in that disapproving tone. Of course, in his house the servants were expected to be emotionless, elegant, and efficient, the three Es of servitude. I gave him an exasperated look.

"Polly loves my visits home." Magnus threw his hat with admirable ease onto a peg by the door. And why shouldn't he feel easy? He'd grown up in this house. His childhood memories were soaked into every corner of every room.

I wished I knew what that was like.

"This is delightful." I looked about. Having lived in Agrippa's and Blackwood's homes, I now saw this place as less grand and more comfortable. The walls were papered blue with faded gold flowers, and peeling at the upper corners. Hardwood floors shone from enthusiastic waxing, even if they were a bit worn.

Listen to me, critiquing a fine London home. *Yes, I've changed quite a bit,* I thought, irritated with myself.

"Mother will be glad to hear you like it," Magnus said.

There were quick footsteps on the stairs, and a woman cried, "Julian!"

A lady rushed down to meet us. She looked to be in her early forties and still quite attractive, her figure slim and her soft brown hair in curls. Her eyes were large and blue. I could read some of Magnus in her, the same pointed nose and the strong, squared jaw. Because of that jaw, most men would call her handsome rather than beautiful, but her smile had probably softened many hearts. She was lovely.

She went to her son, and he kissed her hand. "My boy, home again."

Magnus laughed. "Well, I couldn't resist Mrs. Whist's cooking." He turned her to meet us. "Mrs. Fanny Magnus."

She knew Blackwood and Dee on sight. She warmly gave Dee her hand and curtsied to Blackwood. "My lord, so good of you to visit," she said, turning down her eyes respectfully.

It seemed a bit odd that she should have to curtsy to a boy her son's age, but Blackwood responded with a graceful bow. It wasn't always easy to read his expressions, but it appeared he truly liked Fanny. That put her in rather an exclusive club.

"And this is Miss Henrietta Howel." Magnus winked at me.

"Miss Howel. At last." She was graciousness itself as she took my hand. I could see where Magnus got his ease with people.

Polly trundled down the stairs to meet us again and went to Magnus to pat his cheek, as if he were still some small boy. Blackwood looked stunned, but for my part, I liked it.

"Polly, you're getting prettier every day," Magnus said. "I hope my mother doesn't work you too hard."

The maid squawked at the very idea and scuttled off.

"You keep a nice home, ma'am," I said.

Fanny waved a handkerchief. "Polly's such a dear. I can't give her what she's worth, but she won't leave! Julian sends me what he can from his pay." She smiled at her son. "Once I tried letting our cook go. I offered to help her find a better position, but she cried so bitterly that I had to let her stay!" She led us into the parlor.

"It was always like this growing up," Magnus told me. "A houseful of laughing women."

"It sounds wonderful." I smiled.

"It was." He grinned at me.

We sat down, and I could barely keep myself from gobbling everything at once. The cake was a delicate sponge, filled with cream and jam. The tea was piping hot. I'd been so engrossed in the training that I hadn't even noticed how famished I'd become. I could have eaten twenty slices. Dee went back for third helpings, his ears turning red, but Fanny encouraged him. "Arthur, you know I like to see you boys with healthy appetites," she said. Apparently, Dee was a regular visitor.

Between Magnus and his mother, it was hard to get a word in, or to stop laughing. Fanny had a theatrical air similar to her son's. She would widen her extraordinary eyes when she told stories, and the way she mimicked people's voices was hysterical. There was one tale about losing her bonnet in the park that had me laughing so hard my stomach ached. As the others poured more tea, my eyes lit on a portrait on the back wall, of a striking elderly woman with perfectly set gray hair.

"That's my *grand-mère*, Marguerite. Grandfather met her

over in France during the Revolution," Magnus said, offering me sugar. "She was an actress—and a spy." He seemed particularly proud of that detail. Fanny scoffed.

"Grandmamma was not a spy," she said, sipping her tea.

He mouthed, *Spy*, then continued. "She'd no magic whatsoever. When she first arrived in London, she caused quite a stir." He stared at the portrait with a kind of reverence I'd never seen in him before. "She was the strongest person I've ever met."

"Indeed," Fanny said with a contented smile. "She was the best mother-in-law one could wish for." Magnus looked at his mother with fondness.

I'd lived in Agrippa's great house and in Blackwood's palatial mansion, but this was a *home*.

"I wish I'd known my grandparents," I said.

"Yes," Fanny said, sympathy in her eyes. "The war has done terrible things to families. Of course, it's always possible to expand your family. Isn't it, Julian?" She looked pointedly at her son. For the first time, Magnus didn't seem to know what to say. Blackwood immediately changed the topic to the weather.

Afterward, Magnus, Blackwood, and I stepped into the garden for some air. Dee stayed inside, enjoying the music Fanny played at the pianoforte. The melody followed us into the yard. It was a small, walled-in stretch of grass, but there were also flowering shrubs, and a white-barked tree with a stone bench beneath it stood at the edge of the property. Blackwood moved toward the other side of the garden, looking over my sheet of instructions. I sat on the bench while Magnus made his way around the tree, trailing his fingers along the bark.

"How's Maria settling in?" He poked his head around to look at me. "Has she threatened Blackwood with an ax yet?"

"Don't be too hopeful. She's been helping Rook with his . . . control."

Magnus nodded. "So he's doing well, then?"

"Yes." I hated to lie, but it wasn't exactly a lie. Just stretching the truth. I pretended there was a difference.

"And your arm?" I asked. I'd been watching him all day. Movement at the elbow was stiff, and I'd heard him hiss in pain when making a particularly fast parry with a knife.

"I'll be fine. I always am, after all." He had to force the lighthearted tone.

"Can you continue with the weapons?" I fidgeted with the bone whistle, still dangling about my neck like some ghastly ornament. "I know today was difficult. Well, hellish, really."

"I'd rather train than rest, even if it hurts." He looked up at the darkening sky. "I'm more worried about Mother and the servants than I am my blasted injury. Since the ward's gone down, I've wanted to get them out of the city."

"Where would they go?"

He shrugged. "That's the problem. The only places safer than London right now are Sorrow-Fell and the Dombrey Priory. And they're both so far north, getting everyone there safely would take an army."

"Maybe they could use the Faerie roads?" I recalled what Mab had said about Whitechurch's request. "If Mab would agree—"

"I don't want my mother anywhere near Mab." His expression hardened, and he paced back behind the tree. Why on earth had I brought her up? I could be such a fool sometimes.

"You never told me what she took from you," I said. Magnus came back around and leaned his shoulder against the trunk.

"That's the point, isn't it?" He laughed bitterly. "I don't remember. Though maybe it's a blessing. Happy memories only serve to torment you later." That didn't sound like him at all.

"Does your mother know the truth about . . . ?" I couldn't finish the sentence, but he understood. What Mab had done. Being bitten by a Familiar and nearly dying. Magnus shuddered.

"No. She'd tell me she wants to know, but I can't put those thoughts into her head." He sighed and picked up a leaf that was turning bright red on the edges. "That's a moment, isn't it? When you start protecting your parents, not the other way around?" He let the leaf flutter to the ground. "Perhaps that's the moment you become a man."

"Do you feel like one?"

"Will I ever?" he asked. I knew what he meant. I'd been sure that commendation would bring all the answers, but I found myself still uncertain and scared. Perhaps Whitechurch and the older men went home at night with their stomachs in knots, too, questioning everything they did. What a terrifying thought.

Blackwood came over. "We should be on our way. Eliza will wonder what's happened," he said. And Rook. I wanted to see him.

I tied on my cloak in the foyer while Blackwood and Dee collected their coats and hats. Polly gaped while we gathered the swords and scythes from beside the hat rack. I wandered back toward the parlor, adjusting my bonnet, and heard Magnus speaking with his mother.

"I told you, we don't need more—" Fanny said, but Magnus interrupted.

"You said Mrs. Whist's cough had got worse. Take it, get whatever medicines the doctor prescribes. Bother the cost."

"But what about you? Now that you've called it off, I mean."

I should have turned away, but I couldn't help myself. Called what off?

"Don't worry about me."

I glanced up to see him pressing coins into his mother's hand, and Fanny reluctantly accepting. I pivoted back for the door, embarrassed to have listened.

As we left, Fanny kissed my cheek and asked me to come again. She also pressed a seed cake into Dee's hands, to his wide-eyed delight. At the gate, Blackwood looked for the carriage while Magnus waited next to me. I knew I should stay out of it, but I couldn't help myself.

"Is everything all right?" I asked.

Magnus gave me a knowing smile. "Caught us talking, didn't you?" God, how humiliating. "Don't worry, it would have been difficult to ignore." He took off his hat and studied the brim. "I broke my engagement with Miss Winslow."

My mouth nearly dropped open.

"Oh?" I couldn't help how my voice rose in surprise. "I'm so sorry."

"She was going to Ireland to stay out of the line of fire. Very sensible plan. I wrote to tell her not to feel bound by our engagement any longer."

"Why?"

"My father arranged the whole thing when we were infants. He was the younger son of the family, so there was nothing for me to inherit." He tapped his fingers against his stave. "I told Miss Winslow that we were too young to marry without love."

"She must have been devastated." The poor girl. But Magnus's mouth twitched in amusement.

"Surprisingly, she wrote back in agreement. Sounded rather relieved, which I can scarcely comprehend. Who wouldn't want an eternity with my magnificent presence?"

"Would you like the extensive list?"

The carriage arrived just as the first drops of rain began to fall. With a quick stroke of his stave, Magnus parted the rain so that it fell on either side of us. "You agree with me, don't you? Marriage without love is an abominable fate."

"I do." My thoughts turned once more to Rook, and Magnus noticed my blush.

"Then I'm happy for you," he said softly, and went to help as Blackwood's carriage arrived.

Together, the three of us loaded the weapons. Dee joined us in time to handle the scythe. I got into the carriage, Blackwood following quickly. He closed the door with more force than was necessary.

"See you both tomorrow," I said.

Magnus and Dee waved as the coach rattled down the street.

Blackwood watched out the window until we'd turned the corner.

"Don't worry, I'm fairly certain he won't chase us." I shuffled through the weaponry papers once more. Blackwood began drumming his fingers on his knee.

"He's canceled his engagement." The drumming stopped. "I couldn't help but overhear."

"Yes, now you finally have a chance to snag him. Best wishes," I muttered.

"Does that interest you?"

I looked up, exasperated. Blackwood watched me with a flat, unreadable gaze. He could give the Sphinx lessons in inscrutability.

"*This* interests me." I shoved my papers under his nose. "There's a skinless madman out there who wants us all dead. We've a carriage full of otherworldly weapons, and a book that's supposed to tell us how they all work. At the moment, skinless madmen, weapons, and books are about all I've time for. So if Magnus wants to marry a turnip on Thursday next, I will show up for the ceremony in my best bonnet. All right?"

With that, I went back to studying some incomprehensible diagram that showed the scythe's best elevation for attack, and I bloody enjoyed it.

"I'm not sure you were clear enough." Blackwood sounded bemused. "That's the last you'll hear about it from me." He smiled and took one of the papers. Outside, torrential rain pounded the carriage roof. Lightning snaked across the sky, followed by a startling boom of thunder.

"How do you think it went today?" I finally asked.

"Apart from the blood and pain?" Blackwood didn't say it with anger, though. He took up the tiny dagger and inspected it. "They could be useful, once we adjust to them. But I feel we'd be better served falling back into our own ranks, not looking outside for help."

"So we hide under a ward again?" He handed back the blade, which I put on the seat next to me.

"No. The time for hiding is past," he said, gazing out the window at the storm. "But strength comes from unity. In a strange way, I wish Whitechurch had fought harder to keep us from using the weapons. He let himself be swayed too easily by the queen. By you as well, when you brought him that painting of Strangewayes."

I frowned. "I don't understand. You think he's weak?"

"Definitely not," Blackwood said. "But when you consider the greatest Imperators of history—John Colthurst in the Wars of the Roses, Edward Wren during the Restoration of Charles the Second—they all understood that a man must not yield to the people he leads."

"So the Imperator should never compromise?" This didn't feel right. Blackwood picked up my training sheet once more.

"Good leadership requires compromise. Most of the time." With that, he read until we arrived home.

12

ONCE HOME, I WENT UPSTAIRS TO CHECK THAT Maria was comfortable. The door to the apothecary was ajar, and I heard murmuring. I peeked inside.

She'd finally put on a dress. The gown was a light blue that had been washed so often it had gone gray. She still hadn't put her wild hair up and had now even taken to sticking bits of flowers in it. She picked a purple flower from her curls and crushed it in her hands, dusting the petals over a wooden bowl filled with some strange concoction.

Maria muttered to herself in a voice that was not quite her own. It sounded deeper, older somehow.

"That's it, my love. Now the oil. Quick, don't let it sit too long," Maria said to herself in that rich, womanly voice. She took a flask beside her and sprinkled the contents over the bowl. Grabbing a wooden spoon, she stirred quickly, smiling. "There it is. You see it now?"

I pushed open the door, and her trancelike expression vanished.

"Is Rook here?" I tried to look innocent, but Maria was too smart.

"It's all right. You saw Willie." She took a jug of water and poured some into the bowl, making a paste of the powder.

"Willie?" I sat opposite her, watching as she took a bit of cloth and spread the paste onto it. Folding the cloth in half, she mashed the top of it.

"I've not had many friends," Maria said. Her cheeks tinged pink as she unfolded the cloth and cut a square of the paste. "I was five when I was taken to a workhouse in Edinburgh. Ran when I was ten. Then on, I survived mainly on my own."

"You were in a workhouse?" And at five? I knew enough of the appalling conditions children in York had suffered, slaving from dawn until dusk at looms or wheels without proper food or clothing. At Brimthorn, whenever we felt hungry or cold, the head teacher, Miss Morris, would remind us we were more fortunate than most.

"Aye. After I left, I had to live off the land, learn to hunt, fish, protect myself. So you might say I made a friend in my head." Maria shrugged.

"Why call her Willie?"

"I was never sure." She placed the square of cut paste on the table in front of me. "She always felt like a Willie to me."

Well, far be it from me to tell anyone they were odd. "What's that supposed to do?" I eyed the paste.

"Lavender oil, verbena, water, and gingerroot to strengthen Rook's body." She rubbed her stomach. "Flush out the poison."

There was a small racket by the window, startling me. A cage that I'd not noticed before hung from the rafter, and inside the cage a cream-colored turtledove flapped its wings. Maria made a shushing sound as she got up and unlatched the door. The bird hopped obediently into her hand, and she sat at the table again, stroking the dove's soft head with the tip of her finger. She trilled and whispered, and it watched her with shining black eyes.

"Where on earth did you get a turtledove?"

Maria shrugged. "There was a man selling caged birds, wandering up and down the street. This one called to me." Maria didn't take her gaze away from the creature. "This city is too hard. Soothes me to have something pure and alive near at hand." She cradled the cooing dove against her chest.

Maria whistled gently, the sound like a soft, rushing wind. That bone-deep energy flooded the room again, the kind I'd felt the night I'd seen her rid herself of the Familiar's venom. This was gentler, though.

"Did you have pets when you were little?" I reached out a finger to stroke the dove. It ruffled its feathers in response; it wanted only Maria.

"I don't remember much of my grandmother's coven, but I recall the animals. The turtledoves flocked to us especially. I'd many before the burnings started."

Her warm brown eyes darkened as she placed the dove on the table.

"I don't understand how the sorcerers could be so savage against your kind," I said, unable to help myself. Dimly, I realized I'd said "the sorcerers"—not *we*.

"We celebrate life, yes. But death as well." Maria took another purple flower from her hair and twirled it between her fingers. "You saw what I did with that shrub. For one to live, one must die." Maria's voice dropped once more to that strange, womanly tone. "That's a dangerous power to have."

The door opened, and Rook entered. His eyes were so bright and his face so flushed that for a moment I was afraid he was feverish. But the wide, brilliant smile on his face told me he felt no pain.

"Where've you been?" I asked as he slid onto the bench beside me. His hands were trembling, but he looked excited.

"Wonderful day at work." He leaped up and walked around to Maria. "Have we anything to try yet?"

Well, at least I could be here for Rook's first treatment. Maria handed him the odd-colored square of paste. "The taste'll be strange, but you must have no water for at least ten minutes."

Rook ate the thing in one go. His face puckered.

"Will it work soon?" There was such hope in his black eyes. He sat down beside me again, and his hand found mine.

"We'll find out, won't we?" Maria said. "For now, don't worry."

That seemed enough for Rook. But until the shadows receded, I would keep worrying. There was no way to make me stop.

FOR THE NEXT WEEK, THE BOYS and I met in the barracks' courtyard and practiced with the weapons. We avoided the flutes and the lantern but did our best sparring with the blades. Dee gave up on using the scythe when it wouldn't stop making that horrid noise. Every night when we disbanded, I wondered if we were using them properly. I would read Strangewayes's journal and grow more puzzled. His mind had been a fragmented mess. None of us could be sure.

Then, on the seventh day, the bells rang at dawn.

Before I opened my eyes, I knew these weren't the standard morning bells. Every church tower in London rang at the same time, using the same pattern. *Dong. Dong. Ding ding ding.*

A warning. A call to battle.

I sat up in my bed, my heart hammering. Rubbing my eyes, I tried to remember what the pattern meant. The two solid, long tolls said that it was an attack. The three rapid bells indicated the eastern edge of the barrier. But it didn't include the pattern that announced which Ancient we were to fight.

That was odd, and troubling.

Lilly rushed into my room and threw open my wardrobe without a word. She knew what those bells meant as well as I.

"Did you sleep well, miss?" she asked, sounding a bit breathless. She pushed open the curtains. "It'll be a cool day, I suspect." Lilly hurried about the room, pouring hot water and handing me my wrap. Her face was white, but other than that she showed no panic. I wished I had her courage.

Dong. Dong. Ding ding ding. The bells continued as we got me laced into my corset, tied my boots, and threw on the dark gown Madame Voltiana had designed for me. "Battle ready," she'd called it. It had loose sleeves that let me raise my arms over my head without difficulty, and a less voluminous skirt. Frankly, trousers would have been best, but I couldn't imagine having that conversation with Whitechurch.

When I was dressed, I hurried downstairs to find Blackwood pacing by the door. He'd a sword and dagger strapped to his waist. Without a word, I took the other dagger, put the two-inch-long blade up my sleeve in a sheath, and hung the bone whistle about my neck.

There. We were both prepared. Really, it had been lucky London had not faced a direct attack in the months since the ward fell. We couldn't have expected to stay that lucky forever.

Before we left, I looked for Rook but couldn't find him. The whole house was awake and hurrying up and down stairs, preparing to flee in case . . . well, just in case. Nowhere was safe any longer.

As dawn fully broke, Blackwood and I arrived near Hackney, descending into a sea of sorcerers. Squadron leaders whistled and herded stragglers into neat rows. Joined shoulder to shoulder, with hands upon staves in the customary "resting" position, the men stared at the barrier and awaited further orders. It never ceased to impress me how, well, orderly they were. When I'd first come to London, I'd met the sorcerers when they were mostly idle, taking tea and attending parties. The speed and grace with which they organized—we organized— illustrated the Order's strength. I clutched the hilt of my dagger, hoping it would inspire confidence and ease. It did not.

While Blackwood and I walked past the rows, looking for

our own squadron, I kept stealing glances at the barrier. The dark Fae had created it, and as such it was like something from a shadowy fairy tale, one used to frighten children on winter nights. Tangled thickets rose thirty feet high around us, rife with dagger-sharp thorns. Flowers bloomed with teeth glittering among the petals, and snapped if you drew too close.

We found Magnus and Dee near the end of the squadron lines. Dee was loosening up, running in place. Magnus was still, which was odd for him. "What do you think it is?" he asked.

Part of me wildly hoped that it was only a drill to test our formation time.

"Do you think it's the Vulture Lady?" Dee asked. His right leg jiggled like mad. "I think she's the worst one. Picture her swooping out of the sky and gutting you with her talons. Suppose she starts eating you while you're still alive."

"Thanks for the image," Magnus said dryly as Valens arrived. There was a trace of stubble on our captain's chin, and his eyes looked bleary and red. He counted the four of us, nodded curtly, then took out his stave and created a column of wind to lift him off the ground.

"Come along," he said as he hovered. So we were going up and over the barrier. Glancing down the line, I waited for the other squadron leaders to order their men up and forward, but it didn't happen. They were creating water glasses, as if they were planning to watch. Watch? Were we going over with no backup?

Still, I must obey my leader. So, knees shaking, I made a column for myself and rose. As I crossed over, the thorns snagged the bottom of my petticoats. I had to fight with my skirts as I floated down to the ground—landing in a dress was always a potentially immodest experience.

The boys came down alongside me, and we faced the rubble that had once been part of our city. Before the ward fell, this area had been shielded from violence. Now the remains of buildings stood crumbling around us. Walls of scorched brick loomed overhead, charred memories of homes, shops, and lives now lost. Down the street, a single staircase that had improbably survived destruction stretched up into the sky, leading nowhere.

"What are the orders, sir?" I asked.

"Practice," Valens answered. "The Imperator wants to assess how these magician weapons work in battle. He thinks it better to start small, and I agree." He pointed straight ahead at a two-story building that was still intact. "Familiars have been spotted nearby. Destroy them."

They'd called the entire Order out to watch us battle some *Familiars*? Was there really no better use of sorcerers' time or energy? Every sorcerer in London would witness our victory—or defeat. If the new weapons didn't work, everyone would know, and all faith would be lost.

Whitechurch was a clever fellow. To think that Blackwood worried the man was getting soft.

"What kind of Familiars?" Blackwood asked.

I took my dagger out, determined to make the most of this.

"Ravens," Valens said.

Ravens, eh? They weren't the easiest to battle, but also not the worst. Still, my gut cramped with unease. Something about this felt *too* simple.

Valens retreated to the barrier—*coward*—as we strode forward, finding our way through the rubble. The dawn was blood red, lending a hellish tint to the area. Wasn't there a rhyme about this sort of thing? *Red sky at morning, sailors take warning?*

I needed to find some more cheerful poems.

"At least it's a lovely, brisk morning for a fight," Magnus said.

The four of us clumped together as we came closer to the building. There was the call of a crow somewhere nearby. We stopped, my muscles tensing just to hear it.

Though I had to admit that standing shoulder to shoulder with the boys and waiting for something to come screaming over the horizon felt oddly like home.

Blackwood unhooked his corkscrew sword. Dee had the flute in his hands. I hoped we wouldn't have to use that particular weapon.

Magnus stepped forward and turned in a circle, scanning the area. It was as quiet as a graveyard, and as heavy with death. Blast and hell, I needed to stop thinking that.

"At least there are no Ancients about," Blackwood said, lowering his sword.

"Which is odd." I fingered the whistle that hung around my

neck. "You'd think R'hlem would be attacking us with all his might." With an army at his disposal, why was R'hlem being so, well, *cautious*?

Blackwood looked back at the barrier. "London is still the greatest prize, and he doesn't want to make a misstep. Especially not now that we have the chosen one." He gave me a wry smile. "Once he knows our weak spots, nothing will keep him out."

Wonderful.

Ahead, a pile of rocks fell. Something about the heaviness of the sound made me uneasy. Ravens wouldn't make so much noise.

Three riders on horseback emerged around the corner of the building, the light of dawn at their backs. A man and two women, they had been fully skinned and were slick with blood from head to toe. Their mounts were no different; the beasts had slick, equine heads with no ears, and blood dripped from their snouts. They snorted, pawing at the earth and chomping on their bits. The saddles had been tanned and fashioned from some kind of pink flesh that I didn't think was leather. The power—and stench—that wafted from them made my stomach turn.

So these were R'hlem's personal riders. This was what he'd wanted to do to me.

The creatures paused, assessing us. The rider on the left turned in her saddle and whispered to her friends. They seemed rather baffled by our appearance.

Then again, it wasn't every day four young sorcerers strolled past the barrier to court danger. Few were that stupid.

One of the Familiars, a man, trotted forward with his hand extended. As a unit, we backed away on instinct.

"Come with me, lady, and we will not harm your friends. The bloody king gives his word." The muscles of his cheeks contracted, revealing more of his gums and teeth. He was grinning. "The bloody king wants you alone."

13

THE BLOODY KING. I'D HEARD GWEN REFER TO R'hlem by that title before.

"I'm not a lady," I replied, taking my dagger by the hilt. "I'm a sorcerer."

The skinned rider laughed. "You've brought this upon yourself." He raised one bloody hand to the sky and closed it in a tight fist.

As if on cue, dark forms erupted from the shattered windows, swarming in a deadly mass into the air. Ravens came for us in a screaming black cloud of bristling feathers.

As the Familiars swooped, we panicked and blasted them with fire, forgetting the new weapons to fall back on sorcerer techniques. Billows of flame roasted some of the birds, but not all. They met in the air, congealed, and formed into hideous, manlike creatures with hooded faces and razor-sharp claws. They dove for us, coming in low. We were about to be outnumbered.

"Get the flute!" I called to Dee. He slipped it out of its muter, resheathed his stave, and played.

The exploding sound carried over the battlefield. Ravens

plummeted from the sky, littering the earth. For a brief moment, the fighting stopped.

But the four of us had also fallen to the ground, ears ringing, and the three skinless Familiars seemed better able to shake it off. They galloped for us, drawing out long swords carved from bone.

One of the women tried to grab me, and I swiped with my dagger, fending her off as best I could. The blade whined and vibrated heavily in my hand, twisting my wrist and making me swear. Magnus and Blackwood attempted the corkscrew swords, but the riders easily knocked the weapons from their hands. The boys barely survived. Blackwood launched a quick spell that shook the earth beneath the riders' feet. Magnus followed it with a blast of wind, toppling one of the skinned women off her horse. Blackwood took the opportunity and stabbed her with his dagger. He pierced the rider through the heart, yes, but with an explosion of light that flipped him onto his back.

The ravens began to regroup and circle overhead. God, was no one at the barrier going to help?

I put the whistle to my lips and blew. Not a damned thing happened. The riders and the ravens didn't even blink.

Bother the new weapons. I grabbed Porridge and burst into flames, shooting fireballs and crisping the bastard ravens as they dove. Good. That was progress, at last. I managed to get to the boys, signaling Dee to join us as we regrouped. I kept burning, though my fire faltered a bit—I was using too much energy too fast.

"Knock her unconscious," the lead rider yelled, galloping by on his horse.

Dee unlooped the whip and lashed at him. Violet light erupted from the weapon's tip, stinging my eyes. My nose began to gush blood, my mouth flooding with the coppery taste. The two remaining riders wheeled their horses and prepared to charge us.

"Bother the cursed weapons, Dee. Fight back," Blackwood shouted, dropping his sword to the ground. He summoned stones from the rubble and launched them in a projectile attack. The stones slowed the riders, who had to dodge and weave to avoid them.

Dee and Magnus stood back to back, creating a vortex of wind. The raven Familiars swooped, flashes of white faces and fanged mouths visible beneath their hoods. But they couldn't withstand the force of the wind and were sucked up into the sky.

I could feel my energy draining. Thinking quickly, I ran from the boys and slumped to the ground in a faint. Hoofbeats drew closer, and closer, until . . .

I rolled onto my back and sent a last burst of flame at the rider above me. The woman fell off her frenzied horse and landed heavily. She curled into a ball and died. I lay still, my cheek pressed against the cold ground, unable to tear my gaze away from her charred body. I'd killed a shadow Familiar before, and Korozoth, but not something that looked so . . . human. The smell reminded me of roast pork.

My stomach rippled, and I managed to get to my knees before throwing up.

The lead rider roared. He broke free from the rubble and wheeled his horse toward me, his sword high over his head. Before he could attack, Blackwood rose up behind him, brought his stave down in a whipping arc, and stabbed the skinned man between his shoulder blades. The rider fell, and Blackwood, with two more swings of his stave, kept him down for good.

Blood streaked Blackwood's pale face, but he didn't even wipe at it.

"Are you all right, Howel?" he asked. He was breathing heavily. Looking down at the now-dead Familiar, he kicked it for good measure and came to help me up.

"I'll be fine," I grunted. The nosebleed had stopped, though dark spots wavered in my vision. I spit the taste of copper and ash out of my mouth. "We didn't do much with the new weapons, did we?"

His pained expression gave me my answer.

Now, when the battle was practically done, sorcerers came flying over the barrier to chase the ravens and finish the slaughter. The ravens were in a tizzy, circling and cawing as they sped over the rubble and back toward the horizon. I felt we'd got stupidly lucky, catching them off guard.

We returned to the barrier. Once there, it took us two tries to fly back over the thing, where we found Valens waiting on the other side. Considering we'd failed, he appeared smugly pleased. I wanted to shake him.

"Thank you for watching while we nearly got ourselves killed," I said, beyond respect at this point.

"I'd orders to let you display your so-called abilities." He dusted his sleeves, as though *he'd* somehow been doing all the work. "I'd be surprised if you are allowed another experiment like this."

"We need more time," I said. Valens turned flashing eyes to me. There was anger in him, seething below a thin layer of civility. It startled me.

"Ask the people of Liverpool for more time," he snapped. Liverpool? The four of us exchanged glances, the silent question passing among us. Huffing, Valens contained himself and said, "It's over. Go home and rest. After tomorrow you return to my squadron." He turned on his heel and stalked away, leaving me uneasy.

"Can't say we didn't try," Dee said softly. He took the whip from his belt, slid the flute off his shoulder, and offered them to me.

"Keep them," I said shortly. "We're not done yet."

Blackwood, however, accepted Dee's weapons, then nodded to Magnus. "I'll take yours."

"Think I'll hang on to mine for the time being." Magnus saluted us as he strode away. "Souvenirs."

Dee followed Magnus, while Blackwood and I headed home. Despite being laden down with the failed weapons, he appeared pleased. Really, he looked gleeful to have been disgraced before the entire Order. I let my annoyance boil over.

"You had nothing to say to Valens?" I snapped.

"Perhaps these weapons were always too dangerous to play with."

"We can make them work with proper instruction," I said. Where that proper instruction was to come from, I'd no idea.

"We were almost killed today." Blackwood held up a hand still covered in the rider's blood. "Please. I don't want trouble from Whitechurch or Valens or anyone else but R'hlem." His voice was quiet but firm. We said no more, and I turned over what Valens had said, his anger. Why had he brought up Liverpool specifically? What had happened?

When we arrived home, I walked straight into the obsidian room, taking up a bowl of water and swirling the liquid into the air. I wasn't particularly skilled at scrying, unfortunately, and my water glass resembled a rather limp rectangle instead of the customary square. Footsteps whispered behind me. Blackwood waited in the doorway, arms crossed.

Bother him. I returned to scrying, badly. Blackwood didn't need to be told what I was about. Edging in gracefully, he took up his stave and straightened my mirror into a perfect, glittering square.

I'd never been to Liverpool, but I tried to envision the streets, the port, the clatter of carriages and call of voices, and then—there.

It appeared before us, a smoking ruin.

Blackwood nearly dropped the water glass in shock, and I bit back a horrified cry. Buildings had been ground into rubble. Fires dotted the wreckage here and there, like hideous signatures. Pulling back further, I caught sight of a great lumbering lizard crawling across the destruction, a forked tongue the length of a carriage horse tasting the earth lazily. It looked rather like an iguana, with spikes of red and electric blue fanned out along its ridged back.

Zem, the Great Lizard, opened his mouth and spewed a stream of white-hot flame, roasting the side of a building. It collapsed, and there was movement as people—yes, they were people—fled. Zem's gullet bulged, and he opened his mouth again. . . .

Blackwood swore, swiping his stave at the water glass to change the scene. But I spied something and grabbed his arm. Letters had been carved into a broad avenue, scorched by fire, darkened by ash. The words read:

Give Me Henrietta Howel

Coldness planted itself in my gut as I took over the water glass, moving from Liverpool to York. We'd more sorcerers stationed there, but Familiars still carpeted the area surrounding the city. They were a sea of cloaks and talons and fangs. With so many at the gates, waiting for an opportunity to strike, the sorcerer ranks had to be exhausted. And sure enough, when I went looking at the surrounding area, I found those four ugly words sliced into a green hillside.

"Don't," Blackwood whispered, but I couldn't stop. Hands shaking, I forced the mirror to show me other areas. Kent, Manchester, Surrey, Devon, and on and on. Some areas were less devastated than others. But if I searched the populous towns, I would find the words once more:

Give Me Henrietta Howel

"He's punishing them." My voice was dull.

I knew enough of this war to understand that R'hlem didn't mindlessly destroy. What goods and people he could preserve, he did. Canterbury had been the base of his operations in the east for years, after all. This, however, was sick and wasteful.

He was trying to force the sorcerers' hand to give me over.

"Why does he hate me so much?" I'd destroyed one of his monsters, yes, but why *this*?

"Because he thinks you're the chosen one," Blackwood said quietly, dissolving the mirror and returning the water to its bowl. He leaned against the table as though he couldn't stand properly on his own. "If you're the only one who can defeat him, he won't stop until he destroys you. So he blasts the country until we've no choice but to give in."

"Maybe you should." It was a childish, mad thing to say, but I was on the verge of sobbing. This was where I'd got us all:

a monster rampaging through the countryside, and a chosen one who was not truly chosen. "At least if he has me, he might stop—"

"Don't think that!" Blackwood snapped, swiping the silver bowl to the floor. It struck with a clatter, water splashing onto the black stone. He grabbed me by the elbows, looking desperate. "I know your mind, and I swear to God if you take it upon yourself to go to him, I will drag you home even if it kills me. Do you hear?" His eyes shone with panic. "I'll never let him have you."

He was shaking now. I'd truly scared him. Gently, I extricated myself and picked up the bowl, sweeping the water back inside before setting it in its proper place.

I nodded. "I won't go to him. But," I said, "don't you see? We need those weapons. If only—"

"No, Howel." He cut me off with a look and then stalked out of the room. Apparently he thought that was all it took to settle the matter. He was wrong.

Bother the headaches and nosebleeds, bother that these weapons had been created by a magician: if we were willing to throw something away because we didn't understand it or it made us uncomfortable, then R'hlem deserved to win.

I went right upstairs to get out of my bloodstained clothes. Lilly struggled to keep a calm expression when she saw me, but she did an admirable job. I scrubbed with soap until my skin was raw, and reluctantly let Lilly take my soiled gown for the rubbish after she swore it was beyond saving.

Finally, I pulled out Mickelmas's trunk and tried the *Ever what you need* spell once again. I thought of the weapons; nothing happened. I thought of slashing R'hlem's throat. Still nothing. Groaning in frustration, I thought of Mickelmas, his laughing dark eyes, his gray-shocked beard, his stupid multicolored coat. Above all, I imagined throttling him out of sheer frustration.

That seemed to do the trick. The chest thumped beneath my hand, and I threw open the lid.

Inside was a flyer. Mystified, I picked it up. It appeared to be a carnival poster, the type that advertised the strongest man alive and such. The woodcut letters were blocky, and beneath them was an illustration of a man with a top hat and a curling mustache.

SEE THE WONDERS OF BEGGAR'S CORNER, the poster read. MEET MEN AND WOMEN OF MARVELOUS MAGICAL REPUTATION. CHILDREN WELCOME, PETS PREFERRED. BURLINGTON ARCADE 59, AT PICCADILLY.

The man with the hat held a bubbling potion of some kind, and sparks flew from his open hand.

Definitely a magician. I squinted as I read it over again. Burlington Arcade? But that area had been beneath the ward for over a decade, since the magicians had been driven out of London proper. This poster looked to be much older; the paper was yellowing, and there were coffee stains on the edges.

It must have been from before the start of the war, making it all but useless. I nearly balled it up and burned it but reconsidered. The ward had been gone for months. Suppose the magicians had found a way to move back into the city undetected? Suppose there were now magicians in the heart of London who could help me? Suppose one of them knew about these blasted weapons?

My mind raced. I couldn't tell Rook, not when stress would speed the poison. I couldn't bring it up to Blackwood, since he had a barely concealed dislike for the weapons. Magnus and Dee would be enthusiastic, but perhaps overly so. I imagined Magnus gallivanting into a den of magicians and being turned into a ham. But I needed to tell somebody.

And I knew exactly who that person should be.

The stairs creaked beneath my feet as I hurried to the top floor. I knocked lightly on Fenswick's door, and Maria opened it. Her face and hands were dusted with flour.

"What's wrong?" she asked, wiping herself clean.

"Look at this." I waited until she was neat, handed over the paper, and sat. She scanned the flyer, a wondering expression stealing over her face. She began to grin.

"Mam used to tell me magicians' abilities were grand and strange. Can they turn your hair blue, do you think?"

"Oh, they can do much more than that." Clearly I'd told the right person. "I want to go tomorrow."

"I'll come with you," Maria said right away, sitting beside me. My heart leaped at how easy it was to trust her. Then she frowned. "Have you the time?"

"I'm excused in the afternoon for an outing. Come with me then and we'll slip away afterward." I smoothed the paper, excitement coursing through me. I'd often wondered if all magicians were like Mickelmas. Now I'd have a chance to see.

"Shall I bring my ax along?" Maria grinned again. "Just in case?"

"Yes. Though it'll be a bit out of place at our first stop."

MADAME VOLTIANA'S SHOP WAS STILL FULLY operational, even with the ward down. People might need to barter on street corners for grain or tobacco, but high-society ladies couldn't be expected to do without exquisite tailoring. Dressmaker dummies clothed in elegant, headless fashion waited by the door to greet customers. There were fewer seamstresses working at Voltiana's now, but the purple-skinned faerie was all smiles and enthusiasm when Eliza, Maria, and I arrived, and all business as I was measured for a new gown.

Madame Voltiana clapped her bony hands while she admired my reflection. "You will look as marvelous as I can make you. You're too tall, of course, and not shapely enough, but with my design no one shall be able to tell!"

Lovely. The faerie pinched me while she measured my hips and waist and adjusted my posture. Eliza sat on a plush sofa, choosing between two brightly colored swatches of silk. Maria, who'd been plopped down beside her, studied her surroundings as if she'd stepped onto another planet.

For all of Madame Voltiana's cheerful insults, the shop was a welcome bubble of femininity. In here, it seemed, the war had not come.

"Wait until you see the color. It will be a confection of molten red and rich Indian orange. You will look like a tongue of flame," Voltiana cooed. "I could make your gown like the phoenix, so that at midnight it would burn. Of course, you'd be walking around naked afterward, but we all must suffer for art."

"Since it's Lady Eliza's birthday, that might be too attention-grabbing," I said carefully. Voltiana could be swayed by her muse, as she called it, and forget reality.

"Maybe burgundy for me?" Eliza lifted one of the silk pieces. "Or royal purple." She showed them to Maria. "Which do you think?"

Maria blinked, then picked up a piece of silk that was bright peacock blue. "This one's nice," she said, utterly lost. Eliza clucked her tongue.

"It's lovely, but not my coloring." She held up the purple and beamed. "Yes. This one."

"Oh my lady, you should be in light colors. You are young as the springtime," Voltiana trilled, jabbing me with another pin. I bit my tongue.

Eliza had made up her mind. "Royal purple. I want it to make an impression. You never know who'll be in attendance." She smiled knowingly. "George will probably have several young men as candidates."

I flinched, and this time it had nothing to do with Voltiana's pins. Blackwood hadn't told his sister he was still writing to Aubrey Foxglove? If he didn't have a talk with her soon, I would.

After the fitting, we were climbing into Blackwood's carriage when I gasped and struck my forehead. "Maria, we need herbs from the market, don't we?"

"Aye," Maria said, sounding incredibly stilted. "How could we have forgotten that? Oh, woe." She woodenly put her hands on her hips. She was an excellent warrior—an actress, not so much.

"It's just nearby. Eliza, why don't you go home to tea?" I closed the carriage door with a decisive click.

"What are you up to?" Eliza asked.

"Not a thing," I said, giving a smile that I hoped was convincing. Eliza did not appear convinced.

"Be careful, then. Whatever you're doing." She frowned, and the carriage rolled out of sight. I felt a twinge of guilt. I'd have been happy to take her along, but I didn't want to make her lie to Blackwood. Besides, who knew what dangers we might find?

Maria and I hurried down the street, arm in arm. "Keep your hood up and your head down," she said. "In case any should recognize you."

London was so different than it had been only a few months before. Barricades of sandbags and gravel were being erected along the streets, precautions that would slow certain Familiars but not do much to stop an Ancient. The air smelled permanently of smoke and sweat.

Before, the faces of the wealthy had been relaxed, while those outside the ward's protection had a pinched and harried look. There was no real difference now. Wealthy women in brightly ribboned bonnets and poor patchworked beggars each wore the same haunted expression. Though tearing down the ward had been the right thing to do, I couldn't help but feel ashamed.

More tales of R'hlem's attacks arrived every day, doubling in savagery. Eighty sorcerers had died in a single night on the outskirts of Sheffield—there were whispers that they'd all been flayed alive. Every death now made me recall R'hlem's words: *I will show you horror. Give me Henrietta Howel.*

That's why we're here, I reminded myself as we raced across a muddy street. We're going to make these weapons work. We're going to show R'hlem what horror *truly* means.

Finally, we came out onto a broad thoroughfare. Piccadilly was a large circle, avenues feeding it like veins running into a heart. The old un-warded trade hub, Ha'penny Row, had been ruthlessly smashed during Korozoth's attack. Now all the tradesmen and merchants came here to buy and sell.

I purchased a pair of dubious meat pies, and Maria and I ate quickly while the city roared around us. Hansom cabs and wagons, horse-drawn omnibuses with rusted tin hoods and barouches tore through the roundabouts and roads, narrowly avoiding collisions. I'd never heard such a din in my life, as all around us bodies of rich, poor, and every station in between sweated and pressed and coughed and shoved from one side of the street to another.

While Maria sucked gravy from her fingertips, I led us down Piccadilly toward Bond Street. The arched entrance to

Burlington Arcade soon appeared on our right. It was a long, covered walkway with shops on either side. It had been a fashionable destination before the ward fell, where ladies shopped for perfume or candied fruits. Now the elegant stores shared space with panhandlers and oyster sellers.

"Let's see," I said, pulling out the flyer and threading my way through the crowd with Maria in my wake. The paper said shop fifty-nine, but when we arrived, all we found was an empty ruin. The windows were broken, the door boarded up. Paint peeled in long, curling strips. No one had entered in years.

I chewed my lip in frustration. Had I deluded myself into thinking that the magicians had risked everything to set up shop in their old home? The chest had malfunctioned, most likely. That, or I'd misunderstood what it had wanted to tell me.

"You've got the squinty-eyed look." Maria jabbed me with her elbow. "Shouldn't be so quick to give up."

"What would you suggest we do?"

"Try the blade bit." Maria tugged a thread from her skirt. She thought there was a glamour here, though I felt no magic. Well, why not? I took Porridge, sliced myself much less deeply this time, and coated the thread in blood. Maria held it as I concentrated, cut, and . . .

My hands tingled as a gash appeared in the air by the door. Maria clapped her hands in delight.

"I love that blade bit," she crowed, stepping through the cut. I followed, and behind me the tear sealed itself back up.

What had once been a deserted shop was now a long, crooked alleyway. Magicians, it seemed, had a Burlington Arcade all their own, and it thronged with people.

The place made me think of a house that had long been shuttered and abandoned, and whose windows were only just now being thrown open, its hallways swept, the cloths taken off the furniture.

Stalls had been crammed up against one another, faded velvet curtains separating each shop. Tents and tarps were hoisted on poles, newly painted signs advertising wares beside them. Copper pans, glass vials and jars, brass cages that rattled with gaudy-colored creatures lined the walls. There was the sizzle of a cooking pan, the smell of fat and onion wafting toward us.

The men and women who argued with one another were not unlike the people we'd seen outside, haggling over flour or soap. But here, they were discussing gizzards, the tongues of flamingos, shark-tooth powders, and potions for the liver. One woman stumped across the way, her gait lopsided and odd. She'd a glass bottle in place of her lower leg, with the cork used as her foot.

"These are magicians?" Maria sounded both amazed and appalled. "They're so . . . so . . ."

"Odd," I finished. But my breath caught to see so many of them, ten or twenty, all working together. If the war had never come, if my parents had been alive, I might have spent time in this place. I might have called myself a magician.

We attracted some frowns and attention. Strangers who appeared in the middle of an illegal market *would* be suspicious. Perhaps we should have thought this through better.

As if to illustrate my point, an arm snaked around me from behind and put a blade to my throat.

"What've we here?" a voice whispered.

14

THE VOICE BELONGED TO A GIRL. I STILLED AS MARIA
pulled out her ax.

"Let her go," Maria spit. The girl only pressed harder, the
blade cutting into my skin. Threatening her was clearly a bad
plan.

"There's no need to fuss," I said. It was hard to think with a
blade to your throat. My eyes darted over the people watching
us, eagerly waiting to see what would happen.

My attacker moved the blade slightly, enough to give me
an opportunity. Blue fire rippled over my body, and the girl fell.

"Don't you know it's rude to lay hands on another magician?" I extended a hand to help her up. "I'm Henrietta Howel."

Giving my name was a bit of a gamble. We'd attracted a
great deal of attention by now, and a crowd was gathering. The
girl pushed herself to her feet, dusting off her knees. Absurdly
tall, she wore a bright yellow gown with a green sash. Her
black hair hung loose to her shoulders. Her cheekbones were
high, her eyes dark and brilliant as she stared at me in surprise.

"Wait. Howel?" She whistled. "You're the sorcerers' chosen
girl, ain't you? Why didn't you say so?" She clapped a hard hand

on my shoulder, and I stifled a cry of pain. "You could've asked for the Orb and Owl, you know. Be happy to show you," she said conversationally.

"Er, yes. We'd like to see it," I said, sharing a baffled glance with Maria, who finally put her ax away.

"Name's Alice Chen," the girl said as she led us down the alleyway. I glanced at the wary faces all around me and tried to catch their whispered words. The crowd dispersed, though I still felt everyone's gaze.

Turning a corner, we came to a wooden sign hung over a plain brick wall that said THE ORB & OWL. The sign was carved with a tawny owl alighting on a crystal ball.

There was no doorway. Instead, Alice walked us over to a pair of old, hole-ridden boots and kicked one of them.

With a puff of smoke and dust, the hazy image of a slouching, thin-faced man appeared before us. "Password?" His voice sounded like a sigh on the wind.

I'd read of "ghosts" like this in one of the books from Mickelmas's chest. They weren't the actual souls of dead people. Rather, these were more like echoes of ownership attached to objects, and they could be made to act as guards or enforcers. Not the most skillful of creatures, but useful in their own way.

"Shut up and let me in," Alice said cheerfully.

"Correct password." The ghost disappeared in a puff of smoke, and a door opened in the wall.

"Your people are strange," Maria whispered. Well, she was right.

We stepped into a public house that appeared perfectly normal, as far as public houses went. The walls were brick, blackened in spots by smoke from the guttering oil lamps. A tarnished mirror behind the mahogany bar reflected the room's crowd, which wasn't that spectacular: about ten people all told. Portraits of famous magicians gazed down on us. One of them showed Merlin; another, Strangewayes. In one corner I spotted Darius LaGrande, and in another a man who seemed curiously familiar. . . . When I realized who he was, my throat tightened. I hurried over to look at the portrait more closely. The subject was a handsome young man with dark hair and a round, pleasant face. His smile was warm, open, friendly. The placard at the bottom read WILLIAM HOWEL.

My father had been more renowned in magician circles than I'd ever imagined. His name was carved in Ralph Strangewayes's house, and now this? Unthinking, I touched the portrait, tracing my fingers over my father's face.

I wish you could see me now, I thought, reluctantly stepping back. *I wish, God, I wish I could talk to you.*

Blinking back sudden tears, I took a moment and studied the people in the room to calm myself. Alice had already seated herself at a table and was chatting animatedly with a man. He looked like a normal sort, with light brown hair and a long face, until he coughed up a fish. The silvery creature slid out of his mouth and onto the table. It was alive, flipping and flopping about. With a resigned shake of his head, the man tossed the trout into a bucket by his feet.

I hoped that whatever the spell was didn't last for very long. I imagined that coughing up fish was uncomfortable.

By the side of the room, a little girl with dark skin and braided hair hugged a doll, one that appeared rather badly singed. A shock of light sizzled in her hair, almost like an electric storm. When she caught me looking, she smiled.

A red hawk with beautiful feathers sat on the back of a chair, cleaning its wings.

Surely someone here could help me with Strangewayes's weapons. I was about to start introducing myself when a dark-skinned man appeared out of thin air, right by the bar.

"My truest, most pungent companions," he said, popping onto a stool. "Thank you for meeting me. Our wait is nearing an end, my friends. England will be great once more, with our magic to guide her." He raised his arms, the purple-orange-red patchwork sleeves of his coat falling around his elbows. He received muted, lukewarm applause.

"Oi, Jenkins," the fish-cougher said, lifting his drink in welcome.

Only this man was not Jenkins Hargrove. His real name was Howard Mickelmas.

My mentor, after months of utter silence, was sitting in a pub as though everything were perfectly normal. The bartender passed him a frothing mug of ale, which he happily drank.

"You know him, then?" Maria whispered. She must have noticed my look of shock.

"He taught me everything I know," I muttered, sitting

down at a table. I didn't want him to notice me until I was ready to be noticed.

Despite everything, I was relieved to see him. Though I'd known he survived Korozoth's attack when he gave me his magical trunk months ago, I hadn't known what had become of him. But here he was, drinking and laughing and perfectly alive. I smiled a little as I watched him.

Mickelmas reached into his pocket and pulled out a ridiculously feathered purple hat. "Pass it around, my ostriches. A few coins go to pay for the Army of the Burning Rose."

My smile evaporated. Oh no. No, that could not mean what I thought it did.

"What is it?" Maria asked as I balled my fists. "Do you not like roses?"

"The burning rose is my sigil. My *sorcerer* sigil."

"Ah." She whistled. "I imagine you didn't give him permission to use it?"

"I am going to *kill* him."

"So that's no."

Mickelmas passed the hat around, though most people didn't put anything in it. "Go on. A penny or two for our great army's advancement," Mickelmas clucked. Someone passed us the hat. Maria had to send it on fast, to prevent me from setting fire to it. "And might I add how good it is to see everyone?" Mickelmas looked about the room. I ducked my head to keep him from glimpsing my face. "Yes, Alice and Sadie and Gerald and . . . where's Alfred?" He frowned.

"You're sitting on him," someone called. Mickelmas leaped off the bar stool, which began to rock back and forth on its own.

"Anyone know the counterspell?" He waited, but there was no answer. "Sorry, Alfred. Let's hope it wears off." He patted the leather seat and continued. "Our own flower, seeded in sorrow, brought to bloom in adversity, our dear Henrietta Howel is at this moment living in the seat of power. She has been taken to Her Majesty's most royal bosom and declared the great chosen one. Our success is assured!" he cried. There was some polite scattered applause. The fish man coughed up another trout as Alice nodded at me, expectant. The hat, now lightly jingling with a few coins, returned to Mickelmas, who slipped it back into his pocket.

"Jenkins?" Alice waved her hand. "Now that the burning rose is with us—"

She was trying to introduce me, but Mickelmas jumped onto her speech. "Ah, my dear Henrietta. The brightest pupil I ever taught." He sighed dramatically, one hand over his heart. "She's done such sterling work, infiltrating the monarchy at its highest level. Really, if only I could see her dear, sweet face again." He produced a handkerchief and wiped his eyes. Maria snorted with laughter.

"Here, Jenkins." Alice pointed to me. "Look who I found."

Taking that as my cue, I pushed back my hood and stood. When Mickelmas saw me, it was as though he tried swallowing his own face. I walked over to him, feigning sweetness.

"I'm so happy to see you." I dug my nails into his hand. He gave a small whine at the back of his throat but didn't falter. What a professional. "I'm *so* enjoying my time in the Order."

There were now some murmurs of interest in the room.

"What am I doing after I infiltrate the Order, exactly?" I whispered to Mickelmas, pulling him close. He put an arm around my shoulders and turned me to face the crowd once more.

"Our own burning rose continues our march toward equality, toward liberty, toward the freedom of English magic." I could feel everyone's scrutiny, even the hawk's. I'd an idea what they saw: a magician's girl, born like them but still a stranger. Living with the sorcerers. There was no unkindness here, but there was some mistrust. Well, I couldn't blame them for that.

"Would you mind if I spoke with you for one moment, master dear?" I asked him.

Mickelmas bared his teeth in what might charitably be called a smile. "Oh, to catch up with my prize student. What a balm to my tired soul. But I must turn to fund-raising, my little flytrap. Your army won't build itself, you know."

My army. Of all the ridiculous, insane things.

"Not showing her much of a turnout, are we, Jenkins?" the fish man—Gerald—said with a laugh. *Jenkins.* That gave me an idea. Mickelmas was so careful about hiding his actual identity that very few knew who he really was. And Howard Mickelmas had a terrible reputation.

"Of course I understand, Mr. Hargrove. Wait. It *is* still Mr.

Hargrove, isn't it?" I gave him my most innocent eyes. His mouth became small. "Since you've so many false names—for your safety, of course—I wanted to make sure I didn't slip and use the wrong one."

His wide eyes said he didn't think I would. My expression told him plainly that he was wrong.

"Oh, one moment with my little flower. Privately." He squeezed my arm so hard it brought tears to my eyes. "A round for my friends, on me!" he called to the barkeep, and the place exploded in true excitement for the first time. Mickelmas pushed me through the room while a few of the magicians shook hands with me. Mickelmas shoved me out the door and around the corner. Finally free, I rubbed my arm.

"That's no way to handle a lady," I snapped.

"I've seen you eat a pork pie. There's nothing ladylike about you." He crossed his arms. "What do you want?"

Was this a joke? "Why are you using my name to start a bloody revolt?"

"You think becoming a sorcerer was enough? I'm laying the groundwork for you to rise higher than ever, you stupid pudding." There was a passion in his eyes I hadn't seen before. When we'd worked together in his tiny flat, he told me he'd fought enough for magicians. Now he wanted to plunge back into the fray?

"I thought you went to America."

"Leave when, after centuries on the outs, the time of magicians is rising once more?" He sounded awed by the very idea of it. "The sorcerers will be on their knees to R'hlem in no time."

Yes, because I wouldn't go to him. "We're doing our best," I snapped.

"Oh, don't tell me you actually fancy yourself one of them." Mickelmas scoffed.

"That's what you were training me for, wasn't it?"

"No!" He stamped his foot. "I was training you to become *like* one of them." He looked as if he wanted to shake me. "They'll never accept you. They can never accept anything that isn't the same as them."

My life among the sorcerers was not perfect, but it was a damned sight better than I had ever expected after the commendation ball.

"Isn't that too harsh?" I asked.

"Oh, you're becoming soft. How disappointing. I thought you had the fire of your father in you." He paused. "That came out a lot funnier than I meant it to." He smiled a little. "Eh? Fire? Your father?"

"And *speaking* of my father"—at this he stiffened—"what the hell did you mean about him not having drowned?" If Mickelmas tried to slip away from me again, I was going to hang on to his neck until he told me.

"Oh, why do we have to harp on things that are past? I've said many stupid things to people I never intended to see again."

"Tell me." My hands bloomed with flame.

"I don't know what happened to your father, all right?" He inched away.

"Then how do you know he didn't drown?" That was what Mickelmas had said, in St. Paul's on the night of Korozoth's attack. *Your father didn't drown.* And then in an instant he'd gone, leaving me with the echo of those words in my head.

"Your aunt needed something to tell you when you were a little girl." He wiped his brow. "William left your mother before you were born. He never came back, and I don't know what happened to him. There's the truth."

I'd expected many things, but I hadn't expected that.

What was he saying? That my father could be walking around out in the world somewhere, right now? That he'd abandoned me?

"It's not true," I said softly. Mickelmas pursed his lips.

"It didn't seem fair to keep you ignorant about that."

I kept thinking of that painting in the bar. The young man's face—my father's face—had looked so like mine.

"Do you think he's still alive?" I asked numbly.

"I've no idea," he replied.

I hadn't known I'd feel pain at this. My hands stopped burning.

"I'm sorry," Mickelmas said, looking away. "At the time I didn't think I'd see you again. I felt you ought to know the truth. Stupid idea."

What had I wanted? Some tragic tale or wild explanation? I was a fool.

"That's enough now." Maria stalked out of the pub. That warm, rich, womanly tone was back in her voice. Willie had reemerged. "Don't upset the girl."

"Who is this red-haired person?" Mickelmas looked her in the eyes and froze. His whole expression shifted to something unreadable. "Have we met before?"

Maria shook her head, curls tumbling in her face. "No. I'd remember the pleasure," she mumbled.

"Go home," Mickelmas said, turning back to me. "When the time's right, we'll come for you."

"But I need your help *now*." I unsheathed the tiny dagger from my left wrist, the one weapon I'd brought. He accepted it gingerly, his expression clearing as he held it up. I could tell that he recognized it.

"Where did you get this?" He swiped it once through the air, twisting his wrist in such a way that the blade sparked in the sunlight. Bloody hell, he seemed to know what he was doing.

"We found it in Ralph Strangewayes's house," I said.

At that, he paused. "Tell me everything." While I spoke, he continued to study the blade. Finally, he shook his head. "I don't know about this."

"You don't think they'll work?" My heart sank. He handed the blade back, hilt first.

"No, they will. But these are weapons forged from another world." He sniffed. "They're crafted to use against monsters, *by* monsters."

"I'll take the risk. Can you teach us?" Getting the others

on board with this plan, particularly Blackwood, might prove difficult. But the idea of learning from Mickelmas again was strangely comforting. I'd missed our lessons in Ha'penny Row.

He hesitated. "The sorcerers will never agree to this."

"They've already shut me down. I only need to prove to them that the weapons work," I said.

He smiled a little. "You can't seem to stay out of trouble, can you?"

"You're saying yes?" Relief flooded through me.

"I'll never pass up an opportunity to make your great Order acknowledge magician superiority." He pulled at his beard. "When do we begin?"

THAT EVENING, I SUMMONED MY LITTLE "unit" to Blackwood's house, after Magnus had finished his patrol of the barrier. Maria and I waited in the southernmost parlor, the one filled with Chinese pottery and tapestry. Fiddling with the plain gold locket about my neck, I smiled as Magnus and Dee entered, Blackwood behind them. A footman waited by the door. Oh dear, that wouldn't do.

"Can we be alone?" I asked. Blackwood looked confused but dismissed the servant.

"I'll keep watch," Maria whispered, and ducked out. It was only the four of us now, the boys and I.

"I'm not going to like this, am I?" Blackwood muttered, coming to stand beside me with a weary expression. He frowned. "Where'd you get that locket?"

"It was the best way to make him comfortable," I said, fingering the golden clasp.

"Keep who comfortable?" Magnus reclined on a sofa, hands behind his head.

I slipped the locket off and opened it. Mickelmas exploded out and somersaulted across the floor. Blackwood leaped back, and Dee nearly fell off the sofa. Getting to his feet, Mickelmas turned his head side to side, popping his bones.

"Still not the most comfortable escort I've ever had," he said.

Magnus jumped to his feet, knocking a china tiger off the table beside him. It shattered into pieces on the carpet, a curling tail here, an ocher eye there.

Blackwood looked like a life-sized, bewildered statue himself.

"I remember there being more of you the last time," Mickelmas said to the boys. Noticing the smashed tiger, he waved his hand, murmured, and in a flash the porcelain creature was reassembled and standing atop the table. With a wry smile, Mickelmas wiggled his fingers in another spell, and the tiny creature came to life. It paced from one end of the table to the other, giving miniature roars, its striped tail lashing. Dee made a wondering noise and poked at the little beast. It bit him.

Mickelmas sat down on the sofa. Fluffing his coat, he plumped a pillow and leaned back. "Much more comfortable. Now then. Who's ready for a little magic?"

15

FOR A MOMENT, THE ONLY SOUNDS WERE THE TICK-
ing of a clock and the china tiger's mewls. Dee and Magnus
were each frozen in a different expression: Dee horrified, Magnus elated. Blackwood finally broke the silence. "You brought
him into *my* house?"

I hadn't anticipated his outrage. Evidently, that had been
stupid.

"I'll try not to be insulted, Your Lordship." Mickelmas patted Dee's arm, and the boy jumped. "Glad to see you fellows
still in one piece."

"Oh. Thank you very much," Dee said, brightening.

"Howel, you madman." From Magnus, that sounded like
the finest compliment in the world. He went up to the magician. "Good to see you again, sir! I was afraid you were done
for." They shook hands.

"I remember you. The bold, stupid one," Mickelmas said.

"Bold and stupid is the Magnus family motto." Magnus
pondered a moment. "What's the Latin? *Ferox et stultus*?"

"You *did* remember your lessons! Master Agrippa would be
pleased," Dee said.

"May I see you alone?" Blackwood thundered at me.

He ushered me to the next room, the "armory" that contained the crests of every Earl of Sorrow-Fell there had ever been. His own hung above the doorway: two hands twined in ivy—the standard Blackwood crest—with his own personal insignia, a star to symbolize his status as the family's guiding light.

Right now, an erupting volcano would have been a better image. Blackwood stormed away from me, his fists clenched by his sides.

"We needed help," I said.

"How? Where? *Why?*" A vein flickered in his neck with each word. He made toward an antique clock as if about to punch it.

"He knows Strangewayes's weapons."

"The weapons?" The incredulity on his face gave way to cold fury. "You're lying to the Imperator again. Only this time, you had the audacity to bring the three of us into it!"

My face warmed at the truth. I hadn't wanted to say this, but there was no other choice.

"And your father had the audacity to sacrifice magicians and witches to hide his own sins, didn't he?" Charles Blackwood had been every bit as guilty as Mary Willoughby or Mickelmas when he'd allowed the Ancients into our world, but he had managed to hide his involvement and avoid punishment. For over a decade, witches had been executed and magicians oppressed, but sorcerers and the Blackwood family in particular had thrived.

The temperature in the room cooled, and I shivered as Blackwood drew closer. I was tall, but he was taller. Still, I would not be intimidated.

"You think that's fair?" he hissed, bringing his face close. My pulse quickened, but I stared him down.

"Should everyone be punished for what your father did?"

He struggled for a minute. "No."

"If we defeat R'hlem with magician weapons and training, we can prove to the Order how wrong they've been. You said you wanted to make it right."

Blackwood stepped closer, and I instinctively moved back. He shepherded me against the wall, locking me in a corner of the room. His gaze captured mine.

"Are you sure this isn't about you?" he murmured.

"What makes you think that?" I asked, uneasy.

Maybe it was the dim light, but I could swear pity momentarily softened his features. "Since R'hlem sent that message, you've grown reckless. Insisting we go to Cornwall, insisting on these weapons, seeking out the very magician you were supposed to stay away from!" His anger resurfaced. "You feel responsible, and that makes you take action. *Careless* action. God forbid you wait on anyone else's instruction, oh no. It's *entirely* your fault; therefore, it's entirely *your* problem to fix." It was as if he'd seen me naked, my whole mind and soul exposed to him. "But you aren't alone in this, Howel, and now you've made us all guilty by association!"

With nowhere else to go, I turned my head and studied the very interesting wall.

"Don't be a coward." His voice softened. "It's the truth, isn't it?"

Reluctantly, I turned back to him. Blackwood stepped away. There. I could breathe more freely. "Don't *you* feel guilty for what your father did? You know we have to do this."

With a groan, Blackwood walked toward the door.

"We will." He stopped to look at me, his expression grim. "I thought we had no secrets from each other, Howel." And there it was, the great reason for his anger. For years, he'd carried his father's sin. No one, not even his mother or Eliza, had known their family's darkest secret. When we'd finally trusted each other with the truth—I was a magician, he a traitor's son—I'd become his first real friend.

I'd wounded him without thinking.

My face burned, but he left before I could reply. I trailed after him, back into the parlor.

Blackwood settled into a corner of the room, retreating entirely into himself. Magnus, at least, was enjoying this. He'd picked a vase—Ming dynasty, from the look of it—and was badgering Mickelmas to hide inside it.

"Two pounds says he can," Magnus said to Dee.

"I am not a trained bear, you rascals." Mickelmas laughed. He'd helped himself to the decanter of brandy by the window and was sipping a glass.

"Is it like bunching yourself up tight in a ball?" Magnus asked. "Or do you just sort of shrink?"

Girls' voices sounded outside the door. One belonged to Maria, the other to Eliza, who was probably wondering why Maria was guarding the door.

"Quickly!" Magnus whispered, holding out the vase again. With a groan, Mickelmas leaped into it, disappearing from view. Eliza entered, stopping short at the sight of Magnus gleefully hugging a vase to his chest.

"Oh. Hello?" she said, surprised.

"I, er, love the decorating." Magnus held out the vase. "May I keep this?"

"*What?*"

I looked around nervously and saw that the china tiger had curled up beside Mickelmas's glass and fallen asleep, thank God. Because I'd no idea how to explain that.

"No, Magnus, you can't have it. I think this piece would look better in another room." I snatched the vase and said to Blackwood, "Let's take it out, shall we?"

"Yes. The vase needs a new home." Together, we hurried past a baffled Eliza.

In the garden, I released Mickelmas from the vase in a flurry of purple and orange. He pulled an apple from Blackwood's tree and shined it upon his sleeve.

"We would be honored to accept your help," Blackwood muttered.

"Indeed, your enthusiasm is boundless, my young squirrels." Slipping his arm through mine, Mickelmas led me toward the garden wall, his mirth dissolving somewhat. "You know what you're asking, I take it?" He glanced at Blackwood. "Are you aware that Ralph Strangewayes went mad? Stark raving mad."

Hunting creatures beyond the realm of sanity would do that to a person.

"These weapons are not *natural*," Mickelmas continued. "I heard the stories when I was a boy. They say that Strangewayes's power shattered his mind. Have you experienced headaches, nosebleeds? Have you seen things that aren't there?"

Nosebleeds. Headaches. I went a bit cold.

"The weapons can hurt us?"

"You don't know as much about these things as you might wish." Mickelmas frowned. "Are you certain?"

"Yes." I forced myself to mean it. After all, we didn't need the weapons for long. We weren't hunting; we were fighting. There was a difference . . . wasn't there?

"Very well. Shall we commence our lessons?" Mickelmas addressed the last question to Blackwood, who lurked by the door and resembled nothing so much as a tall shadow with a terrible attitude.

"Not here," he said.

"My thoughts exactly. I find this place to be a bit dour." Mickelmas smirked.

"I've access to Master Agrippa's house," said Blackwood. "Until they sort out the Agrippa heir, the Imperator gave it to me. We can train there."

"Splendid. I've always wanted to reside near Hyde Park. Very chic."

"You're not going to live there?" Blackwood sounded horrified.

"I have to be on hand whenever you all find yourselves with a free moment. Besides, I can't have you coming into town to look for me."

"Fine. Stay out of sight. If you're caught, I know nothing about this," Blackwood snapped.

Mickelmas appeared at my side and kissed my hand. "Farewell, my adorable know-nothings," he said, winking one great black eye. With a flip of his coat, he vanished. Blackwood and I stood alone in the garden.

"Thank you," I said.

"Don't speak to me, Howel. Not right now." With that, he stalked back into the house. Damn. Well, he'd a right to be angry. If the Order discovered our collaboration with Mickelmas, they could throw us all in the Tower. They could strip Blackwood of his title and estate.

Hell, he had *more* than a right to be angry. He'd a right to evict me from his house. That I knew he wouldn't only made me feel worse. But after a while, he'd see that what I'd done was right. We'd laugh about this one day. Hopefully.

I returned to the parlor. Dee stood by the window, looking out into the street. He motioned me over.

"How did it go?" He couldn't raise his voice, as Eliza was over by the fire, talking excitedly with Magnus.

"We've a new teacher."

Dee puffed out his cheeks. "I feel like an outlaw. Never thought I'd feel *that*." Then he nodded toward the sofa. "The tiger's waking," he whispered. Indeed, the little porcelain cat was yawning and stretching. Taking out Porridge, I improvised a quick spell. With a movement designed for freezing water, I wished the creature to become still. It did as I asked—and transformed into a small ice sculpture.

Hopefully, it hadn't been too expensive.

"What are you doing over there?" Eliza called.

"Nothing," Dee and I answered in unison. He sat down on the sofa while I walked over to Magnus and Eliza. As I approached, I couldn't help hearing their conversation.

"*The Winter's Tale* follows the essential plot of *Othello* for the first half, and then deviates into some absurd comedy." Eliza groaned with exasperation. "A bear simply waltzes on to eat a minor character, and then shuffles off. What terrible writing! Shakespeare only did it for the money."

"He wrote *all* of them for the money." Magnus had been eating walnuts, and now he tossed a shell into the fireplace.

"He didn't have to be so obvious about it, did he?"

"Ah, but poetry has always had two chief concerns: lining

pockets and wooing women." Magnus laughed when Eliza made a face.

"You wouldn't know it from some of his sonnets. Remember? 'My mistress' eyes are nothing like the sun'? Such an original way to woo."

I was surprised at Eliza's knowledge and the light in her eyes as she enjoyed the debate. Her face fell a little when I approached.

"I didn't mean to interrupt you," she said, getting up. "Good night." She curtsied to Magnus. As she passed, I followed her to the door.

"I didn't know you loved Shakespeare." I'd meant it as a compliment, but her expression darkened. She really did look like her brother when she was incensed.

"Of course not. I'm no good for anything except parties and dresses." Then she left the room without another word. Magnus waited for me over by the fire, wearing a quizzical expression.

"What was that about?" he asked.

"Nothing." I'd a feeling Eliza was still angry that Maria and I had gone off without her. I hadn't meant to snub her so blatantly.

"So? What does the old fellow say?" Magnus asked.

"We'll meet at Agrippa's."

"I can't believe you found him again." Magnus had none of Blackwood's anger. Rather, he appeared delighted. "You're the boldest girl I've ever known, Howel."

"I daresay you've known a few." The words left my mouth before I could think.

"Perhaps." He played with the wooden charm at his belt. "Suppose I'm a bit surprised you'd rush back to Mickelmas after being thrown into the Tower."

"*Ferox et stultus*," I said, grinning. "Perhaps those are the Howel words as well."

"No, yours would be *I have a brilliant plan*, followed by Blackwood moaning in horror." He let go of the charm. "Blacky doesn't like to take risks. When you're at the very top, there's only one place to go."

I hadn't considered that.

"What's troubling you?" Magnus folded his arms. "You get this little crease in your forehead when you're deep in spiritual turmoil."

"Don't be ridiculous." But I squirmed under Magnus's honest gaze. Blackwood's words about my guilt had rung true. "Well, that bastard R'hlem is going to keep destroying everything in his path. The longer I don't go to him, the better the chance we'll all be killed. That's why I had to find Mickelmas." That was why I'd dragged Magnus and Dee and Blackwood into all this.

"This isn't your fault." Magnus reached out but didn't touch me. Once, when he'd taught me how to fight with warded blades in Agrippa's library, he'd had no problem correcting my arm, the position of my body. Now it was as if a shield separated us.

That was proper, of course. Otherwise, it could prove too dangerous.

"But it *is* my fault," I said.

His features tightened. "You're not the only one who feels guilt, Howel. You can't hog it all."

He was trying to be funny, but I heard the shame in his voice.

"Magnus, what happened?"

He hesitated, staring into the fire. "I don't want to burden you."

"I think you should."

He was so silent that I thought he'd decided not to tell me. Then, "I was on another ship before the *Queen Charlotte*. I lied when I told you I'd never faced Nemneris. About a month ago, we nearly won an assault against her—got a harpoon in her flank. But she dove deep under the water, came back up, and tried to smash us. She didn't pull us down—she was too injured—but the ship couldn't sail."

"Abandoning ship isn't a crime," I said.

Magnus closed his eyes. "It's what happened *after* we'd landed ashore. They were waiting for us, you see, on the beach." The way he said "they" sent a chill through my blood. "The lice. We fought them, but there were more, always more, coming down the sand." He grabbed that token again, holding it the way one might hold prayer beads. "Fifty of us went onto the beach. Nine left it. Later on, when we'd finally got away, I realized I was covered in blood. From head to toe." He passed a hand over his eyes. "It makes you wonder how you managed to survive. Surely you did something cowardly to get away." His voice broke, just once, but once was enough.

I put my hand on his arm. "There's no shame in survival."

He was stiff, unyielding beneath my touch. Utterly unlike the boy I'd known only a few months before.

"Every night I see the lice coming across the sand." He looked at me again. "I'm not the only one with nightmares." It was as though he was defending himself. "The others in the barracks scream in the night, and . . ."

He released the charm slowly.

"What is that?" I said. Magnus smiled faintly.

"Jim Collins. He was the carpenter's mate, all of twelve years old. Bright boy. I taught him how to cheat at cards." His smile disappeared. "And then, when we knew we'd have to abandon ship . . ." He took the charm off his belt and gave it to me. I cradled it in my hands. "Jim told me his mother made this to keep him safe, and he wanted her to have it back. I took it. Didn't know what else to do. Later, when the fighting was done, we found Jim's body lying on the sand." Magnus shuddered. "He'd been bit through."

He rubbed his forehead. "I know he came from Cornwall. But how many Jim Collinses are there in bloody Cornwall? So I keep this with me to give to his mother when I find her." Magnus kept his face stony, but he couldn't hide the painful dance of emotions in his gray eyes. "Do you know, I thought the war would be over in a month once I joined?" He laughed bitterly. It occurred to me then that he played a part for all of us, that the smiling Magnus was like a layer of theatrical paint.

I gripped his shoulder. "I beg you, don't hold this inside. I'm here if you need me."

For a minute, we stayed looking at each other. Magnus's gaze seemed to clear. "Oh," he said, a sound of surprise.

We were so near to each other that I flushed and released him.

"Forgive me," he said as I gave him back his charm. "Living with the Earl of Sorrow-Filled is burden enough."

"Sorrow-*Fell*." I couldn't help laughing.

Magnus went to speak with Dee, who'd been dozing on the sofa. I watched him carefully. He was easy and charming once more; that mask of his was firmly back in place.

THE NEXT EVENING, I SAT BY my bedroom window, surveying the empty streets and thinking on our training plan. The streetlamps cast dancing shadows, but you wouldn't find an actual person out there until dawn. Most refused to venture out at night now, preferring to lock their doors and windows, huddle in bed, and wait for daylight. We all anticipated the night when the monsters would come tearing out of the sky, a dense cloud of claws and talons and teeth.

I was about to prepare for bed when a dark figure coming out of the house caught my eye. It moved down the walk and toward the street.

The figure turned, gazing back at the house. My stomach

dropped when I recognized Rook, his hair hidden beneath a cap. Shoulders hunched and hands jammed into his coat pockets, he slipped out the gate and hurried away.

Where the bloody hell was he going at this hour?

Cursing, I grabbed Porridge, threw on my cloak, and opened my window. A moment later, I used the wind to carry myself to the ground. Wherever Rook was going tonight, he wouldn't go alone.

16

ROOK MOVED OUT OF THE CITY PROPER AND INTO the no-man's-land of the shantytowns. Houses fashioned from plywood, tin, and wire leaned against one another, as if too exhausted to stand on their own. Fires burned here and there, with families gathered about, lined faces accentuated by the glow. Lean, flea-ravaged dogs chased each other through the streets.

I could have caught up with Rook and asked where he was off to, but I sensed that whatever he'd tell me would be a lie. People did not sneak out of the house in the dead of night on perfectly innocent business. When I'd lived at Agrippa's, every moment I could spare had been spent rushing to meet secretly with Mickelmas. Whatever Rook was up to, I wanted to know the truth.

Rook walked slowly, glancing left and right until he came to a halt. Tilting back his head, he began scenting the air. Then he took off at a run, plunging into a narrow alleyway. He went from stillness to action so fast it caught me off guard.

That was when I heard the screams.

Cursing under my breath, I followed where he'd gone

through the labyrinth of makeshift houses. I gagged at the odor of waste and mud, lifting my skirts as high as I dared to keep them clean.

Finally, I came to an intersection wide enough to allow multiple people through at the same time. Before me, two men were locked in a scuffle, one of them with a loaf of bread cradled to his chest. The other fellow beat and tore at him mercilessly. The man with the bread cried out, but no one came to help. No one dared. Finally, the attacker walloped the poor fellow with such force that the man dropped his food.

I prepared to move in, when—

Darkness poured forth in a wave. A cloak of night swept over the screaming thief. Slowly, the wheezing man on the ground got to his feet, snatched his bread, and ran off.

Darkness flowed in a ceaseless tide, suffocating the thief's screams. My eyes tracked to the source as Rook moved into sight, his pace deliberate. He threw his hands into the air, releasing the thief from the shadow. Mesmerized, I could only watch as Rook grabbed the stammering man by his shirtfront.

"If I see you attack anyone else, there'll be no mercy. Do you understand?" There was ferocity to his tone that I'd never heard before.

The man whined, the acrid scent of urine flooding the air as he pissed himself. Rook threw him down and tipped his cap over his eyes. "Go. *Now.*"

The man did not need to be told again, and he hurried

away, tripping twice. Rook cracked his knuckles as the darkness retreated, folding up to neatly fit inside his moonlit shadow. I gasped, and he turned.

"Miss?" he said, "What are you doing here?" His eyes, still a pure black, widened when I removed my hood.

"I could ask you the same thing," I said.

Rook groaned and rubbed the back of his neck, as though I'd caught him stealing a pie instead of threatening a man with the force of black magic.

"We should go. It's not safe for you on the streets at night." Rook came over and slipped an arm around me.

"Not safe for *me*?" I all but pinched him.

"Wait until we get home before you scold me," he replied. I could barely see his face beneath the brim of his cap. He'd pulled his collar up as well, doing an admirable job of blending in with the shadows. Together, we made our way out of the encampment and back to safer streets.

Returning to Blackwood's at this time of night made entering through the front impossible, so we scaled the stone garden wall. Rook climbed it, catlike and lithe, and I floated up and over on the wind. The garden at midnight was lush and quiet, the fruit trees by the wall silver in the moonlight. I sat on a stone bench by the fountain, listening to the gurgling of the water as church bells tolled the hour, and Rook sat down beside me. The scent of lavender and rose should have made this the most romantic setting possible. And it would have been if I hadn't wanted to throttle the boy I loved.

"Don't look at me like that," he said gently. He was being so *patient* it made me want to scream.

"Like I can't believe you're running about in the worst parts of town at night, pummeling criminals? It's a very specific look." When he sighed, I could have exploded. "I don't like being lied to!"

"Bit funny, isn't it?" There was no anger in his eyes, only a kind of weary humor. "When you've done your fair share of lying."

That stung. "I did it to keep us under the ward."

"Which doesn't exist now, so why should I worry?" He shifted in his seat to face me. My heart did a traitorous little flip at his nearness. "Why should I watch you court danger as I stay behind in safety?" Quiet shame tinged his voice.

"It's the sorcerers' job to protect the city." I tried to sound soft and reasonable.

"They defend against the monsters outside, yes, but there are monsters in here as well." His eyes blazed. "You know it's true. That man with the bread was trying to feed his family. If I didn't protect him, who would?"

I hated when he made this much sense.

"I don't want you to risk yourself," I murmured.

He put a cool hand to my face. "I don't want *you* to do that, either, but I know it's who you are." He tilted my chin. "Please don't get in the way of what *I* am."

That was the difference. What he was becoming was monstrous. But should I tell him, *You can't protect people because you're morphing into a hideous shadow demon?* Somehow that seemed the wrong thing to say.

"Can't you wait until Maria and Fenswick make a better treatment?" I asked. He dropped his hand.

"They make me sluggish and stupid." His expression hardened. In the moonlight, I watched as his shadows danced along the garden path like living ink. Whispers slid past me, the whispers of dark things, monstrous things. Whenever Rook became frustrated, the blackness got worse. I held up my hands.

"All right," I said, my voice easy. Slowly, the shadows and whispers died. Rook cleared his throat, bashful.

"I worry that you're ashamed of me," he said at last. Ashamed? I nearly laughed with the absurdity of it. "I do this partly so I can feel *worthy* in your eyes."

"What do you mean?" I whispered.

He took my hand in his own, his skin growing feverish.

"I know that I must humiliate you," he muttered. "Living in that fine house, on someone's charity. You must see what a poor wretch I am, Net—Henrietta."

"You think I care about fortune?" I swung between furious and happy. "You silly, ridiculous . . . thing!" I couldn't think of the right words, or nearly any words. "Don't you know me?"

"Did you call me silly?" He laughed, surprised.

"I love you, for God's sake." I nearly shouted it at him. There. The words were out. I clapped a hand to my mouth. What had possessed me?

"What?"

- 196 -

"I—I only meant—" Then I was silenced.

Rook swept me up and held me close against his chest. I could feel his heart beating, a quick tattoo that matched my own.

"Say it again," he whispered.

"I love y—"

He kissed me, stopping my mouth.

I leaned into him, sliding my arm around his neck. This was madness. We were alone in the middle of the night, like some wonderful scene from a play. But this was no fantasy; no one was pretending. Rook was here, with me, his mouth on mine. At first, his kisses were gentle, feather-light. But then his arm circled my waist, and he deepened the kiss, driving me mad.

His hands trailed up and down my back. Our mouths opened, and I gasped when his tongue flickered against mine.

We pulled apart and I slid my fingers through his hair.

"I don't believe it's finally happened," he whispered, his breath shaky. "I've dreamed of this for so long." His kisses dusted down my cheek until he found my mouth once more. I put my hand on Rook's chest, feeling the thundering of his heartbeat.

When I'd kissed Magnus, it had been wild, frenzied. This was like a homecoming, each kiss, each embrace, a reminder of where I belonged.

I looked into his black eyes, which shimmered with wildness and desire. Fear gripped me, and something else even more shocking: want.

"I don't repulse you?" he breathed. No, the shadows and the scars meant nothing to me, not as long as *he* was here.

His shirtsleeves were rolled up to the elbows, revealing a line of scars along his left arm. I took his hand and put my lips to his callused palm. Then, slowly, I kissed down his wrist until I found the scars, kissing them gently one after the other. His intake of breath was so sharp that I stopped.

"Is it painful?"

"The opposite," he growled. Rook's whole body shuddered. He grabbed my wrists and gazed down at me. "We can't do this," he murmured.

If we kept going, where might it lead? "I know," I said.

And then every hair on my head stood on end; I heard someone else breathing. We weren't alone here. Something crawled on its belly out of the shadows, hissing as it inched across the grass.

The creature had no stag, no terrifying friends. In fact, it was the most pathetic thing I had ever seen. In the moonlight, its tattered black robes scraped over the ground. Smoke curled in feeble whispers over its body, and a black hood cloaked its face from view.

I hadn't seen a shadow Familiar since Korozoth had fallen. The Familiar looked up at Rook and hissed one word: "Master."

The thing bent its head and began to lick the ground. God, it was tasting Rook's footprints in the dirt, lapping them up in adoration. He kicked at the thing, sending it crawling off with a whimper.

"Get away from me, you demon," Rook spit.

Despite the horror in front of us, his violence startled me. The creature only gurgled as it reached for him again. The thing's nails were shredded and filled with grit. This was the most miserable monster I had ever seen.

"Don't fight it," I said, but Rook didn't listen. With a quick sweep of his arm, even more shadows rushed in from every corner and crevice of the garden, covering the Familiar. I listened for the monster's horrified screams.

Instead, a crowing emerged, repulsive in its delight. When Rook uncovered the Familiar, we found it rolling about on its back, ecstatic as a cat in a beam of sunlight. It crawled on its belly to Rook, grasping at his ankles and licking at his feet.

"Leave me alone!" he bellowed. His face was crimson. God, someone would hear us.

The Familiar got to its knees, and its smoke hood rolled away, revealing a face I instantly recognized. Pale, stringy hair, eyes cruelly sewn shut with a black thread—it was Gwendolyn, Master Agrippa's daughter. She'd fallen to R'hlem's influence long ago. Her teeth chattered as she stared mournfully at Rook. Blood tracked down her cheeks like an obscene parody of tears.

"Master," she whimpered. She leaned forward, putting herself nose to nose with Rook as he crouched down. The fury and hatred fled his face. Gwendolyn held up her hands in a pleading gesture. "The bloody king wants her. Come. Come with me, master. Come." She tugged at his sleeve the way a child might beg a parent for a sweet. Rook's disgust dissolved into . . .

tenderness. It was as if some energy existed between the two of them. Shadows bristled and slithered toward the pair.

With a cry, I flung a stream of fire at Gwendolyn. Spitting, she launched herself backward, snatching up her dagger. I grabbed Rook's arm when he started to pursue her.

"Don't! It's a trap," I said, meeting Gwendolyn's oncoming attack with another burst of fire.

Flinging a hand over her eyes to shield herself, Gwendolyn fled into the darkness. With another burst of fire, I looked about the garden for her, but she was gone. Swallowed up by the night.

Rook shifted, unsteady on his feet. Growling, he turned and slammed his fist against the garden wall.

"I didn't want you to see me weaken," he said. "I never want that."

Right then I was on the verge of telling him what he was becoming. Only Fenswick's warning kept me silent.

"I want you to see how I'm mastering these powers." Rook looked into my eyes. "How I'm strong enough to care for both of us." He pulled me closer. "Because I want to marry you, Henrietta." He kissed me again, cupping my cheek in his hand.

"I love you," he whispered when we pulled apart. I closed my eyes, misery welling up inside me.

"I love you, too," I said.

I did love him. And I did fear for him. Very much.

17

THE NEXT MORNING, ROOK AND I SAT ON A BENCH IN Fenswick's apothecary. Maria, her sleeves rolled and wisps of hair sticking to her face, poured some boiling liquid into a wooden cup. Steam rose up in a hissing cloud, smelling of lemons. Maria laid a sprig of something green in the cup, then pushed it over to Rook.

"Drink," she said.

"What is it?" he asked, poking at the leaf with an uneasy expression.

"Mint. Sweetens the taste." She chewed a sprig and caught my eye. After I'd told her what had happened the night before, she'd agreed we needed to try something new. Quickly.

Rook gulped the concoction in one go, then slammed the cup on the table. "What's in it?" He coughed, shoving the cup away as though it had hurt him.

"Dandelion root, honeyed belladonna, certain types of mushroom." Maria deliberately left out the spider eggs she'd mentioned to me, which I thought was wise. The belladonna also worried me. It was poison—treated so that it wouldn't kill him, of course, but poison nonetheless. It was supposed to attack the shadowy parasite that was growing inside Rook. If this worked, we'd kill the thing. No, no ifs—it *would* work.

It had to.

Rook put a hand on his stomach and groaned, climbing to his feet and nearly collapsing.

I rose as he took a knee and pressed his head against the table, digging his fingernails into the wood. The room darkened. In an instant, I had my fire in my hand. The darkness warped while Maria took up her ax. *Please, God. Not like this, not now.*

And then the light flared brighter, and the shadows dispersed.

Rook brought his head up, massaging his forehead with the heel of his hand as if he were recovering from a night of drinking. He blinked at me. His left eye had returned to a pure sky blue.

"Has something good happened?" he asked as he stood, swaying only a little.

Maria beamed and went back to the fire to stir a pot hanging over it. "Very good," she replied as I slid my arms around Rook, laying my head on his chest. He chuckled, the sound resonating against my cheek.

"If it makes you happy, I know it's good," he whispered into my hair. He made a startled but delighted noise when I kissed him. His lips tasted sweet from the honey. Last night hadn't been a dream.

"Didn't know I'd made a love potion as well," Maria drawled.

Flushed with embarrassment, Rook and I stepped apart.

"What's this?" Fenswick waddled into the room, and I lifted him onto the table at once so he could see. He fiddled with a button on his coat, marveling at Rook's improvement. "I'll be sold into the Hollow and made to dance," he said in astonishment. I'd no idea what that meant, but I assumed he was pleased. He examined the dregs in Rook's cup, pouring them into a glass bowl and adding some viscous pink syrup.

"Have you a moment?" Maria whispered to me as Fenswick examined Rook's eyes. We ducked into the hallway.

"You're a genius," I said.

"Aye, that was a given." Her pleased expression faded. "But there can be complications." She curled a ringlet of hair around her finger. "The important thing now is that he remain calm. If his heart beats too fast," she said, hammering her fist upon her chest, "the drug can weaken him. If he's weak, the thing inside him'll fight like the devil to take control."

Sneaking around in the night would be absolutely out, to say nothing of fighting. Maria continued, "You'll have to keep him from *all* excitement. I count the good kind as well as the bad." Her pointed look made me pale. Rook and I had *finally* declared ourselves, and now we couldn't act upon it? I had to keep from arguing.

"Can you give him something to make him tired?" I asked. At least *that* would calm him. What I was asking was little better than drugging him, but Maria nodded in agreement.

"I'll slip something in with the doses. Hopefully, he won't realize."

"Thank you for all of this." I'd pulled on my cloak and was fastening it. Already, the clocks were chiming the hour, and I was late.

Maria smiled. "Are you off to train, then?"

"Would you like to come and watch?" I brightened at the thought, wishing I could invite her to fight as well, but such a thing was impossible. The boys could handle only so many renegades in one week.

"I'd love it. I want to watch your magician in action. He's funny," she said. "I imagine we could take some sandwiches as well."

MARIA GAPED AT AGRIPPA'S HOUSE AS we alighted from the carriage, nearly dropping the basket hooked over her arm. Her reaction was understandable. When I'd arrived months before, this place, with its white Grecian columns and its curling black iron gates, had been like something out of a fairy tale. Now it felt haunted, a memorial to happier times. The great windows on the uppermost floors resembled vacant eyes, gazing down at me in judgment.

"So this is where your great Master lived?" Maria's voice shocked me from my remembrance. "Seems a fair place."

Being here, I thought of Gwendolyn crawling toward us in her pitiful, shadowy rags. Maria noticed my shudder.

"Master Agrippa had a daughter," I said by way of explanation. "They thought she was the prophesied one, you see, before she . . . well, before she went away. I can't help but think of her."

An even more unpleasant thought surfaced. Suppose Gwendolyn *had* been the prophesied girl. Perhaps she had been the one great hope for England . . . and had chosen the side of darkness. I'd worried that falsely accepting the title of England's chosen one meant we were giving up on finding the right person, but what if the truth was even blacker? What if we'd already lost her?

"No sense dwelling on what's past." Maria nudged me from my thoughts. We walked down the path to the front door, where the iron hobgoblin knocker still grimaced. Magnus opened it for us, his coat already off.

"There you are." His smile widened when he saw Maria. "Templeton! My dear, are those sandwiches?" He started poking around the basket at once.

"Count on you to remember what's important." She let him snag one, chopped egg and watercress. Taking a bite, Magnus led us down the hall.

I let them go ahead, chatting together, and gazed about the house. I stopped in the middle of the foyer, dropping the glove I'd just taken off. It felt like a dam bursting.

Memories shouted at me from every corner. This was the foyer where I'd first arrived, turning about in wonder. To my right, the staircase Agrippa had led me up in order to meet the boys on the second floor. To my left, the games room where Wolff had taught me to play billiards. I slowly followed Maria and Magnus, stopping to touch the banister or a framed painting on the wall, anything to rekindle another bittersweet memory.

Entering the library was like coming into the presence of a ghost. Agrippa had sat before the fire with me on several evenings, running over the day's lessons or playing a game of chess with a cup of cocoa. He'd called that his last vice, grinning as he snatched one of my knights in a daring move.

"Are you crying?" Maria whispered, noticing me.

"I'm fine," I croaked, but had to look away. The heart of this room was gone now, and its absence was brutal.

Enough of this. Everyone else had already arrived. They'd moved furniture to clear space for practice. The green armchairs waited by the wall, silent and orderly as a row of soldiers. Mickelmas was coaching Dee, Strangewayes's journal open upon a wooden desk for reference. Blackwood and Magnus watched while Magnus finished his sandwich.

Blackwood frowned at Maria and glowered at me. He said nothing about her presence, though, and proceeded to ignore me even harder than before. He'd not got over the other night. I had a feeling it would be a while before he was ready to speak to me again.

Mickelmas brought a flute's mouthpiece to his lips. Wincing, I waited for that earsplitting scream. He blew into it and began playing the thing expertly, his fingers moving up and down the holes with grace. He looked as though he should be first chair in a concert hall, and in his capable hands the instrument was . . . well, silent.

"Is it broken?" Dee asked as he snatched the flute back.

"No, it's merely being played properly. Handled correctly,

it should emit vibrations that harm only those creatures. The trick is to melt the monsters' brains and leave yours intact." Mickelmas gestured to me. "Henrietta. You see these markings you noticed earlier in Strangewayes's book?" He pointed to a crumbling page. Indeed, there were small black circles on the margins that seemed to have been drawn randomly.

"Yes, the dots," I said.

"Wrong, as usual." He looked pleased with himself. "Musical notes."

No. But looking at it that way, the randomness of the marks suddenly became flourishes of music. How the hell had I not seen this before? Dee adjusted the book this way and that to read all the notes that had been jotted down.

"If you play an up-tempo version of 'Greensleeves,' that should be especially repellent to Molochoron. I hope you're musical," Mickelmas said, handing off the flute.

Dee read the passage over a few times, his fingers flying up and down the length of the flute in practice. Taking a deep breath, he put his mouth to the instrument and began to play. At first there was a slight squealing, enough to make everyone wince, but after a few more attempts, Dee made the instrument silent. He bobbed as he played, practically kicking up his heels. Finished, his face was a splotchy pink from exertion.

"How do you know about all this?" Blackwood asked as Magnus went for his own turn. "How can we be certain this is working?"

"Indeed, Your Lordship. A boy of seventeen's knowledge

is quite comparable to my own," Mickelmas said, selecting a sandwich. "However, please trust that I can interpret Strangewayes's shorthand at least as well as you. For example, those curlicue swords of yours are worked best when twirled *abantis*—counterclockwise."

I'd wondered what on earth that term had been.

"Strangewayes created something like a new language among his followers, as a way to preserve magician secrets. There used to be whole histories of this sort of thing, you know. When I was a boy, they printed biographies of Strangewayes. Revered magicians even had their portraits replicated on pewter souvenir mugs." He sighed. "I miss those days. Magician theory used to be a popular topic of discussion in London salons, passed around with the wine and finger foods." Mickelmas seated himself in a chair, propping his feet on a gold-tasseled stool. "Enough chatter. Knee, let Haggis have a turn."

While Dee and Magnus corrected him on their names, and Blackwood pretended he was anywhere but here, I followed Maria over to the fireplace. She studied Agrippa's portrait with a look of intense concentration.

"That was my Master," I told her. Agrippa's face was younger in this painting, but his smile and his bright brown eyes were the same as ever they'd been.

Forgive me. His last words whispered in my mind.

"Thought he was the man who betrayed you," Maria said.

"He saved my life before he tried to destroy it." To my surprise, Maria scoffed.

"Strange you would remember him so fondly."

Though I'd told her about Agrippa's betrayal, I felt stung.

"He did what he thought was right." What would Agrippa say if he knew we were here with Mickelmas right now, training with magician weapons? He'd probably demand we get these monstrosities out of his house, to begin with. Would he have understood, though? Or was that too much to hope?

"People do what they think is right, but that does not make it good." Maria's voice dropped lower, to that womanly, more musical tone. She rubbed her eyes, as if waking from a dream, then retreated to the window, curling up there to stare out at the garden.

I noticed that Agrippa's prophecy tapestry still hung upon the wall. It had been months since I'd seen that blasted thing with its image of a white hand rising out of a dark wood, fingers tipped with flame. Agrippa's seal, two lions flanking a shield, had been etched into the palm of the hand. I scanned over the "prophetic" lines woven by the Speakers in their priory:

A girl-child of sorcerer stock rises from the ashes of a life.
You shall glimpse her when Shadow burns
    in the Fog above a bright city.
You shall know her when Poison drowns
    beneath the dark Waters of the cliffs.
You shall obey her when Sorrow falls
    unto the fierce army of the Blooded Man.

She will burn in the heart of a black forest;
 her fire will light the path.
She is two, the girl and the woman,
 and one must destroy the other.
For only then may three become one,
 and triumph reign in England.

What a joke it all had been.

"Howel. Demonstrate this, will you?" Mickelmas said, jolting me from my reverie.

He tossed me one of the daggers, then fetched a strawberry and popped it into his mouth. I swiped the dagger through the air, and both times that high keening sound made me wince. Mickelmas sprang to his feet and took the dagger back. "Always have someone incompetent demonstrate first," he told the boys. "It flatters you even more." I restrained myself from kicking at his ankles.

"The trick is to swipe upward." He demonstrated the correct way, with a short, sharp jab. "Ralph Strangewayes claimed he mined these metals from the Ancients' home world. Listen." He flipped open the book, slowly read a few lines to himself, and then spoke: "*Naught but the very melted and molten soil of their ground affects their skins or humors. I fashioned my dirks and cutlasses from their clay and steel, sometimes their very bones.*" The whistle. Had I been putting something from an Ancient's body into my mouth? I felt ill. "*If once you cut them, cut them once again. That is the key.*" He looked back up at us and slapped the page.

"Several of these beasties have unusually tough hides. You'll need a great deal of force behind the blade. You especially, my girl, may not have enough physical strength for some blows."

I wanted to make a snide comment, but after an instant of practicing, I knew he was right. Jabbing up from underneath worked better for me, and the blade did not whine.

"Good. Now that you can use the knife, twist it when you make impact. This little serrated bit on the tip wants to dig into the skin," he said, pointing at it.

"You might have shared all this information with the Order before," Blackwood muttered. "Considering you brought these demons upon us."

Was he really going to be like this the entire session? He remained in the corner, regarding us as though we'd all disappointed him dreadfully. Truly, Lord Blackwood acting a proper ass in Master Agrippa's library was like going back in bloody time.

"In my experience, one tries to avoid those who would like to put one to death," Mickelmas said pleasantly. He ambled over to Magnus, who was jabbing at one of Agrippa's bookshelves with the scythe. Magnus still had one arm wrapped in bandages, and he was making a clumsy job of it. "What, are you trying to pick at it?" Mickelmas adjusted him. "Wide, arcing sweeps, my boy, though perhaps you'd best really go for it when you're out of doors."

Blackwood had not done with his conversation, though. "Why didn't you try this years ago yourself, then?" he snapped.

I'd had quite enough.

"The magicians were scattered and afraid, Blackwood. Can you imagine what that felt like?" I practiced a few more swipes of the dagger.

Blackwood didn't reply.

"How *did* you and Mary Willoughby open that portal in the first place?" Dee asked Mickelmas, finally taking a break from playing.

Blackwood stiffened, but thankfully Mickelmas didn't appear eager to divulge his father's secrets.

"Runes," the magician said, carefully. "But I wouldn't do it again."

"Why?" Dee asked. "Maybe we could send the beasts away?"

"Experience taught me never to play around with such things. All right?" Mickelmas snapped.

Dee blushed to the roots of his hair and played some more.

Mickelmas had us line up and drill with each of the weapons. I could feel the difference when the swords and daggers were handled properly. While I hated to admit it, I wasn't physically strong enough to handle the swords or scythe properly. I was, however, very good with the daggers. Mickelmas applauded whenever I struck a clean, upward blow.

"Excellent. And that tiny little one," he said, plucking the microdagger from my hand. "Well, it's very . . . small." He frowned and flicked his wrist, sending the blade soaring to stick in the front of Agrippa's desk, its handle trembling.

"How will we know if our training works?" Magnus asked, cracking the whip. He did it as Mickelmas had suggested, swirling it once overhead and delivering it in a straight, sharp downward movement. The violet flash of light did not happen this time, and the sound was akin to a clap of thunder. A bit noisy, yes, but it felt right.

"When you're face to face with one of the Ancients, you'll know," Mickelmas said. "Remember, the whip and the flutes are especially good for Molochoron. You don't want to get close enough to use the dagger, as the smell can be quite disconcerting."

I laughed but then grew horribly light-headed. My nose started gushing blood, and the room grew bright before plunging into darkness. Someone guided me to the sofa, where I sat with my head back, pinching my nose.

"Use this," Maria said, giving me a handkerchief. There was a voice whispering in the corner of the room . . . wasn't there? When I turned to find it, a sharp pain stabbed between my eyes. Maria held my head in her hands and shushed my whimpering. "Don't move."

"That'll happen," Mickelmas said. "Boys, raise your hand if you've a headache." The room was silent, then I heard the magician grunt. "Right. Two of you. You must use these weapons sparingly, in practice and in battle."

"Why do they have this effect?" I asked, sounding quite plugged up.

"No idea, but prolonged exposure can have disastrous consequences. Shifts in personality. So do as I ask, and be careful."

I opened my eyes, and the world settled once more.

Blackwood had gone over to the table with the weapons and picked up the softly glowing lantern.

"Don't even think about it." Mickelmas plucked it from the boy's hands and put the lantern back, checking on the latch. "Remember what I said earlier? Never open that unless you must."

"Why?" I asked. I'd missed that particular instruction.

"It's a way to summon the beasts to you," Mickelmas grumbled, tossing a piece of cloth over the lantern. "Strangewayes called it an *optiaethis*. It's not merely an object from another world—it's a living piece of it."

My skin crawled. I wished I'd left the damned thing at Strangewayes's.

"What about the bone whistle?" I looked at the object lying on the table beside the lantern.

Mickelmas shrugged. "No idea what that one does. Never saw any mention of it in the book." He picked it up. "I'd recommend caution."

"Do you think we'll be ready in time for the next attack?" Magnus asked, crouching to one knee and twisting his sword just so. He handled it better, but not perfectly. It sounded like nails scraping down a piece of glass.

"Probably not." Mickelmas took the sword and demonstrated again. "But there's always a silver lining: if you fail, you'll be too dead to be embarrassed."

OVER THE FOLLOWING WEEK, WE SNATCHED every stolen hour we could to train with Mickelmas. There were battles to be fought ten miles outside the city, but those battles were for the army, not the London guard. This gave the five of us time to work quickly. Once we'd got a handle on the weapons, we didn't need to practice as much. That meant the side effects became less frequent as well.

Magnus's arm healed more every day. Soon the bandages would come off, and he'd be sent back to the navy. Once our group dissolved, it would be harder than ever to get the Imperator to change his mind. We needed one more chance to prove ourselves, and we needed it soon.

Then, eight days after Mickelmas had begun to train us, the warning bells chimed once more.

Dong. Dong. Ding dong ding dong. Ding ding, dong, ding. Dong. Dong. Dong. Attack. North. Ancient. And the three large chimes at the end signaled Callax.

So we were to meet the Child Eater at last.

18

WHEN BLACKWOOD AND I JOINED OUR SQUADRON
north of the river, it was clear that fewer sorcerers than usual
had answered the summons. In fact, there were probably no
more than a hundred all told. Perfect—our first sighting of
an Ancient on the city's border in months, and it had to happen when our London ranks were diminished. Yesterday,
Whitechurch had sent several of our squadrons to the border
of Devon, answering a call for reinforcements. Zem was supposed to be down there, rampaging through the countryside,
and our southern forces were taking a beating.

We'd played directly into R'hlem's hands, leaving London
more vulnerable than usual. Blackwood had said the Skinless Man would choose a moment to test our weaknesses, and
now was the perfect bloody time. If he found us lacking today, tomorrow he might decimate our last defenses—and our
queen—in one fell swoop.

My heart was in my throat. We could not fail.

Those of us left assembled directly behind the barrier, four
rows deep, twenty sorcerers per row. The trick was to have
multiple lines of attack, one right after the other. The first row

might use fire, for instance, then bend down and strike with an earthen onslaught while the second row continued the fire assault.

Above us, the air brewed with a storm that two squadrons were creating. Blackwood and I waited as Valens passed by, counting off the people in his division. We had prayed he wouldn't pay us any special attention, with our larger weapons barely concealed. Thankfully, he did not, and I let out a breath as he passed.

"Stay here," I whispered to Blackwood. Balancing on a column of air, I flew up to gaze over the barrier into the no-man's-land beyond. There was no movement on the road ahead, but the air felt weighted with anticipation. Water-glass mirrors were suspended on either side of me, tracking Callax's movement.

"There you are," someone said. I was shocked to find Wolff balancing on a column beside me, his clothes and face spattered with mud. Had he grown even taller since we'd last seen each other? At the very least, his black hair was longer and unkempt, and traces of a beard graced his cheeks. He grinned. "Wondered when I'd see you."

"Wolff! I heard you were in Manchester." I wanted to hug my friend, but that might topple both of us to the ground.

"I was until two days ago. We've been experimenting with shielding. Zem's fire burns hot enough to crack most wards, so we're trying to strengthen our magic." Wolff watched the area ahead with a keen eye. As a warder, he was called upon to provide extra protection when an Ancient attacked. Light shone faintly on the curve of his otherwise invisible shield. "I heard about your weapons. I'm sorry they couldn't let you use them," he said.

"We'll see how that goes," I replied, lifting the whistle out of my collar. Wolff's eyebrows lifted in amazement, or perhaps horror.

"You always were mad." He sounded admiring.

I flew back down to Blackwood, who was watching the water glasses with a nervous eye. As I got into formation beside him, I mentally readied myself for Callax's attack.

The Child Eater, a twenty-foot-tall troll, had plagued the western end of the country for the last two years. He was phenomenal at smashing everything in his way, leveling entire villages. He'd attacked London before, of course, but that was back when we had our ward. Luckily, he couldn't fly, he'd no psychic abilities, and he couldn't breathe fire. But his strength was unequaled, and there was a possibility that the sheer power of his fists could smash the wards and barrier. If that happened, we would have to pray that our powers would be enough to stop him.

Callax was also responsible for Lilly's family's deaths. He'd killed her parents before carrying off her little sisters. It was said he liked to ferry the children he captured away to some cave and eat them later at his pleasure, picking his teeth with their bones. My skin went hot. He wouldn't break through to London today. I'd see to that.

Magnus and Dee arrived and got into position behind me, Magnus with swords strapped to his hips, Dee with the flute snuck under his coat. They both did their best to keep out of Valens's line of sight.

"Lovely day for possible death and dismemberment," Magnus said conversationally, passing Blackwood a sword of his own.

I would have teased him back, but the ground vibrated beneath our feet. My mouth felt dry as cotton as squadron leaders blew their whistles, signaling for us to prepare.

Two sorcerers—the head water-masters—focused the scrying glasses. We four watched as a great, hulking form appeared. The beast's snorts and grunts carried all the way to where we stood.

Callax was a massive creature with a humped spine and long, muscled arms that ended in boulder-shaped fists. Moss-colored patches of diseased skin speckled his torso. His jaw jutted forward, broken yellow teeth protruding. Drool hung in ropes from his open mouth. His eyes were small and deep-set, his head bald and smooth as an egg. Long, pointed ears fanned out to catch every sound.

The thing huffed and then began pounding his fists upon the ground, faster and faster. *Boom. Boom. Boom.* My toes curled in my boots, and I slipped my shaking hand around the dagger's hilt.

With a full-blooded roar, Callax barreled toward the barrier and us, his head down, going faster than such a large monster should have been able to move. Every thundering step reverberated in my bones. Closer. Closer. I could see his flaring nostrils, the hateful glint in his eyes. When he crashed into the barrier, he was going to send all the warders along its edge careening to the ground.

"First shot," Valens cried. He raised his stave in the air and slashed it in three quick movements, shorthand for an earth attack, quicksand. "Begin in twenty paces."

We counted down the monster's strides as he prepared to bulldoze us. On Valens's signal, we all struck our staves to the earth as one. I watched in the water glass as the ground opened beneath Callax, dissolving from stone to sand in one instant. He sank to his waist, clawing at the ground so as not to be sucked away.

Perhaps we could simply harden the sand and trap him there. But with a great, savage cry, he pulled himself out of the pit too quickly for us to stop him.

Valens, undeterred, signaled to the sky above. The purpling clouds swelled and twisted as we turned our staves upward, making five short, sharp movements that rather resembled a lopsided star. Lightning speared from the sky, striking the monster. Callax retreated a few steps, snorting and slamming his giant fists again in rapid succession, *boom boom boom.*

As we prepared for another maneuver, the Child Eater sprang forward and slammed into the barrier. His hand reached over the top and was repelled by one of the warders. But he banged again and again into the thorny wall, and it began to weaken and shred. Leaves, thorns, and flowers littered the ground. One of the warders plummeted with a scream.

R'hlem was testing it, as Blackwood had said. He was proving how weak it—and we—were.

The four of us knew what to do without having to be told. The boys grouped around me, and together we watched as the wall before us trembled with Callax's pummeling. Dee placed his hand on my arm. Magnus gripped Dee's shoulder. Blackwood's hand found mine for one brief instant. We were all beyond words now. Well, not all of us.

"If I should die today," Magnus said solemnly, "I only hope that Blackwood goes first."

Together, as a unit, we summoned wind and flew over the barrier, over the heads of the shocked warders, to stand on the other side.

Landing less than ten feet from the monster, I had an idea of how one felt entering a lion's den. Callax ceased striking at the great wall of thorns, his upturned nostrils quivering as he caught our scent. A thick gray tongue licked his lips in anticipation.

I threw balls of flame at him to draw his attention further. Callax bellowed as my fire scorched his legs, but he recovered quickly. I saw what Mickelmas had meant about a thick hide. I sheathed my dagger and unhooked the whip from my belt.

"Come fight, you great ugly pudding!" I shouted.

"Don't insult the monsters," Magnus said. "They take it personally."

Callax stomped his foot and charged. He was a wall of muscle and cold fury.

If this didn't work . . . It had to.

Dee ripped the flute out of its muting sheath and played, just as Mickelmas had instructed. I heard nothing, but this time the effect was instantaneous. Callax wailed and shook his head like a dog ridding itself of water. Shoving fingers in his pointed ears, he roared in pain.

Blackwood and Magnus dashed forward and, twisting their swords, dug into Callax. Blackwood caught the giant's left leg directly at the knee. Magnus dared higher, leaping into the wind and delivering an upward twisting blow into Callax's side.

They were good, but not good enough; the weapons hadn't broken skin. Dee's fingers slipped on the flute, and for a split second the instrument screamed once more. We all cried out, but Callax was glad for the respite and lifted his fist to mash Magnus into the ground.

Dee took up the tune again, giving Magnus just enough time to roll away, and Blackwood ducked as well.

So far, this was going according to the rough plan we'd mapped out. Dee was to incapacitate the monster while Blackwood and Magnus and I got in shots whenever we could. It wasn't much of a plan, I admitted, but it was better than nothing. At the very least, it would slow Callax until the others flooded over the barrier to help.

Where were the others?

I flew toward Callax. Swinging the whip over my head, I

struck the Child Eater's face. He bellowed as a gash appeared on his forehead and blood poured from the wound. I'd got him, even a little. Magnus attacked again but still couldn't break the beast's skin. I tried the whip once more but missed, my wrist twisting at the wrong angle. Falling to the earth, I cursed as I struggled to catch breath.

We hadn't been in the fight that long, and already I could feel myself growing sluggish. Dee had stopped playing, and my vision was dangerously close to tilting. *No. We can't be ill. We're not finished yet.*

"Dee, give me the flute!" I cried. He began to hand it over, but we were too slow and dropped it. When it struck the ground, it emitted another ear-rattling shriek. The bright bubbles of the ward vanished as the warders dropped their defenses, shocked by the noise. Callax snarled. With him this close to the barrier, there wouldn't be enough time to get the shields back up.

I pulled the whistle out of my collar, not sure what the hell I expected, and blew. Again, no noise.

But Callax halted. His broad, terrible arms fell limp at his sides. His expression slackened, his pupils dilated. His face was blank with astonishment.

What the devil? I tried to "play" a tune, touching the holes along the instrument. Callax winced at some of my playing, then grew calm again at other notes. He took one step, then another toward me.

The beast was following me like a pet.

Magnus took the opportunity and stabbed his sword into

the monster. This time Callax bled, droplets running down the creature's side and raining onto the ground. Callax howled in pain but didn't try to fight back. He watched me, still captivated by the bone whistle's music.

"Keep playing!" Blackwood raced forward with one of the daggers in his hand, and with a cry, stabbed upward into Callax's hide. The beast fell to his knees, bellowing in pain.

If he hadn't been responsible for so many deaths, I would have felt sorry for the creature.

Sorcerers began to arrive at our side, leaping over the barrier and forming a colossal tunnel of wind. My skirts whipped about, and my hair was ripped from its chignon. Callax flattened himself further as Magnus and Blackwood took turns sticking him, blood staining their sleeves up to the elbow.

It didn't seem right, somehow.

Blackwood moved faster than the others. He was absorbed in the task, his expression mixing rage and delight. Droplets of blood spattered his face and ran down his chin. Still blowing on the whistle with my right hand, I approached the monster as well, a ball of fire held aloft in my left hand.

Callax looked up at me. His huge eyes were filled with pain, and he whimpered like an animal brought low in a snare.

Horrified, I stopped blowing the whistle.

"What are you doing?" Blackwood shouted. "Keep playing!"

But I'd already given Callax the time he needed, and the Ancient rose to his feet, black blood gushing in rivulets down his body. He stared down at the sorcerers as they attacked. Nets of fire sizzled his wounded flesh. Shards of ice sliced him. Wild bursts of wind and rain battered him. Keening, Callax lurched forward and ran.

He fled from *us*.

We chased him until he picked up speed and moved beyond our range. Two squadrons pursued, though I doubted they'd bring him down today. If only I'd hung on longer with my whistle, we could have finished another Ancient. I'd been foolish to show mercy, especially as he'd have shown me none.

Still, Strangewayes's weapons had shortened the fight. They had—no, *we* had kept it from being a massacre. We'd kept R'hlem from a great victory indeed.

Blackwood picked up a stone and threw it after the giant's retreating form, such a boyish gesture, and so unusual for him. He came to me, wild with delight. "Did you see it? I wounded a bloody, blasted Ancient!" He held out his hands, stained with the giant's blood.

Magnus and Dee whooped, shoving each other in the particular way of men who've done a good job. And Blackwood rushed to join in, crashing into the others. For the first time since I'd known him, he'd shoved the invisible cloak of responsibility off his shoulders. The boys welcomed him, pounding him on the shoulder as he yelled in triumph. Rain began to rinse the blood from his skin.

He looked young and happy.

Even if we ended up in the Tower, it was a sight worth witnessing.

19

WHITECHURCH RESTED HIS LONG, BLUE-VEINED hands on the alabaster handle of his cane, twirling it steadily. He was seated in a chair by the fireplace. I stood before him, in the center of the rug.

"You disobeyed a direct order." Whitechurch had come to Blackwood's house to have this talk with me, and he'd banished Blackwood from the parlor. I'd scrubbed my face and changed into a rose-colored gown with lace at the sleeves— Lilly had been helpful in choosing it.

"The more ladylike you look, the harder it'll be for the Imperator to punish you," she'd said sagely. Still, I wished I'd kept the dirt and the blood. Perhaps it would have made my case more compelling.

"I didn't think it made sense to forget the weapons before they could be proven in a fight." Hopefully, that sounded respectful as well as bold. "Sir," I added.

The corners of the Imperator's mouth tightened, though whether he was suppressing a smile I couldn't say. "How did you come to make them work?"

"We practiced with Strangewayes's book whenever we'd a

spare moment." I didn't lie. I simply left out Mickelmas's help. But I could swear that Whitechurch glimpsed the truth.

"When you were an Incumbent, your lessons improved miraculously overnight." Slowly, Whitechurch stood. "You had help in that." I stayed still beneath his scrutinizing gaze. "But Dee and Magnus and Blackwood have all corroborated that you worked together. Alone. Blackwood in particular was adamant about it," he said.

I nearly gasped. Of all the boys, he valued the Imperator the most.

"If you did not have their support, I would suspect you of being in league with the magicians." Whitechurch's tone made me wonder if he had entirely got over that suspicion. "But the Child Eater ran today. Korozoth was destroyed in a single night. In nearly twelve years of war, we could not do what you have managed in recent months."

He sounded . . . pleased.

"Then may we continue using the weapons?" I asked.

"I would be the greatest fool alive to forbid it." The footman opened the door, and we passed into the hall. "But you must pay for your disobedience to your commanding officer. I'm removing you from Valens's squadron. For the next month, you are relegated to dawn patrol."

I'd be out of bed at four in the morning every single day. I wanted to groan just thinking of it, but I'd do it. And if Whitechurch thought that not being under Valens's thumb any longer was a punishment, I'd gladly take a second round.

"Thank you, sir," I said, curtsying to him at the door. Whitechurch paused, his sharp black eyes considering.

"Cornelius would be proud of you," he said, and walked to his carriage.

A lump formed in my throat, as it always did at the mention of Agrippa. Before the door closed, Magnus came barreling up the walk. He'd on a sky-blue coat, looking nothing so much like a drop of pure color on the gray London streets. He bowed quickly to the Imperator. Behind him, Dee and Wolff were carrying bottles of what appeared to be champagne—where the devil had they got it?

Magnus burst through the doorway, snatching me by the waist and whirling me around. "Music!" he cried, before setting me down and rushing along Blackwood's cavernous halls.

Bottles clinking, Dee and Wolff grinned as they ducked inside. Wolff's coat collar was upturned, the tips of his ears bright red from the cold. Dee knocked beads of rain from his hat, clumsy as he juggled the champagne.

"Should we leave?" Dee asked me, almost dropping one of the bottles. I caught it just in time.

"Absolutely not," I said, laughing.

Blackwood appeared at the top of the stairs. "Has the Imperator gone?" He paused, looking baffled by the company. "What are you all doing?"

"Celebrations!" Wolff popped a cork and raised a foaming bottle in a toast. Dee went up the steps and dragged Blackwood down by the arm, and we all followed Magnus. We ended up in the music room, with an elegant, polished pianoforte. Normally, rows of chairs would be set up so that visitors could enjoy private concerts. But most of the furniture had been removed for Eliza's debut ball, which was now only a few days away. The buffed parquet floor was simply begging to be used.

"Who here plays? Howel?" Magnus called as we entered. I went and plinked two notes. The instrument was very fine, but I'd always been a lackluster player at best. "No, we need an accomplished musician. Dee? You're good with flutes," Magnus said.

"Never played this before," Dee admitted. Magnus shrugged, slapped Dee on the shoulder, and embraced Wolff. If only Lambe could have been here. If only he weren't still up north, shut away in the Dombrey Priory. There were footsteps in the hall, and a breathless Maria ran into the room.

"You beat him?" she gasped.

Magnus gestured to the instrument. "You don't know how to play, do you?"

Maria grinned. "No, but if anyone loves to dance . . ."

While Magnus tried picking out a simple song—not doing a very good job of it—I got some glasses from one of the servants. Dee and Wolff poured champagne, and we all toasted. Wolff even took swigs from the bottle, spluttering as it fizzed down the front of his shirt. Blackwood, meanwhile, looked as if he'd no idea how he'd got here.

Eliza rushed into the room. There was high color in her cheeks, her shoulders were back, and her eyes were bright and blazing. From the look of her, I expected a fight to break out, but she stopped short as she took in the laughing, shouting group. "George." She stared at her brother. "*You're* giving a party?"

"It just happened," he said, as if he'd been accused of trying to murder someone.

"Play!" Magnus kissed Eliza's hand. "We all know what a genius you are, my lady."

Whatever anger I thought I'd glimpsed evaporated on the instant, and she blushed prettily.

"Well, if everyone would like."

Magnus led her over to the pianoforte, where Eliza struck up a jaunty tune. Maria grabbed Dee and started dancing with him, hitching up her skirts rather daringly as she twirled about. His eyes bulged just watching her, while Wolff clapped in time to the music. Magnus and Blackwood stood against the wall and made room for me to slip in between them. It was so unusual to see them not at each other's throats; this really had been a day of miracles. Together, we watched the dancing.

"Feels like old times," I said.

At Agrippa's, Dee had taught me to dance. Magnus would make fun of us from the side of the room, and Blackwood, seated nearby and studying some document, would shake his head and tell us how incorrigible we all were.

I didn't let the memory drag me down. This was supposed to be a celebration.

"Agrippa would be happy to see us like this," Magnus said

quietly. He raised his glass in a toast to our absent Master and took a sip. "Eliza plays beautifully."

"She does." Blackwood looked proud as he watched his sister. Then, "She probably requires help turning the pages."

"Indeed. Quite rude of me." Magnus drained the last of his glass and went to the instrument. Eliza beamed up at him as he shuffled the music, and Blackwood and I were quiet together for a moment. I studied him from the corner of my eye. He really did have a striking look: his firm jawline and full mouth made him at once harsh and beautiful. That was him all over, a massive contradiction.

"This is the perfect night for dancing. Wouldn't you agree?" he asked.

"Perhaps." I tilted my head. "Are you asking me?"

"That's an idea." He held out his hand, a challenge in his eyes. "Do you accept?"

I put my hand in his.

"Lead on," I said, bemused.

Maria and Dee had stopped dancing, so the floor was entirely ours. Blackwood escorted me to the center.

"How about a waltz? I need the practice." He nodded to his sister, who selected a piece with Magnus's help.

Eliza's fingers glided over the keys. The music was lilting and graceful, the melody wrapping around me like an airy caress. I leaned my head to the side, feeling the waltz's movement. Eliza had an artist's gift, truly. Blackwood slipped his hand to my waist, and I touched his shoulder delicately. We moved as one, back and forth, around and about.

"Thank you for lying to Whitechurch," I whispered. We were close enough that no one could hear. "I'm afraid I'm always getting you into trouble."

"You don't need to thank me for anything, especially not now." He squeezed my hand. "Before tonight, I'd never truly known *triumph*." He made the word sound delicious, although maybe that was the champagne talking. He picked up speed, and I grinned as I managed to keep up. Gently, he pressed me closer against him. We'd never danced like this before, and I felt the surprising strength and grace of his body. We spun and whirled—one, two, three. One, two, three. Faces blurred around us.

"You're not a bad waltzer at all." I laughed. "You don't need practice."

"No." He looked into my eyes. "I don't."

My next words faded. Blackwood wedded his gaze with mine. I had seen such intensity in him before, but it had never been focused upon me. Not like this. I might have compared it to the sun applying all its power on one lone spot upon the earth below. It was overwhelming. Strangely exhilarating. A bit frightening. I could have looked to the side, broken our gaze, but I found it difficult to do so. I half imagined he could see into the hidden compartments of my soul. Something inside me stirred to think of it.

Fanciful talk, that. Clearly, I'd had too much to drink. I

imagined putting up a wall behind my eyes. And gradually, I felt him recede back into himself. The dance became just that, a dance.

Ridiculous to think it had ever been anything else. We came to rest as the music stopped, and Maria and the boys clapped enthusiastically, save Magnus. He watched us with a fixed expression.

I prepared to curtsy, but Blackwood didn't release me right away. His hand still rested on my back, the faintest pressure through the silk of my dress, and I still hadn't taken my hand from his shoulder. Finally, we stepped apart.

"Thank you," he murmured, and bowed.

The lid of the pianoforte slammed shut, startling the room. Eliza stormed away from the instrument. Her face was white with anger.

"I think I should go upstairs. There's a great deal of *freedom* down here," she said. None of us knew what to say.

"Eliza, may I speak with you in the study?" Blackwood said.

"Do as you please. You always do." Eliza rushed out of the room, her heeled shoes echoing sharply. Blackwood followed while the rest of us milled about in silence.

I couldn't help myself—I went out after them. It's not that I wanted to poke my nose into the Blackwoods' anger, but I had an idea what this was about, and I wanted to support Eliza. Blackwood's study was on the second floor, the door half-hidden behind a green silk tapestry. It had been his father's, and he'd told me that he didn't like going in there.

Odd that he should all of a sudden be using it. But it was private, and from the sound of Eliza's voice behind the door, they were close to shouting; I had never heard anything like this from either of them before.

"You had no right to send a letter to Foxglove!" That was Eliza. So I'd been right. "I told you I don't want anything to do with that wretched old man!"

"You are a Blackwood." His voice was calmer than hers, which made it all the more terrifying. "You must marry whom I choose, and bear sorcerer children. That is your function, Eliza."

Her *function* was to be a brood mare for any man with the right pedigree? I had to control myself from walking in there and smacking him myself.

"You said I had a choice!"

"I do not have to explain my decisions to you!" Blackwood shouted, and I flinched. "Foxglove can provide you with safety even Sorrow-Fell cannot match. I know you're still too young to see the good of this decision."

Too *young*? Eliza was only a year younger than he.

"Try to understand. You are all that I care about," he said, his voice gentling.

"You don't want me to be happy because *you* can't be," Eliza sneered. "Do you believe for a second Whitechurch would ever allow it?" Allow what? There was a moment of dead silence.

"You will do your duty." His voice was ice. "Or there'll be no more parties."

It sounded as though she was crying.

"You think I'm some stupid doll." She burst out of the room to find me there, obviously eavesdropping. Her face was blotchy, her eyes glistening.

I didn't know what to say.

"You talk to him," she sobbed.

I tried to comfort her, but she ran down the stairs in a flurry of skirts. Blackwood nodded for me to come in. When I entered, he closed the door and, turning, went behind his father's desk. Rather, *his* desk now.

Charles Blackwood had been a scholar, among other things. The bookcases along the walls strained with the weight of so many books. Yellowing maps papered the walls; a golden astrolabe sat inside a bell jar. Several thick books had been taken down and piled haphazardly on the table, a decanter of red wine placed beside them.

A pulsating glow drew my eye. Strangewayes's *optiaethis* had been placed alongside a volume of Newton. The sight of it chilled me. In truth, Blackwood's return to his father's old study was troubling in itself.

Now was not the time to ask questions, however. Blackwood poured a glass of the wine, drank deeply, then poured another glass. Eliza's words had shaken him, though he tried to hide it.

"No," he said, as if replying to someone. "I won't let this night be ruined." He poured another glass for himself and one for me, then slammed the decanter back down. "We need to celebrate properly." He handed me the wine, which I reluctantly took.

"There'll be other times to celebrate," I said. "We should talk about Eliza."

"Stop, Henrietta." I knew he was serious when he used my first name. "Not now."

My temper flared. "This won't be the only battle we'll ever win."

"This is our first victory with those weapons. Thanks to you." He clinked glasses with me. Leaning against the edge of the desk, he fixed his eyes on my face. "You disobeyed the Imperator and found Strangewayes's house, all against my wishes. You sought out Mickelmas, and now look at us." His lips were red from the wine; his smile looked bloody. "Do you have any idea what you've given me?"

The way he said it sounded . . . odd.

"Today I cut the monster and watched him bleed. *You* gave me that." There were a million unspoken words in his eyes. Carefully, he said, "My father was the Blackwood who nearly destroyed this country. Thanks to you, I'm going to be the Blackwood who *saved* it."

"Thanks to all of us," I said. His focus frightened me again.

There was something about that answer he didn't appear to like. He put his glass down and swept out the door without another word. The Blackwoods were the most dramatic people I'd ever known, and I'd known *many*.

I returned downstairs, hoping to find him, but Blackwood

had vanished. Dee, Maria, and Wolff were gathered around the pianoforte, playing jokey tunes. Eliza huddled by the window with Magnus, talking in low voices. He was nodding emphatically, his brow furrowed in thought. Eliza dabbed at her eyes with her handkerchief.

"Eliza, are you all right?" I asked as I came up to them. Magnus said nothing, but Eliza nodded.

"I will be," she said.

LATER THAT NIGHT, AFTER I'D GOT ready for bed, there was a tap on my window. Mickelmas waved cheerily at me from the ledge, his coat blowing in the wind. I let him inside.

"I take it the day went well." He kept his voice down, since servants might still be in the hall at this hour. Something sloshed in his hand.

"Not more gin." I made a pained face.

"Don't you want hair on your chest?" He held it up to the light, where it glinted red. "A very fine Bordeaux. Come. Celebrations are in order."

Good lord, how much drinking could I do in a day?

He flung his coat around me, and a whirling instant later we stood on the roof, staring down at the street below. I pulled my wrap tighter about my body, shivering in the near-autumn air.

"Here, this'll warm you." Mickelmas thrust the bottle into my hand. Oh, what the hell. I took a swig, wincing. "Here we are, drinking responsibly on a rooftop after a hard day of fighting monsters. It feels like old times," he said.

"Funny. I said something similar earlier." I smiled as Mick-elmas looked out over the city. "Blackwood thanked me, but really our victory's due to you."

"One day, the Imperator will agree." He stroked at his beard. "He'll welcome your army with gratitude."

My army. Heavens. The wine lit a fire in my stomach, making me bold enough to ask a question. "Do you think my father would be proud of me?" It was idiotic, really, to crave the approval of a man who'd never wanted to meet me. I frowned at my feet, which were already turning blue. "Did—did he know about me?"

"He did," Mickelmas said. He paused, then said, "He wanted to be a father."

That made it worse somehow. "Why did he leave?"

"Hard to say. Don't hog the bottle." He snatched the wine back. "I don't know what your father would think of what you've become, but he'd be proud of the person you are," Mick-elmas said. Odd distinction.

"Thank you for being an excellent replacement," I said softly.

He shook his head. "I'm not much of a father figure. But you're a fine apprentice," he murmured. And then he drank.

MY HEAD WAS SPINNING WHEN I got into bed and blew out my candle. The air about me felt chilled as I bundled under the blankets. When I closed my eyes, the darkness sloshed about. Perhaps I'd had too much to drink today.

Mouth fuzzy, I struggled to wake one last time—I felt I'd forgot something—and then slipped into sleep.

Dense gray fog swirled about my ankles, but I didn't feel the chill of it. I tried to get my bearings. Where in God's name was I? The astral plane? But how—

Fenswick's sachet of herbs. I was supposed to put it under my pillow, to keep from coming here. Cursing my stupidity, I tried to force myself awake by pinching my cheeks. Panic thundered through my veins. I had to wake up. I had to, because if I didn't, he could find me.

And then, by my ear, I heard a voice whisper, "Miss Howel. What an unexpected delight."

R'hlem gazed down at me.

20

WAKE UP. WAKE UP. *I STUMBLED AWAY FROM HIM, MY vision lopsided. How had I been this stupid?*

But R'hlem did not attack. In fact, there was astonishment written upon his skinned face. Evidently, he could hardly believe my stupidity any more than I could. He was dressed in a well-tailored dark blue suit and white linen shirt. At least, the shirt would have been white if it weren't soaked in gore. He wrung out his bloody sleeves, a casual gesture.

R'hlem bowed low, bending deeply at the waist. Under any other circumstance, he might have resembled a gentleman asking me to dance.

"I'm surprised you'd return, after all these months of shielding yourself." There was interest in his gaze. He thought I'd done this deliberately. Telling him I'd got drunk and fallen asleep would make me sound even more pathetic than I already was, so I kept silent. As he advanced, I lit myself on fire in warning. "Ah. Yes, your power."

He smiled wider than before.

Make him think you planned this. Act. Now.

"I thought we might talk. After all, you did ask for me by name," I said, doing my best to sound casual and fearless. *"I couldn't help but wonder why."*

"I'd like to hear your own theories on the subject."

I shrugged. "Mine are bound to be incorrect."

"Very likely." He walked about me in a circle, and I always made sure to face him. Church bells rang out through the mist, a bit muted but still distinct.

I prayed that the bells would wake me, but there was no such luck. R'hlem stopped to wring out his sleeves once more. Dark droplets of blood disappeared into the undulating mist.

"What I told you the night you destroyed my beautiful Korozoth remains true. You interest me greatly." His gaze was intense, mercilessly scrutinizing.

"My talent with fire, you mean."

R'hlem laughed. "Yes, quite a peculiar ability. But the fire isn't all that fascinates me. You're surprisingly resourceful, my dear. Those new weapons of yours are most original. I feel ashamed to have overlooked them."

I wondered how he knew about the weapons. Was it seeing Callax's wounds, or had the Familiars reported back to him? And if so, how on earth did they go about it?

"You're picking apart everything I say. Tell me, was our meeting tonight your idea or were you sent by Horace Whitechurch?" He sniffed, which, considering he had no nose, was an unpleasant sight. "I imagine it was your own. The Order would never allow a common magician's brat to use her powers in such an overt way." He tsked.

How? How in bloody hell had he known I was part magician?

He stroked his raw chin with his fingers. "Are you curious how I winkled out your little secret?"

Had someone betrayed us? R'hlem held up a hand; he seemed to guess my thoughts.

"You are acquainted with Howard Mickelmas, are you not?"

"I don't want to hear your lies," I said.

"Then hear the truth from his lips." R'hlem's one yellow eye narrowed. "Ask him what happened on Midsummer's Day in 1822. Ask Mickelmas what he did to me."

And with that, R'hlem extended his arms and ignited in blue flame.

I TUMBLED OUT OF BED, THE blankets tangled around me, and lay on the floor with my head throbbing. Breathing deeply, I waited for the pounding in my temples to stop. My head was still wretched from the wine.

But not wretched enough to ignore what I had seen.

Finally on my feet, I lit a candle, sat at my desk, and wrote: *How can R'hlem set himself on fire? What happened on Midsummer's Day in 1822?*

I slammed the note into Mickelmas's trunk and waited. A moment later, I opened the lid, and the note was gone.

But Mickelmas had never responded to my letters before. Suppose this didn't work? Suppose the notes never went to him? But how on earth could I wait for daylight? I paced to the window and back. Somewhere inside, a voice was crying out, getting louder and louder, and I didn't want to listen.

Damn him to hell, where *was* he?

I turned and bashed right into Mickelmas.

"What have you done?" He'd dressed in a silk gown dripping with golden tassels, and crushed velvet slippers on his feet. His hair, normally tied back, was a massive cloud of gray and white.

"What have *you* done?" I hissed.

Mickelmas winced and rubbed his eyes. He had to clutch the bedpost to keep himself upright; apparently he was feeling as sick as I.

"Come on, then," he whispered, throwing his coat around me. Wind rushed by us, and when he let go, I found myself standing in Agrippa's study. The familiar busts of Chaucer and Homer looked down on me from the bookcase. There was a fire in the hearth, and a cup of half-finished tea sat on the table beside the armchair. Agrippa might have walked in at any moment and taken his customary seat. Somehow, being back in these soothing surroundings made everything that much worse.

"What happened?" Mickelmas fell into the chair.

"I went onto the astral plane by accident," I said, my voice cracking. "R'hlem told me you did something to him on Midsummer's Day, and then he burst into flame. Exactly like me." My voice died on the word *me*.

Mickelmas leaned forward with his elbows on his knees, and for a while he did not speak.

"What do you think that meant?" he asked.

"I don't know."

"That's a lie, or you wouldn't have written to me at three in the morning." He got up and went to a mirror hanging on the wall. Placing a hand upon the glass, he whispered words that I could not make out, wincing in pain as he spoke. The mirror glowed briefly, and there was an odd sucking sound. Finished, he pulled his hand away to reveal a stark white handprint, as if someone had etched it in ice.

I recalled the little hand mirror I'd found in his trunk, the one with the thumbprint. This looked a great deal like that.

I instinctively feared the thing.

"Touch your hand to the surface, and don't take it away," Mickelmas said, reseating himself. "What I want to say . . . is too difficult for words." His voice shook, though whether from the strain of his magic or something else, I did not know. "But you may not like what you find."

I stepped up to the mirror, my pulse pounding, and slowly pressed my palm to the glass.

WILLIAM'S GOING UP THE RIGGING FOR *no damned reason. I swear, he's like one of those blasted tree-climbing monkeys, if the monkey also worked as a solicitor. I toddle across the deck of the ship as a wave swells below us. Whoever enjoys pleasant Sunday cruises ought to be put in an asylum and studied.*

"Howard, isn't it wonderful?" William beams down at me. Foolish boy. He thinks what we're about to do is fun, instead of blisteringly

dangerous. But for some unknown reason, his good spirits lift mine. He's always had that effect.

"Remind me again why we couldn't try this on land?" I call up to him.

"Here, there's privacy." Ah, His Lordship graces us with his presence once more. Charles comes up from belowdecks, an ax in one soft, manicured hand and a rope coiled around his perfumed shoulder. Being the Earl of bloody Sorrow-Fell, you'd think he wouldn't want to take on any of the physical labor. Surely, he'd prefer that a servant set up his feats of magical abomination. But I must confess, he's done his share of the work without complaint. It's true that Lord Blackwood's Sunday activities would normally involve many voluptuous, scantily clad women—I feel rather sorry for his wife—but he's as excited by our endeavor as William is.

Nonetheless, he can be a smug bastard. If he doesn't watch it, he'll get my foot right up his esteemed arse.

William leaps onto the deck with enthusiasm befitting a boy of twelve, not a grown man. When Helena told him a little Howel was on its way, I was certain he'd stop all this nonsense. But impending fatherhood affects all men differently, and for William it increased his desire to accomplish this bloody task.

I wish he'd taken up carpentry instead. I could have at least got a nice bird feeder out of that.

"Youth is wasted on people who annoy me," I grumble as we finally get down to the matter at hand. I pull out the rune chart William nicked from that fellow in Whitechapel, a rough deal made in

a rougher place. William even got stabbed in the arm for his trouble, and who had to patch him up so Helena never found out? I'm entirely too good a friend.

Still, we should remember why the man who sold it to us panicked, why he went for the knife. He thought we'd use the runes. Terrified, he wanted the chart back. When William didn't oblige, the man grew stabby. Kept shouting "Witness the smile" over and over again. Quite troubling, really.

The runes look like a bunch of rude squiggles. "You're sure this is correct, Will?"

"You can trust it, Howard. I got it from a book, after all." Ah yes, William does love his books. Most of the world's agony comes from what people misinterpret in books, the rest from pampered house cats.

The three of us paint the runes onto the surface of the deck in black ink. The basic design is a circle, then undulating lines of runes emanate outward, so it looks like a crude sun. Charles groans to see his pristine ship marked with heretical images. That's why we didn't carve them; he wants to varnish over it when we're done.

Charles's involvement makes me rather uneasy, if I'm honest. What does one of the Order's most esteemed sorcerers hope to gain by trespassing on the wildest frontiers of magician practice? I know what William wants—proof of our power's origin, and justice. Justice for poor Henry, his unfortunate brother. That all makes sense. But Charles? He admires our strange abilities. Rather, he envies them.

Perhaps he's looking for a way toward greater power. Why, not even Imperator Whitechurch could stand against him then.

I've got to stop thinking like this. It's ruining the mood.

Finally, our circle is complete, the paint gleaming wet beneath the sun.

Is it wrong to say that part of me is afraid?

It's almost midday, which means we're out of time. Charles sets the ax to his right and tosses a rope to each of us.

"We should anchor ourselves, on the off chance something happens." He ties his rope about his waist and fastens it to the side of the ship, yanking twice to make sure it's secure. I do as he suggests, and so does William. We're now a triangle of idiots tied to a boat.

William is directly across from me and looks up into the bright sun, squinting. "When the shadows disappear, my lord," he yells.

I know what this summoning means to him. Ralph Strangewayes had a pet named Azureus from some other world. We saw his picture, William and I, when we made our pilgrimage to Strangewayes's home. Well, what if Azureus can be our new pet? What if we can prop him up in a gilded cage before the king and prove, once and for all, that our power is not satanic in nature. Merely different.

It's the least we can do for Henry. Poor bugger.

The sun hits its zenith, and my neck is sweating.

Charles takes out his sorcerer stick-thingy and holds it up, a crease of concern on his face. He's no idea what to do. Neither do I, for that matter.

"Azureus," William says, cutting his hand and bleeding onto the edges of the circle. "We summon thee. Traffick with us now."

When his blood touches them, the runes . . . hiss.

No, that's not it. They hum with energy while the newly dried paint bubbles before us as if boiling.

I feel magic thrumming in my bones, down into my liver and spleen. The circle is waking up, for lack of a better word. A thrill electrifies my blood. I say I'm here to support William, but I can't help my desire to know, to see where our magic comes from.

In the air above the circle, a cloud begins to form, a spot of violent weather in an otherwise pristine day. The cloud purples and churns, and then it . . .

Cracks. The air above the circle cracks as though it's a mirror.

"Is this supposed to happen?" Charles calls, keeping his stave up.

William shakes his head slowly.

"I don't think so," I add, clutching the railing behind me so hard it might break off in my hand.

The cracks grow, forming fissures. Something is wrong, horribly wrong.

"We have to stop," I shout to William, but he doesn't hear me, or he won't listen. He steps forward, entranced by what he sees. Damned fool. He looks so young when he's mystified, like the boy he was when I first knew him. He trails his fingers through the tendrils of vapor leaking from the other side.

"I can feel it," he calls, ecstasy lacing his voice.

The air ruptures, and a gaping vortex of midnight opens in the bright blue summer sky. Screaming voices, banshee wails, insane gibberish come pouring out into our world. Charles screams. I scream.

"Run!" I shout. William takes two steps back to the safety of his post, but it's too late. His feet lift off the deck, and he hangs suspended in the air, tethered only by his rope. He shrieks, legs flailing behind him like a doll's.

The vortex has reached the limit of the runes. Fissures are appearing in the air outside the circle. This other world, this monstrous dimension, is opening into ours.

No. It's going to swallow ours.

The maw is open, hungry. It wants a sacrifice. It wants flesh.

William hangs there.

No. Never.

"Close it!" I shout.

Charles takes the blade on his stave and cuts his hand, flinging blood onto the runes. Blood oils the hinge of reality. The tunnel above us retreats a little . . . then continues ripping apart the sky like a sheet of fabric.

"It's too big!" Charles bellows, the veins of his neck popping.

I keep a tight grip on my rope, and even then my feet start lifting off the ground. Muttering a few spells to weigh down the soles of my shoes, I inch my way to my friend. His hand slips from mine once, twice, and I've almost got him. . . .

Charles lunges forward, slashing with his stave. He's too far away. He's . . . he's trying to cut William's rope.

"We can't!" I scream.

Charles ignores me and grabs the ax next to him.

William sees what this is. He pulls desperately, yanking himself down the rope. I can't. This is impossible. My head is exploding with pain. Grunting, Charles lifts the ax with both hands.

"Help me!" William cries, whipping and battering about in the wind like a child's kite. The thought occurs to me to kill him, to put a blade into his heart before . . .

I can't. He looks into my eyes, and his face blurs because I can't help crying anymore, and I tell him that I'm sorry, I couldn't do it, I can't do anything.

"Howard!" William wails, a sound of pure suffering. "Please!"

Charles throws the ax with deadly precision and slices the rope. For a brief moment, William is suspended in the air, a perfect illustration of shock. Then he is sucked up into the vortex. His hand reaching for me is the last I see of him before the void swallows him whole with an obscene sucking sound.

The fissures retreat back into the circle's frame. The vortex, satisfied with its morsel, withdraws enough for Charles to spatter his blood over the runes. He yells for it to close, and in a flash the cloud disappears.

The sky is bright and blue, and William is gone.

No. I crawl to the bloody runes. The gateway has vanished.

"Call it back!" I touch the wet deck.

"It won't work," Charles says. He appraises the empty sky. "It was the wrong summoning spell."

"No." I reach for the ax to cut my hand, but Charles tackles me.

"Control yourself, man," Charles says as he grabs his stave.

Warding that yellow blade of his, he slashes at the runes, making them unusable. Snatching the rune sheet, he tears it apart and flings the pieces into the water. Even if we wanted to open that gate again, we can't. I didn't memorize the runes needed for the circle, and now they're lost forever.

"What's done is done." He stretches his arms over his head, as if he'd had a strenuous workout. "Interesting, isn't it? Such a shame, the world of Ralph Strangewayes some barren hellscape." He sighs. "Perhaps there are other circles to try. If one fails, another—"

I can't listen to his hateful, hideous voice. I run at him, blinded by my tears—I'm going to rip him apart where he stands. He sent William into that darkness. Charles draws up his ward about himself with ease, and I smash into it, biting my lip and tasting warm blood. Charles then takes me by my cravat. The easy expression on his face has vanished. His nostrils flare.

"Now we're off to the widow." Charles's voice is deadly. "You'll follow what I do and say. If not, magician, you don't even want to know what I'll do."

"I don't care what happens to me," I spit. "Just so long as every-one knows the truth."

"Do you think anyone would believe a magician over me?" He lets me go roughly. "Do you want to spend the rest of your life in Lockskill Castle, your hands chopped from your wrists? No? Best to speak when I tell you, then, like a good fellow."

He says it as if I were a dog. He walks away and leaves me crying for William as the afternoon sun moves farther into the sky.

MY HAND DROPPED AWAY FROM THE mirror. I didn't realize I was falling until Mickelmas caught me about the waist and helped me into a chair. He pressed a cup of water into my hand and helped me drink.

I'd been inside Mickelmas's head. I'd seen the world through his eyes, heard his thoughts as if they were my own. And I'd seen my *father*. Not his painting; not some wistful dream. I'd heard his voice, seen his face as he smiled and laughed. As he screamed. I'd watched through Mickelmas's eyes as the rope had been cut, as my father had been swallowed into that churning . . . I couldn't. I couldn't breathe.

I shoved the water away, spilling it onto the rug, and slid to my knees. I heaved several times, though nothing came up. My throat was raw. Once I could speak, I said, "You let him die."

"For six years, I spent all my money." Mickelmas sounded deflated and, somehow, horribly relieved. "I traveled the bloody world in search of the correct summoning runes." He pulled me up by my shoulders, his gaze locking with mine.

"And I found them, the ones that would allow me to call for a specific person or creature. There was something wrong with our original trio: me, William, Blackwood. We should have had a witch. Such a spell requires all three magical races."

"So you got Mary Willoughby." My voice was weak and flat.

"Yes. We carved the new circle on Midsummer's Day—certain rituals work best at certain times of the year. We summoned William. R'hlem answered. He brought his beasts with him, and the sky turned black." He released me.

I swallowed; my throat felt like sandpaper. "You didn't find him," I murmured.

Mickelmas stood. "I thought long and hard. And then I realized." He walked to the hearth and waved his hand over the fire. Embers lifted into the air. He began to weave words out of smoke.

"William came from a town in Wales called Rhyl," he said.
He wrote,

WILLIAM HOWEL OF RHYL

The words hung in the air. He waved his hand again and
the words changed, the letters shifted, before gradually forming a new word.

RHYL WILLIAM HOWEL
RH'WILLIAM WEL
RH'LLIAM E
RH'LEM
R'HLEM

21

I WAS STANDING, THOUGH I DIDN'T RECALL GETTING to my feet. I stared at Mickelmas's ashen words until they dissipated into nothing and left the scent of smoke lingering in the air.

"You told me he left and never came home." My tongue felt leaden in my mouth. This couldn't be real.

"William left us that day, and the man as I knew him never returned. You interpreted it as you saw fit." Mickelmas lifted his head, as if daring me to challenge his logic.

I *interpreted* it? As though it was *my* fault for not being clever enough to see?

"Don't you *dare*," I growled. Feeling flooded back through my body. My head hurt, my eyes burned, and flame licked up my spine—Mickelmas stilled when he saw what was coming. I walked toward him, sparks raining onto the carpet. "You were going to tell me the truth the night that Korozoth attacked. Why did you hide it?"

"I thought I'd never see you again," he said simply. "When I realized how much better it would be with you on my side, I thought the whole truth would be inconvenient." He held a hand up, as if to appease me. "I'd have told you eventually."

"After I'd murdered my own . . . ?" The word *father* failed in my mouth. No, no, this couldn't be true. Mickelmas was wrong. He'd been tricked all those years ago, when he opened the portal into the sky and R'hlem fell to the earth.

But on the astral plane, R'hlem had been covered in blue flame. . . .

"And now that you know, are you so much better off?" he muttered. With a sweep of his arm, he transported himself to the other side of the room, away from my fire. "This is bigger than any one of us. Magicians can take back this world. Forget this piddling war against the Ancients; we can end the war against *our* people! You'd throw all that away?"

I killed the fire. My skin was cold once more, slight curls of gray smoke rising from my fingertips. I stepped toward him and slapped him across the face. My handprint was emblazoned on his cheek.

He looked slack with surprise, then bared his teeth and stuck a finger in my face. "If you ever do that again, I'll turn you into a chair."

"Go ahead. I'm the last Howel for you to ruin." How had I ever trusted him?

"It's because of my warning that your aunt took you to Yorkshire in the first place." He thumped his chest. "You could show more gratitude."

Gratitude.

"My father's a monster because of you. My mother died of grief because of you. Because of *you*, England could fall!"

I screamed. "You've lied to me since the moment we met. I hate you!" I conjured those words from the darkest place in my soul, then threw out my hands and unleashed a stream of fire. Mickelmas vanished, and I scorched the wallpaper, the red silk curling into charred flakes. Shaking, I took the water on hand—the tea in Mickelmas's teapot—and doused the flames. I didn't want to burn down Agrippa's house. The wet, burnt odor lingered in the air.

Mickelmas reappeared. "Well, I'm the only one left for you to hate, my duck." He counted on his fingers. "R'hlem skinned Charles Blackwood alive; Mary Willoughby was burned at the stake; your aunt took off for God knows where after she dumped you at that school. If you want to blame someone, look at your own precious father. He put magicians ahead of your family." He smirked. "You don't even have his noble excuse. Tell me, will you go to the Order and tell your darling Imperator what I've revealed tonight?"

I hated him beyond anything else in the world. For being right.

"If I see you again, I will kill you," I spit.

"Then we will *not* meet again." There was no remorse in his voice. With a flip of his arm, he sheltered his cloak about me, and an instant later I found myself alone in my bedroom.

Cold. I was freezing cold. I tried to get my shaking under control. I sat on my bed, grabbed the sachet of herbs from my table, and crushed it in my grip, unleashing its bitter floral scent. Why had I gone to the astral plane? Why?

My father is R'hlem.

No, I couldn't even think those words. A sob escaped, and I bit down on my knuckle to keep silent.

I couldn't stay in this room; no, I needed something. Someone.

I needed Rook.

I ran out the door and down the hall, into the gentlemen's corridor. It was improper and impulsive to barge into his room in the middle of the night, but I needed him. I needed his arms around me, needed to listen to his heart beating. I needed to hear his voice telling me I was safe. Turning the doorknob as quietly as I could, I slipped inside his room.

"Rook?" I whispered. He was sprawled upon his bed, asleep. Moving into the room, I shut the door behind me and lit a candle. By the light, I could see that he'd not got out of his clothes yet. His coat was off, and his shirt half-unbuttoned down the front, exposing his chest and a few swollen scars. He lay on top of the covers and gave a soft moan as I drew closer. Sweat stood out on his brow, matting his hair. When I sat down beside him on the bed, I reached out and touched his face . . . and my hand came away slick with blood.

Blood was smeared along his cheek, coating his arms up to the elbow. He moaned again, his eyes fluttering open. He looked up at me, no pain in his expression. I pulled the blankets back and looked frantically over his body to find the source of the wound, only to find him unharmed.

God, the blood wasn't his.

"What happened?" I whispered, smoothing his damp brow. He was a banked coal beneath my hand.

"I'm so tired." His eyes closed again.

Lighting more candles, I poured some cold water into his washbasin and sat beside him again, wiping the blood off his face. Rook sat up, the glazed light of fever in his eyes.

"Henrietta." He kissed my neck. I froze as his lips brushed my skin. Rook was pulling me back to lie down with him. I didn't let myself go with him—God, there was the blood still to clean up, which made my skin crawl. And Maria said I had to keep him calm. And Rook . . . This wasn't like him. That night in the garden, he'd been so shy and gentle. Now he was more aggressive, his hands and lips greedily exploring my body.

"Wait," he said, stopping. "We're not married yet, are we?" He sounded disappointed. I placed my hand over his heart. The skin of his chest was smooth, but the scars throbbed with infection. My face flushed to think of his question. No, we weren't married.

"Not yet," I said. "You need to wake . . . and clean yourself. Something's . . . happened."

Now that he was more awake, Rook took over from me, washing his face, his neck, cleaning out the half-moons of dark blood trapped beneath his fingernails. He stripped out of his shirt. His body was lean and sculpted, even with the scars. I hastened to get him something clean to wear, nervously helping him slide into it. After a few minutes, his hair was damp, his face scrubbed, his shirt unsoiled. He looked all right, yes, but he radiated disease.

This couldn't be the night he turned. No. *No.*

"What's happening to me, Nettie?" The sincere confusion in his voice killed me. Biting my lip to hold in a sob, I rinsed a sliver of soap in the red-tinged water. So much blood, and none of it his. There wasn't a mark on him.

Rook, what have you been doing?

"You're having a terrible dream," I said.

His hands caught my waist and spun me around. Our lips met, the kiss deepening quickly. With a swift move, we were lying on the bed.

"It's become a good dream, then," he whispered in my ear.

My whole body seemed to vibrate as Rook gathered me to him. But it was all too fast. My mind screamed to stop even as I kissed him. Finally, I put my hands against his chest, holding him back. Slowly, very slowly, our breathing calmed, and I pulled away. I still had to learn the truth.

"What happened in the dream? Do you remember?" I asked carefully.

"A man was attacking people." Rook sounded distant, as if he were falling asleep once more. "He deserved what he got for attacking that woman."

He deserved what he got. I did not speak, only moved my head to his chest and listened as his breathing deepened, until finally he was truly asleep. I looked at his face in the candlelight. He looked peaceful now. No one would ever picture this normal, beautiful boy with someone else's blood all over his hands. That wasn't him. That was the *thing* inside him.

But he'd had someone else's blood all over his hands, and now he smiled in his sleep.

"Do you remember Christmas Eve when we were eight?" I whispered, lifting my head to see his face. His eyelids fluttered, but he didn't wake. "I still missed my aunt in those days. I was crying at bedtime, and one of the teachers smacked me and told me to be quiet. After everyone had fallen asleep, I snuck down to the kitchen. You used to sleep near the stove on winter nights, remember?" I traced a finger across his cheek. "You let me crawl into bed next to you. You didn't care that I was crying. You just put your arm around me and let me blubber on and on." Holding back a sob, I kissed his forehead. "I think that was when I knew I loved you."

I laid my head on the pillow beside Rook's, listened to his soft breathing, and tried to collect my thoughts.

R'hlem—I wasn't going to start calling him my father, not even in my head—was the true reason that Rook was transforming. If R'hlem hadn't come back from that alien world, if he hadn't brought the Ancients, if he hadn't brought Korozoth, if Korozoth hadn't marked Rook . . . On and on my thoughts spun in a painful whirl.

If I had to go to R'hlem to save Rook, I would. Finally, fitfully, I slept.

I woke a few hours later to find Maria standing over the bed, looking shocked.

22

"WHAT ARE YOU DOING HERE?" MARIA SAID, PUT-
ting down the cloth and medicine she'd been carrying as I hastened to sit upright. Rook shifted beside me, caught in the grip
of an actual bad dream. Maria's eyes flicked to him, her expression now inscrutable. Finding the two of us asleep with our
arms about each other was compromising beyond belief.

"It's not what it seems," I whispered, struggling to get out
of bed. My head still felt shrunken from the drink.

She didn't sound convinced. "Good thing I found you before anyone else did. It's time for his morning potion." She
uncorked a glass vial filled with that brackish liquid. Another
potion. Another bit of poison to kill the monster. When Maria
leaned over the bed to wake Rook, she gasped and dropped
the vial. The medicine started to spill out onto the sheets, and
I rescued it.

"What?" I asked, but then realized she'd noticed the bloody
cloths by the washbasin, and the water that had turned a cloudy
red. I was a blistering fool. Why hadn't I got rid of those last
night?

"Is he hurt?" She pulled the blankets aside and discovered

that Rook was not, in fact, wounded. Her eyes scanned me. "You're both of you fine." Her gaze darkened. "What in the Mother's name did he do?"

"What makes you think *he* did anything?" Now that I was fully awake, the horrors of last night returned in vivid color. Meeting R'hlem on the astral plane, Mickelmas's revelation, Rook's fever: how was any one person supposed to bear it all? My hands started sparking. "Why wouldn't you suspect *me*?"

"Don't be daft." Maria softened. "If he's too far gone—"

"If he is, who's to blame? You're the one who added poison to his treatments!" I hissed.

Maria's eyes flashed.

"I told you there'd be only so much my methods could do." She spoke in a harsh whisper, so as not to wake Rook.

I couldn't listen to this, so I grabbed the bloody cloths and washbasin. If he woke up and saw them, he'd ask questions. I ran, my feet freezing on the carpeted hall. The water sloshed as I hurried. Inside my room, I threw open the window and emptied the filth onto the garden below, then put the rags in the basin and set them on fire. Maria entered and closed the door behind her, nose wrinkling as I poured water on the now-ashed cloth. Gray smoke billowed upward.

"You can't hide what he's done." She sounded sympathetic, which was worse than anger.

"Leave me alone!" My skin tingled. I was dangerously close to going up in flames.

"Calm down." She didn't show any fear as my hands started

smoldering. Something about her pitying expression drove me over the edge. Without warning, my whole body ignited, and I stared at her from behind a curtain of flame.

Maria stepped forward and summoned my fire.

Blue flame swept into her palm in a ball, hovering just above her fingertips. Putting her hands on either side of her fire, she twisted and twirled it, whirling faster and faster until it spun before her face, a perfect sphere.

She was using elemental magic.

I stood there in shock as the flames died on my skin, only a few telltale embers remaining to sizzle on the cold floor. Maria changed the fireball's rotation, molding it until it grew smaller and smaller and, in a puff of smoke, disappeared entirely.

"If you want to have another tantrum, I'm a bit out of practice," she said, one eyebrow quirked in a challenge.

How?

She jerked her head toward the bench by my vanity. "May want to have a seat. You look a bit put out."

Slowly, I sat.

"Where did you learn that trick?" I whispered. Because it was a trick. It had to be.

In response, Maria merely picked up a vase of flowers from my bedside table and poured some of the water out onto the wooden floor. Waving her hands, she lifted the puddle into the air in a shimmering disc. Without a single word, she turned the water into a ball of ice. With swift, clean movements, she shaped the ice into several elegant images: a figure eight, a seven-pointed star, a perfect rectangle. With a flick of her wrist and a twitch of her fingers, the ice obeyed her most complicated desires. Finished, she melted it back to water and poured it into the vase. Her technique was perfect, beyond anything I'd seen any sorcerer accomplish. And all without a stave.

"I thought you were a witch."

"Mam was a witch." Maria settled the vase back on its table, primping the flowers. "But my father was a sorcerer."

Of course. There could be no other explanation.

"Do you know his name?"

"*You* know it well." Her small face became pinched with anger. "He was your own Master Agrippa."

Back at Agrippa's house, Maria had looked up at his portrait with that distant expression. Her eyes, such a warm brown, had been familiar to me for a reason: they were Agrippa's eyes. I was the stupidest person alive not to have seen it. My mouth fell open.

"He met my mother when he was touring Scotland on some business for the Order, researching the highland covens or the like. He left her flat without knowing she was with child. Not that he'd have married Mam, of course." She gave a sharp laugh. "Who'd want a witch as a wife?"

"He'd have wanted to know about you." My first instinct was to defend Agrippa, even now.

Maria snorted. "Aye. Likely he'd have ordered me burned at the stake with my mother." I froze utterly. "Surely you knew he was the one signed the burnings into law."

Words of defense or explanation evaporated. There was no excusing *that*. Maria continued, "I only know it because I saw his name on the order. The executioners showed it when they came." She breathed deeply and tugged at her hair. "They arrived at dawn, in those black cloaks and black boots, smashing down doors and dragging us all out in our shifts. To this day, I recall only wee bits of that morning. The chickens' white feathers flying. Glint of the dawn's light on a silver belt buckle. Our door splintering to pieces with one kick from the tallest man I'd yet laid eyes on. Their staves, all held in the same position." Maria paused. "Some of the coven resisted, but the only magic powerful enough to stop them was death magic, and no true witch would use it. The sorcerers bound us and put us in carts, all on your Order's blessing. Then they drove us up to the hill, where they'd assembled the pyres."

Here, her voice failed completely. She sat down heavily at the foot of my bed, letting her hair fall like a curtain to shield her face.

I pictured Agrippa sitting at his cozy desk in the library, writing out an order to have a group of women dragged to the stake. I imagined him smiling so kindly, so gently, as the women screamed in the fire.

In a small voice, Maria continued, "They took six from the wagon. I was holding on to my mother's skirt when they pulled us apart. Even now, I can feel the cloth slipping from my hands." Her shoulders shook, but she kept going, her voice pitched higher with every word. "Then they tied them to the pyres as the sun crested the hill. They wouldn't let me look away. Held my head so I could see 'justice' being done; that's what they called it."

For an awful moment, there was no sound but her strained breathing. I went to the bed, trying to think of something to do or say. Finally, wiping her cheeks, she said, "If you were me, would you carry soft feelings for your father?"

"No," I whispered.

"Since I was a child, they spared me and sent me to the workhouse in Edinburgh. Would have been a greater mercy to kill me. That's all my father ever gave me."

I inched toward her, waiting to see if she'd let me near. "I'm so sorry."

"Do you know why I've told you all this?" She pushed her mane of red hair aside and held her chin up, and her eyes, though red, were dry. "Because I believe I can trust you. And I hate to keep secrets. You? You *cherish* yours."

Stung, I said, "That's not true."

"You tried to hide those bloody things. Quite a botched job you made of it, too. When you wake in the morning, you dress in your lies and keep them close. One day you'll wake and even *you* won't know what the truth is." She bunched her knees up to her chest. "So. Talk. Tell me."

Humiliated, I stared at my folded hands. "Rook attacked someone. He—he told me the man deserved it."

"All right." Maria shrugged. "Thank you for telling me what I knew to begin with. But I don't believe you'd do anything so *improper* as go into a lad's room in the dead of night without a reason. Something drove you in there. What was it?"

God, she was crafty. The secret boiled up inside me. I wanted her to know about R'hlem, but Maria could hold it over me, torture me with it. No, I couldn't trust her. I couldn't trust anyone.

Rook needed to be protected; the truth would hurt him. Magnus was too wild, too free to keep such a secret. And Blackwood's father was directly involved in my father's becoming a monster, so how could I burden him? I . . .

I was alone, living life in a glass box: visible, but impossible to touch. I'd end up like Mickelmas, lying about his identity to his followers, lying to me about my own bloody past. Oh God.

Maria touched my shoulder as I buried my face in my hands. "Tell me," she whispered. "What is it?"

The path diverged before me. Truth or lie. Safety or risk. I'd lied to Agrippa. Would I lie to his daughter?

I made my choice and told her everything.

Mickelmas and the astral plane. R'hlem's revelation and Blackwood's father. As the clocks chimed six, I kept talking. By the time I was done, Maria had gone so pale that her freckles stood out starkly.

"So you see," I finished, "it was an interesting night."

The truth sat between us like a living thing that could bite . . . or not.

"See why you'd be anxious," she mused. My laughter translated as sort of violent hiccuping.

"No one can know." I'd given this girl the key to my undoing. But when I looked in her eyes, I trusted her. Not because they were Agrippa's eyes, but because they were Maria's. She nodded.

"As someone who's problems with her own father, I doubt I'll be telling anyone." She twisted a piece of hair. "What are you going to do about, well, R'hlem?"

I stared at my hands, knotting my fingers. "What would you do?"

"First instinct says you should keep as far away as you can get. But then again, he didn't have to burn, or tell you about Mickelmas. If he told you the truth, he probably wants something. Be good to find out what that is."

God, what was I supposed to do? "I'm caught in an impossible place."

"You are." Maria smiled. "But you needn't be caught there alone. Trust in your strength, and trust in mine."

We shook hands on it.

23

THAT EVENING I LAY IN BED, LISTENING AS THE bells tolled the hour. My feet were blistered from a day of marching along the barrier. It was midnight, and Blackwood and I had only just got home from our patrol, so tired that we lurched upstairs to bed without even a good-night. The entire day had been spent tromping through ankle-deep mud, walking the entire perimeter to seek out any weaknesses. Whitechurch had made every available sorcerer do it, including me, even after my dawn patrol. I'd not been able to sit for hours on end. Painful as it was, I'd been glad for the distraction from my thoughts. I should have fallen instantly asleep, but sleep did not come.

Fear overrode tiredness.

The sachet of herbs remained on my vanity table, beside my ivory comb. Thought of the astral plane made my gut tighten, but Maria had made a point. *He probably wants something. Be good to find out what that is.*

As the twelfth and final bell echoed in the night, I closed my eyes. After a while, I began to drift until . . .

ONCE AGAIN, THE WORLD AROUND ME *went gray, the mist neither cool nor warm. I waited for a full minute, every second shredding my nerves. Blast everything, where was he?*

"You're back." That easy tone of his still took getting used to.

R'hlem waited patiently, his blood festooning yet another nice shirt. Instinct screamed at me to wake, but I forced myself to remain calm.

This was likely my only chance.

"I wanted to speak with William Howel," I said.

His skinned face transformed on the instant, the muscles bunching, the tendons stretching. The lack of flesh, of a face, usually made his expressions difficult to read. But when his mouth split into a grin, it could only be joy.

"My child." His arms opened to embrace me. I dodged away— when a flayed monster approaches, rational thought deserts you. Would my reaction make him angry? No, he only passed a gloved hand over the stripped and raw crown of his head. God, what a human gesture. "Of course, you're still unsure. I beg pardon."

I beg pardon. As though any of this were natural.

"I thought we could talk." Damn, even I thought that sounded stilted. But R'hlem appeared eager.

"You spoke with the magician, then?" His voice sharpened at the mention of Mickelmas. But after what I'd seen, I completely understood why R'hlem didn't care for the man.

How should I approach this? Yelling at him, telling him he was a bastard both seemed excellent paths to nowhere. I wanted to know his mind, and to do that, I'd have to create trust.

I'd no experience with parents. How had I watched Magnus with his mother? He had looked safe at home, secure in the love around him.

Make him want to protect me. Make him yearn to indulge me. I'd read of girls in novels who could twirl their fathers about their fingers. How did one accomplish such a thing?

First: be kind, but not too sweet. He'll suspect something if I suddenly become all milk and honey.

"When did you know about me?" There—my voice was soft, uncertain. I forced myself to toy with the sleeve of my nightgown in what I hoped looked like artless fidgeting. Magnus had taught me to act more skillfully than I ever could have dreamed.

"The night you destroyed Korozoth." There was no anger in his voice. "When you told me your name, I knew straightaway. Your mother honored my wishes." He placed a hand over the blood-mottled shirt, right by his heart.

My mother, that long-lost picture on my aunt's mantel of a woman with golden hair.

"You told her to name me Henrietta?" I asked.

"I wanted my child named after my brother, Henry." Henry. Yes, Mickelmas had thought that name several times in his vision. R'hlem put a finger to his fleshless lips, and that burning eye, the one that haunted my dreams, shone. "Now I can see the resemblance so clearly. You look like him, tall and dark. You even have his way of holding himself."

"I thought I looked more like you," I replied. Misstep. He pulled away, receded from me.

"No, I don't want to think of you as that fool William Howel." His words were twisted by bitterness.

"But you're William Howel." I disguised my fear with a laugh.

"That man is dead."

The connection between us snapped. Damn. What should I try next? Ask about my uncle? No, there had to be a reason Aunt Agnes had kept him secret. And I shouldn't bring up my aunt—God knew what R'hlem thought of her. The one person from our past whom he cared for, unequivocally, was . . .

"What about my mother?"

Though this was my first step on the journey to gaining his trust—to twisting him about my finger—I couldn't help how much I wanted that answer. It burned inside me, and the calculating part of me had to admire how well I'd done. R'hlem's shoulders relaxed.

"There are flashes of her in you." He drew nearer, and I let him. Slowly, he put the very tip of his fingers onto my cheek. I could feel the ruined texture of the blood-soaked leather. "Only my Helen's girl would be so bold as to meet me here."

"I'm not afraid now." I forced myself to mean it. There, the trembling in his fingers told me I'd hit right. Victory.

"Good." The word escaped him, quick and hushed. It was born out of deep feeling.

Mickelmas had told me once that my father had been more impulsive and emotional than I. It seemed as though it could be true, though I wasn't about to become easy with him. Not yet.

"There." He removed his hand. "That slight furrowing of your brow—that's your mother through and through."

"What was she like?" I'd drawn up my picture of her—demure and smiling, the model of a perfect companion.

"Surprising." He grinned, the skinned gums a bit disorienting. "No one could tell Helena her mind. We eloped, you know, under cover of night, like Shelley and that girl of his had a few years earlier. We even met in a churchyard—my romantic touch." He spread out his hands, setting the scene. "There I was, standing in the pitch black because I'd sworn there'd be a moon, and of course there was none. I'd a threadbare coat, no hat because I'd forgot it in my excitement, but . . ." Here he laughed. "But I did remember to bring a copy of Shelley's 'Love's Philosophy' to read as we eloped. I couldn't bloody see it with no moon, so I tried reciting from memory as we banged into headstones looking for the gate."

I put a hand to my mouth to keep from laughing.

"Helen had no time for grand gestures—she couldn't carry her bags very far, and her hair was damp with the night mist. She caught cold two days later and wouldn't let me hear the end of it during the coach ride down to Devon. Naturally, I had to read aloud 'Love's Philosophy' over and over again just to vex her." He laughed heartily.

My parents had eloped? Aunt Agnes had said Mother's merchant family didn't approve of her marrying a poor solicitor, but she hadn't told me this. And I loved that my mother had been more concerned with dry hair than poetry by moonlight. For the first time in my life, I felt that she was a part of me, that she would have understood me. And for the first time, I knew what it felt like to miss her, not just long for her.

"I didn't want you to cry," R'hlem said, his voice gentle.

Yes, I could feel the tears on my cheeks. I shouldn't have brought up my mother; now I was too emotional to continue. Too easy to trip up and make a mistake.

"I have to go. I—I need to rest," I stammered.

"You've been patrolling for the sorcerers." He said it with bitterness. *Don't respond.* "That's bound to tire you out. But I will *see* you again."

His certainty chilled me.

The sound of bells began through the mist. Dong. Dong. Ding ding. Dong. Ding ding ding. Dong. Dong. Dong. Dong. *Just as I'd heard them last night.*

"Yes. You will." *Then, without promising more, I left.*

THE WORLD OUTSIDE MY WINDOW WAS pitch black. A bit groggy, I went to my vanity to take the sachet. Might as well try for a few hours' sleep if I could. As I tumbled back into bed, the herbs in hand, something bothered me. I couldn't place it as I lay down . . . until I listened.

There was only silence outside. No church bells ringing whatsoever. But they'd been tolling when I'd woken. . . .

I sat upright in bed, considering. The bells I'd heard hadn't been ringing in London, but rather wherever R'hlem was. It shouldn't have surprised me. After all, we could touch each other on the astral plane. Why couldn't sound carry as well?

Quickly, I ran to my desk and wrote down what I could recall of the bells' pattern. Attack. South. Ancient. Molochoron.

Forget knowing his mind; R'hlem had potentially given me something much more vital than that, and he didn't even know it.

Unlike the lesser Ancients, R'hlem did not choose to display himself much on the battlefield. If he emerged, it was after the fighting was done so that he could creatively flay and dismember the unfortunate survivors. Pinpointing his exact location had been slippery, to say the least.

Knowing where Molochoron was, perhaps we could uncover R'hlem's location as well. Then, if we moved fast, perhaps we could attack with the weapons and—

Are you truly prepared to kill your own father?

There was no good answer for that thought, save for the knot in my stomach.

WHEN THE MORNING CAME, I'D BEEN awake for hours. I needed to speak with Blackwood at once to discuss the bell patterns, though I'd have to be smart in how I went about it. I didn't want him to know everything that had happened—not just yet.

He wasn't at breakfast, which was odd. Eliza drank a hasty cup of tea, toying with the half-eaten toast on her plate. Tonight was her debut; she should have been excited. The past few days, there'd barely been a moment's rest in the house. Bushels of roses and flares of orchids were artfully arranged throughout the halls. Rugs had been taken up, furniture had been moved, floors had been waxed and scrubbed, and through it all Eliza had sat as quiet as the eye of the storm.

Since the shouting match with Blackwood, we hadn't heard a word about Aubrey Foxglove.

"Are you ready for tonight?" I asked, taking some eggs and keeping an eye on the door for Blackwood.

"I'm nervous," she said. But she looked rather resigned. I should have done more to argue in her corner against the engagement. Perhaps Blackwood could still be reasoned with.

"I'll speak to your brother about Foxglove," I said. Eliza looked up, as if properly noticing me for the first time that day.

"You're sweet." She chewed on her bottom lip, the first hint of nerves. "I'll have something to tell you later."

Mysterious. "Why not now?"

The clock struck eight, and Eliza pushed her chair back.

"The timing's not right. Later, I promise." She left the room. Odd. I would never understand the Blackwood family.

He never came to breakfast, and I skirted around the servants as they continued their whirl of preparation for the ball. Great rows of beeswax candles were being lit in the chandeliers and planted all along the walls and tables. Ivy symbolizing Sorrow-Fell decorated the staircase banisters, and faerie lights softly glowed among the tendrils. The Blackwood mansion would be the best-lit building in the city.

Blackwood wasn't in his study or the parlor. The thought occurred that he'd be at practice, but it wasn't like him to miss a meal for it. As I walked toward the obsidian room, I noticed that the air felt . . . off. Thick, somehow. Strange noises emanated from behind the obsidian room's door: high, keening whining like a dog's, followed by a grunting, grinding echo.

Gooseflesh spread over my arms. Pushing in, I discovered Blackwood with one of the swords in his hands.

He'd removed his coat and cravat and undone the top buttons of his shirt, the front of which was damp with sweat. Going into a deep crouch, his legs shook ever so slightly—he was tired. Had he even been to bed? He raised the sword perfectly over his shoulder, arms prepared for a mighty swing, and twisted the blade counterclockwise as he went. The deep, unsettling whine sounded once more.

He finally noticed me in the room's black reflection. "What are you doing here?" He placed the sword against the wall, and the obsidian *warped* when the metal made contact.

Whatever these weapons were, they were against the rules of this place. Blackwood's appearance reflected that: his eyes were glassy. His normally pale skin was red and blotchy at his face and neck.

I nodded at the weapons—the sword by the wall, the coil of the whip on a small table. "What are *you* doing here?"

"Practicing." He picked up a cloth from the table and wiped his face.

"Mickelmas warned us." I noted how he watched the weapons out of the corner of his eye, rather like a dragon guarding its hoard.

"You don't get stronger without practice." He rubbed at the

back of his neck, his eyes closed. Putting down the weapon had drained the bright color from his face; he looked exhausted. Tossing the towel aside, he picked up the whip. Sparks exploded as he cracked it twice.

I noticed a pile of books on the other side of the table. Pulling the stack closer, I recognized them from his father's private study. As I flipped the pages, I discovered small, fine handwriting in the margins.

"You've been making notes." I turned the book to him. Blackwood glanced quickly.

"My father wrote those. He was obsessed with magician craft." *Crack.* He handled the whip with the air of an expert. "He was a bastard, but ahead of his time. He recognized the importance of mastering these forces." *Crack* again.

Mastering was a word Charles Blackwood would have used, not his son.

"You should be careful with what you find."

"When we go up against R'hlem, I want to be ready." The idea made me ill. Blackwood stopped, the whip coiling limp at his feet. "He killed my father, you know." He said it quietly, an admission. "Skinned him alive. When they brought the body back, Mother wouldn't let Eliza or me look."

Dear God.

"So you want revenge." I understood.

"No." That haunted look crept over his face once more. "I want to be the one who *wins*." He cracked the whip again, and again, and again. Each time, the magic washed over my body, soaking my skin. Rolling the whip up, he placed it back on the table and traced his fingers over the handle, a loving caress. "I found myself in the parlor yesterday evening, looking up at Father's portrait."

Yes, I knew the one. It looked disarmingly like Blackwood himself, only with an easier smile. "He never noticed me when I was a child. I think the first time he truly looked at me was the day he went off to die. He seemed to know it, too; that spurred him to tell me what he'd done. He passed the burden of our family shame onto an eight-year-old boy. Do you know what he said then?" Blackwood closed his eyes. "His final words were 'Try not to be so disappointing, George.'"

Crack. He took the whip once more and used it. Breathing heavily, he stared at his own dark reflection. "I hope he can see me from wherever he is now. I want him to choke on my victory."

Blackwood's intensity unnerved me.

"We're going to win," I told him, trying to soothe. He wheeled about to face me.

"Is it wrong to want more?" His eyes searched mine.

"More what?"

He paused, as if afraid. Then he whispered, "Everything."

Blood trickled down his face. His nose had started bleeding afresh. Still, he didn't move as he gazed at me.

"Why shouldn't we take what we can?" he breathed.

I saw in Blackwood's cold smile his father as he cut the rope—

I gave him my handkerchief to stanch his bleeding.

"Forgive me." Blackwood blinked as if emerging from a dream. Turning away, he lined up the weapons on the table. "I should have asked when you came in. Do you want something?"

"I've been considering ways to attack the Ancients, and I can't recall where they're all located at the moment." I paused. "Molochoron, for example."

Blackwood considered, then snapped his fingers. "York. Whitechurch had a dispatch two days ago asking for more men."

So R'hlem was in Yorkshire. I suppressed a shudder at the thought of him near Brimthorn, even though it wasn't close to the city. The sooner I moved on this information, and the sooner I established where R'hlem was, the sooner the girls at my old school would be safe. I had to keep telling myself that. I had to believe it.

Blackwood held open the door for me. Once we were out in the hall, the thick magic bled away, and my head felt lighter.

Blackwood walked with me. "I hope you'll dance the first waltz with me tonight. We've barely had a moment to talk on more pleasant things."

"Of course. I wanted to speak with you, anyway, about Eliza's—"

"My lord." The butler found us. "There's some discussion about what to do with the faerie greeters. The hobgoblin said that he'd some in mind for the job, but they don't seem to have arrived yet, in the typical fashion of their race." He sniffed.

"We'll speak later, Howel," Blackwood said, bowing before heading down the hall.

First, get through Eliza's party. Then find some way to present my findings to Whitechurch. If I could do this—if we could track R'hlem and find a way to move swiftly—the whole war could end.

But with what I knew now, could I even go through with it?

24

THAT EVENING, MARIA AND I WATCHED CARRIAGES pull up before the house in an elegant line. Heavy mist had fallen over London, giving the air around the streetlamps a soupy sort of glow. People came up the walk, and from my window I caught the glitter of jewels and the muted shine of silk. Maria pressed a steaming mug into my hands. She'd made a recipe of calming herbs, which smelled of cinnamon and tasted vaguely like a forest. It burned on the way down but warmed my belly. I leaned my head against the glass and stared out into the fog.

"If R'hlem died, do you think it would stop Rook's transformation?" I handed Maria the mug.

"Well, Rook wouldn't be changing if the Ancients hadn't come." Hell and damnation. What was I supposed to do? "Sure these are fit thoughts when you've a party downstairs?"

The door swept open and Lilly entered, her cheeks rosier than usual and her strawberry-blond hair curled for the occasion. She did love the energy of a ball, and there weren't many to be had in the Blackwood house. She gestured for me to sit at the vanity. I obeyed, letting her work at fixing my hair into the tricky Apollo knot, curls on either side of my face and a high styling at the back.

"Must say, miss, I think the faerie outdid herself this time." She oohed as I stood to make certain everything was in place.

Indeed, the splendid "flame" gown that Voltiana had designed was constructed like a dream. My shoulders were completely bare, the small sleeves hugging my arms, and while the neckline plunged low enough to be daring, it wasn't indecent. The gown's upper half was so tight it looked painted on, while the skirt was voluminous. Bright orange and yellow silk made up different lengths and layers, so that when I walked, it had the appearance of fire.

As a finishing touch, Lilly plunged an arrow made of solid gold through the back of my hairstyle to make it stay.

That was the most decadent part of my outfit, to be sure, a gift from Blackwood. I'd been surprised to find it sitting upon my vanity this afternoon.

"I wish you were both coming downstairs," I told them, taking one last sip of the tea for encouragement. Lilly giggled at my absurdity, but I didn't think it was absurd to have people one liked at a party.

Maria shrugged. "No offense, but I'd rather leap from the window. Wouldn't know what to do, even if I'd a gown."

"That reminds me." I knelt, pulling two slim boxes out from under my bed and handed them over. "To thank you both for everything."

I'd had Madame Voltiana design and deliver them in secret.

Lilly's was smaller, and after she blushed and said she couldn't, she peeked inside. She'd mentioned several times how much she yearned for new gloves with autumn's arrival. These were kidskin gloves, the leather pale as cream and soft as butter, lined on the inside with satin.

"Oh," she gasped, her face going pink. Tears stood out in her brilliant blue eyes, and she could only pet the gloves against her cheek and stammer her thanks. Bemused, Maria took off the lid from her box, mouth falling open as she pulled out a peacock-blue cloak.

Voltiana had insisted on the shade of blue—she'd remembered Maria from earlier. *Some red hair suits blue, not green,* she'd said, and she'd been right. Maria swept the cloak around her shoulders, fastening the leaf-shaped golden clasp at her throat. She wrapped the garment around her body and buried herself in it. "Feels like wearing the air," she murmured.

"You like it?"

"I hate it. How dare you?" She scowled playfully, then tackled me. I'd never been hugged so forcefully before.

Lilly, who was still petting the gloves, cried out, "Be careful of her hair!" She shooed Maria off me. After the uncertainty of the last few months, making people happy felt simply wonderful.

"Looks like they'll expect you." Maria knelt by the window, still wrapped in her cloak. "Best go down."

Lilly wiped her cheeks, fluffed my skirts once more, and sent me on my way.

I arrived at the top of the staircase and looked into the hall below. A crowd was already milling about in the foyer, the buzz of conversation growing louder with every new guest. I frowned as I noticed Lady Blackwood was not there to receive them.

"You look lovely," Blackwood said.

He walked to stand beside me, neatening his cuffs. His eyes widened as they tracked over me from head to toe. "Quite lovely," he said.

I could pay him the same compliment—indeed, my mind went blank as I beheld him. He usually wore dark, somber clothes, which matched his hair—and his general demeanor. Tonight his coat was forest green, golden embroidery curling at his cuffs in the subtle shape of ivy leaves. The coat brought out the deep green of his eyes. His light-colored breeches had been tailored to his long legs. I didn't normally notice the shape or strength of his body, but tonight I couldn't help myself. Every line was elegant, the broad shoulders tapering into his narrow waist. He looked young and wonderfully masculine, a prince from a childhood storybook.

Damn, I could feel myself blushing. Giving him my hand, we began down the staircase.

"I need you to do something," he said as we approached the bottom. "Play hostess in the receiving line."

That was a role for the lady of the house.

"I'm not sure it's my place," I said.

"Normally, it wouldn't be, but Eliza needs to make her

entrance, and Mamma doesn't enjoy parties." Irritation laced his voice. She wouldn't even come down for her own daughter's debut?

"Then, yes," I said. "Of course."

We'd reached the entryway, and I could feel the guests noticing us. Weighing us with their eyes. "Thank you for my arrow," I said as the first partygoers came toward me. "I don't know what possessed you to have it made, though."

"I'll tell you later," he whispered, and brought my hand to his lips.

I watched him as he walked away to meet with a few of the Masters on the other side of the room.

Somehow I remembered everyone's name, smiled in greeting, and didn't stumble over my small talk too much. Enough jewel-encrusted, starched, and perfumed people came through the doors to fill the whole of London. At least, it seemed like enough. I felt some gazes slide over me with puzzlement. Undoubtedly, it struck them as odd that I was playing hostess.

Finally, with everyone assembled, I stepped aside and into the crowd. This was Eliza's cue to enter. A few minutes passed, then another few, and I feared Blackwood would go upstairs and drag her down.

Then she appeared at the top of the staircase, surveying the crowd as gasps greeted her arrival. I'd been rather proud of my dress, but it paled in comparison to hers. She wore a gown of royal-purple taffeta, the sleeves puffed and the skirt a billowing cloud. With her jet-black hair piled atop her head and loosened in artful tendrils, she looked like a Greek goddess who had descended from Olympus to mingle in London society.

Eliza had always been beautiful, but tonight she was radiant. I smiled and caught Blackwood's eye in the crowd. His chest seemed to swell with pride.

An older man who had to be Foxglove bowed and then gave her his arm. He was rather handsome, though unfortunately graying at the temples. Eliza silently accepted him, and he led her through a sea of admirers. She showed no emotion. Chin lifted, she passed among the partygoers as though they didn't exist.

The sight of Foxglove dampened my mood. When Blackwood and I had a moment, perhaps I could try one last time to convince him to let Eliza choose before it really was too late.

Now the party truly began, and people moved freely throughout the house. The whole first level had been made available tonight. Music wafted from several rooms, every one of which hosted tables of food and drink waiting to be sampled.

The house had been made to resemble a glen in Faerie. Brush Fae fluttered along the walls and ceilings, decorating the hall with twinkling lights. Ivy and holly adorned doorways, purple and yellow wildflowers had been arranged in glass and crystal vases, and in the library a trio of goat-hooved pipers played a song that was achingly beautiful.

The food was a marvel: roasted pheasant under glass,

poached pears and cream, turtle soup and gleaming oysters, sweetbreads in sauce, stewed mushrooms, honey-glazed quail, rose and lavender jellies, and spun-sugar confections in the shape of stars and ivy leaves waited inside golden cornucopias or silver urns.

So many people stopped to speak with me, whether it was a lady admiring my gown or a gentleman sorcerer congratulating me upon the victory against Callax. One even asked if I thought we could produce more weapons to send to the fenlands. Moving through the crowd, I recalled feeling like such an outsider when I first arrived in London. Now, a few months later, it seemed as if I'd always been part of this world.

And once again, a terrible secret burned inside me. This time, I could not lay the blame on the sorcerers. It was my own fault, and an unhappy accident of birth, that separated me from them. Whatever giddiness I'd felt at the start of the ball soured at once.

Speaking of souring, I ran into Valens, who was talking with a lovely young woman. His smile evaporated when he saw me. The woman merely curtsied.

"My wife, Leticia," Valens said to me, before encouraging her to take a seat on a nearby sofa. Indeed, she looked pale, and by the swell of her stomach I guessed she was with child. Valens watched her sit, his face relaxing into a contented smile. His tenderness surprised me.

"How are your drills progressing? Do you even practice any longer?" he asked.

I all but rolled my eyes. "Yes, now that I'm not corrected every ten seconds."

He gave a short laugh. "I corrected you because you needed to be at your best," he said. "You hadn't the proper amount of training before the commendation. I would have had my entire squadron drill again because of any man's single mistake." He frowned. "It would be wrong to be any less hard on you because you are a woman. Wouldn't you agree?"

Blanching, I said, "I suppose."

Valens bowed and went after his wife. Perhaps I'd been wrong about him. Had I let my anger toward Palehook rub off on his old pupil? That wasn't an encouraging thought.

"Miss Howel." A smiling Fanny Magnus approached. "You look lovely this evening." She was wearing a beautiful dark blue gown trimmed with lace, and I happily returned the compliment. "You've made an old widow's night," she said, giving a cheerful wink. It was easy to see where Magnus got the best parts of himself. "Julian's been looking for you since we arrived. Ah!" She gave a light wave as Magnus cut toward us. He'd dressed in his naval uniform, complete with cream-colored breeches and a brilliant, deep-blue coat.

Taking his mother's arm, he smiled at me. "Howel. Picture of elegance, as always."

"I'll leave you both to it," Fanny sang before disappearing into the crowd. Oh lord. Magnus shook his head.

"Mother gets ideas about things. You needn't worry."

"I'm not," I said, smiling. "So. Have you any interest in the girls this evening?" Based on the blushes and glances directed our way, I imagined there were scores of young ladies here who would be happy to overlook Magnus's lack of fortune.

"Since you've brought it up, there was something I wanted to speak to you about." He adjusted his collar. "You see—"

"Howel!" Dee practically dove through the crowd. He knocked into Magnus, who cursed as he upset some drinks. Dee was so wildly elated he didn't even notice. "I saw Lilly! She was standing by the staircase, you know, near the servants' entrance. She noticed me! And she even smiled! Can you believe it?" He sighed, as if on the verge of bursting into song about love, flowering trees, and other unsubtle metaphors.

"Dee, if you budge five steps to the left, I will no longer be sitting in the punch bowl," Magnus grunted. As they negotiated who had to move where, Fanny returned and stole me away.

"They're galumphing wildebeests." She laughed. "But I love them. Arthur's practically my second son. When he first came to town, he was miserably homesick. I had Julian bring him home every Sunday for supper."

She guided me into the eastern library, which the faeries had enchanted to look like a medieval castle made of stone, with tapestries and suits of armor on display. Harps floated about in the air, playing themselves. On a raised dais an empty velvet throne sat beside a creature that looked like nothing so much as a white goat with a horn growing out of its forehead. The animal wore a pink collar and chewed some hay.

"That's not . . . Is that a real unicorn?" I gaped. Surely those were extinct?

"Lord Blackwood's spared no expense for his sister's debut." Fanny tutted. "Lady Blackwood isn't here tonight, is she?"

"She stays in her room," I replied.

For the first time, her smile withered. "It's difficult for a boy, his father dead, his mother absent. I had hoped he and Julian would be better friends, but that wasn't to be."

"I don't think Lord Blackwood makes friends easily," I said. Fanny patted my hand.

"What about me?" Blackwood arrived, sleek as a cat.

"Thank you for the invitation, my lord." Fanny curtsied to him. "I'm rarely out of the house these days. Julian insists it's safer if we stay at home."

"In that, he's right." Blackwood said it as if to imply that Magnus wasn't right about many things. "But since you're with us tonight, Mrs. Magnus, I think you should be quite secure."

She nodded to me. "Miss Howel." She returned to the party. Blackwood looked after her, gaze darkening.

"Are you all right?"

"I imagine she was pressing her son onto you. Now that he's thrown away his engagement, she'll be looking for any eligible girl to snatch him up."

I was shocked by his rudeness. "She's a kind woman."

"Yes. She is. Forgive me." He winced. "I—I need to speak with you. Now, if you don't mind. It's urgent."

"Of course," I said. I could not have been given a better chance to talk about Eliza . . . and R'hlem. I'd decided not to make the same bloody mistake twice. Even if it frightened me to my core, I would tell him the truth.

"The aviary is closed to the party. Let's go there." It seemed that he was paler than normal. Together, we slipped away from the guests.

I'd never liked the aviary, which was filled with stuffed birds of prey. Peregrine falcons sat frozen upon perches; glass-eyed ravens hung suspended from the ceiling, their beaks open in a silent cry. Blackwood's father had loved predatory things.

It was chilly here, so I let a tongue of flame bloom in my hand. The whisper of the fire on my skin was a comfort. Kneeling by the hearth, I coaxed it into a bright blaze.

Blackwood studied a falcon, stroking the bird's feathered breast with one finger. This was my chance.

"I'm glad we're alone. I need to speak with you," I said. My heart beat so fast I was certain it weakened my voice.

Blackwood kept studying the falcon. "Do you?"

I went to stand next to the bird; maybe then he'd look at me. "It's urgent." That did grab his attention. Licking my lips, I said, "I . . . I don't think Eliza's engagement to Foxglove is right."

Coward. I would have to build up to it.

"Eliza?" He frowned. "We can talk about her later. Right now I must tell you something." He spoke in a rather stilted manner, as though he'd rehearsed. "The queen's advisors worry that R'hlem is only biding his time, waiting for an opportunity to strike. Even with the success of the weapons, they think it's dangerous to keep you from him."

They had no idea. The admission now lodged itself in my throat.

"Whitechurch is on our side, as is most of the Order, but the fact is, you are an unmarried, parentless girl." I winced— not entirely parentless. "They can push or pull you as they choose until you have a secure position. Do you understand?"

Why did he look at me as though waiting for something? For the moment, I laid my confession aside.

"What are you saying?"

"I went to Whitechurch this afternoon with a proposition. I need his permission, you understand, because . . ." He stopped.

A faint buzzing started in my ears. "What did you ask him?"

"I asked for permission to marry." He looked straight into my eyes. "To marry you."

25

IT BECAME SURPRISINGLY QUIET INSIDE MY HEAD. Blackwood continued speaking, but I didn't hear much of it. *Marry him.* Impossible. I was going to marry Rook. At least, I wanted to marry Rook. We had only so much time left, and I couldn't . . .

I was not going to marry Blackwood.

"I can't," I said, backing away. He didn't react. "I don't mean that I don't—I can't—surely you understand. . . ." Words did not come properly.

"This is all very sudden," he said. "I've never shown you any attention, er, in that way." He finally sat down in a chair, then motioned for me to do the same. "You must admit, it is an excellent plan," he said as I sank onto a sofa. "By allying with my house, no one could touch you."

"Of course." I sighed, understanding at last. "You only offer to save me from my enemies. It proves what a good friend you are."

"A good friend," he echoed. His finger began to tap out a rhythm on the arm of his chair.

"You shouldn't have to sacrifice yourself for me."

"Sacrifice." He kept parroting things. Standing, he moved over to the fireplace. "Why do you think I asked for your hand?"

"To be a good friend," I repeated slowly.

"Then you don't understand." Something stirred in me, a response to the heat I saw in his eyes. No. This shouldn't be. He was my friend, one of the few friends I could rely on.

"I understand," I said, trying to sound cheerful. When I stood, Blackwood put a hand, gently, to my wrist. I was wearing gloves, but even though his skin didn't touch mine, it still sent a pulsing warmth through my body.

"Can you believe how I treated you when we first met?" His thumb brushed the back of my hand. His voice was deep and rugged. "I thought you an opportunist and a liar."

"That was all true." I laughed weakly. He did not.

"Do you not understand how I feel?" He said it almost to himself. "You're my dearest friend." He studied me, as if looking for an opening to strike, only there was no threat of violence from him. Quite the opposite. "When I had your friendship, I thought I could never want for anything more. But over time, I have come to feel for you beyond anything I thought I could."

The passion in his words began to terrify me.

"Don't say anything you'll regret." I turned away and felt him come up behind me.

"I will never regret it," he murmured. "I've fought this feeling. To burn for someone in such a way is weak, and I swore to myself I would never know weakness like my father did." He spit the word *father* like a curse. "I've tried to take myself back to our first days out of Agrippa's house. But that is impossible." I felt him gently touch the golden arrow in my hair. "That's why I had this made. You've brought me down." He took my hand, running his thumb in circles over my palm. Frozen, I couldn't think. I couldn't turn around. He drew closer and whispered in my ear. "I had a dream a few nights ago that you and I were in Sorrow-Fell. No other living soul disturbed us. When I woke, I thought: why shouldn't we be *everything* to each other?"

I had things to say, reasonable things. But he placed a hand upon my bare shoulder. At the touch of his skin, heat unfurled inside me. He wrapped an arm around me from behind, holding me against the hard line of his body. I closed my eyes as every sensible thought scattered. There was only the beat of his heart and the sensation of his hand.

It was like being fluent in a language I had never studied. Something dark and rooted in me, some essential part of my soul, began to stir. I thought of the identical strands of ivy twining down our staves.

There were no coincidences in this world.

His hand traced my bare shoulder, my back. His touch left a trail of heat. *Move.* I had to move away, but it was as if I'd been enchanted. The way I responded, the way my heart pounded . . . I wanted this. His hands, his body trembled. I didn't think he'd ever touched a woman like this before.

Blackwood whispered in my ear, "After the victory against Callax, I felt an intoxicating freedom, all because of you."

My traitorous body flushed as he pressed his lips to my bare shoulder. I groaned softly as he kissed my temple. "That is why I beg you to become my wife," he breathed.

Wake up, wake up. In a flash, I imagined turning and finding Charles Blackwood with his arms about me.

Oh, that did the trick. My body finally listened to my brain, and I wrenched away. Blackwood looked dazed.

"No," I gasped, "I'm engaged to Rook."

"Rook?" Blackwood said it as though he'd never heard that name before. Then understanding dawned. "Rook," he repeated, incredulous.

"I love him. I've loved him since we were children." How could I explain the hours we'd spent to Blackwood? The games on the moor, hiding from Colegrind, sharing what food we'd been able to sneak from the pantry. When Colegrind would beat Rook, I'd be there to soothe his wounds. When the headmaster began to show interest in me, to linger with his hand on me for too long, I had to keep Rook from murdering the man. Our memories, our lives, were linked.

The clock chiming the hour was the only sound.

"There's nothing between us? I misunderstood all of it?" he finally asked. His voice was tight. I wanted to say yes, it had all been in his own head. But had it?

Why had I closed my eyes and, in some dark part of my soul, desired him?

No. Use logic. It was true, I relied upon Blackwood in a way

I couldn't rely on anyone else—as a sorcerer, as my friend. If I said I'd never found him handsome, I'd be lying. But he wasn't Rook.

"I can't give you what you want," I said.

"That didn't answer my question." He sounded hopeful. "My plan might be the only way to keep our friendship intact."

"No one can force us not to be friends." I was shocked by the idea.

"Once you are married, would Rook still allow you to remain in the Order?"

"Rook doesn't need to *allow* me to do anything," I said, stung.

"As his wife, you'd be forced to obey him."

Now I was getting angry. "And if I became *your* wife? Would you lock me up inside the house?"

"No," he said, his voice steel. "We each know the other's soul." He drew nearer. "Can you imagine me telling any other sorcerer girl what my father did?" No. I could not. "If Whitechurch has his way, that's exactly what will happen."

Wait. "*His way?* You said you asked Whitechurch for my hand."

He sneered. "And was refused. 'Bloodlines,' he said, 'must remain pure.' Even with your power, you're a magician's child."

"Well, that settles it." Despite the insult, I was relieved. "We can't disobey."

"Can't we?" His voice was dark. Dear God, was Blackwood

actually suggesting treason? "I think our children would have untold strength. Consider the new world we could show to the Order; the possibilities are endless."

Blackwood was speaking entirely too much about children for my taste.

"We can't do this without permission," I said.

"We can do what we like. We've proven ourselves stronger than most, and the strong should rule." This was insanity. I would have labeled Blackwood as many things, but a rebel was not one of them. "You know me. You know my secrets. And I know yours." I flinched. He didn't know *all* my secrets, but I couldn't tell him about R'hlem *now*. "I will never be as comfortable with anyone as I am with you." He looked into my eyes. "We have so much that can build a successful marriage." He touched the tips of his fingers to my cheek. "I respect you as I respect no one. Do you feel the same?"

He was perhaps the most admirable person I knew. "Yes."

"Do you like me?"

"Yes." It felt as if I were sinking into a quagmire, the irresistible pull taking me down. He put a hand to my waist.

Some part of me was curious how it would feel to press his lips to mine, but I stepped away to look into his striking eyes, his beautiful face. Anyone would call me a fool, and be right to do so. "I want you to be happy," I said.

"The key to my happiness rests in your hands." He wasn't going to make this easy for me. "I think you feel something," he whispered. If only he were wrong, I'd push him away now with a feeling of revulsion, but the revulsion did not come. "I believe that with time, you can love me as I love you. Maybe not with the sweetness of your childhood love, but something real. Something passionate." His gaze hypnotic, he went to kiss me.

"I can't." I retreated to a colder, darker corner of the room, where it was easier to think. "I told you that I'm in love with Rook."

Blackwood kept his back to the fire, his gaze cooling. "I see. Leave aside Rook's poverty and his being Unclean—I know you don't care about such things. Are you entirely yourself with him?" He advanced, one smooth step at a time. "His powers frighten you." He circled me like one of his father's blasted predator birds. "Am I wrong?"

Much as I hated to, I whispered, "No."

"You are hungry for knowledge in a way he never has been. You want to ask questions no one has dared ask before. We can have something that will last for generations. Don't throw yourself away. Don't be ordinary."

I moved back to the fire, but he pursued me. "I would do most anything to make you happy, Howel, if you'd let me. I would become your servant, lay whatever you wanted at your feet. Does that offer mean nothing to you?"

No. But Rook needed me.

"I'm sorry," I said. "I won't break my word to him."

Blackwood was silent then, and despair washed over his

features. But the despair was soon replaced with coldness. He'd shown me his heart and was now locking it away again.

"You'd choose a poor servant over a rich one?" That made me want to snap, but before I could, Blackwood strode out the door, leaving me alone.

Something in the corner moved. I nearly missed the shadow as it swept across the floor and slipped into the hall. It had been shaped vaguely like a person—

Dear God. With a barely suppressed cry, I threw open the door and rushed down the darkened hall. Turning a corner, I emerged into a clutch of people.

I had to move swiftly but without panic. If someone stopped me for a chat, I had to look interested, excuse myself politely, and keep moving. There could be no suspicion, even as I made like hell for the stairs. If anyone noticed my panic, it might draw attention, and then—

Rook had been a shadow, lurking in the corner of the room. If he could do that, how far gone was he?

In the front hall, I was prepared to lose all propriety and start shoving. I managed to navigate the crowd elegantly, but as I neared the staircase, Eliza and Magnus moved onto the stairs. Neither saw me, but I heard them speaking.

"We're doing this now?" Magnus asked.

"George will be back soon," she hissed.

Magnus sighed, raised his stave, and dimmed all the lights in the room. That gained everyone's attention, and the chatter died. All eyes turned to Magnus and Eliza standing slightly above the crowd on the stairs. She smiled, her cheek dimpling, and spoke clearly.

"Thank you all for coming. This has been the most marvelous debut anyone could ask for."

I didn't know much about society's ways, but I was fairly certain Eliza wasn't supposed to speak publicly tonight. Hunting for Foxglove, I found him gazing at his soon-to-be-fiancée with bewilderment.

What in hell was going on? Magnus raised his punch glass and took over.

"Lord Blackwood should be making this speech, but he's missing." Magnus glanced about as if assuring himself that Blackwood was, indeed, gone. Then he kissed Eliza's gloved hand, while she looked the very illustration of excitement. "That makes it my pleasure, then, to make a tremendous announcement. Lady Elizabeth Blackwood has consented to become my wife."

26

THE SILENCE WAS ABSOLUTE UNTIL A TRICKLE OF whispers began. The trickle gave way to a stream, and soon the room filled with confused murmuring. A pocket of commotion erupted near the side of the room as Aubrey Foxglove shouldered his way out, probably in search of Blackwood.

I didn't understand, and right now I didn't want to. I'd no time for any of this, though my stomach gave an unanticipated drop.

As if to cue me, Maria appeared at the top of the stairs, looking about in a panic. I signaled to her, and she waved me up urgently. Launching myself onto the landing, I skirted around the newly engaged couple.

Magnus had the audacity to try to stand in my way. "I need to talk to you," he said, his voice low. Eliza tugged at his arm.

"Not. Now," I said through gritted teeth, and barreled past him and up the stairs. Maria pulled me along beside her.

"He's worse," she whispered.

No. Please, no.

Fenswick was not in the apothecary when we barged in,

but a person was lying on Maria's cot. She grabbed up her ax by the door.

No, it wasn't a person on her bed. A great mound of quivering shadow lay there.

"Rook?" I said, my voice weak.

The darkness developed a form and features, melting into Rook. He lay curled on his side until, shaking, he sat up. His eyes were rimmed in red.

"Were you going to tell me?" he whispered. So he had been in the aviary. He had the power to *become* shadow now.

"How much did you hear?" I asked, keeping my voice calm.

"Enough."

"What's going on?" Maria whispered.

With a curl of his fingers, Rook beckoned me to him. He was sweating, as if he'd been laboring under a fever that had finally broken.

"Let me look at you," he said. Slowly, I did as he asked, and shadows exploded from every corner of the room, extinguishing the candles on the table. Maria cried out as I set my hand aflame and held it up to look at him.

Rook's eyes were pure black.

"How long have you been able to do this?" I asked. Somewhere off to the side, in the impenetrable darkness, I heard a little voice whisper. I couldn't make out the words. When I held up my flame, the voice was silenced.

"I can't see anything," Maria said. I'd never heard her so afraid.

"Please take the dark away," I whispered.

"No. Show me your face." That wasn't Rook's voice; it was too cold, too demanding.

I did as he asked, holding the fire close to my chin. He reached a hand out of the blackness and stroked my cheek. His touch was ice cold. By my light, I could make out the sharp contours of his face.

"Do you love me?" he murmured. I put a hand to his chest. "You know that I do."

He clutched my wrist. "Then why didn't you tell Lord Blackwood he was wrong?" he said.

"I said I wouldn't marry him," I whispered.

"Not before he said I wasn't good enough for you." The shadows knitted together as Rook put his hand to my neck. For the first time in my life, I was afraid he would hurt me.

"I was too shocked to think." I let the flame overtake both my hands, let it creep up my arms and cover my face, which made Rook move away. I wanted to keep him from touching me; I'd never wanted that before.

"I've never known you to be too shocked to think, Henrietta." Once, I'd loved the sound of my name on his tongue. Not now. He drew in a deep, shuddering breath. "How convenient for you to give your promise to one person and then think of taking it away." This was the thing living inside Rook's skin speaking.

By the light of my fire, I could make out Maria's terrified face. I nodded for her to be ready to leave the room. "I'm not going to marry Blackwood. Not ever."

The shadows receded slowly, like a dark tide. Finding a moment of freedom, Maria bolted, throwing open the door. "Come on!" she called, but Rook snarled. If I tried to run, he'd attack.

"I'll be all right," I said. "Just go."

"No, I won't leave you."

"Go!" I focused on Rook until at last I heard the door close.

"Do you promise?" His desperation showed. "Not to marry him?"

"Of course."

My fire went out as he took me into his arms. It was too dark to see him now. "Then end this madness. Marry me," he whispered, kissing me. "Tomorrow, we'll go to the church."

"There's no hurry," I said, petting his cheek. *Keep him calm.* The darkness began to solidify again.

"I can't be sure of you unless you do this," Rook growled.

"You can trust me."

"How can I trust you when I know how easily you lie?" His voice changed, deepened, grew angrier. "Swear that you'll never be his."

"What are you talking about? I'm not *his.* I'm my own person."

"You won't swear it," he growled. "I should have known you'd sell yourself to the man with the best price."

Sell myself? Fury ate my fear as the whispers around us grew louder. I launched flame into the air to keep the dark at bay, then embraced him. Rook clung to me, burying his face in my shoulder, coming back to himself. I felt as though I were walking the ledge of a cliff, one misplaced step away from falling. I kissed his hair.

"Don't you know you're the reason I'm alive?" he whispered, wrapping me so tightly in his arms that I knew there'd be no escape without one or both of us being hurt. "That night the soldiers brought me to Brimthorn, I'd no memory, not even of my own name. I sat in that cellar, fading away. And then I saw your light." He kissed me. "You brought me medicine. You named me. Don't you know that from that moment on, I was yours? All I've ever wanted was you," he said into my ear. "And you'd give yourself to a man who could have anyone else in the world." He gripped my shoulders painfully. "He can't have the only thing I've ever claimed for myself."

I was not some damned bauble to be traded from one man's pocket to the next.

"Rook, stop it!" I flung a spark into his face, and he released me. These had not been Rook's true words. This was not him. "I know what's doing this to you."

"You know?" He looked wild with terror. "Then for God's sake tell me."

Something dark and cold wrapped around my wrist, and I broke.

"You're becoming a monster!" I screamed.

The voices stopped. The blackness rolled away, and I could

see Rook clearly in the window's dim light. "Korozoth's power is poisoning you." I got as far from him and the shadows as I could. "You're becoming less than human."

"Less than?" he said, barely breathing the words.

"That's why Fenswick and Maria have worked so hard to find a cure. That's why you have to take all those treatments. I wanted to protect you from it. Because I love you too much to let it have you." Those last words came out as a sob.

"You wanted to protect me." He stretched out his hands to examine the scars that decorated his wrists. It was as if he'd never seen them before. "But you've lied to me."

"We thought that if you knew, it might hasten the transformation." Rook gaped at me. "I did it to help you."

"Protect me. As if I were a child?" I'd never imagined I could see Rook's eyes full of hatred. "As if I were a pet."

"No!" I gasped. The blackness around me teemed with whispers. My flames began to die as the darkness forced itself on me.

Something was happening: his teeth sharpened, his face grew thinner. "I will not be your toy! Your dog! Do you understand?"

I swore I could hear tendons popping, bones breaking like the snap of kindling.

"I'm sorry I kept it a secret!" My voice was high as he brought me closer to him. "I did it to help you."

"I don't want your *help*," he snarled. "I want *you*." He began to drag me down.

Screaming, I exploded in flame, the blast obliterating the dark container around me. Rook howled. There was an opening through the shadow, and I ran out the door. I thundered down the stairs. Back on the second floor, I sank to my knees and tried to think.

A hand gripped my shoulder.

"No!" I whirled around.

But it was only Blackwood, his stave at the ready, Maria behind him. She handed me Porridge. I clung to the stave.

"Told him," she said breathlessly. Blackwood made to go upstairs, but I prevented him.

"What on earth is going on?" he snapped.

"Something dreadful's happened," I said. "We need to get everyone out of here *now*." Below us, music lilted and the laughter rose and fell. All of sorcerer society was here tonight.

They were in danger. They could kill Rook.

"What is *happening*?" Blackwood blocked my exit.

The candles and the lanterns throughout the entire house snuffed out at once, plunging us into pure darkness. Women screamed below. I relit the wall sconces nearby, but the flame thinned, a breath away from being swallowed again.

"He's here," Maria whispered. I could feel some presence, some animal intelligence that dwelt in the shadows. *Don't fall down. Don't scream. Work.*

"We need to get everyone out," I said, rushing downstairs. "The party is over. Thank you for coming," I called.

Everyone stared at me now, and mumbles of confusion and anger began to surface.

"What the devil is going on?" Magnus said, slipping through the crowd with Eliza in tow.

"Get the women out of here." I stepped around him and walked onto the floor, preparing to tell the crowd something, anything, when screams erupted from down the hall. Several maids raced into the foyer, caps askew, not giving a damn about the party or anything else. They kept looking behind them, into the black entrance to the downstairs hall.

"There's a Familiar in there," one of them shouted. "In the dark!"

The sorcerers summoned what meager flame we had onto their staves and moved forward to investigate. The cold kiss of the black air ate at my fire. Protecting one another's backs, we headed silently down the hall. When the grandfather clock chimed the hour, it felt like an explosion going off.

"Does anyone even know what we're looking for?" Valens asked.

Something rustled ahead. We heard the clicking sound of claws on a marble floor, and the world froze.

"Rook?" I whispered.

The beast came out of the darkness.

He lunged at me with his mouth wide open, fangs gleaming. Hooked talons reaching out to catch me. Soulless black pits where his eyes should be, lengthened bones, a face twisted by cruelty.

He wasn't human. Not anymore.

Several sorcerers fell, their flames extinguishing. Screams, then gurgling cries, then silence and the smell of wet blood. The shadows pulsed, feeding on the dead.

"Attack!" Valens swung his stave, shooting a stream of flame.

I joined him, shooting fire into the monster's face, and Rook shied away, hurrying back to the shadows.

Together, we drove the monster into the main hall with waves of flame. Rook curled in on himself, darkness flowing over his body like a cape of protection. He grew larger, more monstrous—the new shadow and fog. But he did not know how to control it, and he shriveled in the face of our assault.

We were going to kill him.

"Stop!" I shouted, trying to push through to Rook. He roared in pain, leaping into the air.

Someone screamed at the corner of the room, by the staircase—Eliza. God, she hadn't left with the other women. She gaped up at the beast, her face white with terror. The sorcerers were all caught off guard by her cries. With shadows bristling on his spine, Rook roared toward her.

Someone threw herself before Eliza.

"Run!" Fanny shouted, her body protecting the girl.

Rook dragged Fanny to the floor as Eliza escaped. Fanny's legs kicked wildly as he buried his fangs in her white neck, and I could have sworn I heard the smallest, most sickening crunch. He began tearing and thrashing like a dog shaking the life out of a rat. Even in the near darkness, I could see the blood gush onto the floor. Fanny stopped striking at Rook. I attacked him then, blindly, because I knew that it wouldn't hurt Fanny. Horrified, I knew she was beyond all that now.

And I heard Magnus's wail.

The sound was agony itself. He charged into battle with a mass of fire at his fingertips. Rook leaped off Fanny and snarled, his mouth dripping with rich, dark blood. Magnus launched fire, strengthening it with wind, and all the others joined him. The onslaught sent Rook crawling across the floor like an animal. Magnus moved to shield his mother's body, his face illuminated, his eyes frenzied.

The front door blasted off its hinges with a squeal of metal. Splinters of wood rained onto the floor. Dark figures in the doorway surged forward, cackling gleefully. Too fast to make a sound, several sorcerers fell, blood gushing from their necks.

"Kill them!" someone roared.

We opened fire on the shadow Familiars, catching two, three, five of them. But there were so many. Two landed on either side of Rook—of what had once been Rook—and lifted him high up into the air.

"Little lady sorcerer," one of the Familiars cackled. I knew it was Gwen. "The bloody king has claimed what is his. You should have gone to him!"

Shoving forward, I exploded in fire, a searing column that took out a group of Familiars. They tumbled to the ground, crisping as I went after Gwen while she laughed and laughed. The men about me shouted to stop—I was going to take the damn house down with me.

There was enough reason in me left to know they were right. The column disappeared, and the room around me was all smoke and darkness and death again.

Gwen and the remaining Familiars flew back out the door with Rook between them, leaping over the threshold and up into the night sky.

I ran alongside the other sorcerers, though I was barely conscious of what I was doing. Pouring outside, we discovered the Familiars and Rook had vanished utterly. The night sky was clear.

Amid the screams and shouts of terror from the guests, Blackwood was shaking me, saying my name. I could barely hear anything, couldn't feel anything.

Until I went back inside the house and found Magnus sitting on the floor, his mother's body cradled in his arms. The candles and lanterns had flickered back to life, illuminating the garish scene. Crimson blood had spattered everywhere, most of it pooling in the center of the room. People had tracked through the gore, leaving red footprints in wild zigzags. Five sorcerer bodies lay upon the tile, gazing vacantly at the ceiling. The ashed corpses of Familiars littered the staircase. Magnus rocked Fanny back and forth, sobbing into her hair. She looked so small now, so fragile. Eliza clutched the banister, weeping openly. Her and Magnus's cries blended in gruesome harmony.

My legs gave out, and I slumped to the floor. I was useless to them, as useless as I was cruel.

Cruel and useless: the Howel family motto.

27

SORCERER FUNERALS ARE HELD AS SOON AS POSSI-
ble. The magic of the earth clamors for its own, so they say. A
day after they had taken Fanny's body from her son, washed
her, tended the horrible gashes in her neck, and dressed her in
her best black gown, we were at the churchyard saying goodbye. The men who had fallen last night would have a grander
ceremony tomorrow, with the queen's blessing. It was a miserable morning, the sky an oppressive gray and the air thick
with bone-chilling mist. Rain would have at least been something.

Blackwood, Eliza, and I listened to the minister's promise
of everlasting life. Eliza crushed a handkerchief and wept as
the final blessings were said over the casket. Then, one by one,
the mourners left, stealing away as awkwardly as dinner guests
who've overstayed their welcome. The undertakers lifted Fanny's shrouded body from the coffin. Sorcerers were never buried in wooden boxes—caskets were for the funeral service. A
sorcerer was wrapped in black silk, head to toe, and placed directly into the ground, to be absorbed by the earth that much
faster. Though Fanny had never had a sorcerer's powers nor

wielded a stave, she had been a sorcerer's daughter and had given birth to a sorcerer son.

I thought about the laughing, happy woman I had met only a few weeks earlier. I could not understand how such a lady now lay under the earth, her body called back into the dirt and the darkness. I thought of the way she'd greeted me when I'd come into her home that first time, as though I were already a friend. As though she could trust me.

Even in my numb state, tears began to fill my eyes. I had allowed Rook to transform and damn himself with her murder. I whimpered so softly only Blackwood noticed.

Magnus stood by the grave's edge, his face pale against his mourning clothes. I had never seen him in black before. His rich auburn hair stood out starkly against his bleak garments and the gray of the day. He dropped the first handful of dirt onto the body, then stayed staring into the grave. There was no flicker of life in his face.

"We'll stop by the house to pay our respects," Blackwood murmured to Eliza. "Since you are his fiancée."

He didn't have to say it so cruelly, I thought.

At the house, black-garbed sorcerers moved silent as shadows. Only the occasional hushed whisper, or the creak of a floorboard, indicated that anyone walked these rooms at all. Sheets had been hung over all the mirrors. On the dining room table, someone had laid out a circle of candles. They were all lit, save one in the very center.

"The unlit candle signifies the sorcerer's extinguished life."

Blackwood stood beside me in the doorway and spoke low. "After sunset, they'll light it and leave it burning the entire night. It's to represent her soul as she moves from this world to the next."

In the parlor, Eliza was sitting beside Magnus, her cheeks stained from crying as she spoke to him gently. He was hunched over with his elbows on his knees, staring at the floor.

Eventually, people drifted out the door. The house grew even quieter, until there was only the ticking of a clock and the muffled sobs of Polly in the kitchen. I looked in to find her sitting down, her apron over her face, wailing bitterly. Through the front window, I saw Dee standing by the side of the house, near a cherry tree. He was leaning his forehead against the trunk and biting on his fist. He would not share his tears with anyone.

I wanted to go to them and offer what comfort I could, but it was as if my voice had been stolen away. The words would not come.

Returning to the parlor, I watched Blackwood collect his sister. They went to gather their hats and cloaks while I sat with Magnus for a moment.

"I'm so sorry," I whispered, finding my voice at last.

It seemed he had not heard me. Then he said, "I could've seen them all safely outside, but I had to go back. I wanted to see what all the *excitement* was about." He laughed bitterly.

"You can't blame yourself."

"I wanted to speak with you before the announcement." He

looked up at me finally. His eyes were clear but cold. The laughing, carefree part of him had been buried back in the churchyard.

"Why?"

"To explain. Our engagement was only to protect Eliza from marrying Foxglove. We planned to end it once a suitable period of time had passed."

My stomach clenched. "Why did you want to tell me?"

"Can you not guess?" He truly looked at me. "You forbade me to speak of my feelings ever again, and I agreed," he growled. "But I couldn't bear to have you think I'd regressed to being a fortune hunter."

"I wouldn't think that," I whispered.

He got up and went to where his grandmother's portrait hung. Leaning against the wall, he said, "I blame myself for what happened. If I'd only told Agrippa, or the Imperator, when I knew Rook was transforming, maybe . . ." He didn't finish his thought but looked at me again. "Then I remembered how you rushed up those stairs, like you knew what was at the top. Tell me." He could barely get the words out. "Did you know what was happening to him?"

My composure finally shattered, and I wept. Magnus slammed his fist into the wall, the sound an explosion in the still house.

"What is it?" Blackwood hurried into the room.

"Nothing. Tend to your sister." Magnus's voice was dull and heavy. Blackwood looked wary of my crying, but he reluctantly obeyed.

Magnus strode over. "I want you to leave, Henrietta," he whispered. Rage was in the deadly tone of his voice. He sat down on the sofa again and stared out the window. "Leave. *Now.*"

I nearly ran from the house. Eliza caught up with me on the pavement, slipping her hand into mine. I was grateful for her strength. We leaned against each other in the carriage on the way home. Blackwood sat across from us, gazing out the window and saying not a word.

When we arrived home, Blackwood went at once to his study. Walking to the stairs, I passed the spot where Fanny had died. Even though the blood had been cleaned, I could tell exactly where it had been. The precise place and moment where everything had changed.

Upstairs, I entered the study to find Blackwood sitting behind the desk, the pulsing glow of the lantern casting harsh shadows over his face, creating a chilling effect of dark sockets where his eyes should have been.

He picked up a gilt-edged book and leafed through it, looking as if he'd crawl into the pages to avoid me. Finally, he spoke.

"It's not that you tried to help Rook. It's not even that you rejected my proposal in favor of him." A muscle jumped in his cheek. He was fighting some deep emotion. "But you lied again. I was a fool to think you'd changed."

Right though he was, I'd had enough guilt today to last a lifetime.

"You might have told me you were ignoring Mickelmas's orders about the weapons, you know." I was on the verge of shouting. "You might have told me you were digging further into your father's research, because . . ."

I stopped, for I still hadn't told him about our shared family histories. Well, he was right about one thing. I hadn't much changed at all. He slammed the book closed, causing an eruption of dust.

"I imagined you as my wife. My best self. I pictured Sorrow-Fell as a type of Eden, and you my Eve." He sounded furious, and more than that, disappointed. "I was wrong."

"Perhaps it's for the best," I said tartly. "Adam and Eve made a pretty pathetic end."

Without waiting for his reply, I stormed out. Going down the stairs, I gripped the banister to keep myself upright. The butler awaited me below, a tray with the post balanced in his gloved hand.

"Miss Howel, a letter's arrived for you."

I thanked him and took the note, ripping the envelope with shaking hands. Immediately, I recognized a familiarly loopy script.

> *Howel,*
> *Come at once.*
> *Poison.*
> *Lambe*

I rushed to grab my cloak and bonnet, called for the carriage, and went straight out the door.

WOLFF AND LAMBE HAD TAKEN ROOMS in Camden, preferring privacy to life in the barracks. Their surroundings were humbler than most sorcerer boys would accept. Their neighbors were charwomen and stallkeepers, and the flat they shared was small. But they had made it their own, and quite comfortable.

Several paintings of countryside and waterfowl, amateurish by the look of them, lay against the wall waiting to be hung. A breakfast tray hadn't been cleared yet, eggs congealing upon a plate, cold tea growing cloudy in a cup. In a corner of the sitting room, Wolff's cello and Lambe's violin rested against each other, a strangely comforting sight, as though they were propping each other up.

Wolff let me in—it was surprising to see him home at this hour. His normally neat hair was spiked all over his head. Thick stubble coated his chin. He didn't bother to ask why I'd arrived—instead, he guided me quickly into the parlor.

"He said you'd be here. He needs to tell you something."

Dear God. Lambe was laid out on the sofa, his hands arranged over his chest. He keened softly.

Poison.

Wolff knelt beside Lambe and placed a large hand on the other boy's forehead. Lambe's eyelids were so translucent and thin that one could make out the tracery of every blue vein. His breath came in worrisome gasps.

"What did he take?" I asked Wolff.

"Nothing. He wouldn't eat or drink these past few days—

he was too weak to attend Lady Eliza's party." Had Lambe foreseen what would happen at the ball? No, I didn't think so. His prophetic powers didn't work so clear as that. "This morning, he wrote that he wanted to see you, and then fainted. I've tried waking him." Wolff's voice cracked with fear.

The first thing to do was revive him. "I need chamomile and gingerroot, if you've got any." Maria had told me how soothing those ingredients could be. "And some clear broth." Wolff sent me downstairs to the landlady, a broad-armed woman who tsked to see an unmarried young lady in a gentlemen's flat, sorcerers or no. But she gave me what I wanted.

I brewed Lambe a cup of tea and forced him to drink. Most of it ran down his chin, but it was a start. His eyes fluttered open, and Wolff groaned in relief.

"Are you all right?" I whispered. Wheezing, Lambe tugged at my sleeve.

"You will. Won't you?" he asked. His pupils were dilated.

"Won't I what?" I said. He slurped more tea, and Wolff managed to give him a few spoonfuls of hot broth.

"Help the girl defeat the woman. It's the only way," he whispered. Then, "Poison." He said the word twice more, emphasizing it.

"Someone poisoned you?" I whispered.

Wolff swore, but Lambe shook his head. He took more broth, mopping it in a piece of bread. Faint color returned to his waxen-looking cheeks.

"Listen. Poison. Belladonna. You must take it. Take the

belladonna when you can," he rasped. Belladonna was incredibly lethal. Lambe was clearly delirious. "Take the belladonna and you'll finally know the truth. The poison will show you."

"I don't know what he's talking about half the time." Wolff swiped the back of his hand over his eyes. "I warned him about drinking their damned Etheria juice."

"Why did he go to the priory in the first place?" I laid a cold cloth on Lambe's face. "I thought he wanted to stay in London."

"He said that there were things he could only learn up north."

"I'll get some more cold water from downstairs," I said, wringing the cloth and taking up the basin.

I walked out the door, but halfway to the landlady's rooms I realized I'd forgotten to bring the tray. I ran back up, opened the door . . . and stopped in my tracks.

Wolff had Lambe tight in his arms. Lambe murmured gently while Wolff kissed his forehead, his cheek, his lips. Lambe's pale, thin fingers tangled in the other boy's hair. Their embrace was tender, passionate even. What in the devil?

I backed away and accidentally knocked into the door. Wolff released Lambe and shot to his feet. We stared at each other, neither seeming to know what to do. What had I seen? A tortured moment ticked by in silence.

"I should leave," I said, setting down the basin as I tried to find my cloak. I'd no idea how to behave. Wolff trailed me as I walked around the room, bumping up against one of the chairs.

"Why won't you look at me?" He sounded heavy.

"I don't know what you mean." Forcing myself to stay calm, I brought my eyes to his. He sighed.

"I can see how much you loathe it. What we are," he muttered.

"I could never loathe you." The idea of it shocked me from my stupor. Damn it all to hell, this was Wolff. My friend. Shoving his hands into his pockets, he sat next to the sofa. Lambe reached out his hand, and Wolff took it. I was struck by the honest fearlessness of that simple gesture.

"You'll run straight to Whitechurch now," Wolff said.

"No. Never." I found my normal voice at last. They could be excommunicated if anyone knew about this relationship, perhaps even jailed.

Wolff brushed a piece of hair out of Lambe's face, his expression full of tenderness.

"I won't give him up. Not for the world. Maybe it's a half life, living this lie, but it's the only one I want." He looked up at me. "No matter what I do, I'm trapped." His voice wavered.

His pain was palpable, and I recognized that sensation of living and breathing a lie. Damned if I would let another friendship be ruined, I sat beside the sofa, took up the teacup, and offered it to Lambe once more.

"I don't bloody care what you do. Whitechurch will never hear about it from me." As far as I'd seen in my life, love was too rare to squander.

Wolff touched my shoulder before going to the table. He

picked up a plate of food and then returned, and together we tried to get Lambe to eat something solid. After a while, Lambe was able to finish half of some cold mutton stew. His cheeks regained their color.

"You're all right," I said, relieved.

"Yes. There's one more thing to discuss, though." Lambe focused on me. "The bells."

I nearly dropped the cup. "Bells?"

"Molochoron at York. Yes, and the Skinless Man is there as well." He quirked an eyebrow and took a bite of potato.

"How . . . did you . . ." I couldn't finish.

"I returned to London because I am to be your mirror, Howel, now and in the wars to come." He nodded. "I will help you with the Imperator."

"Thank you," I breathed. Yes, we would hunt down R'hlem together.

Because I'd decided something, watching Magnus cry over his mother's body and Rook scream like an animal. My father was responsible for all of this, and I would stop him . . . no matter the cost.

28

WHITECHURCH WATCHED THE HOVERING SQUARE of water glass, brows furrowed. Lambe waited in the front row of the obsidian cathedral, his pale hair visible from where I sat. I crossed my fingers in my lap as Whitechurch scanned scene after scene until he came to what he wanted.

"That," he said with quiet excitement, "is R'hlem."

Indeed, we caught faint glimpses of a man striding through a swarm of Familiars. He was taller than most, his face slick with blood. R'hlem was there. He hadn't moved from his position outside York.

When Lambe had come to Whitechurch two days earlier with tales of his "vision," Whitechurch had at first been hesitant to believe it. But he'd investigated on his own and located the Skinless Man. Every few hours since then, he'd watched and waited to see how R'hlem moved, what he did, if his days held a particular pattern. The rest of the Order was brought in to observe, and soon it became obvious that R'hlem had stationed himself. He was not moving.

Now would be the time to strike.

Blackwood sat beside me, but he might as well have been

on the moon for all he acknowledged my presence. Since our arguments in the aviary and then the study, he'd become like a stranger. Fine. I could ignore him just as easily.

"The time has come." Whitechurch melted the glass, returning it to a ball of water and draining it into the elemental pit.

Sorcerers began asking questions, but I'd a fair idea of what was coming. We'd march to R'hlem, the boys and I armed with our weapons. Several squadrons would protect our little group, forming a block on all sides. If we moved swiftly, without alerting the other Ancients, we could surround R'hlem and take him down. Yes, his psychic powers could be extraordinary—I knew that from firsthand experience—but with sorcerers attacking from every direction, he'd be overwhelmed. That would give us the opportunity needed to strike. And by us, I meant me.

It had been the queen's particular wish that I strike the final blow.

My heart hammered to think about it. Even after all of this—Rook, Magnus's mother, the death of so many people—even now I didn't know if I had such an act inside me.

To kill one's own father required something monstrous.

"How are we to approach him, sir?" Dee called.

"I believe I can be of service in that particular area," a delicate, feminine voice said. Queen Mab stepped out of the shadows, arriving from Faerie between one heartbeat and the next. God knows how long she'd been listening. At least she'd worn a more modest gown for this occasion. The sleeves were long, her bosom fully covered, though the fabric still seemed to be woven from spider silk and dusted with moth-wing powder.

Blackwood stiffened. We both knew what was being suggested.

"My Faerie roads are the surest path across your country." Mab twirled a piece of hair on a pale little finger. "You can be in the north after two hours of marching, and the Skinless Man won't be able to track you."

There was much happy murmuring among the sorcerers. I noticed Magnus in the crowd, deliberately facing away from the faerie queen. He'd put on his naval clothes once more, though he kept a black band tied about his upper arm to signify mourning. I knew he did not want anything to do with Mab. But needs must.

"Indeed," Whitechurch said. "We join with Mab's forces. We march north. We circle. We divide the Ancients and vanquish R'hlem. We end this war." His voice boomed upon the obsidian walls. As one, the Order rose to its feet, the applause thunderous. Mab beamed and waved at the crowd, as though she'd won something.

"Do you think we're ready?" I asked Blackwood. For the first time since the day of Fanny's funeral, he looked at me straight on.

"We'll have to be." That was all I got from him.

THAT EVENING, I MADE MY WAY upstairs to the apothecary, half of which had already been scrubbed and packed away. Fenswick didn't want the Order finding any of his "experiments." He was squatting on the table, stacking bowls when I entered.

"I'm so sorry," I said.

The hobgoblin only laid three bronze measuring spoons into a napkin and tied it up.

"I should have informed the Order myself." He held a dried yellow flower of some kind to a candle flame and watched it burn. The smoke was cloyingly sweet, like incense. Maria came out of the back room, a few small objects gathered in her apron. She wiped her eyes with her sleeve.

"We've destroyed nearly everything dangerous." She sniffed. I handed her my handkerchief, my initials embroidered upon it in blue thread. She blew her nose, then said, "I should go. If they find me out, you know what they'll do."

"Where can you go?" My heart wrenched at the idea.

"Maria shall come with me into Faerie," Fenswick said, packing two velvet pouches into a little wooden box. "The roads can take her wherever she wishes."

"Will *you* be all right?" she asked me.

"Of course." I forced myself to mean it. I didn't want to part with either of them, but keeping her and Fenswick safe was more important than anything else. Together, we finished cleaning the shelves, scrubbing out the evidence, and packing their few bags. Soon it was as if no one had been there. "Until we meet again, Miss Templeton," I said.

Miss at least made her smile. "Until then."

Maria tried to return my handkerchief, but I closed her fingers around it. "Give it to me next time," I said.

I needed to pretend there would be another meeting.

"We must move quickly," Fenswick said as Maria picked him up and shouldered her pack.

"One last thing." She took her ax from its place by the door, though Fenswick grumbled about the iron. Then she walked to the corner of the room and, under Fenswick's guidance, stepped gingerly into a line of shadow. They vanished at once.

I found myself alone once more. Even the turtledove's cage was empty. Maria had set the creature free.

29

THREE DAYS LATER, ELIZA AND LADY BLACKWOOD were sent north to Sorrow-Fell, along with most of the servants and an escort of five sorcerers. We'd tried to get them access to the Faerie roads, but Mab had been strict about who could use them. Besides, I didn't like to think of them wandering those paths beneath the earth. Lilly was one of the few who stayed behind with the house. When I tried to get her to go with the others, she simply shook her head.

"If it's all the same, I feel safer here. And I'll be waiting to greet you when you come home victorious, miss." She smiled.

The remaining household all turned out to see the ladies off. Lady Blackwood walked out of the house and climbed into the carriage without so much as a word or a look. She was swathed totally in black, from her lace shawl to her gloves, and a thick, opaque black veil covered her face entirely. Not an inch of her was visible. She passed me as though I did not exist. Eliza came next. I kissed her cheek, and she embraced me. "Why won't you come with us?"

"It's my duty," I said. I spoke the words with all the passion of a novice actress in a theatrical company. These days, my duty did not please me. Inside the depths of the carriage, I heard Lady Blackwood coughing. "I'm sorry for what happened at your ball," I whispered to Eliza. She waved away my apology.

"Don't worry about me," she said softly. Leaning closer, she whispered, "It's a pretend engagement, you know." Eliza sniffed. "Magnus was never on my list of prospective suitors. Poor as he was, how could he be? But I confess the idea of it makes me happy, even knowing it's a lie." She tried to grin and climbed into the carriage. "I'll see you at Sorrow-Fell." She said it hopefully. The footman closed the door, and they departed. A cart filled with the servants bumped behind them down the road, and the sorcerers rode alongside on horseback.

Blackwood had not come out of the doorway. He watched the carriage until it disappeared. When I went to speak with him, he vanished into the house.

I KNOCKED AT HIS STUDY THAT evening, receiving no answer. But the lantern light seeping from beneath the door told me he was inside. That night, and the night after, I had my meals alone, walked alone through echoing halls. It was like living in a marvelous tomb. I would sit by the fire in the library and imagine Rook coming in to say good night. Or I would go to the place where Fanny . . . it became difficult to even think the word. I would sit on the stairs, smooth my skirts, and listen to the utter silence. The memories sat beside me, laid their heads in my lap.

There was nothing else to do but reflect and prepare.

Whitechurch was selective about who would undertake

the mission, choosing the fittest and strongest fighters. Valens, Wolff, and Lambe were among the few warriors chosen to remain behind, to keep the barriers secure.

Blackwood, Magnus, Dee, and I worked every day, planning how we would ambush R'hlem. Despite being constantly near one another, we had as little interaction as possible. Magnus actively avoided me. Blackwood would address me always in an impersonal tone. Even Dee was distant.

Every time we practiced the final moment—Magnus and Blackwood at the sides, Dee behind with the flute—I delivered the killing blow, a short upward jab with my dagger, careful to avoid the rib cage. And then a slash across the throat, just in case.

R'hlem, the skinless monstrosity, dying at my feet. But William Howel, the man who'd read my mother poetry as they eloped, bleeding alongside him.

Every night, I lay in bed and asked myself if I could do it. And every night, silence was the only reply.

FINALLY, THE DAY ARRIVED. WHITECHURCH SPENT the morning in consultation with his Masters, appraising R'hlem's movement. They'd got his pattern down and had selected a hilly terrain ideally suited for attack on the high ground. The time had come to march.

I drank tea with a shaking hand while Lilly prepared me. Every button hooked, every pin placed, every lace tied had the weight of goodbye. If this failed, we would never have this routine again.

"You look very nice," Lilly said when she'd finished. I wasn't sure who moved first, but we embraced quickly. She was so short that my chin nestled in her hair. The bells began tolling outside, calling the squadrons into position. Today, it seemed that all of London held its breath. The street corners were silent, the windows of every tavern and shop shuttered.

We assembled by the river, standing side by side in the early morning as our robes moved in a breeze off the water. I'd the bone whistle around my neck, Porridge on one hip, a dagger on the other. The little dagger rested in its sheath up my left sleeve.

Thorn knights with oaken armor walked through our ranks, inspecting us. The faerie creatures congregated at the head of the line, raising twisted-looking horns to their lips to sound the signal to advance.

As one, we marched forward, following the Fae.

The transition from our world to Faerie was immediate: the air chilled on my skin, the wind died in my hair. We followed a road lined on either side by tall, bony-looking trees that pointed upward like accusing fingers. The sky—for there *was* a sky—was speckled with constellations I didn't recognize. There was no Ursa Major, no Orion's Belt.

I was in the front squadron with Whitechurch, Blackwood, and Magnus. The Goodfellow we'd seen before in Cornwall stopped us in our path.

"Halt," the faerie said, wooden joints creaking. "Imperator, Her Majesty wishes for you and these four," he said, pointing to Magnus, Blackwood, Dee, and me, "to meet in her chambers."

"We've no time to entertain Mab," Whitechurch said, sounding impatient. Blackwood sighed; he knew the Fae did not appreciate rudeness. But the Goodfellow didn't seem put out.

"Her Majesty says it's a matter of a toll."

Magnus flinched, and I barely kept from cursing. Still, there'd be no progress until we appeased Mab, and Whitechurch seemed to understand that as well. The creature led us away, and the call for the squadrons to hold position rang out. Soon we'd lost them in the dark.

After a few turns down a rocky road, we arrived at a wooden door in a great rock face. The Goodfellow tapped his spear against the door and it swung open, revealing a low-ceilinged room, rather like a burrow. The place smelled peaty and damp. I rubbed my hands together, willing myself to take heart. We'd be gone from this place soon.

Mab appeared quite literally from nowhere. Her midnight-blue dress, studded with pearls, was so low-cut it went to her navel. Much was revealed.

"Is it time for the war yet?" She clapped her little hands like a gleeful child.

"We are prepared to move, Majesty," Whitechurch said. He already sounded tired of indulging the queen.

"Oh, I'm sure you are. And you *will* be moving. Shortly."

She smiled, showing a bit too many sharp teeth for my liking, and played with the skirt around her legs. "My tall one will be quite safe. As for the rest of you, who can tell?"

I didn't like the way she'd said that. The wooden door had vanished, leaving a wall of solid earth. Whitechurch's words became clipped.

"Enough of this. When do we leave?"

"You leave now." Mab reclined onto a chaise of moss, wriggling her bare toes. "What a shame, tall girl, that your friend turned so terribly shadowlike. Such a disappointment."

It became difficult to breathe.

"How do you know about Rook?" I murmured, gooseflesh creeping up my arms. Mab giggled, as though I'd asked a silly thing.

"Because I ordered it, of course. Where's my little doctor?" She peered around the room, one hand shading her eyes for dramatic effect. Someone moved in the corner, and then Fenswick appeared, holding his four hands behind his back in an apologetic fashion. "Your human was healing, apparently. Someone had to fix that. What would dear R'hlem do without his Shadow and Fog?"

I couldn't have understood what she'd said. But the way Fenswick averted his eyes, his ears drooping, was undeniable.

Rook had been healing, and Fenswick had *poisoned* him.

"Madame, are you saying you had knowledge of the Ancients' hold on that boy?" Whitechurch reached for his stave.

Mab opened her mouth and screamed. Her scream pierced

my brain and rattled my vision, a siren song from hell. My ears felt as if they might explode.

Something twined about my arms and pulled them to my sides. Vines sprouted from the earth and coiled down from the ceiling. A loop of vine cinched around my waist, dragging me to my knees. Blackwood, Dee, and Magnus shouted as the same happened to them. Soldiers, the Goodfellow among them, burst from out of the very walls, going from clay to flesh in an instant, and forced Whitechurch to his knees. They held his arms and pulled his head back to look the faerie queen in the eye.

"You treacherous creature," Whitechurch spit. He struggled against the guards. "Why?"

"Because you are too greedy, Imperator." Her girlish tittering died. "You never thank me for the bodies of my lovely subjects lost fighting your stupid wars. R'hlem understands. He knows the Fae are not his enemies. So the bloody king has offered a marvelous bargain," Mab cooed, flicking her fingers at Whitechurch's eye. He jerked in pain. "He burns your kingdom and gives my people the north again." She sighed. "And we receive ten thousand Englishmen as slaves. Isn't it glorious?"

I began to set fire to the vines. One of the knights took a blade of bone and held it to Blackwood's throat. Mab lifted an eyebrow.

"Would you care to use your power now?" she asked me sweetly. Blackwood winced as the knife cut him.

My fire disappeared at once.

"Howel, do what you must," Blackwood snapped. Mab patted his cheek.

"Isn't your sister on the road to your estate, my little lordling? Would you care to test me?"

"You demon." Magnus pulled against his bonds.

Mab huffed and turned back to Whitechurch. She leaned closer, a malevolent light in her eyes. "You know, there's a toll to be paid for using my roads."

Whitechurch didn't flinch as Mab trotted over to one of her soldiers and drew a long, savage-looking bone sword from his scabbard. She grinned, licking her teeth. "I think your head will be payment enough," she said, pointing to Whitechurch with the tip. Then, to me, "Frankly, I'd take yours, but he wants *you* without a hair out of place. Can't imagine why."

The perfect image of William Howel I had carried in my heart was gone forever. Of all the reasons to hate R'hlem, that might have been the greatest.

"And you." She sniffed at Blackwood, Dee, and Magnus. "Well, I'll make up my mind later."

"Sorcerers." Whitechurch looked at us. He no longer struggled against his captors. There was no fear in him. He refused to give her that. "Her Majesty commended you."

While the boys screamed, I could only stay silent in horror as Mab sliced off Whitechurch's head in one clean sweep.

30

"I THINK HE'LL LOOK QUITE NICE ON A MANTEL," Mab said conversationally, shaking Whitechurch's head by his hair. Drops of blood rained onto the earthen floor. "Though I'm not sure what a mantel is. Hmmph." Mab chucked the head across the ground, then gestured to her soldiers. "Take their weapons."

They took our swords and daggers, snatched the whip and the flute off the boys. They ripped the bone whistle from my neck and grabbed my dagger as well, piling them into a corner along with our staves. I wanted to cry out for Porridge, as I felt strangely sure my stave was crying out for me.

I stared at Whitechurch's crumpled form. I wouldn't allow myself to shrink away from the image. I memorized the slumped angle of his body, the blood-speckled collar of his shirt.

Her Majesty commended you. What had the queen said the night I became a sorcerer? *I grant my commendation, that you will take up arms in my defense, that you will live and die for my country and my person, and that your magic shall find its greatest purpose in the service of others.* Whitechurch had ordered us to remember.

Feeling surged through me. We were *not* going to die in this place.

Mab went to Blackwood. "Lord of Sorrow-Fell." She said it with mockery. "I don't care if it's my sister's property. Humans settling Faerie lands? Disgusting." She spit in his face. Blackwood didn't move a muscle.

"I doubt Your Majesty has read much of Dante. According to him, the lowest level of hell is reserved for traitors," he murmured.

Mab snorted with laughter, then frowned at Dee. "Who are you? Oh, wait." She slapped his face. "I don't care."

Finally, she moved to Magnus, whose eyes glinted with challenge. Mab purred, sliding her hands through his hair.

"Mmm, such a handsome young man. The epitome of beauty." She pressed herself against him. With the vines holding his body, Magnus was helpless. "I was going to kill all three of you boys, but I think I'll keep you as my pet. You really will look so nice chained to my wall. You'll be *such* fun to play with." She traced the tip of one finger along Magnus's jaw. "As long as your youth and beauty last, of course. Then you'll be scrumptious food for my little goblins." Leaning forward, she licked his cheek. "What do you say to that?"

"Madame." Magnus gave a breathtaking smile and instructed her to do something with herself that was physically impossible. The faerie went rigid. "Would you take that as an answer?"

"Maybe I'll feed you to my goblins now," she growled.

"Good, because I'm rather bored by the company."

My mind raced. If I freed myself, I'd be too late to keep Mab from killing the boys. How the devil was I to manage this?

Something fluttered into my lap. It was a handkerchief, with *HH* embroidered at the corner in dark blue thread. It looked exactly like my old handkerchief.

Because it *was* mine. I peered up at the soldier standing watch over me, a short creature with a wooden helmet and a visor of bone. Impossible to see who it was.

The vines at my wrists gave, and the one about my waist went slack. The soldier was cutting me free with . . . yes, an iron ax. No one noticed. All eyes were upon Magnus and the queen.

Maria's voice whispered in my ear, "When I signal, fire."

No music had ever sounded as sweet as her voice in that moment.

Across the room, Fenswick put one clawed finger to his lips: silence.

"Let's begin by cutting something off," Mab mused, laying the edge of her sword on Magnus's arm. "You won't need your hands. Will you?"

The last vines fell. I would have only one chance at this. Leering, Mab raised her sword.

Maria threw her ax, splitting open the head of the soldier who held the knife on Blackwood. Mab squealed, and while she was distracted, I stood.

Throwing out my hands, I unleashed my powers.

Flame billowed from my fingers, consuming the pale queen in one violent burst. She dropped her weapon with a scream and crumpled to the ground. I didn't stop, even when her shrieks died and her body shriveled. I kept my flame on her, the smell of charring flesh and burnt hair making my eyes water. She wanted to put Whitechurch's head on a mantel? I wouldn't stop until there was nothing left but a greasy smear.

Maria wrenched her ax from the dead guard and attacked the Goodfellow and his soldiers. Fenswick, meanwhile, proceeded to cut the boys from the vines. They grabbed their staves from where Mab had put them by the side of the room, and joined the fight. Soon all the faerie knights formed a crude pile on the ground, and the queen was left in a smoldering heap. We retrieved the weapons as quickly as we could, strapping on swords and daggers with shaking hands.

"Wait," Magnus growled as he marched toward Mab. "I've appendages to remove."

"There's no time!" Fenswick touched the earthen wall, and the wooden doorway reformed. "You need to return to London—now!"

Maria pulled off her helmet, tossing it to the side as she shook out her hair.

"Did you know about this?" Blackwood demanded.

"She's innocent." Fenswick moved before her protectively. "I thought they'd let her pass safely, but they took her prisoner."

"The doctor only just got me out," she said to me, "else I'd have gone back to warn you."

"You can't expect us to believe that," Blackwood said.

"Well, seeing as we narrowly escaped having our limbs chopped off, I'm willing to go on some faith." Magnus strapped his sword about his waist, and we followed Fenswick back onto the smoky darkness of the road. Ahead was an empty path choked with black brush. The other squadrons had vanished from sight.

Blackwood hoisted Fenswick into the air and shook him. "How could you?" he shouted. Fenswick's legs kicked uselessly.

"I'd no choice. R'hlem wanted another Shadow and Fog, to seal the bargain between our races."

My heart twisted. No matter the cost, I'd take all the rest of his beloved pets from him.

Focus. We've no time for this now.

I made Blackwood stop shaking the hobgoblin, then yanked on his ear while he squealed. Was I being rough? Undoubtedly. "Where are the squadrons?"

"Gone." Fenswick swallowed. "They're being butchered as we speak."

I could hear the faint cries already fading on the wind. Leaving the others, I ran down the path while Fenswick shouted at me to come back. Branches tore at my clothes, slowed my speed. Eventually, I had to stop altogether.

"I can't see them," Blackwood whispered, coming up behind me. It was difficult to see anything at all. Above, the stars had gone out, the slate of constellations wiped clean.

"They've been trapped in the shadowed realm. No one who goes can ever return." Fenswick twitched his ears. "You must get to London."

"Why must we do anything you say?" I wanted to *kill* him.

"The roads are now open for R'hlem's army," he said. That shut all of us up. "They'll be able to march past the barrier. With half the forces gone and no Fae intervention, it'll be an open season."

"My God," Dee breathed.

"If R'hlem starts now, he'll be there in only a few hours. You must evacuate the city before it's too late."

The queen was in residence at Buckingham Palace. R'hlem could end this war today.

"Let's go," Blackwood said, guiding us back down the path. Somewhere in the blackness, I swore I could still hear the voices of sorcerers crying for help. I imagined the men drowning in eternal blackness. Every step I took was a necessary torture.

"Hurry," Fenswick whispered as we tripped and smashed into each other. I didn't dare use my fire, as it would be a beacon for any monster that wanted to hunt us. My palms prickled, though, my impulse to ignite a burning whisper in my skin. No matter how many breathing exercises I performed, the rage did not die.

As we walked, I swore I heard *something* moving about on

the path behind us. But tendrils of mist and the wet smell of moss were all that confronted me when I looked. Still, some invisible thing scraped closer.

"Fast. Fast now," Magnus said, leading the charge. Dee hoisted up Maria when she tripped, and Blackwood summoned a minor gale to keep the thing back. We rocketed through the bramble, my skirt catching on a branch and ripping. If we survived this, I would get a pair of bloody trousers.

Finally, we entered a clearing. Two winding paths diverged ahead of us, and Fenswick cursed. "I always get lost around here. One leads to London."

Darkness moved on the path behind. Something breathed.

A creature charged out of the wood. Maria swung her ax, sending the thing skidding backward. The beast had a hound's rudimentary form but bristled all over with mushrooms and branches. Its clawed feet raked the earth, and the stench of it— boggy and rancid at once—made my eyes water. Snapping back its head in a howl, it revealed a mouth jagged with thorn-teeth.

Cursing, Magnus led us in a group spell that drained the horrid thing of its water. A puddle formed before us as the beast cracked open like drying mud. But then it began to twitch, re-forming and reshaping as water filled it once again. We couldn't hold it forever.

"Keep going!" Fenswick leaped out of Magnus's arms, gripping the monster by its face. His small talons dug in as the hound shook its head, Fenswick clinging for his very life.

Blackwood pulled me down the right-hand tunnel. *Please,*

let it lead us home. Let it be correct. Behind us, the sounds of pursuit and struggle died, and soon there was only our harried breathing in the darkness. I used Porridge as a torch and held it aloft.

Some murky light formed ahead, marking the tunnel's end. We stopped, boots sinking into the mud.

"What if it's the wrong way?" Magnus cursed as howling echoed behind us. Fenswick hadn't been able to hold the beast off.

No time to second-guess. I charged ahead.

We catapulted into sunlight. The air was clear, the sky above a bit hazy and overcast. But we were outside, in the natural world once more. I could have fallen to my knees and kissed the ground.

We stood upon a grassy slope, a dense forest at our backs. That was the first troubling sign. Gray and white gulls wheeled overhead, while nearby waves crashed on a beach. Salt laced the wind.

This wasn't London.

A signpost on the road ahead pointed in two opposite directions. The first advertised DOVER, 5 MILES. The second, pointing north, read LONDON, 70 MILES.

"We're in Kent," Blackwood said, his voice lifeless. Magnus threw down his stave and screamed, while Dee sat heavily. We couldn't go back into Faerie; the risk of the roads was too great.

We wouldn't reach London in time.

31

BLACKWOOD ADJUSTED THE WATER GLASS, SHOW-
ing a new location as we all watched in shock. We'd used it to
peer ahead down the road and found swarms of Familiars—
ravens, skinless, shadows, lice, trolls—roaming the area. They
flooded abandoned villages and gnawed like animals on bones
picked clean. Kent had been one of the "red zones" in the war
ever since R'hlem had taken Canterbury three years earlier.
Like an infection, his influence had spread. "Going over ground
won't be easy." Blackwood released the glass, and the water
rained down.

If only I knew how to use the magician porter runes. I
should have begged Mickelmas to teach me when I had the
chance.

"Well, there might be a boat." Magnus dusted his trousers.
He'd swallowed his earlier rage and was all business again.

"This area's deserted, but best of luck," Blackwood muttered.

Maria followed Magnus and Dee down the path toward
the beach while I pulled up fistfuls of grass and tried to think
of anything useful. I was no sorcerer Master; I knew only the

most rudimentary magician spells. All I really had was my fire ability, and that wouldn't help us.

"This is my fault." Blackwood put his head in his hands, his raven hair a tangled mess. "I didn't see through Mab's lies. I've lost the war," he groaned.

But he hadn't been the one to decipher R'hlem's whereabouts and send everyone down the blasted Faerie roads. Nor had he been the one to suggest using the weapons, which had started this all in the first place. No, that had been my own brand of selfish pride. I must *always* be the one with the answer.

"Magnus found a boat!" Maria called, running up the hill and rousing us from our self-pity.

We followed her to the beach, passing the shattered remains of a town. The stone houses had been ripped down to their foundations; sun-bleached carts and wagons were swallowed by overgrown grass. The hill sloped down to the beach, the earth giving way to white sand and sea grass. We'd come to a small cove, and anchored fifty feet off shore was a fishing vessel. Magnus waved aboard the deck, Dee beside him.

Blackwood took Maria by the waist and floated them both toward the boat. I followed, growing more unsteady the closer I drew to the water. I narrowly made it onto the deck before falling. My corseted ribs ached as I tried to get up. Maria, however, looked perfectly comfortable as she helped unfurl the canvas sails. Magnus frowned at her. "Should you really come with us?"

"Think I can't handle myself?" She spit into the sea.

"My dear, you can handle yourself better than most men. But this is *magical* war."

Maria gave me a pointed look.

"We can't leave her behind," I said. Her abilities weren't my secret to tell.

As Magnus steered us out of the cove, I peered over the ship's side and noticed its name: *La Bella Donna*.

Take the belladonna, Lambe had said. I bit my lip. Bloody psychics. Hopefully, he had foreseen our victory as well.

AN HOUR LATER, MARIA AND I were leaning against the railing, listening to the taut snap of the sails and the slap of water against the hull. Blackwood provided wind to keep the vessel moving. Dee sat beside him, and Magnus continued to steer. I would relieve Blackwood of his position soon, but for now there was nothing to do except sit and prepare.

"How much do you think I'll be gone?" Maria asked.

"God knows." My eyes tracked the faint coastline, and I imagined that rolling green replaced by a vision of my father atop Buckingham Palace's steps, surveying London's carnage with pleasure.

My father. The shock and horror of his discovery had worn off, and a cancerous sort of admiration had wormed its way into my heart. What orphan child doesn't dream that her parent is a long lost monarch? William Howel, humble solicitor, had metamorphosed into a king of nightmares. He did not cower or bow. He did not lie.

When I met him in the flesh, would I find any remnants of goodness? Or had his greatness burned that humanity away?

As the sun neared the horizon, we entered Southend-on-Sea, the gateway to the Thames and to London. Land appeared on both sides of us, far enough away that it was difficult to pick out details. Large, round rocks and boulders dotted the shoreline.

Blackwood stepped up beside me. The wind had a bite to it, and I shivered. Without saying anything, Blackwood took off his coat and draped it across my shoulders. When I tried to return it, he stopped me. "I'm all right."

I buried myself in the coat, still warm from his body. It smelled of the dark earth of Faerie, twined with his own particular scent of clean soap and linen.

"I'm afraid to see London," he said, a quiet admission. He looked down into the sea. "Whitechurch is dead." His voice sounded so small with realization.

"Who will be the new Imperator?" If there would ever be a new one. If the Order, and the queen, and London, and a free England still existed tomorrow.

"In times like these, the monarch appoints one until the Order can hold a proper vote." A wave stretched up over the side. With a quick, graceful sweep of his stave, Blackwood sent it back down into the sea. My shivering had stopped.

"Here," I murmured, slipping out of the coat.

He took it, staring at it as if he'd never seen one before. Then, "I'm sorry." The words were so soft the wind nearly carried them away. "I should never have shut you out."

"You've no reason to apologize," I said.

"But I do. I wanted you to yearn for me." He put on the coat, his movements slow and mechanical. "But I realized that you don't need me as badly as I need you."

"I need you," I said, and meant it. But Blackwood seemed resigned.

"It can't be the same. You grew up in the open air, with Rook." He gripped the railing. "I was raised in a dark place. The only two people who knew my secrets disliked me." His voice quavered. "You are the first and only person who saw me and still cared. How could I not love you? How could I hope you would understand what *need* is in that kind of love?"

He choked on the last word. I felt that I'd unlocked a door hidden at the back of a dark house to find the most essential part of him: a lonely little boy watching out the window for visitors who would not come. Gently, I laid my hand on top of his own, feeling the strain in his fingers.

The boat came to a sudden, jerking halt. We all fell forward, Blackwood nearly tipping over the side. The wind still filled the sails, making them taut, but the boat rested.

"What—?" Magnus went to the back, puzzled. Then, "Everyone, come here." His voice held an edge. Just below the surface of the water was a shimmering mass that clung to the bottom of the boat. At first I thought it a kind of weed, but when I touched it, it stuck to my fingers like a web.

A spiderweb. I yanked myself away, stifling a scream.

"Don't pull on it," Blackwood hissed, grabbing my hand.

Maria whistled. "It may be too late for all that."

In the distance, by the eastern shore, one of those large boulders I'd noticed earlier stirred. It shifted and began to move toward the boat. Inch by inch, foot by foot, the boulder rose higher, revealing itself to be no rock at all but an *abdomen*.

Her fifty-foot-long body glistened in the weak light. Mottled brown in color, with violent green and purple decorating the pulsing sides, the enormous abdomen belonged to a creature with eight legs as long as trees. Three round eyes, each large as the window of a house, eased out of the sea to study us. Dripping pincers emerged.

Nemneris the Water Spider perched on her web, front two legs moving rhythmically up and down, a silent monstrosity.

She was beautiful in her hideousness, a totemic god. Such a massive thing should not be so deathly quiet, but she was—it was a moment born from the most feverish nightmare. With that jerking crawl peculiar to arachnids, she made her way toward us. The boat shook with each pull of the web.

We were frozen, until Maria shattered the hypnotic peace with a short, piercing scream. As if a spell had been broken, we acted.

This couldn't be the end. We still had to get to London; I still needed to fight R'hlem. Dimly, I recalled something of that prophecy tapestry in Agrippa's home, something about a drowning poison. After all, shadow had burned above the city when Korozoth was destroyed. Perhaps this was *meant* to be. Perhaps the great Water Spider would die today.

Or at the very least, perhaps we would not. Hope flooded my veins, spurring me.

We considered abandoning ship, but it wouldn't work. The western shore was too far away, and it would be impossible to reach on one gust of wind alone. We'd fall into the water and into her web.

As Nemneris crawled forward, we lined up on the starboard side with our staves and the new weapons. Maria kept behind me, squeezing my shoulder. I'd never seen her so afraid before.

"I don't like spiders," she muttered.

Dee pulled out the flute and began to play. Nemneris stopped in her tracks and rose up. Her scream was more horrifying than her silence, the sound insectile and shrill. Webbing shot out of her pincered mouth, aimed directly at our boat. I launched my flame high into the air, and the boys guided the fire to snap the webbing. It plopped uselessly into the sea on either side of us.

"Keep playing," Blackwood shouted to Dee.

The bone whistle. I reached for it . . . and found it wasn't about my neck. *Of course, the faeries snatched it underground.* Like a fool, I'd left it behind.

The Spider dove off her web and into the deep water. We each took a corner of the boat to watch. Dee paused playing to catch his breath. I guarded the stern, hearing only the slop of the waves.

"Is she . . . ?" Maria stopped herself from asking the question.

The Spider exploded from the sea, toppling me back onto

the deck. Her eight legs clung to the sides of the ship as she rose above us. Maria hacked at a limb with her ax, screaming bloody murder all the while. Dee played again but was knocked off-balance and slammed against the edge of the boat. The flute tumbled out of his hands and into the water.

I nearly threw myself overboard working a spell with Porridge to bring the damned flute back, but it didn't resurface. My arms ached from the fruitless maneuver. Magnus and Blackwood tried stabbing Nemneris as her eager fangs tore into the sails, shredding them to useless rags. The mast splintered and fell. I launched another torrent of flame at the creature, screaming in frustration. She hissed as my fire licked her face, but she did not release us. It wasn't enough.

"Come on, then!" Magnus roared, using his sword to hack at the monster. He thrust upward, getting her beneath the jaw. Black blood coated him as Nemneris's high-pitched squealing shattered my ears. She rose onto her legs again and spewed a jet of white foam.

Dee shoved Magnus away and fell beneath the liquid. He shrieked, trying furiously to wipe it away. There was a hissing sound like acid, and then the smoke of burning flesh.

I ran to help Dee as the Spider released the ship and slid back beneath the waves.

"Maria!" Magnus bellowed, ripping off his coat to wipe at the foaming venom that still covered Dee. The boy lay unnaturally still. *Please, no.*

I reached them as the bottom of the boat ruptured. Below

us, three hollow black eyes stared up as the boards tore apart like thin paper. I stumbled for the railing, flinging myself over and twisting before plunging into the cold waves.

She's supposed to die! Dammit, the prophecy said, "You shall know her when Poison drowns beneath the dark Waters of—"

Wait. *Poison drowns beneath the dark waters.*

Our ship's name was the *Bella Donna.* Belladonna was a type of poison.

Nemneris wasn't fated to drown. God, perhaps our ship was fated to sink.

I pulled my head up just enough to break the water's surface and take a breath. There were no more screams. The ship had vanished completely. Chunks of debris and canvas bobbed around me, ensnared in her webbing. The silence was more awful than the fighting.

Her webbing. My arms and my back were practically welded to the web. Despite my thrashing, I couldn't break free. Porridge was still in my hand, at least. But I was a fly awaiting certain death. I let out a frustrated cry.

Magnus and Blackwood both shouted, but I couldn't see them. Thank God, they were alive.

"Who else is there?" I yelled.

"We're bloody stuck!" Magnus cried. The web jostled beneath us at his attempts to break free.

"Dee's beside me." Blackwood sounded stunned. "He's not moving."

"Maria?" I waited for her response. There was none. *No.* I called for her again, tears in my eyes as I yanked my head away from the webbing. It took probably half my hair to do it, but I was able to crane my neck and look about more. The broken bits of ship, the boys, the lowering sun on the coast. I could see it all except Maria.

Once more the web jerked. My breath lodged in my throat as Nemneris clambered out of the sea to stand over us, lifting her dripping body high. She regarded us with those bulbous eyes.

She was relishing this kill.

Blackwood ordered us to try freezing the web, to light her on fire. But if we couldn't move, we could not do any sorcerer spells. When I attempted burning, the water extinguished my flame. Swallowed by the sea, I was worse than useless.

The boys' thrashes and screams ceased as we realized the truth. I lay before the monster, helpless; the only bitter triumph was the fact that R'hlem would lose me to the jaws of one of his own beasts. *Let that haunt him.*

Her Majesty commended you. Whitechurch had died for nothing. His message had been for nothing, and rage boiled inside me to see that creature deciding which of us to devour first, like dainties in a shop window.

Her Majesty commended you.

"God save the queen!" I yelled into the hideous thing's face. "God save the queen!"

"God save the queen!" Magnus took up the cry, and so did Blackwood. We shouted in unison, our voices rising as Nemneris opened her jaws.

And then the world exploded.

The sea went wild; white-capped waves shot ten, twenty feet in the air, as though an underwater volcano were erupting. Nemneris squealed in surprise as Maria rose up atop that column, red hair streaming behind her like fire. She'd her arms out, palms turned to the sky.

With her whipping hair, her bared teeth, her outstretched arms, she resembled some great and terrible god. She sized the Water Spider up . . . and attacked.

With one sweep of Maria's arm, the wind rose into a frenzied gale, battering us like toys. Waves peaked and sloshed over me, water flooding my nose. I strained for air. She pointed one hand to the sky, and clouds brewed with a violent storm. Nemneris backed away as Maria put another hand toward us.

The web beneath me froze into ice. At Maria's gesture, the ice shattered, plunging all of us into the sea. My skirt, petticoats, and boots filled with water, dragging me below the surface. But a current caught me, and as one the boys and I were raised up on a steady column of water.

When we were safe, Maria turned again to the gargantuan spider. Nemneris had got over the shock and spewed more of that venomous foam. Maria was too quick: a barrier of water enveloped the girl, and the foam was harmlessly absorbed. Nemneris gave a thin, nervous chittering.

Maria brought her hands together over her head and then swung them down. Lightning forked out of the sky, striking the Ancient. She fell backward, eight legs flailing as three more bolts shot through her. The smell of something burned and rotten wafted over me, and I gagged.

With Nemneris down, Maria stretched one hand back into the sky and made a fist.

"Now!" she screamed. I swore I heard two voices come from her mouth, her own and that honeyed, deeper, womanly voice. The waves swelled up and covered Nemneris's stunned figure, rolling her. Maria clapped her hands together, and the webbing on either side of the shore ripped up, twining itself about Nemneris. The waves rolled her again, entangling the Spider in her own web. The monster screamed but didn't free herself. Her bulk vanished beneath the waves.

Was she dead? If finding out meant staying here, I'd rather not.

Maria's water column began to lower us back to the sea. Even with her level of power, she couldn't keep this up forever.

"Summon the wind," Magnus called. He caught Dee, whose face and body were scarred.

Blackwood and I hooked a current of air, while Maria created a platform of ice beneath our feet and we rode a wave in toward shore.

Her strength finally gave out about fifty feet from land, and we plunged back into the water. I coughed as I paddled forward. Just when I thought I was about to sink, my feet scraped the rocky shore. I dragged myself out, dripping and ragged. My sodden skirts weighed me down even further, and my legs were rubber. My head stung from where I'd ripped out my hair. When I touched my scalp, I found blood on my fingers.

Magnus had already got ashore and laid Dee on the ground. I groaned in horror as I beheld the damage: his right leg below the knee was splintered, bone poking out of his shin. His left arm below the elbow was *gone,* a few strips of torn flesh all that remained. Lines of scarring crisscrossed his face. One eye had been shut forever. His flesh was white with shock.

"Move!" Maria shoved me and got to work. "Make me a tourniquet. *Now!*"

I tore at my skirt, hands shaking. We tied off the bleeding at his arm, and she rotated his leg so that his pain wasn't as intense. Maria laid Dee's head in her lap. Still, he didn't wake.

"Too much blood loss," she muttered, wincing. "That leg may have to come off."

Dear God. Blackwood and Magnus stalked about in a circle, looking painfully helpless. When Maria bid me set my hand on fire and cauterize Dee's wound, I did, even though I tasted bile while he screamed.

Still, after rechecking his pulse and breath, Maria nodded. "He could still die of the shock. But he may live. He *may.*"

The immediate emergency began to dissipate. Now we had time to consider our escape from Nemneris.

"How the hell did you do that?" Magnus cried, crouching beside Maria. She became mute. While Blackwood questioned her as well, I held Dee's hand. And then, slowly, I recalled those prophesied words I'd hung on to earlier:

You shall know her when Poison drowns beneath the dark Waters.

And Lambe's words: *Take the belladonna and you'll finally know the truth.*

My entire body went cold.

Maria was Agrippa's daughter, a girl of sorcerer parentage who had seen her mother burned: *A girl-child of sorcerer stock rises from the ashes of a life.*

How had it taken me this bloody long to realize? I stopped the interrogation, making a noise somewhere between a sob and a laugh. When I had the boys' attention, I said, "She's the chosen one."

The three of them regarded me as though I'd lost my mind.

"I'm what?" Maria asked.

I practically crawled to reach her. She looked frightened as I said, "You were foretold by the Speakers. You're meant to save us." Should I kiss her hand? Throw my arms about her ankles? How did one embrace a savior?

Maria paled.

"But she is not a sorcerer!" Blackwood found his voice at last. I couldn't tear my gaze from Maria as I answered him.

"She's Master Agrippa's daughter. That makes her more of a sorcerer than I ever could be." The boys gaped. Recalling the tapestry's image of the white hand with Agrippa's seal burned into the palm, I smiled in realization. "The prophecy must have meant the chosen one would come from Agrippa's bloodline,

not that he'd find the girl." So simple. I'd been so close, thinking it was Gwendolyn.

My trance dissolved when Maria pulled away from me.

"No." Despite her exhaustion, she looked furious. "I don't
want it."

"Howel, you could be right." Blackwood ignored Maria's
words, lost in his own thoughts. "I've never seen such power."

"I don't want to be your *anything*!" Her anger fed the wind,
which picked up sharply. "Why should I risk myself to save
murderers?"

"You've risked so much already," I said, stunned.

"For you, and for Rook, and for my friends, I'd risk
everything. But for the *Order*?" She spit on the ground. Blackwood rose angrily. Waving him down, I approached Maria
with care.

"Please." Maria watched me, her brown eyes wary. "Forget
the Order. What of England?"

"England's done nothing for me." She balled her fists. Beneath us, the earth shifted in response to her passion.

I sank to my knees, to Maria's bewilderment.

"What are you doing?"

Taking her hand once more, I bowed my head. When I was
a child, Rook and I had played at something like this, acting
a scene from the Arthurian tales. A knight knelt at the king's
feet, pledging his loyalty and service. My desperation resonated
through my body and into hers. I could sense it.

"I am at your service, now and always. I'll fight for you, die for you if need be. From this day forward, I swear no one will harm you."

Maria watched me, wearing a stunned expression. I'd no right to ask this, but I would, because she was stronger than I. From the moment we had met, she was the stronger, the better, the kinder, the wiser person, and England needed her. And while I was not much, I was a servant of England, now and always. "How do you think the Order will feel when a *witch* is their champion?" That gave her pause. I pressed one final time. "Show the sorcerers the full horror of what they did."

Maria turned and walked away up the beach, hair whipping about as she gazed out to where the sea and sky met on the horizon. Behind me, the boys remained still and watchful.

Maria came back to us. "Someone must stop that bastard R'hlem." She gave a tight smile. "Might as well help."

I wanted to sob as relief and exhaustion swept over me. Maria helped me up while Blackwood tromped over to us.

"Very well. If you're truly the one prophesied, your timing is perfect." He looked north. "We've got to get to London."

"What about Dee?" Magnus was doing his best to comfort the boy as he moaned in pain. God, he'd be awake soon, and then his agony would truly begin. "We can't leave him."

"We can't help him." Blackwood winced but continued. "We need to get to town—"

"And what? Warn people?" Magnus shouted, his eyes red and wild. "The place has probably been under siege for hours by now!"

"We will go and fight," Blackwood said, every word precise and clean. "That is our duty."

"To leave a fellow sorcerer to die?" Magnus snapped.

Blackwood glared. "Don't force me to say these things. His body is broken." Here, he quieted, in case Dee should hear. "He can't handle a stave anymore. What can be the good—"

"The good of saving a friend?" Magnus boomed, moving toward Blackwood until they were practically nose to nose. Dee shifted, groaning in pain. Blackwood relented somewhat.

"Howel, stay with Magnus and see that Dee is comfortable until . . ." Blackwood didn't finish. "Maria and I will go—"

"No. I can heal him." Maria returned to Dee's side, helping Magnus adjust his body. "We can manage."

"If you are the chosen one, this cannot wait!" Blackwood barked, all but throwing his stave to the ground in frustration. But Maria was right: without her, Dee would die. The capital might collapse, yes, but Dee *would* be gone. And if Maria was our chosen one, rushing her unprepared into the most brutal kind of danger might be foolish.

"This is our plan." I interrupted them all. "Maria, you and Magnus stay until Dee is stable, then come to us. Blackwood, we're going." I prepared myself for flight, but Blackwood snagged my arm.

"You don't have the authority!" he cried.

"Neither do you." Summoning the wind, I lifted unsteadily onto a cushion of air. Magnus ran over.

"Stay," he said. Unlike Blackwood, he didn't make it an order. "If R'hlem captures you, God knows what he'll do."

I imagined that *I* knew. A chill walked down my spine, but I was resolved.

Maria understood, because she said, "Let her go. We'll meet again in London." Then she returned her attention to Dee. Magnus and Blackwood started arguing; to save us all time, I took off.

I flew half a mile before I had to rest, and drifted to the ground. Kneeling, I waited for Blackwood to land beside me.

"We find our chosen one, yet somehow *you're* the one who faces R'hlem." He sighed. "Why is that?"

"I'll tell you if we survive." Before he could ask more questions, I harnessed the wind once more. He caught up and did not speak again until we'd reached the outskirts of London.

We landed by the river, while across from us clouds of dust and smoke stained the sky. Bells tolled at random, like the screams of madmen. Even from this distance, I could see the flicker of orange light as buildings burned.

London was on fire. The Ancients had come to town.

32

ASH COVERED THE STREETS LIKE A SINISTER SNOW as we walked through what had once been Whitechapel. Blackwood and I followed the shouts for help and the distant, bestial cries. Figures darted out of the clouds of rubble, racing for the river. The men and women and children who ran didn't even glance at us as we calmly made our way deeper into the city. Before too long, we'd gone up Fish Street to the Monument, a column memorializing the Great Fire of London. High above us, the fat black shape of On-Tez the Vulture Lady landed atop the pillar, spread her wings, and cawed.

Fitting.

God only knew how long the Ancients had been here. Blackwood had kept close to me since we landed, his arm before me like a shield. I would have told him off, but as we turned onto Monument Street, we stumbled upon a collection of bodies. There must have been thirty of them all told, rich and poor together. Familiars knelt over the dead and gorged themselves, tearing flesh in leathery strips.

From the scaled appearance of their skin and the clawed

hands that sliced open the corpses to get at the more tender organs, I could tell these Familiars were Zem's. One looked up, its serpentine eyes frenzied with bloodlust. It wiped a sleeved arm across its gory mouth, a chillingly human action.

When the creature charged, I summoned as much water as possible from the ground beneath and created a long, sharp blade of ice. Together, Blackwood and I shot it right through the lizard's heart. The thing took two jerking steps and fell over, the ice dissolving quickly as the thing's fiery blood ate at it.

Blackwood ripped stones from the street and formed a cage around the other two lizards. Inside, we could hear them pounding and bellowing; they began to breathe fire, turning the stones to powder.

R'hlem was here. I knew it in my bones. I had to find him, wherever he might be, but every time I moved so much as a foot away from Blackwood, he shadowed me. There was no way in hell he'd let me go alone.

My moment to run came when a stampede of people erupted out of the haze of dust and blood. Forty or fifty people pounded up the street toward us—they'd seen our magic and were clamoring for help. A woman with a ripped gown and a bloodied forehead stumbled sobbing into Blackwood. As the crowd swallowed him, I stole away into the darkening streets. Blackwood shouted my name but couldn't immediately follow without hurting someone.

It was cruel to leave him like that, but it would be crueler still to take him with me. My hands gripped Porridge on one hip, the hilt of the dagger on the other. I wished to hell and back I had that bone whistle.

Coughing, I quickly made my way through the streets, stopping dead when I heard a man's scream. Dimly, I spotted a louse Familiar attacking someone on the ground as the man cried out for help.

"Get off!" I threw warded force, knocking the creature onto its back. Its bright green underbelly flashed and its legs writhed as it tried to right itself. Grabbing the dagger from my belt, I plunged the blade into the monster's chest. Black blood coated my hand, warm and thick as tar. The beast curled its legs into itself and died. Wiping my hand on my skirt, I went to help the gentleman on the ground. "You're all right now, sir."

"Late, as always," Mickelmas said, taking my offered hand and getting to his feet. He smoothed his impossibly messy hair. "Impeccable timing to save my life, though. Your army seems to have got away from me." He looked about, as if they might be hiding in an alley.

"What, all nine of them?" My astonishment gave way to anger. Even with England falling down about our ears, the sight of him made me want to scream.

"Ten, now. At least, there are ten if Shanley made it. I lost track of him when Molochoron attacked." He shuddered, tugging at his coat. "Poor bastard."

"The army probably ran, if I know anything about magicians." I shoved past him.

"Well, I don't think your darling father is running, chick-pea. Certain you'd like *him* as a role model?" Mickelmas stalked beside me, kicking away bits of debris and a dented pail.

"Go to hell." I walked faster.

"Very winning argument," he called as I pulled ahead. "Speaking of dear Papa, I imagine you'd like to find him?"

I slowed. "Do you know where he is?"

"Buckingham Palace, I shouldn't wonder. Fortunately, Her Majesty has an awful lot of rooms to destroy. He'll be so pre-occupied she might even escape."

I knew that the queen had a plan in place in case of attack, so secret only her closest advisors knew where she'd be. But R'hlem wouldn't stop hunting her, and his patience was great—he'd find her eventually. "Then I need to go to the palace." Straightening my shoulders, I pressed on.

"You *could* walk. Or?" Mickelmas dodged in front of me, holding out his arms. Much as I hated him, I'd be an idiot to ignore the offer. Grudgingly, I let him wrap me in his coat. One heartbeat later we stood before the palace.

The iron gates had been pulled down, the bars twisted and discarded like pieces of straw. Bodies of red-liveried guards had been left to rot in the open. Some of their faces resembled raw meat; R'hlem had skinned them where they stood. Black flies dotted the corpses. Shuddering, I barreled toward the entrance.

"Come on, then," I called, but Mickelmas stayed put. "The queen needs us."

"I'm afraid I have to get back to it." Mickelmas didn't even attempt to look ashamed. "I, er, don't think he'd be terribly pleased to see me."

I'd no energy to argue.

"Goodbye, then," I said. What more could I expect?

He vanished, and I hurried to the entrance. The doors had been smashed open, allowing me easy access.

God, I could *feel* him here. The tension in my stomach would not ease, like a tightening thread tied to my gut, pulling me along now-deserted corridors and out into the courtyard.

Of course R'hlem would go to the obsidian cathedral. I should have known.

His power settled on my skin like a fine dust, something both foreign and intensely familiar about it. Both sensations were equally horrifying.

Boom. Boom. Boom. I followed the sound, the growing sense of his magic a bad taste in my mouth, and entered the cathedral.

R'hlem stood atop the dais, studying his reflection in the walls. He'd worn clothes again, an impressive suit of rich green and brown. Fire burst from his hands and flooded the room. Shards of black volcanic glass rained onto the floor. The glass crunched beneath his boots as he ambled to the elemental pit. Muttering a few words, he created a fireball so powerful that it smashed the sacred thing, destroying it thoroughly. It felt like the deepest kind of profanity. R'hlem kicked shards of the ruined glass.

His laughter grew, and my stomach turned to hear it.

"Pardon me!" I shouted.

R'hlem turned, one hand raised and ready for attack. When he recognized me, he lowered his arm.

"Henrietta?" His eye widened in shock. "The devil are you doing here? Why aren't you with Mab?" It was such an ordinary way to respond, as if he were scolding me.

Here in the world outside the astral plane, he was not quite as I'd thought he would be. He was tall, yes, but not a giant. The bloodiness of his face was not a bright crimson but a duller red, like raw meat left out upon a table. When he spoke, the tendons of his neck stretched, the sight more grotesque than I'd have thought. A fly circled overhead, buzzing as it landed upon the side of his face. He waved it off without thinking, like it was a daily occurrence.

"Surrender now," I said, my voice echoing. Foolish words, of course, but I needed to keep him off guard.

"I beg pardon?" He chuckled, as though I'd said something precocious.

"Surrender, or you'll be forced."

"And who, might I ask, will force me?" A smile tugged at his fleshless lips. Taking Porridge in hand, I steadied myself.

"I will," I said, and attacked.

33

I BOWLED HIM OVER WITH THE WIND. GOOD, BUT I knew he wouldn't let himself be caught off guard like that again. I spun Porridge overhead, attempting to transform the current of wind into a cyclone, but my arm erupted in pain as if the blood inside my body were rebelling. Screaming, I dropped my stave. An instant later the agony had vanished, leaving me to cradle my arm as R'hlem approached.

"This is not what I wanted from our first true meeting, my love." He sounded bitter.

When I covered him in flame, the fire washed over his body harmlessly. Damn it to hell, his abilities were like mine; of course fire would not hurt him. With a nod of his head, the muscles in my back and arms tightened, locking me into place once more. I toppled over, then felt my body mercifully relax as he released me. R'hlem merely waited for me to grab Porridge and get to my feet. He was *indulging* me.

He held up his hand. "I don't want to fight you. Why do you think I waited all these months to attack London in full force? I had to be certain you were out of harm's way. Please, don't make me hurt you now, after all this."

Attack in a way he won't expect. I snared one of Mickelmas's spells in my mind, willing the shards of obsidian glass to form a hand and pin him down. But I'd misjudged how differently this would work with glass instead of earth. The shards splintered into tinier pieces, yes, but did nothing else.

"That wasn't pure sorcery, was it?" R'hlem came closer still. "Mickelmas trained you in our ways." His eye narrowed. "I should thank him for giving you *some* proper instruction."

Attacking would only make me appear more foolish. R'hlem came closer and sighed in frustration as I retreated.

"My darling, all I want is to talk," he said. In response, I burst into flame. It would do nothing, but it sent the message that I didn't want him to touch me. Rather than grow irritated, he crouched on the balls of his feet and looked me over, as though he was appraising me.

"You've better control than I did at your age." He sounded like a doting father whose child has taken its first step. "If your mother could only see this." Hearing him speak of my mother made me blind with fury.

"She'd kill herself if she could see what you've become."

He paced around me. For the first time, something I'd done wounded him.

"It's a cruel blow of fate that you don't resemble her in the slightest." His gaze gentled. "But I do glimpse her defiance in you." He took off his coat, dropping it to the floor. Blood stained the loose sleeves of his shirt like some garish design. "I want to see more of what you can do." He held out his hands, beckoning. "Attack."

He was *playing* with me.

With a sweep of my arm, I sent the jagged shards of glass flying. He melted them with his fire and shook his head, disappointed.

"Your magician abilities aren't terribly strong. You're hampered by that *thing*." He glared at Porridge. I hugged the stave to my chest. "You've nothing to fear. I know your life depends on it." He sneered. "But I will burn them all for chaining you so."

Conjuring up an old spell of Mickelmas's, I twisted Porridge at my heart and created three perfect illusions of myself to surround my father. Hoping to distract him enough to land a blow, I attacked . . . and skidded to a halt as *dozens* of bloodied, flayed men surrounded me, every one wearing that smug grin. Tripping on my damned skirt, I turned smack into the real him. He looked down on me—he was quite tall—but allowed me to dodge away up the stairs. I made it to the second level and stopped, my chest heaving.

"Nicely done," he said. "But there is no trick you can perform that I cannot match. Once you're with me, I'll teach you better techniques."

I would not go anywhere with him. With a shout, I slashed Porridge through the air, throwing pulse after pulse of warded force. He batted the blows away easily but was distracted enough for me to rush down and slash at him with my dagger. He growled, putting out his hand. My body froze once more, and I tipped over. My head struck the floor, the world around me rippling. While I lay there, dazed, R'hlem squeezed his hand into a fist.

Every muscle in my arm jumped in agony. I howled, the sound trapped in my clenched jaw. He kicked my dagger away.

"That's a weapon from Strangewayes's, isn't it? Unfortunately, you'll find they have little effect on me. I was *re*born in the Ancients' world, my angel, not born. I am a mere imitation of my beautiful monsters." He sneered again. "Just as you are a pale approximation of a sorcerer." He jerked his hand; I was sure my muscles would shred. *Anything. Do anything he wants, only if he'll make it stop!* I whined deep in my throat. He relaxed my body, but only slightly. "I wanted you to join me willingly." He sounded so remorseful. "But if I must hurt you to save you, I will."

The invisible force gripping me could not be budged. R'hlem raised his hands and shouted in some, unknown guttural language. But I recognized one word: *Korozoth*.

A shadow swelled by R'hlem's feet. Slowly, a body rose up from that shapeless pool, darkness flowing like drapery from his shoulders.

I recognized the flash of pale yellow hair, the gentle profile that had hardened and grown bestial. Fangs jutted over the soft lower lip. Fingers were tipped with elongated talons. Rook knelt before R'hlem's feet and bowed his head.

"Such an obedient servant." R'hlem stroked Rook's hair.

All the kindness and strength in Rook's face had been

snuffed out, his body made vacant to allow a monster to crawl inside. R'hlem eased the tension in my jaw so I could speak.

"How could you?" I shrieked. The pain tightened in my wrists as R'hlem turned Rook to face me. The shadow cloak whispered about his body, fluttering open around his chest. A slice of white skin and the inflamed scars that decorated it were on display.

"You can have him, my love. I would not mind."

R'hlem ceased binding me, then sent his "servant" to help me to my feet. Rook put an arm about my waist to steady me, but there was no familiarity in his touch. To him, I was a stranger.

"I want us all to be a family," R'hlem soothed.

I ignited in Rook's arms. He flew backward, baring his fangs. R'hlem sent me to my knees once more in a flash of pain.

"So be it. I'll have to take you like a common prisoner of war." His voice was mournful as Rook advanced to gather me up. This was how it would end. I'd been a fool to think I could defeat him.

"William!" The voice echoed in the space. R'hlem whipped about, shocked at hearing his old name.

Mickelmas entered the room, kicking aside bits of glass. He stopped twenty feet from us, hands behind his back.

I tried to scream—*Get out, run away!*—but my jaw ached. I struggled so hard to open my damned mouth that I nearly passed out.

"*You?*" R'hlem sounded dumbstruck. The muscles in my body loosened.

"She's your own flesh and blood." Sweat glistened on Mickelmas's face. He was doing his best to mask his terror.

"*You* lecture *me?*" R'hlem's awed whisper began to develop into a powerful roar. "You sent me to *hell*." He burst into flame, bright blue fire churning into the air, reflected upon the thousands of pieces of obsidian—it looked as if we were *all* in hell now. Mickelmas flinched.

With a furious cry, R'hlem shot a fireball at the magician, who dodged it. With a wave of his hand and some shouted words, Mickelmas made all the shards of black glass surge into the air. They formed sharp-winged, dagger-beaked little birds that circled and pecked at R'hlem. While the Skinless Man fought, Mickelmas vanished and reappeared by my side.

But then, with a scream of pain, his whole body went rigid. R'hlem had taken control of him as well. Instantly, the birds crashed to the floor, and R'hlem stormed over and ripped the multicolored coat from Mickelmas's shoulders. As we watched in horror, R'hlem set the garment ablaze and tossed it to the floor. It burned quickly, reduced to a pile of ashes.

"Let's see you hop about now." R'hlem seized Mickelmas by the throat.

To my horror, Mickelmas began to cry. "Punish me, but leave the girl alone. She's innocent."

"Of course she is. In time, when she's by my side and sees

all of England spread out at her feet, she will appreciate all I've done," R'hlem rasped. He slammed the older magician to the floor and leaned over him, blood dripping from his face and onto Mickelmas's cheek. "You know what they did to me."

"I can see," Mickelmas gasped.

"Not my beauties, no. The *sorcerers*. You saw what they did to my brother. To Helen. You kept my girl away from me." His voice shook with terrible feeling. "The last human piece of me; the final scrap of her mother. You turned that into one of *them!*" He roared that last word in Mickelmas's face. "After everything they've done to our race, you bow like the servant you are." There was nothing of the calm bloody king left in R'hlem. Over a decade of misery and blame flooded out of him. *"I hate you."*

I'd said the same words in the same way to the same magician. Mickelmas was sobbing now, tears streaming into his gray beard.

My body screamed as I sat up, the pain finally ebbing. R'hlem was so fixated on Mickelmas he'd taken his attention off me. I knew now, beyond any doubt, I could not win against him. I wasn't strong enough.

There was no way.

"I flayed Charles Blackwood from the top of his scalp to the bottom of his feet." R'hlem bared his teeth in Mickelmas's face. "What can I do to *you?*"

R'hlem made a fist, and Mickelmas howled as the flesh of his left hand began to twitch. With excruciating slowness, the skin tore apart with a dreadful rip. Blood ran down his arm.

Mickelmas wailed and pounded his other fist into the floor, but he could do nothing. R'hlem was skinning him alive before my eyes.

"No, please!" I wept, crawling forward. "Please, Father!"

R'hlem paused. Slowly, he brought his arm down. Mickelmas keened, clutching his torn hand to his chest.

Wonderingly, R'hlem said, "Say that again."

Shaking, I unsheathed Porridge and tossed it to the side. My dagger already lay by his feet. Then, broken, I collapsed and sobbed, "Father, please. I can't bear it any longer."

My cries reverberated in the space around us as I buried my face in my hands. My grief—for Dee, Whitechurch, London, Rook—all flooded out in one painful rush. I wept until I couldn't breathe, until my stomach ached.

I could not fight him. Against such power, victory was impossible.

There was the crunch of a boot on glass, and the sense that someone stood before me. R'hlem knelt, and with a gentle shushing sound took my hands from my face. That metallic tang of magic all about him eased as he helped me stand.

"There, now." He plucked a surprisingly unbloodied handkerchief from his breast pocket and wiped my eyes.

"Please just let him go," I whimpered, my teeth chattering uncontrollably. He pressed me to his chest. The damp, cold feel of bloody silk met my cheek, but I didn't flinch. He passed a gloved hand over my hair.

Despite everything, I let myself be folded against him.

R'hlem rested his chin on top of my head, and then whispered, "Helena. Darling, I have her."

I trembled at those words. And even with all this horror, for that moment, I let myself feel safe. I returned his embrace. With my eyes closed, I could picture us as we should have been: in a house in Devon, me at his knee growing up, him holding me when I cried. Fathers were supposed to keep your nightmares at bay. I let him wrap me in his protection, listened to him whisper my mother's name, and cried. He hushed me, soothed me, stroked my hair.

"There, now. I'm sorry, sweetheart," he murmured, pulling away and touching my cheek. His one eye shimmered with unshed tears. Here was the spark of goodness I had prayed for. Love revealed the man behind the monster's facade. I trembled to see it. "Can you forgive me?"

"If you'll forgive me."

I made the one small dagger—the tiniest, most insignificant one I'd taken from Ralph Strangewayes's house—shoot out of its wrist sheath and into my hand.

My father could not be defeated by strength of arms. His goodness, his love, was my only weapon against him.

I plunged the blade deep into his heart.

34

R'HLEM WENT TO THE FLOOR, AND I WENT WITH him. I gripped the back of his neck, feeling every pulse and twitch of his muscle. He looked at me, shocked, as if trying to understand. Blood spurted onto the front of my gown as I fumbled with the blade's handle. Ripping it out, I prepared to drive it once more into his body . . . but the betrayal burning in his eye paralyzed me.

I stabbed my father in his heart. The blade slipped from my hand, my fingers too numb to grip properly. No matter how much I saw the beast in front of me, I also saw the man.

R'hlem roared, the sound shaking the cathedral to its very foundation.

Shadow overwhelmed me, plunging me into pitch black between one heartbeat and the next. Rook threw me to the floor and straddled me, his knees pressing into my sides. One clawed hand to my throat, his lips pulled back to reveal wicked fangs. Lunging forward, he sank those sharp teeth into my shoulder.

Pain shredded muscle and bone. Darkness poured into me like the ocean crammed inside a thimble.

My vision failed, my screams becoming unnaturally thin.

A void seemed to rupture in the air above me. If I looked into it, I would forget my name, my past, my friends, everything. . . .

No. I fought against the void and lit myself on fire. Rook was engulfed as well, and he sprang away from me.

My whole body was warm and wet with blood; my shoulder gushed. The *pain.* A thousand hot needles jabbed into my flesh; a continuous river of acid flowed through my veins.

Rook threw his arms over his face and howled at my fire. I could now make out threads of black twisting in the blue flame. Why? Why should that be? With one last effort, I burned as brightly as I could.

Screeching, Rook flew to R'hlem and brought me back into the daylight. I lay there, every breath I drew like fire in my lungs.

Mickelmas, his hand still bleeding profusely, circled R'hlem. My father struggled to rise, slipping in his own blood. *I'd done that to him.*

Gore dripping from his fingers, he reached into the air. "Come! Korozoth!"

Rook swallowed his master in a flurry of shadowy wings and robes and dissolved them both like smoke on the wind. Mickelmas and I were alone.

The magician struggled for breath. "I brought this upon us all." It sounded like a revelation. "And my coat. My beautiful coat." He gazed mournfully upon the pile of ashes.

When I tried to sit up, the pain sank its claws deeper into

me. My vision fractured—somewhere, as if from a distance, I heard my screams. Mickelmas was at my side, whispering words in my ear. As if by a miracle, the pain abated. It still had a tooth in me, but only one.

"It'll keep you from bleeding to death," he whispered as he hoisted me to my feet. I was a ghost, surely, floating over the floor and out into the courtyard. Soon we slumped against each other outside the palace doors, surveying the damage of the city streets. Smoke still shrouded the landscape.

"What happens now?" I croaked. My legs gave out, and Mickelmas gently sat with me. I pressed my face into his velvet sleeve.

"We'll see if the Ancients follow their master. Perhaps they'll remain and hold the city for when—if—he returns."

If I'd silenced R'hlem's mind forever . . . I didn't know how to feel about it. I had not paused to exploit his weakness. The man in my father had given birth to the monster in me.

Mickelmas hissed in pain, clutching his hand. "The time has come for me to atone."

"What do you mean?" The pulsing agony was abating moment by moment; his spell had done its job. Gingerly, I wiped at some of the drying blood on his face.

"I hid for years when I should have gone hunting for the answer to our problem. Now would be the time to get started." He squeezed my good shoulder. "I'm giving you the Army of the Burning Rose. My little magicians need someone to look to for strength." He touched my head in the manner of a blessing. "God forbid, if R'hlem survives . . ." Neither of us wanted to dwell on that possibility. Mickelmas sniffed. "I know you can't forgive what I've done," he muttered.

Forgive me. I would not make the same mistake as I had with Agrippa. Though I couldn't put my arms around the magician, I patted his hand.

"Once we finish this war, I'll have years ahead to badger you about it," I whispered.

"You always were a smart-mouthed creature." Mickelmas frowned. "God, that injury. Stay here—no, don't stand up!"

But the world had gone hazy once more. The queen. I should find her, wherever she was, and make certain she was safe. But my vision split as I dragged myself to my feet, over Mickelmas's protests.

I didn't remember falling.

"Wake up." A wet cloth soothed my brow, and hands lifted my head. "Drink."

I spluttered at the hot liquid rushing down my throat, which tasted like butter and basil and wet leaves. My eyes opened. Light stabbed me through the brain, but the blurred image of the person above me came into focus.

Maria. Her hair was plaited down her back, and the circles under her eyes indicated she'd spent a sleepless night. Sitting up, the world scattered a moment, but with a few more sips of her drink I could see clearly. My shoulder, now covered in gauze, throbbed like an impatient reminder.

We were in one of the palace's rooms, though the fine furniture had been removed and the elegant rugs rolled up. Several pallets and cots had been laid out about the place. Paintings had been taken down, leaving obvious squares on the wall where they had been. Through the window, I caught a glimpse of two men on patrol, staves in hand.

The Order hadn't been completely demolished, then.

"How long have I been asleep?" My voice sounded like it belonged to an old, weary woman.

"Two days, miss." Lilly sat beside me, rinsing out a cloth in some cool water. Her strawberry-blond hair had come thoroughly undone, and her face was smudged, but her hands were steady as ever as she put the cloth to the back of my neck.

To Maria, I said, "Dee?"

"He's survived, but I'm making him sleep." She lowered her eyes. "He'll need to adjust."

Lilly made a noise as she wrung out the cloth.

"And the others?" My heart beat faster. "The queen?"

Maria counted on her fingers. "Her Majesty's safe." She nodded to the sorcerers by the window. "The monsters are moving out, but slowly. The Order's had to set up shields all around the palace until they decide what to do."

"What about the citizens? How many of them are here?" I asked. At that, Maria and Lilly shared a brief glance.

"Don't worry about that now," Maria said, putting her cup to my lips. "This'll manage your pain for a bit, though we'll have to think of something more permanent."

"Permanent?" I didn't understand. If this wound wouldn't kill me . . .

"Rook bit you." Maria didn't make that a question. "He's an Ancient now, of a sort." Her gaze met mine, kind but honest. Always honest. "You're Unclean."

My thoughts went quiet. Gently, I touched the gauze, pain murmuring beneath my skin. I knew what that meant. Sneers and looks of revulsion as you passed, the world treating you as though you were invisible, or the devil himself. Absorbed by the pain until you were a mere vessel for the monster that marked you. Rook—the thing that had been Rook—was my master now.

"Does the queen know?" I finally managed.

"Aye. She knows, and so does—"

The door slammed open, and Magnus exploded into the room. God, it really was him. He was a sight, covered in dirt, his auburn hair gray with ash. His coat was gone, his shirt torn, but he looked elated as he fell beside me. A long, ugly gash snaked over his forehead, and his face was puffed and yellowed with older bruises, but he was alive. Though soot rained down upon me, I didn't mind. I clasped his arm, noted how the dirt on his face was lined from tears.

"You bloody genius. How the devil did you manage it?" His gaze lit on my shoulder. "Does it still hurt? How badly?"

"Which question do you want answered first?" I smiled up at him.

"So, aye, this one knows." Maria slapped at Magnus, forcing him off. "Lord Blackwood as well."

"He's alive? Thank God."

"More than that," Lilly said, but was cut short. The doors opened again, and two sorcerers outfitted in red soldier's livery entered.

"She's awake," one of them said, eyeing me. I could not read his expression. "The Imperator wishes to see her."

"She needs rest," Maria argued, but they did not listen. *Imperator?* So Her Majesty had appointed one. Likely a Master, or perhaps a squadron captain.

The Imperator entered and stood before me.

It was Blackwood.

35

HE WAS UNHARMED AND SURPRISINGLY CLEAN. Somehow in all this madness, he'd found a pristine white shirt and an unsoiled jacket. His black hair shone in the sharp square of sunlight coming through the window. The contrast between Magnus and him was incredible. In the middle of a ravaged city, Blackwood looked better, healthier, than ever before.

And he was the Imperator of all English magic? A boy of seventeen who hadn't even had time to test for the rank of sorcerer Master?

"How?" My throat was dry, and Lilly gave me some more water.

"May we have privacy, please?" Already, he sounded in control. The others obeyed him at once, even a grumbling Magnus. After all, he could not disobey his Imperator. Moments later, we were alone, watching each other, as though calculating how to move. His gaze homed in on my bandaged shoulder.

"I'm Unclean," I said.

"Yes." It was a breath, so soft I nearly missed it. His lips formed a thin, tense line. "What happened?"

"I put a knife into R'hlem's heart." It sounded so simple that I began to giggle uncontrollably. Giggling turned to hiccuping, which in turn bordered on tears. I swallowed more water as Blackwood processed what I'd said.

"How?"

I didn't have the strength for the whole story. "I found an opportunity. He summoned Rook, and Rook bit me." Even mention of his name made the pain in my shoulder flare. "Then I fainted. What happened to *you* once—"

"Once you abandoned me?" He didn't sound angry, though. More like he was trying to puzzle me out. "I fell in with a squadron near St. Paul's. We had a devil of a time. Our losses have been . . . extensive."

Here, he looked over the empty cots, the blank spaces on the walls where art had previously hung.

"Every man in those Fae tunnels was lost," he said. "Half the sorcerers who remained in London are also gone."

Most of the men I saw daily, gone within hours. My stomach felt leaden.

"How many of us are left?"

Blackwood flinched. "Able-bodied men? No more than five hundred."

That was a blow beyond any I could have imagined. "Only five hundred left in London?" I whispered.

"You misunderstand." He looked to the ceiling, as if reading his lines off it. "The Ancients and Familiars took full advantage of the Faerie roads, striking every city and town with a strong sorcerer presence. There are five hundred commended sorcerers left in the whole of England."

Extermination. R'hlem had shown no mercy.

"Women and children?" I whispered. My strength gave out, and I slid back to lie on the floor. Blackwood gave me his hand.

"We're not certain yet," he said gently. "Come. I must address our Order." *Our* Order was an odd thing to say. "Can you walk?" With help, I got to my feet, and he called Maria and Lilly inside. Between them, they escorted me into the courtyard, but they had to let sorcerers take hold of me at the entrance to the obsidian cathedral, since only the commended could enter that hallowed space.

Wait until they find out what Maria is, I thought darkly, letting myself be led inside.

The numbers barely filled the first two rows. Some men, the younger ones, stared blankly ahead or were rocking back and forth. Others were hard at work sweeping up the shattered obsidian with small gusts of wind. I didn't see any blood left in this place; they must have washed it away. Glancing at the room, I noted something disturbing: most were either very young or old. R'hlem had swallowed up the majority of our best warriors in one go. I saw a few in their twenties, like Valens, who was among those cleaning. But most were either sixteen or sixty.

Simply being back here made the pain in my shoulder

flourish, and I crumpled. The men holding me tried to pull me up rather roughly.

"Howel!" Magnus was there in an instant, breaking through the men to hold me himself. Wolff and Lambe came to greet me as well.

They were *alive*. My wound screamed, as if furious that I'd ignored it for half a moment. Wolff carried me to a seat, settling me in between the boys.

Lambe whispered, "You took the belladonna. You saw." He smiled.

"Yes. I saw."

Wolff patted my arm. Somehow we'd all come together again. Damn everything that had happened, I was luckier than most.

The room quieted as Blackwood climbed the dais. There was no throne for him to sit upon. Its remains lay piled in a corner, a broken reminder of all we had lost. Tension rose as Blackwood took his now rightful place. Sorcerers waited to pounce on the boy Imperator. Why on earth had the queen assigned such a crucial role to someone so very young?

Then again, as I'd noticed a moment before, we did not have a large selection from which to choose.

"I know we have suffered a great deal." Blackwood's voice rang out. "I know many do not approve of Her Majesty's choice of Imperator." Dead silence met this statement. At least one person had the decency to cough. "Let me explain, then. Much of Her Majesty's government was slaughtered in the ambush.

What's left of the army and navy is scattered about the country. The prime minister is alive but badly wounded. All of our old safeguards have been ripped away." He scanned the room, clearly watching everyone's reaction to his words. "The queen requires sorcerer counsel, and I made Her Majesty an offer of safety that I could ensure only if I held the position of Imperator." I could sense him slotting everyone into the columns of ally or enemy. "My estate in Sorrow-Fell is the best safehold we have left, besides the Dombrey Priory, and Dombrey has neither the space nor the resources to house the rest of sorcerer-kind."

Murmuring began. One man in the back called out, "What are you suggesting, sir?" His tone was harsh. *Enemy. Blackwood didn't falter.*

"We go north to Sorrow-Fell and stay behind the faerie protections."

There was instant and explosive arguing about the faeries. I tried to piece together how he intended for this to work. Blackwood held up his hand until order was gradually restored.

"Sorrow-Fell was a gift from one of Queen Titania's nobles, of the light court. Mab's army cannot cross those boundaries any more than Titania's can. It is physically impossible without an invitation from me. Thus, the estate becomes the one place in our kingdom where we are completely safe from both Ancients *and* faeries."

He was right. I heard people reluctantly agreeing.

"What about the survivors in London?" Magnus asked, standing up.

"Yes." Blackwood sounded regretful. "We can take only those who are most essential. Therefore, all survivors who are non-sorcerer must be left behind."

At that, there was full-throated shouting, and if I hadn't been so weak, I'd have joined in. Leaning against Wolff, I recalled a night at Agrippa's where Blackwood and I had hotly debated protecting the strong over the weak. I couldn't have heard him right just now. He had once said no innocent life is worth more than another, and now this? Abandon the people we were sworn to protect?

Her Majesty commended you.

"It is the only way to ensure survival." Blackwood waited until everyone was calm enough for him to continue, though there was still angry buzzing at the back. He looked blank, as though he'd anticipated our reaction, anticipated every reaction. It dawned on me that he was fully in his element. "Those innocents who die in the coming months will be a hard burden to bear, but the generations that come after will exist because of what we do today. There *is* hope ahead. We have the weapons. We know that R'hlem has been severely wounded." His eyes found mine. "If we rely solely upon one another, victory could be mere weeks away."

Some were not prepared to move on, however. Valens stood, livid with anger.

"This goes against everything in our commendation vows!" he cried, and I quite agreed. A hush gathered as he kicked aside a pile of broken obsidian. "We cannot leave these people to slaughter!"

"We hid beneath the ward for years." Blackwood's voice was icy. "I'm asking for months."

"Monstrous," Valens snapped. Blackwood closed his eyes, and a cold wind sprang up, chilling me to the bone. The men cried out in surprise. Blackwood looked at every one of us in turn, power surging from him and out to us, just as it had with Whitechurch.

But Whitechurch had never used his power to silence us. When Blackwood ceased his warning, no one spoke.

"United, we will survive. Divided," he said, looking quickly at Valens, "we won't last the winter. We will be safe, but not complacent. Palehook performed monstrous acts to keep us sheltered from reality, but I will have none of that." His eyes blazed as he reached out to us. "We will work tirelessly until the Ancients have been destroyed. Who in this room has not lost a friend in this attack? A brother? God forbid, a son?" Some of the older men placed hands over hearts. Blackwood had them now—he had them in his very palm. "I lost a father to these monsters long ago. I will be *damned* if I lose another member of my family." He beat his breast. "And the Order is my family, now and always."

He was *lying*. He didn't grieve his father; he had no great love for the Order. But right now, the boy who hated artifice above all else was reveling in it, because they were all turning to *him*. Following him. Believing in him. Cursing, Valens returned to his seat. He knew he'd lost.

"Give me your trust this one time. Let us work together to end this war. Then, when peace has been restored, I will step down as Imperator." He bowed his head. "You've my word."

He burned with sincerity, and the crowd broke into applause. In a matter of minutes, he'd won them all over, desperate as they were for someone to take charge. The boys and I, however, were silent.

"As I say, we shall provide a united front, and I must have the best possible advisors by my side. Which brings me to another, more joyous announcement." He held out a hand to me. "Henrietta Howel is to become my wife."

Magnus gave an astonished laugh. The rest of the room buzzed once more, not angry so much as bewildered. I merely stared at Blackwood. In fact, I smiled. *Smartly done.*

The Imperator had the job of dictating the Earl of Sorrow-Fell's marriage. Blackwood had maneuvered things brilliantly. Somehow, I began to laugh a little.

"What's so bloody amusing?" Magnus sounded incredulous.

How could I explain that, between Eliza and her brother, Blackwoods were expert at springing surprise engagements?

Soon after these revelations, the meeting broke up. There was much to do, loading wagons and carriages with provisions, assigning a guard for the queen's protective unit, bandaging the sick so that they would be able to travel, and simply devising a clean exit out of the city. London was to be left to rubble and ruin with the hope that one day, we'd be back to rebuild.

I was able to hobble up the stairs to the Imperator's—Blackwood's—chamber on my own. Magnus had wanted to escort me, but I'd declined. This was between Blackwood and me.

R'hlem hadn't touched this place. Even the china bulldog remained on its customary table, waiting for a head pat that would never come again. Already, the *optiaethis* lantern glowed in its own private corner. It had survived the ambush, then. I hated the sight of it. Blackwood appeared to have anticipated my arrival, because he was seated in a chair and doing a poor job of looking casual. When he saw me, there was a mixture of triumph and concern in his face. I tried to sit with dignity, but the pain twisted like a knife. He rushed to help, but I stopped him.

"I can manage," I said. He sat opposite me. For someone so bold that he could announce a public engagement, he averted his eyes. "That was a shock," I said flatly.

"I don't know what came over me."

"Liar." I didn't say it harshly. "You wanted to put me in a position where I couldn't say no; at least, not in the room." I lay against the back of the seat, which ordinarily no lady would do. But the pain became easier to handle.

"You know me well," he whispered, sounding pleased. His eyes tracked over my form again, the overt longing in his gaze heating my face. He couldn't desire me now that . . . well, *now*.

"I've become Unclean." There was no point trying to pretty up the reality. "You can't mix a Blackwood bloodline with my degenerate—"

"Don't say that!" He rose, his features livid. "I don't care what you become. I want *you*."

All my coldness thawed, and I found myself near tears.

"Everything that's happened is my fault," I whispered.

"How is that *possible*? You're likely the reason there are any of us left at all. If you hadn't landed that blow on R'hlem . . . How the devil did you do it?"

This was an order from my Imperator. Even now, the impulse screamed, *Lie! Lie for your life!* But I was too tired and too hurt.

"R'hlem is my father," I said. Odd that a few small words could so thoroughly change one's life.

The muscles in his face went slack. "What?"

"He was thrust into the world of the Ancients years ago, during a failed experiment he performed with Mickelmas." I paused. "And with *your* father."

Blackwood slumped in his seat.

I told him what Mickelmas had revealed about the runes, and how I had convinced R'hlem to get close enough to strike. Every word seemed to deflate him further. When I described my injury from Rook, he put his head in his hands.

I told him what *his* father had done: cutting the rope that sent my father to his doom. When I'd finished, Blackwood was still.

"You must hate me." Finally, he looked up, his eyes red. He

teetered on the edge of emotion. "Of course you could never love me knowing *that*." Every word was soaked in self-loathing. He pounded the side of the chair, the violence startling me, then got up and walked away. "My father poisoned everything else in my life. Why not you as well?"

"When I rejected you, it had nothing to do with your father. I loved Rook."

Loved. Because Rook was gone now. The wounds at my shoulder throbbed, reiterating my failure.

"Loved?" Blackwood said the word tentatively. Hope was in his voice and eyes. "So you don't love him anymore." No question. It was a veiled order. Gritting my teeth, I climbed to my feet. I would not be told what I could and could not feel, not even now.

Agony burrowed deeper, kicking my knees out from under me. Blackwood caught and cradled me while I grounded myself in the steady rhythm of his heart. The silk of his waistcoat was cool, his small ivory buttons biting into my cheek. He murmured apologies.

"At least we're honest with each other again," I whispered.

"Yes. Your secrets are mine." That slight edge of delight pervaded his voice. His grip became possessive. Here was that tiny part of his father, the bit that sought to master. But Blackwood was *not* his father.

"I suppose it's up to you, as the Imperator, what to do with me." If he wanted to throw me into a prison wagon and drag me up north, I wouldn't fight.

"We'll keep it quiet, of course, but if R'hlem survives, we can use you to our advantage."

I'd stabbed my father in the heart. If we met again, I doubted he'd be at his most cordial.

"You're taking this rather well," I said cautiously.

"I can hardly judge you for your father, given what you know of mine." Blackwood circled his arm around my waist, helping me to sit. My shoulder throbbed, but the pain diminished as his slender fingers cupped the back of my neck. "In a perverse way, it makes me feel nearer to you." He brought his lips close to mine. "I know I don't have your heart the way Rook did, and I don't enthrall like some." Magnus's unspoken name hung in the air. "But I can promise you my love, Henrietta." His voice caressed my name. "I want you to rule at my side."

Rule the Order? I didn't think I was fit to *rule* anybody.

"I'm not sure that's the best idea," I said carefully. The desire I glimpsed in his eyes overwhelmed me.

"You could be the second-most powerful person in English sorcery, and you don't think it a good idea?" He sounded baffled.

That was the problem, sorcery itself. We were now an endangered species, about to isolate ourselves further from the world. Perhaps it was wise, but it didn't feel right. Besides, Mickelmas had left me with the Army of the Burning Rose— well, the promise to protect it, at least. So . . .

"May I bring magicians to Sorrow-Fell?" I would simply come out and say it. He blinked. "Mickelmas has gone away and left me his army." Blackwood's bewildered expression deepened into concern. Sensing his disapproval, I added, "My father may try to court their favor the way he did with the Fae."

Blackwood wasn't a fool.

"If we find them," he murmured, "you may take them on." He traced my cheek with the tip of a finger. "Let it be a wedding gift." In one small moment, Blackwood had maneuvered me perfectly. He might not even have known he'd done it, but it was his way, as surely as it was a spider's nature to spin a web. Passing the back of his hand down my cheek, he whispered, "Despite everything—your lies, your wounds, I cannot help but love you. I'm helpless against it. Be my wife."

"If I said no, would you force me?" As the Imperator, he could. And there was a shine in his eyes, something that came alive with the word *force*.

"I wouldn't," he said at last, "but no position will be safer for you than the seat at my side." Then came the most unexpected thing of all from him: the threat of tears. "My responsibilities frighten me. *I* frighten myself," he whispered. "Help me. Save me."

Save him, indeed, as he'd offered to save me. It was even more than that, really. There was the matter of our fathers, of that odd trick of fate that had bound us together. Our staves bore matched ivy insignias, and I could imagine those tendrils knitting us snugly together. Destiny lay in his touch as he cupped a cool hand under my chin. Something dark that slept inside me stirred, opened one eye. It was as though a secret part of my soul had been designed for his.

Yet he frightened me, too, with the way he *wanted*.

Still, perhaps this was where my path had always been meant to lead. Perhaps the monster I concealed within myself could only be governed by him, and vice versa. And I had my magicians, wherever they might be, along with the non-magical folk shut out from sorcerer protection. They would need someone to speak for them. So, taking a breath, I nodded.

"Yes?" Blackwood sounded amazed.

"Yes, I will marry you," I said. He kissed me.

His lips were soft, but that was the only gentle thing about his embrace. There was no heated teasing as there had been with Magnus, no sense of homecoming as with Rook. His hand gripped in my hair, he claimed my mouth again and again until he was satisfied. When I moaned in shock, he ran a trembling hand down my body. The sleeping *thing* inside me awoke and unfurled itself, responding to his call. Despite my pain, I also found my lips parting with an unexpected flush of pleasure. Only when I was returning his kiss did he let me go, to make me crave more.

He took me to my feet, his eyes glowing in triumph. At last he'd got what he wanted.

It was both thrilling and frightening to see.

"We will be happy together," he whispered, tipping my chin and catching my lips until I pulled away.

"Above all," I said, "we will be strong."

36

WE LEFT LONDON THE NEXT MORNING, OUR CARTS
and carriages banging over the rubble-strewn streets. The
sorcerer army assumed the rough shape of an arrow, with
Blackwood and his most reliable Masters at the front, and the
uninjured men fanning out behind them. This allowed Her
Majesty, the provision wagons, and the wounded to be protected on all sides. As we passed out of the city, a sense of gloom
permeated the air.

For the first time since the Norman Conquest, there would
be no sorcerers in London.

I should have ridden with Blackwood but instead lay shuttered inside his carriage, wincing at every sharp movement.
Maria was trying to keep me asleep as much as possible to ease
my pain, but even she could not stop the dreams.

My nightmares had teeth, and they dogged my heels. In
sleep, I glimpsed yellow eyeballs and curved talons, heard
whispers in a language that should not exist. When I resurfaced
from another fevered rest, shaking and sweating, Maria would
feed me some broth or another potion. When I couldn't drink
any more, she'd sit with me.

Had it been this way for Rook? The feeling that, day by day, the dark washed over him with the relentlessness of waves on a beach?

The first day, we covered a lot of ground. When we finally rested in the evening, I pulled up the carriage's blind to look at the camp. A perimeter of sorcerers circled us, hands on staves, ready for battle. They stayed that way throughout the night, only moving for the changing of the guard. Already, Blackwood was running his Order like an army.

The next day, I woke up feeling slightly better, which meant I wasn't in mind-breaking pain. Though Maria seemed unsure, when we stopped for a rest, I left the confines of the carriage and walked in the sunlight. Had it always been so painfully *bright*? Shielding my eyes with my hand, I spotted the cluster of wagons used for transporting the wounded men and searched for Dee.

He was lying upon plush cushions so fine they must have been stolen from the palace. We were like bandits, ransacking the best bits of London and making off with them. He stirred when my shadow fell across him, and he opened his one good eye. Weakly, he smiled.

"Glad to see you, Howel," he croaked.

He tried shoving himself up to sit properly, but it was hard with only one good arm. The stump below his left elbow had been expertly wrapped in white bandages, while his right leg had been splinted—Maria had saved it, after all. That was something, at least. A cloth mask draped the right side of his face, as cover for his blind eye. The swelling had gone down, but ridged lines of scars still crisscrossed over his cheeks and jaw.

I poured him a cup of water. He drank while I settled blankets around him.

"Thank you." When he smiled, he was still the same blushing young man I'd met at Agrippa's.

God, I didn't want to cry in front of him. I found a book beside him, *Ivanhoe,* and began to read aloud. For a few minutes I could forget the pain in my body and in my mind. The book and the words soothed me in a way no medicine could. When I finished, Dee closed his eye.

I thought he'd fallen asleep, and I was prepared to slip away when he murmured, "Want to know something funny?" Dee's cheeks tinged pink. "My father will be so disappointed."

"Oh?" That was all I could think to say. Who would be *disappointed* to see his son mutilated?

"I've only met him three times, you know. It's because my mother was . . . That is, she *wasn't.*" Dee plucked at the blankets. "She was governess to his children. My real last name is Robbins."

Oh. Dee was illegitimate. In any part of our society, that would have been frowned upon, but the sorcerers had a strict law against natural children becoming members of the Order. It was a blisteringly stupid law, of course, but one they upheld. How had he even been allowed to train?

"Father cast mother out when they found she was expecting, but my grandmother let us live on her estate. No one ever thought I'd receive a stave of my own, until my half brother, Lawrence, died in combat. My father got the Order to grant me legitimacy. Hard to do, since you need the Imperator's written consent, but he was desperate for an heir." Dee sniffed. "I didn't like giving up my name. Robbins sounds far better than Dee, I think."

He flipped *Ivanhoe's* pages.

"Funny part is, after all the trouble he took, he'll be so disappointed that I'm . . . as I am."

"Brave?" I snapped. The idiocy of some people never ceased to amaze.

"Ah well. Who needs him when I've my friends about me?" he said mildly. Settling back against the cushions, he fixed me with a pointed stare. "When I first came to London, everyone was horrid to me about my mother. Until Magnus started fighting anyone who dared speak. After a few bloodied noses, they became dead quiet. He's a good friend."

Before I could respond to that, Lilly climbed up into the wagon, a tray of food balanced in her hands. Dee whipped his face away from her. I'd the feeling she'd been listening a while—she smiled warmly as she set the tray onto Dee's lap.

"Time for your medicine, sir." She offered Maria's pea soup–like concoction. Dee still wouldn't look at her.

"I'm sorry you have to do this," he muttered. "It must be hard to see." Lilly blushed.

"Proud to do it, sir." She handed him a forkful of steaming potato. "I like looking after brave men."

When she said *brave*, I thought Dee would pass out. He looked spellbound as Lilly picked up *Ivanhoe*. "Someone's left off in the middle. Would you like me to continue?"

"You would read to me?" Dee's smile widened as I slid out of the wagon to give them some room.

As I walked across the clearing, I studied the company around me. The sorcerer perimeter remained in place, in rigid anticipation of an attack.

Pain flared again through my body. Like magic, Maria was at my side, grumbling as she supported my weight.

"Can't believe I have to chase you around camp. You're worse than a runaway pup."

"I wish I could take a shift." Joining the guard would have meant *I* was in control of my traitorous body.

"You'll be able someday, but not soon, and not as you used to." A lump formed in my throat; yes, nothing could be as it used to.

We returned to the carriage. I didn't want to climb into that small, hot box, but I hadn't much choice. As I placed my foot on the step, Maria said, "Though I don't know how they'll manage the guard with that squadron leaving. His Lordship's mad as a hen about it."

"Which squadron?" I stopped.

"Valens is taking a handful of men and riding off to aid Her Majesty's army in the north. Told Blackwood he didn't want to sit behind glass walls any longer." She tucked a curl behind her ear. "Magnus is going with them."

Shocked, I slipped from the step. "Where is he?"

Maria tried to stop me, but I ran, ignoring the increasing bite of pain. Sure enough, to the north of the perimeter, a group of men were saddling horses and tying up sacks of provisions. Magnus was among them, cleaning out the hooves of his chestnut bay. The men had all dug up spare red coats for the army; his hung loose on his frame, designed for a bigger man.

This was bloody suicide. Heart in my throat, I stopped in front of them.

"Howel." Magnus looked surprised to see me. "Here to say goodbye?" He put the horse's hoof down and stroked her neck; her ear flapped in appreciation.

"Where are you going?"

"Northumberland. They say there are more Familiars pouring in against the eighth battalion." He tried to make it sound easy, but I knew what horrors awaited them. "Blackwood—I mean, *the Imperator*—was in a snit, but I think when he found I'd volunteered, he agreed to let us go. Don't believe he's terribly keen on having me in the family." Jokes. Always jokes with him.

"You'll be killed!"

At last, the merry facade fell. He looked bone-weary; there was no life in his gray eyes any longer. "I don't pretend to be necessary. You're the burning rose, Maria the chosen one, Blackwood the Imperator, but I?" He shook his head, his auburn hair catching the sun. "A soldier, nothing more. One dispensable brass cog in the great war machine." His voice faltered.

"The only person who needed me died while I stood there and watched." He fastened a strap on his horse's saddle, then closed his eyes tight. "It was cowardly of me to blame you for Rook."

"No, you were right." My voice shook. *Make him stay.* His was a presence I'd taken as a given, and it was only now, when he was riding into oblivion, that I realized how badly he was needed. He was a spot of light in an ever-darkening world. Such a person shouldn't—couldn't—throw himself away. "Magnus, we need you." I paused. "I need you."

"No. You need Blackwood." He sounded resigned. "There's no reason for me to stay when you have him."

That was all he said, but his eyes and voice expressed more. *You forbade me to speak of my feelings ever again,* he'd said, *and I agreed.*

My face went hot. "Eliza needs you, for God's sake."

"If I die, she'll be in mourning for a year. I've saved her from Foxglove. At least I could be useful once." He took out his stave and presented it to me with a low bow—a sorcerer's bow. "There's nothing left for me in this world, Howel. Let me find some meaning in the next, at least." Sheathing his stave, he mounted his horse and took the reins. "Goodbye."

"I won't allow you to do this," I said, positioning myself before the horse. Magnus's shoulders slumped.

"You have to let me go," he said.

Before I could reply, Valens whistled, summoning his squadron. Magnus rode to join his fellow soldiers. Together, the ten of them cantered ahead, breaking through the perimeter and heading north. I watched until a cloud of dust and the faint pounding of hooves were all that remained of them.

Magnus had gone.

I accepted the agony in my shoulder as I made my way back. Blackwood was waiting for me at the carriage, holding the door open.

"So they've left, then?" He said it with some degree of satisfaction.

"You should have forced them to stay," I muttered.

"Them?" he asked pointedly. "Or one in particular?"

My silence mollified him. Cupping my face in his hands, he kissed me. "Come inside. The sun is too hot."

He helped me into the dark of the carriage.

37

DAYS BLURRED INTO ONE ANOTHER WHILE THE nightmares tugged at me. Upon waking, I'd often find Blackwood and Maria in the carriage, monitoring me. Apparently, I'd taken to sleepwalking and had nearly got outside the camp one night. It was just how Rook had been in the early days of his illness. My head ached all the time now, even when I slept.

Would I become like Rook? A vessel for Korozoth's hatred and power? Maria and Blackwood, perhaps, should kill me. But I knew they wouldn't, and I didn't have the strength to do it myself.

We had come to Yorkshire; I could tell it without even pulling up the blind. The air tasted different here, like stone and frozen earth. The north was harder, and hardier. Even the light had a slate-gray appearance. Soon we'd wake to frost on the windowpane and snow on the breeze. I'd been happy to leave this place once, when my greatest problems had been Colegrind and a meager breakfast. How could I have been so stupid?

"We should be home soon," Blackwood said when I awoke on the third day. I sat up, pushing off my blanket and hissing as Maria undid the top of my dress. Blackwood turned away to give us privacy as she exposed my shoulder, peeling off the gauze. I winced, then looked at my marks.

They were black as night, the punctures neat, round, and surprisingly fresh. Maria rubbed in ointment, which stung so badly I cursed and accidentally kicked Blackwood's shin.

"Will they always be that black?" I asked through my teeth.

"Aye. It would appear so." And why shouldn't they? Rook's scars had always been inflamed. Working my shoulder, I studied Maria as she put her bottles back inside a wooden chest balanced on her knee.

"When do we tell them we've found our true chosen one?" I asked. Blackwood and Maria both looked up in surprise.

Blackwood lifted an eyebrow. "Do you think that's wise?"

That was his way—ask a question, then let the answerer fall into a trap of her own making.

"*Isn't* it wise?" I asked.

Maria stopped our arguing. "I don't want anyone else to know. Not yet." She pulled up the blind halfway and gazed at the rolling countryside. "I like being invisible to them for now." She still didn't trust sorcerers.

"Quite." Blackwood breathed more easily. "We'll wait for the best opportunity."

I kept silent until the carriage stopped for a rest, and Maria climbed out to tend the other patients. "You're trying to keep your power," I said to him.

Blackwood rolled his eyes. "She wanted to hold back."

"Oh, don't play games. If everyone can at least pretend I'm the best we have, your support is stronger."

"No, I'm doing this to protect the woman I love." He squared his jaw; apparently my accusation had stung. "We need to keep your position secure. You're Unclean, and if the truth about R'hlem ever gets out, even I may not be able to shield you." The light from the window threw half his face into deep shadow. He climbed out the carriage without another word.

Uneasy, I settled back and sank into sleep.

The black of my dreams faded to gray. Around me was a world of nothingness. Hell and damn, I was on the astral plane once more. That could only mean . . .

R'hlem appeared, one hand over his chest. He was barely standing. The left side of his body was bandaged, blood seeping through the gauze. Well. At least we were both hurting.

"You've broken my heart," he said.

He was alive. Despite the terror of knowing that, I couldn't help feeling somewhat relieved.

"You left me no choice," I croaked.

"You had a choice. You chose your sorcerers." He grunted in pain; the astral plane around us flickered. This had to be taking much of his energy. "You joined the men who condemned your own mother." What the devil did my mother have to do with this? *"You preferred murderers to me."*

"You are also a murderer," I said, my tone icy.

"You chose the men who turned me into this," he snarled, gesturing to his own skinned face.

"I chose England over you, and I'd do it again."

"Is that so?" He sneered at my words. Once again our surroundings warped slightly. "Then the sorcerers are no longer enough for me. England will pay the price." His expression filled with pure hatred. "The Kindly Emperor comes. You will all bear witness to his smile."

I snapped back to consciousness with a cry, my shoulder burning. Blackwood had returned to the carriage and laid me against him while I slept. Instantly, he brought a flask of water to my lips.

"Are you all right?" he asked. I finished drinking and wiped my mouth with the back of my glove. Most ladylike.

"R'hlem," I whispered. "Still alive."

Blackwood took a shuddering breath. "At least now we know." For a while we sat in silence. I buried myself against him, lost in the pine and snow scent of him. He had been out of doors, in the fresh air. I envied him for it.

Then, as if making a decision, he whispered, "Here." Taking my left hand, he gently unbuttoned my glove at the wrist and slipped it off, a daring move. "I risked a trip back to the house for this. It's tradition for the future Countess of Sorrow-Fell to wear it."

He produced a ring from his pocket and slid it onto my finger. It was big for me, but hopefully I would come to fit it. A plain silver band, it housed a tiny pearl. I marveled at its small, perfect beauty.

"Thank you," I murmured.

He kissed my bare wrist, my pulse elevating at the touch

of his lips. Alone in the carriage, his strict Imperator facade melted somewhat.

"Don't be afraid of me," he whispered. Damn. He could feel me shivering beneath his touch, but I couldn't help it. The light sculpted his face in just the right way to make him look exactly like his father.

"I'm not afraid." I meant it. Mostly.

The carriage came to such a lurching halt I nearly fell into Blackwood's lap. He knocked on the roof.

"What's going on?" But then he closed his eyes in relief, as though he could sense the answer. "We passed the barrier."

I could feel it as well, a light tingling on my skin. Not the same pressure in my head that the ward had provided, but something more soothing and natural.

"Come," he said, climbing out of the carriage. "I want to show you." He helped me down and walked with my arm through his.

The mist was heavy all about us but dissipated as we came to the hilltop. Ahead of us, the most spectacular mansion glowed in the early-morning sunlight.

It was like something carved out of time. A marble colonnade decorated the front of the multistoried house, calling to mind temples of ancient Greece. Hundreds of windows sparkled, jewel-like, as the sun struck them. As the length of the house continued, it morphed from classical to the medieval. It bore the rough outline of a castle, but the turrets were corkscrew, the windows positioned at chaotic angles. It gave the impression that gravity did not apply, as though one might run down a staircase and somehow end up dancing upon the ceiling. In truth, it was a perfect estate from Faerie.

Nearby, a pond glittered, and an emerald lawn reached all the way into a dark fringe of trees. Black forest waited on every side of the estate, ancient beyond anything. Magic perfumed the air.

I thought again of the prophecy tapestry, how the girl's white hand stretched out of a gnarled, dark wood.

It was all coming to pass, wasn't it?

Blackwood whispered in my ear, "I'd hoped to bring you here alone, after we were married." His lips grazed my temple. "But that can wait."

Maria trotted up to us, her peacock cloak fastened about her shoulders. It was resplendent against her hair. "Good to be home?" she asked Blackwood. Her face had better color than I'd ever seen. Something about nature, and the north, appeared to agree with her.

"Very good," he replied.

Maria grabbed my hand. "Come along. You must keep up your exercise." She led me away as the other carriages and wagons pulled up the hill, and Blackwood turned away to deal with them.

"Look at it." Maria parked us beneath the shade of an oak. "Did you ever think to see such a place?"

Did I read some fear in her eyes?

"Never." I nudged her. "Are you ready for your great destiny?"

"If you'll stay with me." She sounded breathless. "Can't see how I'll do it alone."

"Then we shall remain together, always." As far as I could see it, she was now my great duty in life.

"Aye. Two of a kind, that's us." She stepped into the sunlight, which fired her red hair. I hung back, leaning against the tree. Maria strode farther into the light. Healthy and fearless, she was the ideal savior. While I, well, I found comfort in the shadows. Lighting my hand, I watched the fire play over my knuckles. Black still threaded itself through my blue flame. What could it mean?

Bother that. I focused on Maria.

Below us, Sorrow-Fell waited, the sight enough to ease my pain. Looking at the house, I noted the lush growths of ivy that decorated the walls and twined up the brilliant white columns, and I touched Porridge's carved design. We were meant to come here, the stave and I. Even without prophecy, it had the touch of fate. Here, the kingdom hung in the balance. Here, all our destinies would be decided.

ACKNOWLEDGMENTS

If book one is the courtship, book two is the marriage. In the first book, everything is wide open and wonderful, filled with possibility. The second book requires work and planning as much as love. Thankfully, there were many great people involved in this particular marriage. An odd thing to type, yes, but still true.

First thanks have to go to Chelsea Eberly, who is never too busy for a phone call, never less than certain that something will work out even when I'm convinced it won't. Thank you for being a brilliant plotter, a helpful listener, and a tireless champion for these books. Every day I'm grateful that I get to work with you. I don't deserve such luck, but I'll happily take it.

Thanks to Brooks Sherman, who treats every question I have with intelligence and care, even when I ask something truly ridiculous. Thank you for making time, no matter how inconvenient it is. You're a tremendous agent, an equally wonderful person, and a peerless brainstormer. Thank you for being in my corner.

Thank you to the incredible team at Random House, who have put so much into this series. Special thanks to Allison

Judd, Casey Ward, Bridget Runge, Mary McCue, Hannah Black, Melissa Zar, and Mallory Matney. I'm proud to be a Random House author. Thank you, Ray Shappell and Christine Blackburne, for the gorgeous cover. Thanks also to the team at the Bent Agency, especially Jenny Bent and Molly Ker Hawn, for insight and support.

The greatest part of the publishing experience has been meeting and learning from many brilliant, talented, and kind-hearted people. Thank you to Amie Kaufman, Jay Kristoff, Kiersten White, and Arwen Elys Dayton for your wisdom and humor and for eating cold pizza while driving to Denver. Thank you to Stephanie Garber, a jewel of a human being and a powerhouse author. Thank you, Roshani Chokshi, for dispensing invaluable advice, being one of the kindest people I've met, and having the most fabulous Instagram of all time. Alwyn Hamilton, for drinking great champagne, being a GIF goddess, and just being a friend. Emily Skrutskie, for not freaking out when my car broke down three times. Kelly Zekas and Allison Senecal, for talking about hot Victorian men with SO MANY CAPS LOCKS. Kerri Maniscalco, for pizza and sweetness. Rosalyn Eves, for being my historical-fantasy buddy. Nicole Castroman, for Poldark in all his glory. Tobie Easton, Audrey Coulthurst, and Romina Russell, for being LA writer friends and genius women. Hannah Fergesen, for notes, laughs, and Other Girls. Most of all, thank you Traci Chee and Tara Sim for being the other parts of my triangle. Whether DMing like mad, giving helpful advice, or freaking out, having you two with me is the greatest gift of all.

I have so many people in my day-to-day life who make even the most difficult tasks fun. Gretchen Schreiber, Brandie Coonis, Alyssa Wong, the entire Clarion family, Josh Ropiequet, Jack Sullivan, Aidan Zimmerman, and Martha Fling, thank you for your belief and your acceptance of my crazy. Most of all, thank you to my family for laughter and for never giving up.

Finally, thank you to the readers, librarians, and booksellers who have found these books, loved them, and recommended them. A writer really is nothing without a reader, and I'm so grateful and glad you've come on this journey with me.

ABOUT THE AUTHOR

JESSICA CLUESS is a writer, a graduate of Northwestern University, and an unapologetic nerd. After college, she moved to Los Angeles, where she served coffee to the rich and famous while working on her first novel, *A Shadow Bright and Burning*. When she's not writing books, she's an instructor at Writopia Lab, helping kids and teens tell their own stories. Visit her at jessicacluess.com and follow her on Twitter at @JessCluess.